MW00807324

FAGIN THE THIEF

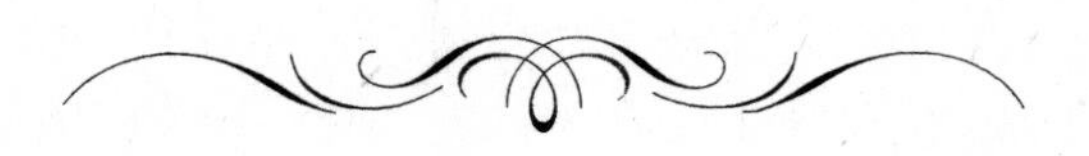

ALSO BY ALLISON EPSTEIN

A Tip for the Hangman

Let the Dead Bury the Dead

FAGIN THE THIEF

A NOVEL

ALLISON EPSTEIN

DOUBLEDAY NEW YORK

 Published in the United States by Doubleday, a division of Penguin Random House LLC, New York, and distributed in Canada by Penguin Random House Canada Limited, Toronto.

www.doubleday.com

DOUBLEDAY and the portrayal of an anchor with a dolphin are registered trademarks of Penguin Random House LLC.

Jacket painting by John Atkinson Grimshaw.
Photo © Chris Beetles Ltd., London / Bridgeman Images;
(pocket watch) Kuchin Viktor / Shutterstock
Jacket design by Emily Mahon

LIBRARY OF CONGRESS CATALOGING-IN-PUBLICATION DATA
Names: Epstein, Allison, author.
Title: Fagin the thief : a novel / Allison Epstein.
Identifiers: LCCN 2024005691 (print) | LCCN 2024005692 (ebook) |
ISBN 9780385550703 (hardcover) | ISBN 9780385550710 (ebook)
Subjects: LCSH: Fagin (Fictitious character)—Fiction. |
London (England)—History—19th century—Fiction. | LCGFT: Novels.
Classification: LCC PS3605.P6456 O97 2025 (print) |
LCC PS3605.P6456 (ebook) | DDC 813/.6—dc23/eng/20240207
LC record available at https://lccn.loc.gov/2024005691
LC ebook record available at https://lccn.loc.gov/2024005692

MANUFACTURED IN THE UNITED STATES OF AMERICA

1 3 5 7 9 10 8 6 4 2

First Edition

For my parents

When such as I, who have no certain roof but the coffin-lid, and no friend in sickness or death but the hospital nurse, set our rotten hearts on any man, and let him fill the place that has been a blank through all our wretched lives, who can hope to cure us?

—*OLIVER TWIST*

The villainy you teach me I will execute, and it shall go hard but I will better the instruction.

—*THE MERCHANT OF VENICE*, ACT 3, SCENE 1

PART ONE

1

1838

LONDON

The sun isn't yet up over Bell Court, and already someone is screaming.

It's not, however, a familiar scream, and so Jacob ignores it. There's a select circle of people whose screams he knows intimately, and for surety of whose well-being he will sacrifice the sear on a pan of sausages to investigate a cry in the dark. But whoever's screaming through the uncertain light slipping into the narrow court is a stranger, and one who sounds more angry than frightened. Well, Jacob thinks, twirling the toasting-fork so it catches the firelight, there's a great deal in the world to be angry about. If some stranger can't bear the trials of life without howling in the streets about it, that's none of his affair.

He flips one of the sausages—a little early; its exterior is beginning to toast but is not yet fully browned. He settles into his chair, drawing his scarlet dressing-gown back from where it slipped to expose his throat and the ridges of his collarbones. Behind him, an old clothes-horse sags under the weight of some two dozen squares of patterned silk, which he'll spend the day laundering and ironing and sorting when the sun is properly up. The value of stolen goods, he's learned over the decades he's been dealing in them, is at least half in their presentation. Properly pressed and folded, this collection of ordinary pocket-handkerchiefs could go for three shillings, provided someone with a suitably respectable demeanor is brokering the deal. And while a respectable demeanor isn't something he possesses, he knows several places where one might borrow an upright-looking individual for a reasonable fee.

The screaming is closer now. Some thief, he gathers, wasn't as subtle as the profession requires, and what should have been a quick maneuver devolved into a chase. As long as it's not one of his boys, it's all the same to him. After sentencing a thief Jacob doesn't care about to six months in Bridewell, the police will move on, leaving the thieves he does care about to their business. Certainly Charley isn't to blame for the commotion outside: just now, he stumbles into the room with his hair in disarray from sleep, his shirt creased and drooping off the left shoulder. At eleven, Charley Bates looks even younger than when Jacob met him at nine. Then, the boy was all hard edges and anxiety, but two years with a roof over his head and someone to cook him breakfast if he steals the raw materials have rekindled his childishness. It makes him a liability in their line of work, but Jacob can't bring himself to frighten the endearing brainlessness out of the boy. Charley sits cross-legged in front of the fire, eyeing the sausages with intent.

Jacob kicks at him with the side of his slippered foot, like nudging a dog away from a roast. "Wait your turn, Charley."

Charley scowls. "Dodger's not here. 'S only me, and I don't see why I should wait."

"Because you'll eat the lot of it, you shameless little tramp, and in this house those who work first eat first."

"I'll work," Charley insists.

"I'll expect it. You know I'm not in the habit of paying in advance."

Flipping the second sausage reveals that he's waited the proper time—the poorly ventilated room begins to smell of toasted meat, and if that won't call Dodger in, Jacob isn't sure what will. He spears one of the sausages with the toasting-fork and holds it out to Charley, who seizes it so eagerly he hardly seems to notice his burning fingertips.

The door at the end of the passage bangs open, and for a moment the sound of shouting from the street surges to full volume. It's cause for attention, but not yet for alarm. Still, beneath the surface, Jacob is always ready to run underground. There are ways out of this house that no one knows about, not even the boys, and he intends to keep it that way. It's not that he specifically doesn't trust them to know about the passage downstairs, more that he's never trusted anyone with anything, and this attitude has seen him reach the age of fifty-one with all his limbs still attached.

"You're late, my boy," he calls to the person he assumes is Dodger. "You know I don't like it when you're late."

"And when have I ever changed how I live to suit what you like, Fagin?" a woman calls back.

"Nan!" Charley cries in delight. He wolfs down the sausage almost without chewing and launches himself toward the door, where Nancy Reed stands with a felt hat jammed over her unbrushed hair and what seems to be half the mud of London on the hem of her skirt. She smiles as Charley seizes her round the waist in a crushing hug, but Jacob can see the distance between her smile and her eyes, and he knows she didn't come for company. His nerves, newly loosened, wind themselves again.

"Once or twice, my dear," he answers her, "if memory serves. That carrying-on in the street had nothing to do with you, I hope? Unbecoming for a lady, causing commotion."

Nan snorts and pushes Charley off, swatting him good-naturedly on the back of the head. She sweeps the hat off her own and thumps it businesslike against her thigh, dislodging a cloud of dust. He has half a mind to tell her his home isn't a barnyard for all and sundry to knock their dirt free in, but he's under no delusions about the state of the house. With the water pump a fifteen-minute walk away and the line for it usually twice that, no one in Saffron Hill can afford to have standards.

"You know I never cause a commotion unless I want one," she says. "Was Toby again, the heavy-fingered idiot. Expect he'll crash in here before long, sweating like a pig from outrunning the law."

Jacob sighs. So it was one of his after all. Toby Crackit is twenty-two now and only an occasional visitor to Bell Court, preferring to spend his evenings at the gin-palaces or buried up to his hips in some girl or other. Even so, Jacob's known Toby since the lad was six, and his strongly held principles of *us* and *them* make it clear what side of the equation Toby falls on. "That one will find himself collared before the year's out if he isn't careful."

"You taught him everything he needs to know," Nan says. "If he didn't learn, that's his funeral. But I didn't come here to talk about Toby."

Over the years, Jacob and the children who stay with him have developed an unspoken language. All it takes is one look as sharp as the toasting-fork, and then Charley scurries upstairs murmuring his regards to Nan—though not, Jacob notes, before snatching another sausage, leaving a trail of grease in his wake. Jacob doesn't like animals, never has, but some days he thinks taking in a pack of stray cats would at least have been neater.

He waits until the door at the landing bangs shut before gesturing at one of the chairs. "Tea?"

She sits. "How many times have you used the leaves?"

"For you, Queen of Saffron Hill? Fresh."

"You spoil me, Fagin."

He drifts toward the hob, removing the kettle, pinching out tea leaves with unnecessary ceremony. When he turns back, the distance between her eyes and her smile remains the same, for all the lightness in her voice. He leaves the tea to steep in the pot and returns with two mismatched cups, the chipped one done up in pale blue chinoiserie and the intact one with a bloom of roses. They were both part of fine sets at one point, though their quality didn't survive the loss of their mates.

"Now," he says. "Talk to me, Nan. I assume it's Bill."

Nan gnaws her lower lip, confirming it.

"Right then. What is it this time?"

"He's frightening me, Fagin," Nan says quietly.

What Jacob thinks, but doesn't say, is that if Nan is only just now becoming frightened of Bill Sikes, she hasn't been paying attention for a very long while. To give her time to collect herself, he returns to the teapot, pours two cups, nudges one toward her. She stares into it the way he's seen suicides stare at the Thames.

"He wants Charley," she says finally.

Jacob doesn't know what he expected her to say, but this isn't it. "What on earth for?"

"Next job. Says there's nothing like a boy for getting into and out of tight spots. The house he's after, it's near twenty miles out in Chertsey, half a day's journey just to case it, and you know the owner has dogs and servants who aren't afraid to shoot. Almost makes me wonder whether he's trying to get caught."

She isn't saying it, but Jacob knows what she's thinking. If Bill goes down, he's taking everyone within arm's reach down with him. And no one these past twenty-five years has been closer to Bill Sikes than Jacob has.

"He's met Charley before, hasn't he?" he says finally.

Nan laughs, surprised into it. "You know one boy's the same as another to him. He doesn't know Charley will run off chasing a butterfly halfway through the job. But you tell him that and he'll only make you find him another."

He nods, but he's hardly listening anymore. The black eye Nan came to see him with last week is nearly gone now, though she keeps her sleeves pulled down almost to her first knuckle, and he's known Bill and Nan long enough to suspect what that's meant to hide. He's tried to voice that concern more than once, only to be dismissed each time with the same grim laugh and the same "You're one to talk, Fagin." Granted, he *is* one to talk. But that's why he knows he's right.

A person who was properly afraid of Bill would not be in Jacob's situation, would not be the one Nan comes to in times of crisis. He's not Bill's keeper, is not Bill's friend, is not Bill's father. Every time he tries to think of what Bill is to him and he to Bill, he is made aware anew of the vast holes in the English language, the voids into which the men society casts off can slip, and where they must form categories and semantics of their own. He is Bill's, and Bill is his, and no dictionary in the country can put the matter more precisely.

"I'll talk to him," he says. "About all of it, not just Charley. I know how he gets better than anyone."

"Anyone but me," Nan says, her chin lifted.

"Anyone but you," he concedes. "You have my word. I'll talk to him."

Nan laughs. "Your word? Damn my eyes, what is your word good for?"

He sips the tea, grimacing—the tea leaves may be fresh, but they are not good, and at the moment he lacks so much as a splash of milk to make them more palatable. "More than you'd think, in some circles. He's at the Cripples?"

"Will be. Still asleep when I left him. He didn't come back until past three last night. The dog turned up without him, and for two hours I thought the traps had pinched him."

"Not Bill," Jacob says. "Not like that, in dark of night. If they ever take Bill again, I promise you, the whole of London will know about it as it happens."

Nan seems prepared to remark that this is a singularly cold form of comfort when the door thumps open again, and two sets of footsteps rattle down the passage. Both Nan and Jacob fall silent, listening. Their two visitors are clearly of opposite temperaments. One swaggers in with great clomping steps, as if a brass band appeared to herald their entrance. The other—so quiet that less-attuned ears than Jacob's and Nan's might not even hear them—creeps with an air of apology.

He nods to Nan. "Not to worry," he says. He knows what such footsteps signify. He's been here many times before.

Sure enough, Jack Dawkins bursts into the room with his hat under one arm, a grin stretching the sides of his thin face. The boy looks as if he got into a fight with a penned-up swine and came off decidedly the worse: mud and dust cling to the hem of his coat, and a smear of dirt swipes across his cheek and chin in a way that puts Jacob in mind of a gentleman's sideburns. There is, of course, nothing gentlemanly about the self-styled Artful Dodger, despite the elaborate bow he gives to introduce his companion.

The owner of the apologetic footsteps is a boy of indeterminate age, somewhere between six and twelve. A workhouse boy, Jacob would bet his life on it. Children stumble out of such institutions simultaneously too small to walk the streets on their own and too old to laugh or shout or smile. The boy, whatever age he might be, is fair-haired and fine-featured, and his wide blue eyes dart across the room, taking in the seemingly random furnishings. He lingers on the clothes-horse bedecked with pocket-handkerchiefs before proceeding to the three sausages still left in the pan, which catch his attention and keep it.

"Haven't you any manners?" Jacob says to Dodger. "Do we not introduce guests anymore, just let them wander in like sheep?"

Dodger's grin becomes, against all laws of anatomy, wider. "Oliver, this is old Mr. Fagin, him as I told you about," he says. "And Miss Nancy, a friend. Fagin, Nan, this is Oliver Twist. Walked here from Tadley, so he tells me. I met him on the way."

Despite himself, Jacob stares. Tadley is fifty miles from London if it's an inch. The improbably named Oliver Twist watches him with something between terror and defiance, two things Jacob is perfectly prepared to work with.

"Not a bad distance for a morning stroll, my boy," he says, recovering his composure. "Come, sit. There's sausages left, if you've worked up an appetite."

Oliver stares at him with the same wide, hungry eyes Fagin remembers seeing in Charley's face, and Dodger's, and Toby's, and, in what feels like another life, the reflection of his own. "Yes, Mr. Fagin, sir," Oliver says. "Please."

It's impossible to say who laughs first or loudest, Dodger or Nan or Jacob himself. Regardless, it's Dodger who thumps the boy on the back and steers him into the chair, still chuckling.

"Keep your 'sir' to yourself in Saffron Hill," he says merrily. "Manners will only get you marked down as green, and being green will get you cut."

Oliver receives this wisdom with some alarm, though it's tempered by the arrival of the sausage, which he nearly swallows whole. Jacob shrugs, then tips the remaining two sausages onto the boy's plate, ignoring Dodger's indignant exclamation. The boys can scrap for them if it comes to it, but Jacob suspects that Oliver will smash Nan's teacup and use the pieces to stab anyone who comes between him and his breakfast, and that sort of initiative deserves a reward.

"Dodger told you about the business?" Jacob says, setting the empty pan back on the hob—he'll have Charley clean it later, as the boy in question bounds back down the stairs, informed by his friend's voice that whatever private conversation was taking place is over now. Jacob gives Charley another sharp look, preventing him from leaping at the newcomer with the unbridled energy that frightened off more than one prior visitor not prepared for it. Charley scowls but takes the hint. He settles in front of the fire with his legs crossed, watching Oliver like a curious bird.

"He said you're in the used goods business, Mr. Fagin," Oliver says, "and while I haven't any experience in the trade, I'm happy to do whatever I can to help you, as payment for the good Christian kindness you've shown me." The words are, granted, a little difficult to follow, as the boy gets them out around a mouthful of sausage. Either Oliver is the slowest-witted boy for twenty miles in any direction, or he knows exactly what's going on and is prepared to play the game. Jacob is inclined to think it's the latter. Walking alone and unprotected from Tadley to the East End is by no means an easy feat, and he doesn't think a total imbecile could manage it.

"That's very kind, Oliver, my boy," he says. "I'm sure we can find a use for you. Now, eat up, and, Dodger, see if you can't find him something to wear that isn't more holes than cloth. Nan, I'll see you to the door, shall I?"

"Like a right lady," Charley says with a laugh: apparently the thought of Nan being waited on respectably is a source of profound hilarity. Both Nan and Jacob give him a rude gesture, hers ruder than his, though coupled with a curtsy.

"I'm sure I'll see you by and by, Oliver," Nan says, as she and Jacob retreat down the passage. Oliver, overwhelmed by the presence of company and also breakfast, makes no great reply.

Nan follows Jacob through the dim passage, but she stops at the door, one hand on the handle. The house on Bell Court has escaped the alderman's notice for years because it presents such an outward state of disrepair that powerful men can't fathom anyone choosing to live in it on purpose, and so while the passage is in dismal condition, Jacob deliberately hasn't put any effort into mending it. Better a darkened entryway with wood nailed over the broken glass in the door, better a smattering of cobwebs, better barred-over windows than some Mayfair swell sauntering in with the intention of renting it by the week to eleven families at three shillings a head and throwing Jacob and his boys out into the night. He leans against the wall, cloaked now in both shadow and his dressing-gown. Nan, more than likely, can scarcely see his face, but he, long accustomed to the dark, can see hers. He rests a hand on her forearm.

"I'll speak to him," he says. "This afternoon."

"Be careful," she says.

"Not a word to anyone, mind," he tells her. "If he were to find out you came to me…"

Nan scoffs. "How do you think I've lived so long, Fagin?"

"Smart girl," he replies. "Hurry on now. Never say die."

It's the right thing to say. She flashes him a grin, one with her old fire in it, and tips her crumpled felt hat in his direction before leaving him in the passage.

He lingers there another moment, imagining her making her way west toward Bethnal Green, the path from his lodgings to those she shares with Bill as well-traced as the scar of an old wound. With a sigh, he turns aside, and the shadow of a man, who appears out of the darkness of the passage as if summoned, turns with him, his insubstantial figure as silent as ever. Jacob hardly spares him a glance anymore. This presence has become so familiar, as much a part of his surroundings as the broken window and the boarded-up door. They walk together, Jacob and the shadow of a man whose footprints do not disturb the dust, back toward the front room. Within, Charley and Dodger and Oliver are engaged in a spirited argument over whether they've split the third and final sausage into equal parts. He hesitates, wondering if their chatter could be a suitable distraction, then turns aside at the last moment, and both Jacob and his shadow leave the boys to it, drifting instead upstairs to the low-ceilinged room where he sleeps. He sits on the end of the bed. The man—whose reddish hair is now visible in the clearer light, precisely the same color as his own—lingers near the doorway, arms folded.

Jacob watches him in silence for a long moment. Thinking of ringed bruises around a woman's wrists, around a man's neck. Thinking of what it truly means, *Never say die.*

"What will I say to him?" Jacob murmurs aloud.

The silent man shakes his head. Before the negation is finished, the room is empty again. Jacob sits alone, listening for a response he knows isn't coming.

2

1793

"I named you Jacob," his mother says to him one day, when he is six years old, "because I knew you could be great, if you put your mind to it."

He looks up from his seat on the floor and tries to work out whether she's mocking him. He can read his mother better than anyone in the world, and while he hears a sideways jibe in the remark—*if you put your mind to it, which you haven't yet*—she seems, on the whole, to mean it. Satisfied, he returns to the job at hand. Leah always sets him the task of sorting her fabric scraps, placing fragments large enough for practical use into one pile and leaving the smallest bits to be woven into mats or stuffed into pillows. He says nothing to the pronouncement that she expects greatness of him. Generally, he only says anything when he's alone with his mother, and just now, they have company.

"Jacob was the cleverest of the patriarchs," Leah goes on. She sits in one of their two chairs, a stretch of pale blue fabric spread across her lap. Her needle darts in and out like a silver fish, turning the expanse of cotton into the hem of a skirt, which she'll sell in Rosemary Lane later that week for barely any money. "He wrestled with angels and won, could talk anyone into or out of anything. It's not a bad namesake, I don't think."

Jacob blinks.

"Don't expect an answer," says Esther Singer, the rabbi's wife, who lives on the floor above. She, too, is sewing, though—Jacob's filial loyalty aside—he's certain his own mother's stitches are finer than anything Mrs. Singer ever produced. Mrs. Singer is lucky her husband is a holy man: the other women in the tenement have to command respect on their own merits. "Nathan says he's never heard that boy say more than one word at a time. Is he simple, do you think?"

Leah's lips tighten. The Fagins aren't important enough to argue with the rabbi's wife, but Leah lacks the ability to keep what she's thinking out of her face. Jacob can almost hear the tirade his mother will unleash as soon as they're alone: *Small-minded busybody, sticks her nose in other people's business to forget that she hasn't got any children of her own.* The pleasant secret of their shared hatred glows inside him.

"Jacob's not simple," Leah says. "He speaks plenty when he has something to say."

"Is that so?" Mrs. Singer says. She frowns down at Jacob. "Prove it, child. Tell me what you're thinking. Anything will do."

Jacob shrugs. Mrs. Singer clicks her tongue. Leah's cough very obviously began life as a laugh.

"Better to have named him after Laban's sheep, Leah," Mrs. Singer says.

"Count yourself lucky," Leah says. "I waste my breath every day praying to God this boy will *stop* talking."

This is true, though most of the families in their Stepney tenement wouldn't believe it. Thin, awkward, ill-disposed toward making friends, Jacob is silent everywhere except at his mother's feet, where he sits making her laugh with his eerily accurate impressions of their neighbors or bullying her into telling him stories. Those she reads aloud to him are not appropriate for a boy of six—sensation items out of the *Times,* Pitt and the Tories opining against the bloodshed in France, melodramatic penny-novels she buys used from the bookseller on Ford Square. The other boys taunt him for how tightly he clings to Leah, call him *coward,* call him *molly,* call him *lapdog,* and though each name gives him a new reason to hate them, he keeps his anger close. He is small and they are bigger, and however stupid they think he is, he knows not to pick a fight he can't win. Besides, he doesn't need them. He has his mother, and that's enough.

"My sister's youngest was simple in the same way," Mrs. Singer says, refusing to acknowledge that no one is interested in her opinion. "They apprenticed him to a chimney sweep when he turned eight. No need for great thoughts in that trade, and he earns his keep. It's honest work yours needs, if you ask me."

"Odd," Leah says. "I don't remember asking."

Jacob laughs, and his mother spares him a quick wink before returning to her sewing.

"Don't encourage him," Mrs. Singer says sharply. "He'll come to no good end, mark my words. Just as his father did."

The air in the tiny flat chills. Jacob reaches for a scrap of fabric—dark green, like he imagines the fine lawns of St. James's Park must be—so he can clench something that isn't his mother's hand. He recognizes this mood in Leah. If he asks her for affection now, she'll slap his hand away.

Mrs. Singer has crossed a line. Nobody speaks of Jacob's father in front of Leah.

"It's to be expected," Mrs. Singer goes on. "I don't blame you, Leah, you've done your best. And the Lord doesn't punish children for the sins of their fathers, but even so, the path to the gallows is in this one's blood, and if he doesn't improve he'll end by swinging the same as his good-for-nothing—"

Leah slams her sewing onto the table. He sees fire in her eyes, not the fond irritation she tries to suppress when she disciplines him, but genuine anger. If that anger ever turned on him, Jacob would run away like the coward he is. Now, insulated from the force of her rage and feeling only the hurt behind it, Jacob rises to his feet with terrible suddenness.

Mrs. Singer hurt his mother, and it's his job to make her pay for it.

Hate floods through him for everyone who would cause Leah pain: the rabbi's wife, the whole respectable world, his own father.

His blood rushes in his ears, and he wants to fight them all, the living and the dead, on her behalf.

She gave you a name, he thinks. Use it.

And he begins to speak.

"Toshiv lohem gemul adonai kema'aseih yedeihem. Tittein lohem meginnas-leiv ta'alosecho lohem."

Leah and Mrs. Singer recognize the words at once: Eicha, the book of Lamentations, which the rabbi is reading to the boys in the tenement's makeshift Hebrew school. Mrs. Singer, who sews in the bedroom while her husband teaches the boys in the sitting room, knows this. She knows, now, that Jacob understands, that he can hear, that he can think. But that isn't all Jacob wants her to know.

Jacob is an ugly and unimpressive child, but as he raises his chin, he feels something he's never had before: power. His father might as well have risen from the grave to stand at his back, whispering the words in his ear. He continues to speak in the same rhythm and cadence of the holy books, but now the Hebrew words are his own, from no text either woman has ever heard: old men who wander through mountains with bare feet, flames licking at their heels, pursued by angels driving them like sheep from the promised land. Mrs. Singer retreats as he pushes on, frightened without knowing of what. Good. She has to acknowledge him to fear him. He speaks about the taste of rich black earth between his teeth, about a sky ablaze and cannons that hurl metal through wood and brick and stone, about serpents thick as chimneys that writhe through the currents of the deep. He could continue speaking forever, if only to see the horror on Mrs. Singer's face. She expects wickedness from him, and he can deliver.

As the final word flies from his lips, he sinks to the floor in what he knows is a convincing faint. His small body goes very still, and he waits, heart thumping, for a response.

"The boy is touched," he hears Mrs. Singer exclaim beyond his closed eyes. "My God, I have never, never in all my life—"

"I think you should go, Mrs. Singer," Leah says. "Let me see to my son."

"Leah, surely—"

"Now."

Though Jacob keeps his eyes closed tight, he imagines Mrs. Singer's flinch. A small disturbance follows as she gathers up her sewing, and then she flees the room, leaving Leah and Jacob alone. A long silence stretches in her wake. His mother crosses to the door and closes it with a snap. He cracks his eyes open. Noticing, she sits on the floor next to him with her legs crossed under her skirt, regarding her son sternly.

"What," she says in a perfectly level voice, "was that?"

Jacob sits up and folds his arms. The performance drained him, but it was worth it, knowing Mrs. Singer might see him again in her nightmares. "She deserved it," he says, "for making you angry."

Leah sighs and tilts her head back. He knows her well enough to see the slight tug at the corner of her mouth, the crinkles at her eyes. For all she's tried to teach him to honor the word of God, she knows what the Singers are like, and she's trying not to laugh. "You are my trial in this life."

"You won't tell?"

"What would I tell?" she says. "That I've raised a liar and a hellion? That my son is six years old and already he spits in the eye of God and his mother?"

"I wouldn't ever spit at you," Jacob says seriously.

Leah closes her eyes. A beat too late, Jacob realizes he should have defended himself against blasphemy too, but after this performance, that might beggar belief. Likely Leah agrees, because she gives in and opens her arms wide. Jacob doesn't need to be invited twice. He clambers into his mother's lap and rests his head on her shoulder. Very soon he will be too big for this, but for now his mother's arms still feel like the safest place in London. A few locks of light brown hair escape her tichel, and Jacob treasures the glimpse as one of the many secrets he and Leah share, the brightness of her hair against the pale green fabric, something few other people have seen.

"You need to be careful, *ziskayt*," Leah says, holding him close. "You can't only be clever. You also have to be smart."

"Is that what happened to my father?" Jacob asks. "Was he not smart?"

Leah stiffens, and he tenses in her arms, holding his breath. He's pushing further than he's ever dared to. People whisper, here and there, that his father met a brutal and early death, but he's never been sufficiently brave to ask his mother about it. In this moment between risk and consequence, she might say anything. His father might be an angel of the Lord. He might be a bloodthirsty murderer buried at a crossroads.

"He was clever like you," Leah says quietly. "Very like you, in fact."

She means it as a warning, but Jacob feels as if he sits three inches taller.

They never speak again of his performance in front of Mrs. Singer, but word passes quickly through the building, from the rabbi's wife through her impossibly broad network of gossips. Before the week is out, the general consensus is that Leah's son is destined for a bad end, the only question being how quickly he'll reach it. He could change their minds, could force them to see him properly, but he isn't interested. He feels a strange desire to hold his own power close, dissuading others from smudging it with their fingerprints. Finery only lasts so long as you're careful about when you use it.

Besides, he got what he wanted. Mrs. Singer continues to give Jacob a wide berth. Jacob and Leah are left alone, and the subject of his father does not come up again.

3

1797

Jacob wouldn't trade Leah for any woman in the world, but as mothers go, she's unusual. He can't set foot outside their tenement on Copley Street without bumping into a mother, and they all seem more or less the same: serious, tired women with handfuls of children and husbands they love or cannot stand or both at once. Leah is only thirty years old, and Jacob loves her youthfulness fervently, that spark in her eye that hasn't yet outgrown mischief. He's always been the only man in Leah's life. Family in Stepney signifies overcrowding, shouting, obligation, debts, but for Leah and Jacob, family only means each other.

To Leah, family also means home, narrowly defined. Despite the great sprawl of London that stretches from their door, she rarely ventures more than a mile from home. She prefers the costermongers on Ford Square who will sell to her at a fair price, knows there's a butcher in Sidney Street who sells kosher beef and lamb, and even if she can't afford brisket more than once a year for Pesach, still she feels better knowing where she might find it.

"The people here might not like me, but they know me," she said once, when he asked. "These days, I'd rather be known than guessed at."

Jacob couldn't disagree more. Their tiny enclave of the Stepney slum is home to some four hundred Jews who have, to all intents and purposes, built their own country, half a mile square in which they need not be outsiders. To Leah, it's a safe haven; to Jacob, it's a claustrophobic nightmare where everyone knows everything about everyone. He itches to go someplace where he can be just one face among thousands, not the troublesome boy with the dead father.

One morning, when he's ten years old, he decides to set out and find it.

It's a gray morning, already spitting rain, and Rabbi Singer has just concluded Hebrew lessons for the day, which means all the boys in the tenement have a choice to make. They can join their mothers and fathers at work, crafting or buying or selling or washing to bring back a few extra coins. Or they can shirk responsibility and take over the second-floor hallway, using an old rubber ball and a broken umbrella to play an elaborate game they've invented themselves, similar to cricket but with more shouting and a higher likelihood of bloodshed. It's an easy choice for most. The hallway is pure bedlam, and more than one of the tired mothers sticks her head out her door to add her disapproving voice to the din. It couldn't be simpler for Jacob to duck through the crowd and disappear. Another boy might make people worry, going off alone like this, but no one's likely to notice he's gone.

He whistles as he wanders, crossing Whitechapel Road and taking care to sidestep the parts that have already turned to muddy soup. No one looks at him. He is a boy in a worn-out shirt with the sleeves turned up, a length of cord supporting his too-large trousers in the optimistic belief that he will grow into them. There is nothing less remarkable on a London street than he is.

To untrained eyes, the neighborhood he enters would look exactly like the one he left, but Jacob knows he's in a new world. People pass by in droves, umbrellas lofted against the rain, shoes slapping the mud, tall hats and watch-chains and pocket-handkerchiefs that add a spice of finery to otherwise utilitarian clothing. There are easily three dozen people within eyesight, and Jacob does not know a single one of them.

Grinning, he roams down Brick Lane and east toward Spitalfields Market, which rises like a beating heart. Stepney Parish has its own markets that cater largely to Jews, and he sometimes joins

Leah on trips to Petticoat Lane to sell the clothing she makes and mends, but Spitalfields strikes him as rich and bloody and foreign. The merchants shouting from their booths do so in English only, and they hawk a dizzying array of foods: barrels of oysters like severed ears in their mottled shells, tangled knots of black eels he thinks will feel like earthworms that rise after the rain. Adults mill through the damp to haggle, while packs of drenched boys his age circle the stalls like crows, hoping for scraps.

A group of six boys stalking the market catches his attention. They seem about his age, all as poorly dressed, a few of them taller but none of them better fed. What they do have—what he can't look away from, as he shelters from the rain beneath a baker's awning—is fearlessness. They move as if they have a perfect right to be where they are. As he stares, one of them lobs a punch at another, catching the boy on the shoulder. It's clearly meant as a joke, but it lands hard nonetheless, and the scuffle expands like ripples in a puddle, each boy taking the opportunity to throw an extra shove.

That could be me, he thinks. I could be like that.

He intends to retreat without saying anything, but his staring attracts the attention of the tallest of the boys. Suddenly the whole pack crosses the market square toward him, the tallest at the front and the others fanning behind. A smarter boy would run, but Jacob stands where he is, waiting for his fate to reach him.

The tall boy shifts his weight onto his back foot and folds his arms. "You want to get cut, lurking like that?" he drawls, his voice the purest Cockney Jacob has ever heard.

Jacob wants to be the kind of person who stands his ground, but he takes a step back. The deep pockets of the boy's coat could easily conceal a knife. "I'm sorry," he says. "I didn't mean anything by it."

One of the other boys whistles, loud and low. "Bloody Christ, Sam," he says to the leader, "you've caught an out-and-out ikey swindler."

Sam narrows his eyes, looks down his nose at Jacob. "That true?"

They're speaking a language Jacob has never heard before, and his face grows warm. "Is what true?"

"You a mucky little sheeny?"

That word he does know. They must hear it in his voice: he speaks English and Yiddish equally well, but he learned both from his mother, who prefers Yiddish and carries a Prussian accent across both languages. That, or there's some sign in his face, his hair, his bearing that gives him away. It's possible. These boys speak a dialect he only half understands; it seems likely they live in a world where everyone's secrets are written plainly on their faces.

"Yes," he says.

Silence, for a moment. And then Sam and his boys trip over one another to ask questions, each less comprehensible than the last.

"What's it *like*?"

"Why do you lot dress like that?"

"Have you ever killed someone?"

"Where's your bloody horns?"

Jacob blinks rapidly at the last question and takes a beat before he answers. Later, he'll wonder whether he should have lied, pretended to be the same as them. But what cause would they have to notice him if he were just the same? Different is frightening, and having someone around who can frighten others is useful for boys like these.

"Not killed anyone yet," he says. "But the day's young."

The punch Sam lands on his shoulder feels better than any embrace.

He never meant to repeat his excursion to Spitalfields, but his original plan didn't account for Sam Fisher and his boys. It would be an exaggeration to say they welcome him, but he slips into their shifting mass nonetheless, not the strongest or the oldest but a curiosity worth keeping nearby. Their attention is intoxicating, and there's very little he won't do to keep it.

At first, he tells Leah he found work near Wapping, running errands after lessons for dockhands who pay him with supper and a few pennies. It's the sort of thing many of the tenement boys do, particularly those who don't have fathers with trades, and Leah doesn't argue with the free meal. At least not for a week or so, until he returns one evening with dust in his hair and a fresh rip in his trousers. Only then does she look sternly at him and command him to sit on the end of the bed, which he knows is the signal for a conversation he doesn't want to have.

Annoyed, he thumps onto the bed, tossing up a leather ball he hadn't owned that morning and catching it as it falls. The arc it traces from his hand and back is infinitely satisfying, made that much sweeter because of its previous owner, a self-righteous little child who dared to sneer at Sam that afternoon. Sam knocked the boy down with two punches, rolled the ball forward and back in his palm once, then tossed it to Jacob, as casually as if they shared possessions all the time. As if they were friends.

"Don't suppose some captain at Wapping gave you that," Leah says.

"I have friends, Mum. I see them too, when I'm out."

"And would I like these friends?"

Jacob shrugs, which isn't an answer, but then how should he know, really?

"All right." She sighs and sits next to him. "God knows I wouldn't talk to my mother either, when I was your age. But I want you to make me a promise, so listen."

He flops onto his back and continues tossing the ball in the air, catching it before it strikes him in the nose. There's a sweet thrill that comes with the act of not paying attention. Before he met Sam and the others, he could count the number of times he ignored Leah on one hand.

The next time he tosses the ball, it doesn't come down. His mother shoots out a hand and catches it mid-arc. Jacob sits up, indignant.

"Mum," he snaps. "Give it."

"You want it back, you listen," she says. "I want you to promise me you're being careful. That's all."

He scoffs. They've been speaking Yiddish until now, but he switches to English, unconsciously mimicking the sharp Cockney of Sam and the rest of the boys. "Course I'm careful. 'M not stupid enough to get myself sent to the jugs, am I? Christ."

With the hand not holding the ball, Leah cuffs him on the back of the head. He yelps, rubbing the spot and scowling. It doesn't hurt—she only ever hits him for emphasis, not to cause pain—but it stings his pride.

"Don't speak like no one raised you," she says. "Rabbi Singer taught you better. Use words."

Jacob's scowl deepens. He doesn't know what kind of school, if any, the Spitalfields boys go to, but he knows for certain that Sam Fisher's mother doesn't care a farthing whether he drops his h's or blurs his th's into f's. Sam and his friends speak like the poor, rough boys they are. It feels dishonest not to pick up their mannerisms when he's around them.

"That's how people talk, Mum," he says.

"I don't care how people talk," she says. "You aren't people."

"Won't have any friends at all if you carry on making me talk like a newspaper," he mutters.

Leah grins, and despite his anger it almost makes him laugh to see her tossing the ball from hand to hand. She's doing it to taunt him: something Sam just knocked down a boy for trying, but from her it elicits an undeniable warmth. "They aren't friends worth having, if they only like you when you're stupid," she says. "No man's reputation ever suffered because he was bright."

Reputation, he wants to tell her, can mean many things. The Spitalfields boys have built his reputation for him out of a wild and various store of nicknames, creating a person Leah wouldn't recognize. *Professor, rabbi, penny-wit,* when they're being harmless. *Swell Street mouth, flash-kiddy, toad-eater,* when they want it to bite. *Christ-killer, Shylock, blood-drinker, sheeny,* all with the same casual lack of ill will as if they used his given name, until he answers to "Jew" the same way he'd have answered to "Jacob" or "Fagin" if the boys ever used them. This is London, he thinks but does not tell his mother. Other people make your reputation for you, and if they don't hate you for one thing, they'll find another. Why not take it as it comes?

As though she can read his thoughts, Leah shocks him out of his musing by tossing the ball straight at him. He flinches and flings up a hand to catch it, avoiding by an inch the ball cracking him square in the nose. Their eyes meet, and she smiles with such childlike wickedness that he can't help but return it. No one—he's absolutely certain in that moment—will ever know how to love him the way Leah does.

"I understand you're a great big man now," she says, and she eases a book out of the pile stacked in the corner. "With his own job and his own friends. And great big men are too important to have stories read to them, aren't they? I'll read to myself then, and you do what you like."

This splits his heart in half. Just that afternoon, Sam boasted about the sixpence he stole from the jar on his mother's mantel. He showed the coin around the group so the metal glinted in the light, crowing that his mother watched him do it and was too frightened to say a word. If he wants to be like Sam, he has to harden himself. Has to be the one who makes people tremble when they hear him coming.

The book Leah took from the stack is Lewis's *The Monk,* a new edition she secured from the bookseller gratis in exchange for mending a gown for his wife. It's newer than any of the other books in the pile. Leah has a wonderful voice for reading, and it's the kind of story he loves best, tales of villains and scandal and black magic and gore. He's confident at least three people will be brutally murdered before the midpoint of the novel.

"I can stay at home tonight," he says, careful to enunciate the h, "if you promise to read an extra chapter?"

She laughs and reaches for the bottle of gin balanced on top of the pile of books, taking a quick swig. "Ah, we're bargaining now, are we? Very well, *ziskayt*. I'll take those terms."

4

1798

Jacob always knew he'd never leave London. By the age of eleven, he's decided that he doesn't want to. No other city on earth could possibly be so vibrant, the streets always alive with something to look at. Either someone is singing for coins, or the police are dragging furniture from a debtor's house while the wife shrieks from the doorway, or the traveling rat-trainer has set up shop with his band of vermin running up and down his shoulders on command, a farthing for the privilege of watching. Best of all are the fires, which throw the whole city into a holiday atmosphere that can last for days on end. Families bring picnics and camp on nearby rooftops to watch the hellish spectacle, the shouts of men with buckets mingling with the celebration of the crowd, sparks dancing in the light like diamonds in a lady's ears.

Today, there's a juggler at the south end of the Haymarket, and Sam and the others idle there to take in the show. They're loud, challenging a world that doesn't want them by taking up twice as much space as they need. Jacob stays toward the rear of the pack, watching them shout and shove one another with not a little jealousy. He's not big enough to frighten anyone on his own, not strong enough to make anyone get out of his way.

Jacob sees the impatience in Sam's broad face—clearly he'd prefer some bloodier form of entertainment, and if there isn't a fire at hand he's more than willing to set one himself. But Josiah, one of their youngest at only seven, has a gleam in his eye like he spotted the man in the moon, and Sam has given in, unwilling to drag the child away. Besides, the juggler is good. When they first arrived, the man had five silver balls aloft at the same time, passing through his hands easy as water. Now, sensing his audience's attention waning, he sets the balls aside, taking up long metal batons dipped in pitch at the ends.

Sam elbows Jacob in the ribs so hard it hurts. "Maybe he'll burn down the bloody market, eh? At least then we'd have a show worth watching."

Jacob laughs. His side aches, but he knows it's a sign of favor. "Wouldn't mind seeing that."

He should have said something cleverer, something rude and daring. That's the way to catch Sam's attention—be the smartest, the strongest, the most *something*. But he's too slow, and Sam's eyes already rove about for someone else to entertain him.

"Joe!" Sam roars to another of the gang. "You still sweet with Nell down near St. Katharine's?"

"Why?" Joe calls back. "Your girl tired of dancing your hornpipe?"

"My girl don't run a gin-palace where drinks are free for swells she's keen to bounce around the bush with," Sam says. "Enough of this, eh? Get us a drop, you owe us that much."

With the absolute clarity of the prophet he once pretended to be in front of the rabbi's wife, Jacob sees what will happen in one week's time, or two. Sam will keep him around as long as it's less trouble to let him stay than to shake him off. But when someone else turns up, a boy stronger or taller or smarter or louder than he is, there will no longer be a place for him. They won't say it to his face, that he's been shut out. They won't need to. He knows what he is: a stringy boy with dirt under his fingernails and a bump on the bridge of his nose, unruly reddish hair, one crooked front tooth. The adventure of being a different sort of person will end soon. It frightens him how much he'll miss being important.

Sam begins to herd the others south, no doubt in search of the alluring mistress of the gin-palace. Jacob lingers, watching the juggler light his batons and send them tumbling through space. It's a delicate dance, each movement tapping against the brink of catastrophe before swerving away, and the crowd is vocal in its appreciation.

It's then, by the glowing light of the batons, that Jacob sees the man who will change his life forever.

The man draws attention to himself on purpose, the way a magpie stockpiles bright objects to compensate for its drabness. He's perhaps thirty-five, running toward stout in the middle, with dusty wheatlike hair and a previously broken nose, but given the brilliance of his turquoise velveteen frock coat and black silk cravat, he could be mistaken at a distance for a handsome gentleman. His hands draw Jacob's particular attention: broad, each long finger nearly squared off at the tip, almost all bedecked with rings. Jacob has only ever seen married women wear rings, and those are dull, ugly ornaments, bare silver or gold tarnished over decades of being passed from mother to son to wife. This man's rings are gaudy as peacock feathers, and enormous. The wide bases contain jewels cut in ovals and squares—emerald, topaz, one he doesn't know the name of, black as a dead man's pupil.

Jacob cannot imagine anything more impractical than these cumbersome rings. He's never wanted anything more in his life.

The man with the rings is on the move, strolling through the crowd with the languid grace of someone who has spent time in much finer company than the Haymarket. Jacob leans forward, determined not to miss what's to come. This is a man with his next steps firmly in hand.

A moment later—Jacob's breath catches with the wonder of it—the man brushes up discreetly alongside a gentleman with a silver-topped walking stick passing in the opposite direction. Before Jacob can track the movement, the gentleman's watch is in the gaudy stranger's palm, and then in the pocket of his frock coat. Every eye except Jacob's remains caught on the flaming batons whirling overhead, which cast queer shadows over the thief's face as he saunters away. The gentleman will notice sooner or later, but not before he's home, patting down his pockets in confusion that turns into impotent anger. The thief, Jacob thinks with a surge of joy, has won.

The thief changes course, leaving the bustle of the street. He moves so fast that in a moment he'll be entirely lost to view. Detaching himself from the crowd, Jacob weaves around the crush of bodies, tailing the flash of turquoise. It's not difficult for a boy his size to stay unnoticed, and he's better at it than most. Keeping a few cautious yards back, he moves in the thief's shadow as the man enters an alley that winds northward, into the hushed space between the main streets.

In the new quiet, the rasp of Jacob's breath gives him away. The thief whirls round and flinches violently when he sees a boy standing behind him.

"Christ be damned." The thief reaches for his pocket—not the one with the watch. Jacob freezes. He knows the behavior of an armed man when he sees it. "Starting the sneaks younger every day, I see? Don't tangle above your weight, boy. Policeman ain't here to save you, whether or not you've been paid."

"I'm no sneak," Jacob says. He puffs up his chest as if that will make him seem older than eleven.

The thief's eyes narrow. Jacob can see him weighing the evidence in front of him. Would the Bow Street Runners waste a shilling on an informant as small and untrustworthy looking as Jacob? Surely they could do better. Jacob folds his hands behind his back, not sure whether he should try to look more respectable or less. In either case, he knows he can't let the man send him away.

"All right," the thief says. His hand drifts away from the pocket, though it doesn't go far. "Say you aren't a sneak, then. What in hell are you doing skulking about? Damn me, you'll get yourself killed watching the wrong fellow that way."

This is his chance. Until now, being a member of Sam's gang has given him protection, but if he's going to last on his own in a world wider than his mother's doorstep, he needs a skill that feels like juggler's magic in his palms, that makes every movement bright and powerful as a flame.

"I want to do what you do," Jacob says.

The thief blinks. His eyebrows descend into a single horizontal line. "Then do it. No rules to this life excepting those you make."

It's a dismissal, but Jacob won't be shaken off so easily. "Give me one week," he says. The man laughs, but Jacob doesn't leave time for the incredulous remark he knows is coming. "Show me how you do it, then one week. If I don't bring in twice what you're earning now, I'll go, never bother you again, never say a word to the law. You'll be done with me."

The longer he talks, the deeper the man's brow furrows. It may be wishful thinking, but Jacob doesn't believe it's anger. He can be persuasive when he needs to be. If only the rabbi's wife could hear him now. She'd know there's more in his head than cobwebs and dust.

"And if you do?" the man asks.

Jacob grins. "Then you've earned twice what you would have. I'd be pleased, in your shoes."

The man shakes his head, chuckling. "You've a lot of spirit for someone tall as my elbow. What's your name?"

"Fagin," Jacob says. It's out of his mouth before he's thought it through, though there's no particular reason he shouldn't give the man his first name. But it strikes him that he would prefer this fellow not call him by the same name his mother does.

The man laughs brightly. "Ah! A Jew small enough to hang by a watch-chain." He bends down, resting his hands on his knees so they see eye to eye. "All right, Fagin. Anthony Leftwich, if it please you. Stick with me a week, eh? Let's see if all your high-and-mighty talk is worth anything."

Jacob grins and thrusts out a hand. Leftwich takes it as if he's striking a bargain with a man grown, and they shake.

"When do we start?" Jacob asks.

"Eager little mite, aren't you?" Leftwich says. "All right. We start now. Come on."

And he's off at a rapid clip, heading west down Oxford Street. Jacob needs to run to avoid being left behind.

Lesson number one, Leftwich says as he walks and Jacob jogs, is to avoid habit at all costs. "You can double back to somewhere with rich pickings all you want," he says over his shoulder, "but do it irregular-like. As soon as you're known as someone with a usual hunting ground, you'll get cut, either by the Runners or by someone who wants the same pockets you're after. So stay light. Stay on the move. Understood?"

Jacob nods, fighting to breathe through his nose. *Stay on the move.* He's panting by the time Leftwich slows his pace, in a part of town Jacob has never visited before. Farther west yet than Spitalfields, the neighborhood appears well-to-do to his untrained eyes, though not so fine that his own dirty clothing draws attention. A mix of shop-girls and servants and merchants taking a stroll chatter in at least three languages. The air smells of wood and dust and sweat, strong but not unpleasant. Jacob suspects Leftwich selected the street on purpose, a betwixt-and-between place where poverty and riches brush elbows. Someday, he decides, he will have the same encyclopedic knowledge of the city and everyone in it.

"There now," Leftwich says. He doesn't point, but nods minutely toward a draper's shop, outside which the seller has arrayed a table with fine linens and handkerchiefs and cravats. "An easy start, they've laid it all out like a banquet. Go and steal us one of those fancy wipes, eh?"

Jacob stares. *Show me how you do it,* he said, not *Let me get myself arrested.* "How?"

"How?" The thief scoffs. "How, he asks me. You either have the touch of it or you don't, Fagin, and there's only one way to tell. Do it, and we'll see."

A smart person would turn away, understand this to be a sure path to Bridewell and find another way to make his name. But Jacob takes a breath, then nods.

Look alive, then, he thinks.

As he did when trailing Leftwich, he weaves through the crowd, keeping to other people's shadows. Taking care not to jostle anyone, he must move slowly, but gradually he approaches the draper's table at an oblique angle. How did Leftwich do it at the Haymarket? It seemed so easy from a distance. Jacob would give anything for one more opportunity to observe. He would like to sketch diagrams, take measurements, plan his first theft like a tailor laying out pieces for a fine gown. But this, it seems, is a skill he must learn by doing.

He falls into the wake of a woman with petticoats wide enough to nearly hide him from sight. There, safely concealed, he toys one final time with the idea of running away. No one would know. It would be as if nothing ever happened. Leftwich would chuckle at his failure and feel superior for ten minutes, and then even he would forget the whole episode.

He grits his teeth and clenches his fists. His bare knuckles ache, his dirty palms pierced by his own nails. These hands are all he has, but they will have to do.

They are nearly past the shop when the woman pauses, eyeing a bolt of fabric at the far end of the table. "How much?" she asks the shopkeeper, pointing.

"Three shillings the yard," the shopkeeper says. "As fair a price as you'll find anywhere."

It isn't. But the goods have her attention. No one is looking at him now. Fast as lightning, Jacob darts out a hand toward the opposite side of the table and crushes the nearest handkerchief in his palm. The silk against his skin feels like the finest thing he's ever touched. The woman is still asking about the quality of the fabric.

Triumph. It is intoxicating. He can barely contain himself as he walks easily from the table, hands in his pockets clutching his prize. He is a natural. His first time, no instruction, and he managed it, right under the shopkeeper's nose. Gold, jewelry, food, money, fine clothes, all of it parades before his mind's eye, a dancing troupe of ghostly objects made animate by his own skill. He will have them. He will have everything.

And he's nearly out of sight too, before the cry goes up.

"Thief! Somebody stop that boy!"

Jacob takes off running.

He isn't fast, but he is desperate, and right now that's enough. He bolts like the prince's hunting dogs are after him, shoving people out of his way heedless of their protests. No one tries to grab him, but it's a matter of time—the street is too crowded, the cry too loud for him to disappear properly, and every person in London knows what to do at the words *Stop, thief.*

He darts into an alley, and then it's as if God has smiled on him, for he spots it straightaway. An overturned cart with a broken axle, which some frustrated vendor left behind to become the city's problem. He almost weeps when he sees it. A quick glance reveals that no one has followed him around the turn yet, though he has only seconds left. He vaults over the cart and clambers beneath it, still clutching the handkerchief.

It's filthy and dark below the cart. The street has turned to mud, and it squelches under his knees as he crouches there, seeps through the holes in his shoes and chills his sweat. A scuffle comes from near his left shoulder. He glances toward it and stifles a shout with the handkerchief as a pair of rats blink their button eyes up at him, startled out of their nest by his thumping about. They chatter irately in his face before scuttling into the street, where Jacob can only pray their exit will not attract attention. The smell of mud and shit and damp enfolds him.

Holding his breath, heart roaring in his ears, he waits.

It's debatable whether what he's doing could be called praying, but he doesn't know what other name to give it. Please, he thinks, don't let them find me. I'll be better, I'll learn everything there is to learn, only let me get away this first time.

The footsteps thunder nearer. Jacob stops breathing. He hears voices, some women and some men, conferring nearby. Makes out a stray word here and there. Then—and whether God is to thank for it or some power altogether less holy, he doesn't know—the footsteps and the voices begin to dwindle and die.

Silence, when it comes, seems to weigh a thousand pounds.

He remains where he is far longer than he needs to, listening to his own heart. Thank you, he thinks to no one in particular. Thank you. I meant it. Then, like a rabbit emerging from its hole, he climbs out from beneath the cart. Mud tracks up his trousers from calf to thigh. Some of it, he notes distantly, has the distinct grittiness of rat droppings. He is covered in sweat, and his knees are trembling despite his best efforts. But he is alive. He is safe. And Anthony Leftwich is standing at the mouth of the alley, leaning his turquoise-clad shoulder against the west wall, watching Jacob with faint amusement. After a beat, he raises his ringed hands and applauds slowly.

"You have it?" he says.

With all the dignity an eleven-year-old with rat shit on his trousers can manage, Jacob crosses the alley and presses the handkerchief into Leftwich's outstretched hand.

"Yes," Leftwich says—his face serious but his eyes glittering. "This, I can work with."

5

1800

With Leftwich's arrival, it's as if Sam and the Spitalfields boys cease to exist. To Leah, Jacob's habits appear unchanged—he still attends lessons with the rabbi each morning, if only to keep the peace at home, then claims to go scout work at Wapping the moment Rabbi Singer releases him. He can't tell her the truth: that he spends each day closer to Leftwich than the man's shadow, watching every movement of his wrist, every dip of his shoulder. Jacob has never studied anything as intently as the practiced thief's mode of weaving through the world, filling his pockets with the wealth of others. He wants to learn everything there is to know from him.

One bright summer day, Leftwich and Jacob are back near the Haymarket, a hunting ground they only visit every other week at most. At eleven, Jacob could be found there picking fights with smaller children alongside Sam and his boys, hoping the glow of their good opinion would last one more day. Today, at thirteen, he hardly considers these familiar streets worth walking through.

These past few weeks, Leftwich has begun to let Jacob take the lead in their thefts, identifying the targets and proposing the choreography. He's come a long way since his first bungled attempt. Practiced now, he knows how to find a likely target. Spotting one, he nudges the thief with an elbow, bringing them both to a halt. The teetering cart of the costermonger on the corner makes the most of every inch of space, jars of honey and mustard and preserves arrayed neatly while the little room that remains is packed with whatever merchandise will fit, bundles of radishes and great clear jars full of pickled cucumbers steeping in spiced brine. Jacob's mouth waters as he looks at these, suspended like brains in an anatomist's laboratory. He hasn't eaten since the previous evening, and the thought of the sour-sweet brine floods him as if he's already opened the jar and bitten one in half. It's come to the point that he can taste food more clearly when he's thinking about it than when he's eating it.

"What do you think?" he says, nodding at the stall.

Leftwich looks, considering. "Not exactly the crown jewels."

At the beginning of his ad hoc apprenticeship, Jacob would have winced at the reprimand. Now, he only scoffs. In addition to the finer points of thievery, Jacob has also learned how to talk back. "If I could eat the crown jewels, I'd go for them."

"Animals think with their stomachs, sheeny."

"And people who want to live. Can we do it, or do you want to stand here talking all afternoon?"

Leftwich laughs, then pulls a mocking half bow, touching the brim of his hat. "You want face or hands this time?"

"Face," he says confidently.

"Care to tell me why?"

"Because I don't look like I escaped from a traveling circus."

Leftwich glances down at the sterling silver tiepin glittering near the collar of his burnt-orange frock coat and chuckles. Jacob is right: they're both well positioned to cause a distraction, but Jacob can cause the right sort, while Leftwich's gaudy appearance will draw more eyes than they need. It's a maneuver they've executed dozens of times. While Jacob engages the vendor in conversation, Leftwich will dart behind the man's stall and fill his pockets with biscuits and hard cheese and oranges, clearing out before anyone's noticed. Though Leftwich will sell the extra for ready cash, Jacob will get enough to fill his belly before that.

"Go on, then," the thief says, waving a hand toward the costermonger. "All's clear. Dazzle me."

Jacob grins and starts to saunter toward the stall. A familiar voice stops him short.

"Jew-boy! Thought you'd bloody died."

It doesn't take him long to find the source. Sam Fisher is leading the pack of boys across the Haymarket toward Leftwich and Jacob. Seven of them today—the gang expands and contracts to account for whoever turns up, only one person's presence truly required. Sam wears a hat with a red silk band, cocked so proudly anyone would think he'd stolen it from Pitt the Younger. The other boys mill around Sam, turning to look at Jacob like one many-headed animal. Some he recognizes; others are new since his time. They greet him with a collection of smiles and an undifferentiated crush of voices. Once, their attention was the greatest joy in his life. Now, it's a dull, dusty consolation.

"Sam," Jacob says, but does not move.

Leftwich raises his eyebrows. "You know them?" he says. It's clear what he means: *I hope not, for your sake.*

Jacob leans against a pile of crates at the side of the road, watching Sam's expression hover between expectation and surprise. Beside him, Leftwich is the perfect foil: adult and well-dressed and impressive, clearly capable of anything.

"I used to," he says, and he hooks his thumbs into his pockets, addressing Leftwich. "Come on. We have work to do."

It's a clumsy performance, but Sam and his gang have never been subtle, and the rage rises in Sam's face right on cue. Sam moves in until they're less than an arm's length apart. Jacob doesn't blink. He knows Sam could break his nose with a single blow, but the important thing is that he doesn't let Sam see he's shaken. If he looks like he isn't afraid, then there's no reason to be.

"D'you want to say that again?" Sam says.

The rules of their conversation are already set. Sam has to pick a fight: can't afford to let the rest of the gang think they might simply walk away if the mood strikes them. What Jacob knows, though Sam doesn't, is that the older boy has already lost. Sam is no longer the strongest or most interesting person on this street. What follows is only for show, and Jacob has lost interest in acting.

"You're playing games, Sam," Jacob says, turning to go. "I'm too old for that now."

"You hear him, boys?" Sam says with a laugh. "Sheeny thinks he's too good for us. Take your clown of a pimp and get out of here, and keep off streets that don't belong to you."

Leftwich doesn't react. He keeps his arms folded, sparing Jacob the smallest of sidelong looks. He's amused. On another day, knowing Sam was on the defensive would satisfy Jacob. But seeing Sam's broad stupid face, the one he once tried so desperately to impress, has pushed him beyond common sense. He already knows what he's going to do, and the thought fills him with such preemptive pleasure that he doesn't even have to fake the parting smile he gives to Sam.

"Fair enough," he says. "Good day to you."

And he sidles away, into the crowd of the Haymarket. Leftwich is at his heels.

"Fine friends you keep," he starts to say, but Jacob stops him with a curt shake of the head. He isn't finished, and one wrong word will give the game away.

The target presents itself at once: a tall man with a fine mustache, thinning hair that reveals glimpses of a pale, freckled scalp. He has a loaf of bread already under his arm and is browsing root vegetables arrayed on a nearby stall. By no means a rich mark, but Jacob knows what to look for by now, and the man's jacket pockets droop in a way that suggests there's something worth having inside them. Leftwich, following his eyes, signals agreement with a tilt of his head. *You go, boy, and I'll follow. Show me what you can do.* Leftwich is smarter than Sam or his gang will ever be. He doesn't need anyone to spell out a plan.

Jacob steps forward and ducks his head. "Pardon me, sir," he says to the man, dredging up every ounce of proper diction to make the words sound humble and sincere. Leah, he thinks, would be both proud and outraged. "I hoped you could help me."

Leftwich taught him the sleight of hand needed for a successful theft, but Jacob never needed any instruction to lie convincingly. The waver in his voice seems to presage real tears, and he hunches his shoulders as though expecting the man to chase him from the stall with a blow. The man's stern face softens, and he shifts the bread under his arm and stoops to see eye to eye with Jacob. It's unnecessary to the point of being patronizing, but it makes the role Jacob's playing more convincing, and so he glances up, then away again, shying from an imagined rejection.

"I suspect the help you need can't be bought at the market," the man says.

Jacob lets his eyes fall back to the street. It looks like bashfulness instead of misdirection: if he looks up, he'll see Leftwich sneaking behind the man, fingers poised to relieve his jacket pocket of its burden.

"It's my mum, sir," he says. "She's sent me to find the apothecary, who has the medicine she needs for her cough, but I've gotten so turned around, and I'm not sure where I've gone wrong—"

He breaks off with a single, rather loud sob, and Jacob can see the man setting aside his suspicions in favor of the impulse to be helpful. The directions spill from him like the man's waited all his life to point a child to the apothecary. Jacob chokes out his thanks along with a stream of silent tears that are no less convincing for being utterly fake. He keeps the fellow talking until he sees Leftwich melt back into the crowd, then bows and peels off himself.

"Give me that," he whispers.

Leftwich's eyes are alight with amusement, but he doesn't waste words on questions. He hands over the full purse, and Jacob pauses only long enough to tip a healthy lining of coins into his own pocket before setting off again. Sam's red-banded hat flashes gaudily in front of him, leading the way. Easy as anything to creep up unseen behind them, the gang already distracted by a pretty girl selling flowers two for a penny. Easier still to slip the purse into the pocket of Sam's too-large jacket, the principles of theft just as straightforward when executed in reverse.

Easiest of all to shove Sam so hard he jostles several strangers and shout at the top of his voice: "Stop, thief!"

If there are two words in the English language whose effects are more predictable, Jacob doesn't know them. The Haymarket freezes as each member of the crowd instinctually checks their pockets, and then Leftwich's victim lets out a cry and takes off running toward Sam, misinterpreting his stumble as the beginnings of an escape. Sam, panicking, runs in earnest, but the robbed man now has the entire market on his side, and it's a matter of seconds before Sam is pinned to the ground, voices shouting, policemen sent for, the rest of the gang scattering to the four winds.

Jacob, unmoved and untouched in the center of it all, makes his way out of the market and into a nearby alley, grinning ear to ear. Leftwich's eyes are shining as he follows. He looks at Jacob as though he's never seen him properly before.

"You're a snake, aren't you?" he says. "A heartless little devil."

Jacob shrugs, though pride sparks like a candle catching flame. He closes his eyes, the better to hear the commotion still going on in the Haymarket, the shouts and the piercing whistles of policemen newly arrived on the scene. Sam will be taken to the station house, tossed in a holding cell, then sent to Tothill Fields for at least six months, longer if Jacob's mark is particularly angry and gives the magistrate a reason for stringency. And when he comes out, half eaten by lice and the tips of his fingers blue with cold, he'll know better than to make an enemy of Jacob or his friends. It's a victory—a cruel one, and all the more satisfying for it.

No one will make him feel small without his consent.

The glow of his triumph spills over into the next day, and even Leftwich seems caught up in the excitement of it. Rather than resort to their usual tactics of large crowds and brutally efficient thefts, Leftwich leads Jacob that afternoon all the way to St. James's Park and pauses just inside Buckingham Gate, in the shade of a large beech tree. Beyond, graveled walks extend between the trees at sharp, uniform angles, while ducks paddle alongside the odd pelican through the brownish water of a long artificial canal. Jacob has never been here before; frankly, he isn't sure he should be here now. His clothes are not suited for a respectable stroll, though Leftwich could blend in with the fashionable men promenading past if he made an effort.

Leftwich, though, hardly seems to notice their surroundings. He leans against the tree trunk and cocks his head to one side, as comfortable as if they're lounging outside the pub. "All right then," he says. "Have at it."

Jacob stares. "You're not going to—"

"Oh, I am." Leftwich flicks the cuffs of his jacket up past his wrists; Jacob thinks of a gourmand at a tavern preparing to tuck in, almost expects the thief to lick his chops. "We're going to play a little game today. Call it a contest, if you like."

Immediately, Jacob is paying attention.

"Be back here in half an hour," Leftwich says. "Whoever has the best prize gets to keep the lot."

This is not wise. This is a risk they have no business taking.

This will be the most fun Jacob has had in months.

He salutes Leftwich and trots off into the park, blood singing with the hunt. Before, he always sought out the sure marks, maximum reward for minimum risk. But this is sport now, not work, and he lets the wave of leisure-seekers in the park wash past him, searching for one who will be worth pursuing. A rattling sound comes up close behind him, followed by an annoyed shout, and Jacob steps off the path into the springy grass. A trap drawn by two horses barrels by, containing an older man who scowls at him as he passes. Jacob considers sending the man on his way with a rude gesture, but the insult barely registers. He's on the brink of victory, and nothing can sour his mood.

The pressure of the time limit only adds to the thrill, and before long, he makes his decision. There's a spot toward the east end of the canal where the water splits round a peninsula so narrow at the point it's practically an island. Near it, two gentlemen—one some six inches taller than the other—show off their tall hats and brilliant silk waistcoats for a coterie of ladies taking shelter from the sun under their parasols. Both men are decked out in their finest, but just now Jacob's interested in the smaller of the two. The fellow wears a broad gold ring on the index finger of his right hand, polished to a proud shine. A personal seal, Jacob suspects, or a sign of membership in some club or society. It doesn't look as if it fits terribly well.

"'Scuse me, sirs," he says in his very best Cockney. The tall man looks askance at his companion, but neither of them leave. "Sorry to disturb, but I hope your honors can help me."

The gentleman with the ring blinks twice. "With what, in heaven's name?"

"Alms," Jacob says, and holds both hands open. "For the orphans of St. Giles Parish. Them what's taken care of by the Sisters of Mercy. The ones littler than me, sirs, and nothing but gruel to feed their bellies. Please, sirs. Anything you can spare."

He laid it on a little thick at the end, but it works just as he planned. The man with the ring glances over his shoulder at the women. Charity, the man thinks, is an admirable quality in a gentleman. Certainly ladies think so, at any rate. He puffs out his chest like a prize pigeon and reaches into the pocket of his frock coat for a purse, from which he extracts a bright sixpence.

"Of course, child," he says, pitching his voice to carry, as he places the sixpence in Jacob's hands.

"Oh, thank you, sir," Jacob exclaims. Pocketing the sixpence, he shakes the man's right hand with both of his own, pumping it up and down in a shameless display of gratitude. "Thank you, God bless you."

He almost wants to linger, watch the gentleman play up his selflessness to his tall friend and their uninterested audience, but Jacob knows better. Any moment, the man will notice his right index finger is more naked than it was ten seconds ago. By that time, Jacob intends to be on the other side of the park.

Leftwich is already waiting for him near Buckingham Gate,

leaning against the beech tree with a smug smile. "What've you got for me, mouse?" he drawls. "Something better than this?" He's holding a cigarette case inlaid with pearls—the sort of thing that ordinarily would make Jacob's palms sweat with want. Today, it's nothing.

Jacob grins and holds up the ring.

Leftwich stares. "Hell and the devil," he says incredulously. "The cove wasn't *wearing* it, was he?"

Jacob nods, then takes the bright silver coin from his other pocket. "And he gave me sixpence."

The laugh that flies from Leftwich is more of a cackle. He slings one arm around Jacob's shoulders—they aren't of a height yet, but they're getting steadily closer. "Damn me blind. All right, viper. You win. Keep it."

He's so pleased with himself that he doesn't even remind Leftwich that the promised prize was the lot, ring and cigarette case both. Today, Jacob won respect, which is worth more than the rest put together.

The whole day is that way—instead of returning to work, Leftwich pulls Jacob into a gin-palace and buys him a drink, then another. By the time Jacob makes his way home, though it's still earlier than usual, he is buzzing with liquor and satisfaction. He lets his footsteps fall heavy on the stairs, and when he sees Leah sitting at the table cutting out pieces for a jacket with an old pair of shears, he doesn't think. He reaches into his pocket and tosses the gold ring onto the stretch of brown wool.

It lands with a thud. Leah stops her cutting to stare at it.

"Take a rest," Jacob says brightly. "There's enough for the week in that. Just give me time to flip it."

Her silence drains away the warmth of the gin. He is growing more sober by the moment.

"This is how they pay errand-boys now?" she says quietly.

"Mum, it's not—" he begins, but falls silent, because of course it is.

"How long? The whole time?"

Not the whole time, but close enough that the truth will not help him.

Until today, Leftwich has always pawned the take and meted out Jacob's scant share in pennies before pocketing the rest for himself. Jacob has never been able to hold on to the prizes themselves before now. A sixpence here and there can come from honest work. A ring like this has only one explanation.

He should say something. He should say *anything,* any lie, but he can't think. Leah whips out a hand and curls it around his wrist, and he is too shocked to shake her off. Her nails dig half-moons into his skin.

"Come with me," she says.

It doesn't matter how much he would rather not follow. He does.

6

The late-afternoon sun weights down the air as Leah pulls him through the streets, still keeping tight hold of his wrist. Jacob is all bones and angles, and he stands some inches shorter than Leah, but even if he were a man full-grown, he's too frightened to do anything but allow himself to be propelled along. The child he is now bears almost no resemblance to the bold, successful thief of St. James's Park hours ago. Here, he is Leah Fagin's son, and something terrible is in store for him.

Leah steers him west with the confidence of someone who has traced this path many times before. It's nearly three-quarters of an hour before she begins to slow. By then, he's worked out where they're going. The realization sends a spark of terror through him. He tries, uselessly, to tug his hand free from her grip.

"Mum," he says. Until now he's been silent, but he's never encountered a situation where it's more urgent to beg. "Please. I want to go home."

"I'm sure you do," Leah says, and she pulls him into the crowd that surrounds Newgate Prison.

He tries once more to worm himself free, but he elbows another spectator nearby and only earns himself a cuff to the head for his trouble. It's impossibly hot, and between the thick air and the furious pounding of his heart, he's certain he's going to burst into tears.

At least a hundred people have gathered in the square. Jacob's heart is fluttering so fast he can't guess their number more precisely. All around him, the atmosphere is jubilant, the same wild cheer that accompanies a fire dancing from rooftop to rooftop. More than one person brought their own liquor or beer, and conversation jangles like discordant bells. They've converted every building around the square into box seats for a gruesome theater, people setting up tables at open windows or spreading picnics on their own roofs. Jacob tries once more to plead with Leah, but she keeps her gaze straight ahead. She hardly looks like his mother then. Seems a decade older, and harder than he has ever seen her.

He doesn't know how long they wait there, shoulder to shoulder with the macabre crowd, sweat dripping from his brow and beading from the tip of his nose to his lips. All he knows is that the world stops as they bring the condemned man out.

"Watch," Leah says.

He does.

The man is short and slenderly built, but that's as far as Jacob can judge; he can't see the prisoner's face. They must have placed the burlap sack over his head at the foot of the scaffold, while the crowd still concealed him. Through the ringing shock that descends, Jacob finds it in himself to be surprised. He pictures hangings more often than most boys of thirteen. Ruminates on them the way other boys daydream about the naval ships their fathers sailed away on or the foreign battlefields where their fathers are buried. In all his past imaginings of the hangman's noose, he wasted so much energy picturing the jeering crowd, the wood between his feet, the dangling coil of rope. It must be so much worse to see nothing but the rough weave of burlap. Sweat spilling from your brow into your eyes. The hot cloud of your own breath, like a child with a blanket pulled over his head. What does it sound like? What does it smell like? His imagination didn't give these senses their due.

"That man," Leah says, "is being hanged as a thief."

"Mum," Jacob begins, but his mother digs her fingers into his hair and wrenches his head back, which silences him. He wants to press his eyes shut, but he doesn't dare.

"Be quiet," Leah says in Yiddish. "Do you know who else was hanged here as a thief?"

He knows the answer but doesn't give it. Leah doesn't release her grip on his hair. Wildly, he half-expects his mother to slit his throat.

"Your father," she says. "I stood here with you in my belly, fourteen years ago, and watched them break your father's neck, like they're about to do to this man. I want you to watch the way I watched. And imagine it's your father again. Or your friends. Or you, who think you're too clever to get caught, because you aren't. No one is."

Jacob twists out of his mother's grip, disregarding the sharp pain in his scalp. He gets only about a foot away before Leah grabs him by the collar and yanks him back. Panic starts to claw up his throat.

"Let go," he says. "Let me go, please."

"No," she says. "I want you to see this. Stand there, be a man, and watch."

He screws his eyes shut, which is all he can do to escape, but Leah, sensing it, shakes him sharply.

When he opens his eyes again, the thief on the platform is not alone.

The figure of a man stands behind the condemned thief, slouching against the arm of the scaffold. A lean figure, rough bearded, the beard and hair the same reddish color as his own. The man is dressed in a long black coat, and around his wrists Jacob spots a glint of silver, as if of manacles, but brighter than any dull iron, polished to a shine. The crowd is enormous and rowdy, but the figure looks directly to where Jacob stands, with Leah's hand still fisted in his collar, and their eyes meet. Seeing that Jacob is watching, the man winks. The corner of his thin mouth twitches toward a smile. Before Jacob can speak—before he's sure what he saw, before the question forming on the back of his tongue can spill past his lips—the man shakes his head, and then either Jacob blinks or something shifts independently of him, because there's only one man on the scaffold now, face obscured by burlap, and the crowd roars as the man is pushed from the block and swings. The sun beams down overhead, impassive.

Jacob stands there, eyes wide, as the thief dies. He is not breathing.

Gradually, Leah's grip on his collar weakens. It's no longer necessary—he isn't going anywhere. His throat tightens under an unseen pressure. The crowd senses that its entertainment has come and gone, and soon those on foot begin to disperse. From a balcony overhead, Jacob hears the sound of wine pouring into glasses, the clink of a toast.

"Jacob," Leah says.

She shakes his shoulder, not as a reprimand but to bring him back to himself. He can't imagine what he must look like through her eyes.

As the ringing in his ears fades, he remembers who he is, and where he is, and he can't think of anything more unbearable than either. Like he is a child of seven again, he bursts into tears.

Leah sighs, then rests one hand on his shoulder. "You see now," she murmurs, and kisses him on the top of his head. "You see, my dear. I can't lose you."

He saw, that much is certain. What the sight will drive him to do, he has no idea.

Jacob spends the next two weeks keeping close to Stepney. Leftwich, though he knows where Jacob lives, doesn't come in search of him, and Jacob tries to slip back into the quiet life he left behind when he began his instruction at the thief's side. Mornings learning the holy books with Rabbi Singer, afternoons playing football in the muddy street or running meals from the cookhouse for a penny an hour, evenings listening to Leah read. It's safe. It's a life, though it isn't much else.

With every passing day, the terror of the noose fades. In its place rises a desperate hunger, a bone-deep itch.

He is terrified to die, but he cannot live like this.

Before the month is out, he's back on the streets, walking in Leftwich's shadow. Leah knows where he's going—he sees it in the way the corners of her eyes tighten, the way she won't speak to him for a quarter of an hour after his return in the evenings—but she doesn't stop him from doing it. There's nothing she could do shy of taking Mrs. Singer's advice and selling him as apprentice to a chimney sweep, and however angry with him she is, he knows she couldn't bear to send him away. Easier to pretend, and to let the memory of the hanged man do the rest.

Leftwich doesn't ask Jacob where he's been, and Jacob doesn't offer any explanation. It doesn't matter. Life is only the present moment, the past a fairy story and the future speculation. He is here now.

"Aren't you afraid?" Jacob asks Leftwich late one afternoon, a few weeks after he turns fourteen. It's only four in the afternoon and the sun is already slipping away, but even so, Jacob feels an ease in his chest, a quickness to smile that hasn't come often lately. It's one of those startling February days, the first brilliantly bright one after an endless London winter, four months straight of gray that leave you no choice but to grit your teeth and shove your way through it, dreaming of spring. Energized by the sudden brightness, Leftwich has led Jacob farther west than ever, all the way to Battersea Park. They picked a few pockets along the way, lined their own coats with pennies and a disappointingly thin wallet each, but today is less about making money and more about waking from a long winter's sleep. Even now, the sunset sparkles on the Thames like a handful of crushed diamonds.

Maybe it's his sense of well-being, or the pleasant ache in Jacob's legs and feet, or the bottle of beer he's been pulling from as they wander the city, free from any responsibility other than their own whims. Whatever the cause, Jacob is happy, and because he's happy, he stupidly asks the question that's never far now from his mind.

"What?" Leftwich says—a reasonable response to such a question.

"Afraid of being caught, I mean," Jacob says. "Of dying. Everything."

Leftwich laughs and takes the bottle from Jacob. Before he answers, he drains it dry, then tosses it aside. The glass shatters in the gutter, stabbing into the mud.

"What's this?" he says. "My little viper losing his nerve?"

Jacob bristles. "Never."

"Good," Leftwich says. "Because it doesn't matter if you're afraid. There's nothing else. We'll both end just the same. A pile of bones buried behind Newgate. Enjoy what you have while you have it. None of it lasts."

It sounds less awful when Leftwich says it. In Leftwich's voice, it seems obvious that a life like the one they're living won't extend long into the future. Theirs is a short story, the beats achingly familiar.

With a laugh, Leftwich surges forward, swinging one arm around Jacob's shoulders. He's drunk already, Jacob's beer far from Leftwich's first drink of the afternoon. Jacob almost buckles under the man's weight, but he braces himself and holds his mentor up, steering them on toward the river.

"We're living on borrowed time, you and me," Leftwich says, the words slurring together. "So you know what we've got to do."

"What's that?"

Leftwich grins. "Steal as much more as we can."

7

1803

It's three weeks past Jacob's sixteenth birthday, still in the dead of winter, and despite the damp and cold, it's been a productive day. The February air draws a cough out of him as he mounts the stairs to their third-floor flat, but he stifles it in the crook of his elbow and keeps moving. He knows what a cough sounds like when it's nothing and when it's worth worrying about. So long as his body isn't slowing him down, he isn't concerned.

Jacob isn't stupid: he knows his partnership with Leftwich hasn't been worthwhile for months now. If he isn't the better thief already, he will be within the year, and half the time Leftwich watches approvingly from the shadows as Jacob does most of the work. Leftwich still owns the relationships with London's fences, though, which means that most of the money from Jacob's thefts disappears into his mentor's pockets. Until recently, Jacob thought of it as paying off a debt to his teacher, but now the imbalance is grating. There's nothing for Leftwich to teach him anymore: Jacob was born for picking pockets. He's all skin and bones and quick movement and daring, and if anyone looks at him oddly he can spin a convincing excuse out of thin air and walk off with his victim none the wiser.

Today, he came away with a teak-handled clasp-knife, which Leftwich magnanimously decided was worthless enough for Jacob to keep. Its original owner, a sailor on leave, was too overcome by the temptations of land to notice its absence. Jacob amuses himself by flipping the blade in and out of the handle as he mounts the stairs, watching the knife glitter terribly in the light. It seems finer than jewels, brighter than glass. Not having owned many fine things, he preens over it like a magpie. This must be what rich people feel like all the time, surrounded by objects with no purpose.

When he opens the door to the flat, the oil lamp is still lit, and Leah sits in its unsteady light, gazing at the unfinished mending in a pile at her feet. His chest tightens. He expected to find Leah in bed by now. She wakes at four to deliver her work before any of her customers depart for the day, a schedule that usually leaves her drooping with fatigue by late evening. Jacob, a notorious layabout who, so Leah says, would gladly reverse the Lord's rhythm of creation to sleep away the sun and prowl the streets at night, can't remember the last time he came home to see the bed empty and his mother watching for his return. The close room buzzes with the scent of something animal, musky and frightening.

"Mum," he says quietly.

Leah flinches. Swears. Runs the back of one hand across her eyes. "What's the time?"

"Past midnight," he says. "Did something happen?"

She shakes her head, though not in answer. This tired, abstracted woman with the pale face bears only the slightest resemblance to the Leah he knows. This isn't his mother, he thinks wildly. Someone replaced her with a weak copy while he was out, and the illusion is starting to fade.

"Mum," he repeats, and lays a hand on her shoulder. "Are you all right?" Even through her pale blue cotton gown, he can feel the searing heat of her flesh. He draws his hand back as if from a hot iron.

"Fine," she says brusquely. "Stare at the stitches long enough and your eyes start to cross, you lose track of yourself. You know how it is. Or you would, if you'd ever done an honest day's work in your life."

It's the same speech she's given him a thousand times before, but her heart isn't in it. It leaves a foul taste in his mouth. He wants to spit out the suspicion, let it rot on the floor.

"Here," he says, and he crouches down beside her chair. "Let me get you to bed."

Jacob isn't a helpful child. If he's offering to assist his mother without being cajoled into it, it's because he knows the circumstances are extraordinary. And though many of their neighbors still privately believe Jacob to be an idiot, his mother always knew better.

"How old do you think I am, *ziskayt*?" she mutters. "All right. If it will stop you hovering."

With a great show of tolerance, she lets him tuck his bony shoulder under her arm, hoist her from the chair, and guide her to bed. Once she sinks into the mattress, he eases off her shoes. Her feet are stiff and swollen, and she winces in both pain and relief as she flexes her toes. Leah is still not yet forty, clever and practical, unstoppable as a draft horse. The woman before him who is too weary to stand on aching feet must be someone else. She sighs, and he draws the coverlet to her collarbone.

"You're a good boy," she murmurs, eyes closed. "All evidence to the contrary."

An unfamiliar feeling twists through Jacob's stomach, and it takes several moments before he identifies it as guilt. There's a self he keeps tight between his own cupped hands and there's one he's crafted to show his mother, the same at the root but with a different shine, less hateful. Codes of behavior govern Leah's world, and what the neighbors murmur before they snap their doors closed at night is cause for concern and not for ridicule. A world with consequences. If he could cut those consequences to pieces with the knife, he would, never mind how bloody it became.

"I can read to you a little," he says. "If that would help you sleep."

She closes her eyes and smiles. "You have a nice voice for reading. Everyone says so."

This seems like an exaggeration, unless by *everyone* she means herself, and also Rabbi Singer, once, when grasping about for something inoffensive to say about Jacob's Torah portion. Still, it's something to do, and sitting in silence with his worry seems like torture, so he scans the familiar stack of books before easing one out from the middle. It's Richardson, whom Jacob can't stand, but Leah has a sentimental streak, and it's her tastes he's trying to match just now.

He settles down on the end of the bed, crossing his legs in front of him and resting the open copy of *Clarissa* on his thighs. With a gesture that suddenly feels daring as any theft, he rests one hand on Leah's ankle, the barrier of the coverlet between them. He closes his eyes and thinks of anchors, of ropes and doors and locks and walls and everything that can keep a body where it's meant to be.

Then he begins to read.

Morning comes, and Leah is worse. Jacob can barely rouse her, and when he finally does, her eyes are unfocused, and her skin is still hot to the touch. She sits up to take a sip of gin, but as soon as the bottle leaves her lips, she nestles back under the covers again.

"I'll run for Dr. Thompson," he says.

"Don't throw away the money," she says, already closing her eyes. "I'm only tired. Let me rest a day or two, and I'll be right again before Shabbos, you'll see."

"Mum, you're not well. If it was me, would you—"

"Yes, I would," she mutters. "Although it would never *be* you, would it? What work would tire you out? Go, and make sure you eat something today."

Jacob isn't used to being a dutiful son; he's even less used to his efforts being rejected. "Are you sure? I could stay, keep you company. Finish the sewing—"

"Child, if you touch my sewing I'll whip you raw when I'm better," Leah says sharply. "Stop trying to take care of me. It makes me nervous. If you want to be helpful, get out and let me rest, and bring supper with you when you come back."

This, somehow, is the worst sign of all. She knows what he'll do to find supper. No matter how tired or ill she's been in the past, she's never too weary to be angry with him for his chosen profession.

"All right," he says, backing toward the door with his palms raised. "All right, I'm going."

He leaves but doesn't go far. Closing the door behind him, he sits on the landing, wrapping his arms around his knees. Though it can't possibly be true, he imagines he can hear her breathing through the door.

She will not die. People do not die from fevers.

If people do not die from fevers, Jacob will make a deal with God, and he'll study properly, he'll stop stealing, he'll observe all the holy days and devote his life to healing the sick. He'll knock on the door of every shopkeeper until someone offers him an honest job. He'll walk the two miles every Friday to the temple near Aldgate, barefoot if that will make God happier, and his voice will be the loudest in all the songs. Jacob Fagin is a liar and a cheat and a thief, but he also drives a hard bargain, and if God holds up his end, Jacob can be counted on to hold up the other.

Terms set, he makes his way back toward Spitalfields, where he knows Leftwich is waiting. Whether God follows through or not, he'll still need money.

8

It's a prime working day—so rich Jacob wonders whether God isn't showing his hand early, indicating he's accepted the terms of their bargain. Under Leftwich's approving eye, Jacob selects the dense crowds of Rosemary Lane for their work and helps himself to whatever strikes his fancy: a pair of spectacles poking rakishly from a lady's reticule, a snuffbox that looks like silver from a distance but annoyingly proves to be tin up close. Usually there's at least a frisson of danger to the act of thieving, one cove who turns round too quickly or a close shave with a shopkeeper, but today there's nothing of the sort, and Jacob fills his pockets like a bee in a rose garden. Leftwich will take the goods to a fence in Blakesley Street, though the exchange will take the better part of a week and Jacob will see little to none of the return. Still, with the tenpence Leftwich offers as an advance, Jacob haggles his way into some cold chicken and a penny-loaf from Leah's preferred vendor on King Street.

Only as he mounts the stairs to their flat does he feel the warmth of his luck start to fade. He doesn't know what he'll find when he enters, but it suddenly seems terrifying that he has to find it alone.

The room is dark, he notices first. What little light reaches their flat is gone this time of year by half four, and it's hours beyond that now. It's dark, and Leah didn't light the lamp. He does it himself, disgusted by the trembling of his hands. Lighting a lamp is nothing, the basic machinery of living. If he senses some kind of fatalism in the darkness, it's only because his own fool imagination put it there.

The light casts long shadows on Leah's face, pale against the pillow. Warily, he sits on the bed, reaching one slow hand to stroke her brow. She is white-hot to the touch. Though her lips move to speak, the sounds she makes are barely audible. He isn't sure if she even knows he's there.

"I'll be right back," he tells her softly.

Then he takes off at a run.

It's a twenty-minute walk to Dr. Thompson's, but Jacob closes the distance in well under ten. He's never moved so fast in his life. Jacob doesn't think of Thompson as a friend by any means, though the medical man from Stepney Parish has delivered babies and set broken bones for the Jewish families on Copley Street as far back as Jacob can remember. The doctor supplements his treatments with long-winded attempts to convert his patients to the Established Church, but the spirit of Christian charity has at least one benefit: it compels Dr. Thompson to provide quality care at a fraction of the cost of other doctors in the area. Jacob pounds on Thompson's door until at last a startled-looking young woman in a white cap and apron appears on the threshold.

"The doctor is out, I'm afraid," she says.

The words bounce against Jacob's brain and fall back unabsorbed. "He's what?"

"There's an outbreak of scarlet fever in Whitechapel," the girl says. "He was called in urgently. I don't expect him back until morning."

"Then what—"

"Try Whitby, in Sidney Street. It's where I'd go."

The door closes in his face. He stands there a long moment staring at it. Then he's off running again.

Thompson's door is far from the last one to slam in his face that night. Dr. Whitby is in, at least, but when Jacob gives him the address of their slum, the professional interest drains from the man's face. *Go to Dr. Fowles,* he's told through the crack of a closing door, *that's the right fellow for your part of town.* Fowles, of course, feels differently, and sends Jacob in search of a Dr. Giles—*Early in his career, that one; can afford to cut his teeth on people of your persuasion.* Soon an hour has passed, and Jacob is out of breath, sweat pouring down his face and murder in his heart. He stands on a stoop in Shadwell, nearly a mile and a half from home, glaring up at the nameplate declaring it the practice of one Bernard Long, MD. No matter who opens the next door, he tells himself, Dr. Long will be his doctor. He doesn't care if he has to break every law in London to make it happen.

"Dr. Long?" he says to the gentleman who emerges to scowl at him.

"The same."

"Here." Jacob thrusts the shilling from his pocket toward the doctor. It's the last one he has, one he keeps on hand for emergencies, for which this certainly qualifies. "If that's not enough, I'll find more when you get there. Just please, come with me. My mother is dying and no one will see her."

Dr. Long glances down at Jacob from behind the rim of his spectacles. Jacob has seen sailors look with more affection on their ships. There is no charity in his eyes, but there is also no hatred.

"Good God, boy, there's no need for hysterics," the doctor says, tucking the money neatly into the pocket of his waistcoat. "You're lucky I'm at liberty this evening, or I'd have the watch called on you. Mrs. Huxley," he calls over his shoulder. "Fetch my bag. I'm going out."

Dr. Long closes the distance between his practice and the Fagins' flat at a snail's pace, and by the time they scale the stairs and the doctor enters the room, Jacob is so anxious he wants to tear off his own skin. The hand Dr. Long extends to check Leah's pulse is narrow and pale and anemic looking. Jacob has to press down the urge to slap the hand away, to prevent something that so closely resembles death from coming near his mother.

Dr. Long's examination is precise and businesslike. He presses the back of his hand against Leah's brow, listens to her breath, checks the skin of her palms and the bottoms of her feet. Jacob hasn't the faintest idea what the man is looking for, and Dr. Long isn't the type to narrate his actions. The entire process cannot take more than five minutes, and Jacob isn't sure he breathes during any of it. Routine done, Dr. Long stands and unclasps his bag, reaching within for a vial of oblong white tablets, which he hands to Jacob.

"See that she takes one of these each evening," he says.

"What are they?"

The doctor seems miffed that Jacob has the temerity to question a medical man. "Purgatives. Will clear her system of the miasma that's troubling her. If you administer them properly, I should expect a complete recovery by week's end. I will call again on Friday to assess her progress."

"But what if—"

"Good evening." Dr. Long shakes Jacob's hand with the air of someone who intends to wash after, then gathers up his belongings and passes into the corridor—where, Jacob sees now, half the women in the building gathered to watch the doctor at work. An unknown medical man in the Fagins' room is both cause for worry and fuel for the inevitable cycle of gossip. Jacob sees the women glance from him to one another, then back at him, then away again. He recognizes women whose children his mother minded, whose skirts she mended, whose flats she visited with food or a listening ear. Leah always knew when she was needed. No one has ever needed Jacob before.

He sinks down at the table, holding the glass bottle the doctor gave him. A task, and thank God for it. Give her the tablet, then wait, and she'll be better. It's that simple. Any idiot off the street could do it.

His mother protests the tablet, dribbles water down her front, but on the third try he persuades her to take it. That done, he sits in the lamplight, staring at an open book he's not reading. The women vanish in twos and threes without a word to him, and before a quarter of an hour goes by he is alone with Leah again.

Dr. Long first visits on Wednesday evening. By Thursday, Leah is barely lucid, drifting out of dreams now and again only to reach for Jacob's hand. More often than not, her eyes slide past him, toward the corners of the room, rich with dust. He doesn't allow himself to follow her gaze, afraid of what he might see. Sometimes she seems to know it's him sitting next to her, his hand she's holding. He tells her he loves her in these moments. It seems likely that she hears him.

The tablets, he thinks stupidly. That's all it's meant to take. If I do them right, she'll be fine.

Jacob doesn't take the chance to beg a blessing from his mother, much as he knows he should. He's no fool, and the inevitable ending of this slow, slipping dance is as clear as if he is the one dripping sweat into the pillow. But knowing what will happen next is not the same as believing it, and he is incapable of comprehending that this may be his last chance to feel his mother lay hands upon him. He is too much of a failure still, too much of a disappointment. His mother named him Jacob after a clever and self-sufficient patriarch. She can't die until he's done something to deserve it.

Didn't you hear me? he asks God. I'll study four hours a day, five. I'll say a blessing over every meal. I'll honor you, I'll do as you ask, but if you made me then you know what I need to survive, and you can't take it from me without giving anything in return.

If God is listening, the only sign is that it moves quickly.

By Friday morning, Leah falls into a sleep beyond words, staining the sheets with sweat, her fingers picking at loose threads as though she wants to take her needle and mend them as she's always mended every other broken object that comes her way.

By the time the doctor arrives, near to sundown on Friday, she is gone.

Jacob feels as if he should be screaming, but he is silent when it happens. He stands there, useless, the stupid half-full bottle of white tablets still clenched in his fist. It all happened so suddenly, with no time for his mind to catch up with what his body knows. He can't understand a loss of this size, and so he shoves it aside in favor of one thought: he's done the treatment wrong, he didn't listen. It's guilt instead of grief, like he still expects Leah to shout at him for dragging their name through the mud. His mother is dead. These rank sheets, this pale face, will be his last memory of the woman who raised him, a corpse stiff in bed. All he can seem to feel is shame, for being too young and slow-witted and powerless to do as he was told.

It is sundown, and Dr. Long packs up the bag he barely opened, tips his hat to Jacob in polite but disinterested sympathy. It is sundown, and everywhere else throughout the tenement, candles will wink into view like stars, and loaves of challah will be sliced thin to serve more mouths than they were meant for, and the familiar chords of prayer will drift through the halls. Everything will happen the way it always does, because it is sundown, it is Shabbos, and for every family here, this is the holiest time of the week. Every family except for Jacob's, which lies in wreckage at his feet. He wants to overturn the candles. He wants to set the whole world on fire. At least then he would know what to feel.

He hears a soft rustle behind him and turns away from the bed. A cluster of women stand outside the door, their mouths tight but their eyes soft. All are dressed in their Sabbath best, the suit of clothes they set aside and patch with particular care. All of them abandoned their own homes, their own children, to stand here for him, the broken boy in need of God. He hates them for it.

"Go away," he says, and turns back to his mother.

He doesn't want them, these women who edge out of the way as he passes and whisper condemnations of his father like it's prophecy and not history. Who stand here now not out of love for him and his mother, but out of duty for that callous God who heard his bargain and brushed it off with a shrug. He wants Leah, not any of them.

"No," says Mrs. Singer, who steps first into the room.

The disdain he expects from her is there, but muted. Her response is so soft it threatens to tip him over the edge into tears, though whether it's grief or anger he doesn't know.

"Every seventh night is a Sabbath," she says, "but a woman as good as Leah only dies once. And I'll not let her memory be harmed by leaving it in your hands. Now move."

He stares at her, and he sees it, then, why they're here. He's not a good man the way his mother was a good woman. They don't love him because of Leah; they love Leah in spite of him. Numb, he retreats to the corner, out of the way, while the dark-colored cloud of women floats into the room, familiar ghosts offering comfort he can see but not touch.

They work quickly, as they've done many times before for other women, other mothers. As he looks on, they wash Leah's body, prepare her for prayers. They know what to do, for which Jacob finds it within his rageful heart to be grateful. He only attended school for his mother's sake. Nowhere in Rabbi Singer's lessons does he remember hearing instructions to drape the windows and mirror with fabric to prepare for shiva after the burial, or how to speak the kaddish in a way that makes the prayer feel somber yet gentle, like a black velvet glove. These are things the women who encircle his mother know.

He looks up as the prayer ends, and with a thud in his chest that is neither horror nor truly surprise, he sees the figure from the Newgate gallows standing at the head of the bed. The man holds the metal filigree of the headboard, which glints in the new candlelight like the silver manacles around his wrists. He hasn't changed his appearance in the slightest, as ragged and filthy as ever, but there's something in his eyes now that wasn't there before. It's not only coal-black humor any longer. There is tenderness too, and a terrible pity.

Jacob clenches his fists until his knuckles ache and stares with all his might at the figure. Maybe if he looks carefully, he'll see a second figure rise from the bed to stand beside the first. Shorter, hair brown instead of red, the lines of hard living and laughter crinkling outward from her heavy-lidded eyes. If he looks long enough, he'll see that pale face still flushed with sweat, those nimble hands that could transform any scrap of fabric into something magical. Maybe the new figure will speak to him.

He stares until his eyes cross, but the man remains alone and watchful by the bed. When the tears welling in his eyes force him to blink, the red-haired man is gone too.

9

Time passes, absorbing him as it goes. He could stay here forever, eating the scraps of food neighbors bring by to honor his mother by not letting her son starve, watching the black fabric over the windows ripple in the draft. But just as the women know the choreography of the rites, they know when it's time to bring this interlude to a close. The undertaker must be called, and the burial should take place as soon as possible, and he should take charge of it—sixteen, nearly a man grown—but if his mother's friends are already setting it in motion, then who is he to stop them? There's no question of burying Leah Fagin beside her husband, whose bones lie—restlessly, it seems—somewhere in the dust behind Newgate. But the Jews of Stepney have buried their dead in the Alderney Road Cemetery for a century, and if the women put up a collection for the services of an undertaker from the community and for a tombstone to be erected at the end of sheloshim, at least she will be in familiar company.

The undertaker comes past sundown on Saturday, barely an hour after the prohibition on work is lifted. A dark-haired man with a thick beard that reminds Jacob of a bramble patch, he is quick and methodical about his business. Jacob stays out of the way as the man measures Leah's body for a coffin. It feels as mechanical as the day years ago when Leah saved up to buy their bedstead from a secondhand shop, the way she measured the doors and the widths of the stairway to ensure it would fit. Jacob wonders what the undertaker will do if the coffin is too wide for the door. Surely he's encountered such difficulties before, the East End being built up the way it is, more rabbits' warren than habitable housing. Maybe they leave those bodies where they lie, and that's why Stepney is so full of rats. It's easier to think this way than to listen to the undertaker, who has an unpleasant habit of humming tunelessly to himself as he works.

Finally, the undertaker straightens up with a grunt, counterbalancing the ache in his joints with both palms on his lower back. He nods to Jacob, informs him like any other shopkeeper that he'll return the next day with the coffin, as well as a boy to help with the journey to Alderney Road. It's so dispassionate that Jacob briefly loses himself, as though they're discussing the purchase of a sofa and not their actual business, the body on the bed that he still won't call by its proper name. What did he expect, the undertaker to linger, to take tea? A hundred other lives will have found their terminus today, whether by natural or unnatural means. The undertaker can't waste time on anyone when his peculiar set of skills is in such high demand.

"Evening, sir," the undertaker says as he leaves, tipping his hat to the man standing in the doorway.

"Good evening," Anthony Leftwich says to the undertaker.

Leftwich remains on the threshold of the flat, watching Jacob silently. The thief looks like a parrot escaped from the king's menagerie, his yellow paisley waistcoat and the brass buttons of his navy surtout lurid against the black-draped silence. Jacob stands mute. Leftwich has never come to his home before. Then again, Jacob is not in the habit of vanishing without a word. Leftwich's visit is nothing more than a master checking up on a wayward servant. The answer to the thief's question is obvious without asking, lying as it does on the bed beneath a sheet.

"So, little viper," Leftwich says. "What will you do next?"

Jacob doesn't answer. It never occurred to him to wonder what he will do next. The moment the doctor's cold-fish hand brushed his mother's brow, Jacob fell out of time, between the cracks of *then* and *now; next* is some forbidden country he doesn't dare enter.

"No father, eh?"

"Dead." They've worked together five years. It seems impossible Leftwich doesn't know this.

"Neighbors you can gull into taking you in?"

You, he almost says. You're the only person left who knows or cares that I'm alive. You, Anthony Leftwich, who've been by my side through all of it, your gaudy rings and your cruel little eyes watching, measuring the distance between my feet and the gallows. That isn't love—he's more sure now than ever, he did know what love was, once—but Leftwich sees Jacob when he looks at him. Just now, he doubts whether anyone else could say the same.

"Couldn't I—" he begins.

Leftwich takes a startled step backward. Jacob has seen him pull back the same way from a rat that lost its head to a carriage wheel in the street.

"Good God," he says, with a single alarmed laugh. "No."

Whatever door Jacob briefly allowed to open in his heart is closed now. Of course not. More fool him to wonder.

"The landlord will be by once they remove the body," Leftwich says. He spins the ring on his right middle finger with his thumb, and the stone catches the light in each rotation. "He'll want to let the place again, charge two families twice each what he charged yours. And he'll send for the beadle, who'll drive you out and chase your hide straight to the workhouse."

Jacob closes his eyes. The workhouse is at the center of countless stories told throughout the neighborhood to frighten shiftless children. He'll be given a uniform and a scrap of floor for a bed, which he'll share with the fleas and the rats and whatever stains have worked their way into the floorboards over the years, piss and sweat and vomit. They'll set him to working the crank, or picking oakum until his fingernails bleed. They'll drag him to the parish chapel too, and make him mouth Christian prayers with the rest, dunk his head into their baptismal font and pull him back up before giving him the chance to drown properly. Entering their chapel and saying their prayers will mean turning his back on the God Leah gave him, the God who took Leah away. If he can't hate the God who took his mother, he'll have nothing left.

"Mark me, little lost Jew," Leftwich says, as he drifts toward the door. "You're running out of time. My advice as a friend? Make a bolt, and quick."

Jacob waits only until Leftwich's footsteps die away on the stairs. Then he forces himself into motion. He gathers the belongings scattered around the room, the worthless leavings of sixteen years of life. A spare shirt, a handkerchief, his mother's silver candlestick, the knife lifted from the sailor. He can't possibly take all the books, but he selects *The Monk* and *Richard III* from the stack, not because they are particular favorites but because they are small enough to fit in his pocket. After a moment's hesitation—foolish, to hesitate with no one left to judge him—he opens the jar inside the clothes press and shakes the shallow layer of coins inside into his palm. It isn't much, the entirety of Leah's savings: one pound six. It still means he need not starve tonight. As far as inheritance is concerned, it's more than he deserves. Everything fits neatly into the pockets of his overcoat. Gathering them takes less than five minutes.

He stands there in the center of the room, hands hanging open, looking in silence at his mother's body. The rich people listed in the newspapers as survivors of the dead, he thinks, don't know how lucky they are. They can distract themselves dividing up possessions, disposing of a house. There's nothing else he can think of to do that will prolong his departure. Nothing at all to take care of.

The storm of women will look around at Leah's burial tomorrow and mutter to themselves when they see Jacob is gone. *Didn't love his mother enough to bury her. God defend me from such a son.* He ought to have left the first stone at her grave, ought to have sat shiva in their empty flat for seven days. So much he ought to have done, but what does any of it matter? His mother is already gone. Everyone who ever cared for Jacob has left him. It's his turn to leave now, if leaving will keep him alive. Better to cut his losses and care for himself, because this is the price that must be paid when someone else cares for you, the searing, ever-expanding pain when they inevitably disappear. Iron hearts can't break. It's a lesson he will remember.

He bends down, kisses the sheet covering his mother's brow, and goes, into the world.

Without a destination, he wanders. He weaves between carts and takes long jumps over puddles, mud splashing the hem of his coat. Few people know the streets of Stepney Parish better than he does, but he won't feel safe until he no longer recognizes anything around him. He reaches the Thames before that happens, the dirty banks of Ratcliff Cross Wharf, where rickety skiffs lean against their moorings like drunks in the courtyard of a public-house. There's a low wall separating the muddy bank from the street—decades of talk in Westminster about a formal stone embankment have come to nothing, least of all here. He braces himself against it and looks out at the wavelets chattering across the surface of the river. He was crying, he realizes, though he's not anymore. He runs the back of his hand along his cheeks, hastily smearing the evidence with the dirt from his knuckles.

And then he thinks, why?

He always hid his tears whenever they had the gall to appear. The East End is not kind to weakness. But there is no one here for whom he must adjust his expression, no feelings to account for other than his own. Only his grief, his need, only the unthinking animal of his body.

With every step away from Leah, the ties securing him to the world weaken—and at some point, when he doesn't know, they snap. He is loose, drifting. It hurts too badly to be freedom, but he doesn't know what else to call it.

He follows the river westward for half an hour more before turning north, following Leman Street into Whitechapel. It's not terribly far from Stepney, but it's far enough, and he sees no familiar faces in its shabby curtained windows, hears no familiar voices raised in laughter or reprimand drifting from the homes or the shops or the alleyways. No one he knows will ever think to look for him here. They'll reason—not wrongly—that Jacob's survival will be hard enough already without trying to achieve it in Whitechapel, where church bells ring out an hourly warning that here he's the outsider, that here he doesn't belong. No, they'll think, if Jacob is to be found anywhere, it will be in the familiar streets near Stepney Green, and if he's not there, he's likely to be dead.

Which he will be, if he doesn't come up with a plan.

Whitechapel is an even grimmer and narrower slum than Stepney, and the voices he hears within the dense little haunts are far from welcoming. He will need to start asking after rooms to let, but the memory of a stream of doctors' doors slamming in his face leaves him exhausted, and tonight he'd rather not try than be turned away. He settles for the scant cover of a doorway, huddled in his coat with his hands in the pockets, tight around the handle of his knife. Only after he stops moving does he finally lower his defenses enough to feel.

It hurts more than he ever imagined.

Jacob cries silently, the only sign of it the quiver of his shoulders against the wall. Men and women pass by in the street, shadows that avert their gaze and adjust their paths. Maybe they don't hear him. Maybe they do. Just as his survival depends on hiding his tears until it's safe to drop them, maybe theirs depends on not taking any grief that isn't their responsibility. Children have been orphaned before today. More will be orphaned tomorrow. It's only to him that the pain feels unprecedented.

He doesn't sleep at all that night, only presses his eyes fiercely closed and thinks of Leah's hands, the regular darting of her silver needle, the glow of candles against the darkness. He leans against the wall with his left hand clutching the knife until the pattern etched on its case imprints in his palm.

When the sun rises the next morning, the sleeve of his coat is damp from tears, but his course is set. He rises, stretches his aching back, and sets off.

He hammers on door after door, which sure enough results in rejection after rejection, until at last he arrives at a dirty house on Harrow Alley. A very young woman opens the door with an infant on her hip. It might be his imagination, but even the baby seems to look at him with suspicion. It doesn't bode well, but Jacob is getting desperate, and sundown is coming on again. He can't feel the tips of his fingers any longer. Besides, she hasn't closed the door.

"Rent isn't till the first," the woman says tiredly. A girl, really: she can't be more than a few years older than he is. "I'll have it for you then."

"No," he says, "not that." He extends a hand, remembers after the fact that her arms are fully occupied with the baby, but she shifts the child into a one-armed hold and it would be ruder to take his hand back now. "Jacob Fagin. I'm searching for lodgings."

She laughs as she shakes his hand. Her grip is firm, though the ridges of her knuckles are swollen and protrude unpleasantly. He wonders where she works to earn hands like that. A laundry, is his first guess. Not the factories nearby, if she's home at this hour. It might be the power of suggestion, but he fancies he can smell lye on her skin.

"And a desperate search it must be too, if you're looking around here. I'm May Walpole. And this nuisance is Margaret."

"Must take after her father that way," Jacob says.

May raises her eyebrows: this is a bold approach for someone looking for a favor, but she takes a moment to size him up and decides the threat he poses is minimal. "You have work, Mr. Fagin?" she says. The unnecessary title is a jibe, but a light one.

"Manner of speaking," he replies. "Work tends to find me."

May sighs deeply; clearly his type is nothing new to her. "Come in," she says. "Have a look, at least."

The room is so narrow he suspects he can touch two walls if he stands in the center and stretches. It's a simple space, barely furnished: one iron bedstead, a sack stuffed with straw a few feet away. The only window looks directly on a solid wall—May lives in one of those permanently dark houses with taller buildings fronting it in either direction, though at least she can crack the window to swap the stagnant air within for the stagnant air without. An unfriendly looking gray cat skulks in the corner with its ears low and flat against its head. Man and animal lock eyes, and then the cat hisses at Jacob and vanishes under the bed. It's all the same to him. The best thing the animal could do is break rats' necks and stay out of the way.

"How old are you, Mr. Fagin?" May says.

"Twenty," he lies, reasoning he's less likely to be cheated if he rounds up. He isn't sure whether he can pass for twenty, but the people of Whitechapel always look skinnier and smaller than their ages, made that way by a lifetime of stooping in shadowed factories and dark courtyard houses.

"And you haven't any family?" May asks.

He shrugs as if the question doesn't sting and wills her not to press harder. He's putting on a brave face now, but he's cold and he's hungry and he's been an orphan less than forty-eight hours, and if she asks him to explain what happened he'll start to cry right here in front of her. "Had. You know how it is."

He sees her weigh the foolishness of what she's considering. She is a woman alone raising a child, and he is a dirty-looking youth who could, as far as she knows, want absolutely anything from her.

"Here," he says to May, and extends his arms. "I can hold her. Rest."

May's indecision crescendos, the allure of the word *rest* against the terror of relinquishing her child to a total stranger. But he knows how to be persuasive when the moment calls for it—has for the most part used the skill to distract shopkeepers from the fact that he's midway through robbing them, but the same tactics can get him something else he wants. He smiles and raises his hands, fingers spread. *No harm.*

"I know," he says. "Hard to trust someone with a face like mine. But it's in my best interest to make you like me, isn't it? If I want you to let me stay? If you can't trust a stranger to be kind, at least trust him to be selfish."

Some wall behind May's eyes crumbles, and she passes Jacob the baby. For a moment, he's afraid he's overestimated his abilities—it would be just his luck, that his attempt to curry favor ends with a screaming baby and infant bile dribbling down one of his two shirts. But Margaret only squirms in his arms for a few moments before she settles and nuzzles her downy head into Jacob's shoulder. He holds Margaret the way he saw Leah do when the neighbors brought their newborns on their Sabbath visits, one palm stretched wide across the little girl's back. He's not a sentimental person, doesn't consider himself a particular lover of children, but it's still remarkable that an entire human life can fit between his little finger and thumb. God might have felt something similar when he created the world, the same power and patronizing fondness.

"You have a way with her," May says. "Maggie hardly ever lets anyone take her."

"She's a good judge of character." On the contrary, any baby who relaxes in his arms like it's a safe place will be lucky if she lives long enough to walk. "I can watch her when you need. I know how to make myself useful."

"Rent is ten shillings a week," she says. "Bring in three and help me mind her when I'm at work, and you can stay. It's only the floor, I'm afraid. Bed is taken."

Three shillings and a little acting. It's the best price he's going to find in Whitechapel.

"Miss Walpole," he says, "you have yourself an accord."

In fact, it isn't as good a bargain as it seems originally. When May said the bed was taken, she hadn't meant by her: a family of six, the Forresters, also shares the diminutive room, and they pack themselves onto the mattress each night layered foot to shoulder like tinned herring. The straw sack provides bedding for May and the baby, leaving Jacob to sleep on bare boards with only his overcoat for cover until he can better outfit his corner of the room. Even so, as he lies down that night listening to the rain pounding the street to mud outside, a rush of safety crashes over him like a bucket of cold water. He lives here now, and no magistrate or beadle will ever find him. And if staying alive here costs only three shillings a week, his trade will more than cover that. His mother is dead, but he's alive, and he knows how to stay that way.

He's still too tightly wound to sleep, so he reaches into the pocket of his coat and takes out *The Monk*. The idea is to avoid thinking at all costs, but instead of opening to a random page, the book falls open naturally to a spot three-quarters through, where, he sees now, someone has tucked a folded piece of paper between the leaves.

His blood flashes cold as he unfolds the paper. The handwriting is familiar, though messier than he's used to seeing it. She's written in Yiddish, the language in which she felt most comfortable. The creases in the paper are deep enough to fade some of the letters. He can't tell how long ago she wrote this, whether she ever planned to give it to him at all, how long it's been sitting between these pages waiting to be found.

All he knows, as he squints to read in the poor light, is that she waited too long.

10

Jacob,

Do you know how ridiculous it feels to write to your own son? Your son who lives with you? A last resort when you don't listen, and I can't talk. I get too angry when I look at you, and the words come out wrong, so I've stopped trying. The neighbors love to ask after you with that look on their faces like they've smelled something vile, offering their condolences for how you've turned out. Someday soon I'll fight Mrs. Singer in the street over it. Don't laugh—it isn't funny. I don't want their sympathy. I want my boy, home and in one piece.

That's all I wanted you to understand, that day at Newgate. But you don't listen. These days, I'm not even sure you hear.

So let me tell you a story, love. You listen when I read to you.

Once upon a time, long ago, a girl left her home with her family when she was very, very small, to live in a great city on an island farther west than she'd ever been. Never mind why they left. Fires, hunger, knives, guns, smoke, horses, uniforms, broken glass. I've told you these stories all your life.

The girl and her parents found a place for themselves in that new city, built up on both sides of a new river. It wasn't easy there, but nowhere is, and as the girl grew up, she liked it better than her fading memories of home. She had only been four years old when she left. There were other children in this new city for her to play with, and she helped her mother with her mending and sewing, which with her father's work at the butcher's shop nearby brought back almost enough money to eat. They were safe, if not quite comfortable.

This could be the whole story. This ordinary, cozy little story. I could tell you about every corner of her life then, build out the world until it was one you wanted to live in too, one worth being careful to protect. The day the girl found a lost dog sitting near a shop door and brought him home, persuaded her father to keep him. How that dog let her sleep every night with her head on his belly, snoring like an old man. Or the day the girl and her mother went to watch the soldiers parade down Pall Mall in their robin-red coats before they were sent over the sea, and how the girl's mother started to laugh and cry at once because for the first time she could look at a soldier holding a rifle and think, These men are here to protect me. I have almost fifteen years of that story, so much of it you've never heard before.

But I know you, Jacob. You aren't interested in these kinds of stories. So let me tell you one you might like.

The girl was nineteen when she met the boy. You hate romances, but I can't help it, that's the way this story goes. He saw her walking with her dog along the river and came to join her. They talked all that day and into the evening, and even though the girl's mother shouted at her for coming home late and missing supper, the girl hardly heard it, because all she could think of was the next morning, when she'd promised to meet the boy, so they could walk again.

No one else understood what she saw in him. Not her parents, not her friends. They called him cruel names to the girl's face, no doubt worse things behind her back. He was poor, they said, and dangerous, a fast talker, too well-known in the taverns, a gambler, estranged from his own parents, Jewish by birth but not by much else. They didn't understand, but I think you would. Talking to him was like drinking fire. Everything was bright and hot and alive when he looked at it. His world was so much larger than the girl's, his cleverness a London sort of cleverness, quick and deep like the river.

She wanted to know what he knew. Even if it meant losing her parents, her friends, that ordinary cozy little story. And she did lose those things. But she could bear it, because she had him, his biting wit, his daring, his agile hands.

She had him, until she didn't anymore. And then for months she had no one.

Until she had a son.

I could continue the story, but that part isn't what I want you to hear. You're barely here anymore, in and out, always thinking of the next time you can leave. You think I don't know you're still thieving, as if I'm not the one who raised you, as if I didn't learn every trick you have along the way. I know if I want you to listen, I have to be very, very clear. So read carefully, and I'll put it plainly.

I'll never leave you, Jacob. Not like the girl's mother left her.

But in return, you have to promise not to leave either. Not like the boy left the girl.

Those are my terms, and I'll hold to them if you will.

The story isn't finished yet. I left off at a terrible place. My favorite character had just entered the tale. But I don't know how it ends yet. Promise me you'll be the one to tell me the rest, and mean it.

Mama

PART TWO

11

1838

The afternoon is well underway before Jacob gets Dodger and Charley out of the house with Oliver in tow. The delay, he knows, is his own fault—thinking the parish castoff might be a natural, he approached the new boy with unwarranted optimism and ran him through the standard tests straightaway, challenging Oliver to lift a handkerchief from Jacob's coat pocket undetected. Oliver is by no means the least talented boy he's ever come across, and with time he'll learn, but he's no Dodger. He second-guesses himself like he's spent every day expecting a blow to descend from some quarter. After several rounds of flinching failure, Jacob cuts the unproductive lesson short and urges Oliver merely to stick closer to Dodger and Charley than their shadows.

"Watch everything they do," he says, clapping the boy on the shoulder, "and you won't go wrong. Dodger's a regular artist. No one better to show you the ropes."

At length, they go, Oliver tramping after the other boys and looking even smaller from a distance. As soon as they're clear from sight, Jacob sets out across Hatton Garden and south, toward the juncture of Snow Hill and Cock Lane where the Three Cripples stands. He can get to the pub by many routes, but this one is fastest, though it's also the one he likes the least. The buildings that loom over both sides of the road remind him unpleasantly of Copley Street, where he and Leah defended their own little world, where he watched his childhood drift away without realizing it was happening.

It feels the same, but of course, it isn't. Stepney is some three miles farther east, and besides, the community there these days isn't the one he remembers. Most of the people Jacob grew up with have either moved on or died—some from cholera, some from consumption, some from the weight of hard years piling up on the will. The makeshift Jewish colony is still there in a sense, but its members are more recent émigrés now, Poles and Russians and Romanians with little money and less English fleeing violence to the east. Jacob has seen some of the faces from his childhood here and there. The boys who once struggled to stay awake next to him as Rabbi Singer droned on have taken over their fathers' trades, or else they peddle glassware in St. Giles or drag wheeled carts of secondhand clothes down Charterhouse Street. They don't recognize him now, which suits him fine.

Before long, his path takes him flush with Smithfield Market, and the ghosts hissing in his ear are lost to the sounds of vendors and horse-drawn carts and a woman damning her husband's eyes for purchasing eggs at too dear a price. Familiar music at last. The natural order is inverted here, as if God took Mayfair and turned it wrong side out before setting it back to earth as Saffron Hill. Here, in this bent and fractured world, dangerous places feel most like home, nighttime safety and daytime risk. This is topsy-turvy London, where the sunrise barely displaces the shadows and dreams only become more real upon waking. Here, he can drink gin and water for breakfast, and sing to himself over dinner, and walk the streets confident no one will stab him in the back unless they are either very green or very suicidal. In the web of streets between Little Saffron Hill and Bishopsgate, he is a man with no past.

What he has here isn't power, but it's close. It isn't dignity, but it resembles respect. It isn't freedom, but in a world governed by the shriek of the factory whistle and the slam of the workhouse gate, where bodies float to the surface of the Thames faster than the longshoremen can fish them out again—bodies like his, meant only for the inside of a coffin or the wrong end of a rope—in such a world as that, freedom is difficult to come by, and he will accept a substitute.

He arrives at the Cripples in good time, but it's still too late. From behind the bar, a Jew of Jacob's acquaintance, a nervous fellow named Barney, gives him a panicked glance before busying himself with a near-empty bottle of Madeira. Otherwise, the room is empty. Stained oak tables are scattered throughout, and the walls are thick with the same detritus that's served as decor since Jacob was less than half his current age: horseshoes nailed points upward for good luck, a lady's fan spread open to bare its tobacco-stained feathers, a portrait of Queen Victoria in the same dirty frame Jacob has seen house two Georges and a William. It feels like home, but far from a safe one: the weathervane of Barney's unease makes it clear which way the wind blows.

"He's here already, isn't he," Jacob says quietly, leaning against the bar.

Barney's beard shivers like a tree in a thunderstorm as he nods. "Heard broken glass already. You owe me sixpence for it."

"Not my fault if you were fool enough to give Sikes something that smashes when he throws it."

"What would happen if he threw you, Fagin, I wonder?"

He laughs, not because it's funny but because he knows it will make Barney think he isn't afraid, and if Barney thinks he isn't afraid, he won't listen with one ear to the keyhole, which is a sure path to getting both their heads broken, either by Bill or by the police, because Barney can't keep a secret.

"Why do you think I eat so many eels, my dear?" he says. "Makes it impossible to get a proper grip on me. I just slip away, you see."

"You're mad," Barney says, stowing the Madeira beneath the bar. "Get in there, before he calls for me again."

Jacob raps his knuckles on the bar twice for luck before darting into the back parlor.

The Three Cripples' private room is a sunken space, two steps down from the main tavern. Two windows punctuate the back wall, but as they look out on a dirty courtyard that itself is blocked by another building some ten feet away, they admit almost no light. The tavern-keeper, an old acquaintance of Jacob's named Travers, hung a pair of mismatched curtains over them to hide the grimness outside. A handful of lamps are laid across the tables, their oil running low and the flames beginning to sputter. In the unsteady light, a white bull terrier sits under the center table, his queer triangular eyes darting toward the door. The dog gives a shadow of a growl. He recognizes Jacob but does not like him. The feeling is mutual.

On the far side of the room, Bill Sikes leans against the wall, both thumbs hooked in the pockets of his brown fustian breeches. At the table in front of him is a young man Jacob doesn't know—flaxen hair, dressed too well for the Cripples. Jacob cannot see his face. Bill, hearing the click of the door, glances in Jacob's direction, then, satisfied the intrusion is no threat, turns back to the business at hand. Beside the pale-haired young man at the table sits a bottle of gin, no more than a third full. One sturdy glass rests at his elbow. The other lies in pieces on the floor.

"You don't understand," the man says. Jacob raises a single eyebrow. It's been a long time since he's dared to tell Bill what he doesn't understand. "If I don't have the money by Friday, they'll call the law in, and it'll be the Marshalsea for me by sundown."

Bill leans his head back until his eyes are cast toward the ceiling. The movement exposes the line of his throat, dark with stubble. On another man, the posture would seem vulnerable. On Bill, it reminds Jacob of a wolf catching a scent on the wind.

"And would serve you right, Fred," Bill says, his hard Cockney accent making the other man sound even frailer and more foolish, "for wasting two fortunes at the card table. Can't see where you got the notion I care."

"I promise you the Carmichaels are in Bath for the fortnight," Fred says. "Not a soul at the house but the old butler, and you could handle him with one finger. I'll give you the keys, I'll tell you where the plate and jewels are, and when you pawn them, I'll give you twenty percent for your trouble. It's an easier job than you'll find anywhere. I'm handing it to you."

The man, Jacob knows, has heard stories of the fearsome housebreaker Bill Sikes, but he hasn't understood them. He heard about the towering, quick-fisted man who can move faster and more secretly than the night itself, and in this specter he seeks the sort of devil he can make a deal with. But Fred sorely misjudged his position, if he thinks he'll be setting the terms.

Jacob leans against the wall, waiting silently for Bill to finish. Fred, with eyes only for the robber, doesn't notice they're no longer alone, but Bill takes the opportunity to put on a show. Like old times, Bill feeling the urge to impress him.

"Twenty percent," Bill repeats. "Twenty, for putting my neck in the halter and trusting you not to throw the trapdoor."

"I wouldn't—" Fred begins.

"And of course you'd say that. Because you think I'm soft enough in the head to believe you. Ain't been to your fancy schools, ain't been brought up with your folderols and your by-your-leaves, you think I can't tell a man who's set to cut my throat when my back is turned?"

Bill pushes himself off the wall and takes two steps toward Fred. His hands drift out of his pockets, and Jacob, like Fred, finds his eyes skimming Bill's body, searching for where he's concealed his weapon. Trouser pocket, he suspects: there's something heavy near Bill's left hip.

"Let me tell you something," Bill says. "Bill Sikes looks out for himself first. And if you want to get the better of him, you have to get up damn early in the morning to try it. Do you hear?"

Fred nods so quickly Jacob pictures his head toppling off his skinny neck.

"Good," Bill says. "Then clear out."

"But—"

"Out."

He doesn't wait to be told a third time. Fred shoves back his chair, whirling to the door as if to make a dead sprint for it. This, of course, brings Jacob into his line of sight for the first time. Fred cries out in alarm. His face is as insipid from the front as Jacob suspected from the back. Jacob gives him a small, fluttering wave.

"Don't let me keep you, my dear," he says.

Fred slams the door so hard it rattles.

Bill chuckles and crosses to sit in Fred's now-vacant chair. "Gave him the fright of his life, you did."

Jacob shakes his head. "All your doing, I suspect. Drink? I'd offer to pour, but it seems we're down a glass."

"If I have to look at your ugly face, I'll need more than fits in a glass." Bill pours out three fingers of gin, nudges the glass across the table, then drinks straight from the neck of the bottle. "Sit down, if you're going to stay. Don't loom there like an old bat in a cave."

Jacob sits. To stop himself wringing his hands, he settles them in the pockets of his greatcoat. It's cold outside for September, and the heat from the fire doesn't seem to reach him.

From close up, Bill looks dreadful. Since their last meeting two weeks prior—the last time Bill stomped drunk into the house on Bell Court with Nan on his arm and the vilest curses Jacob has ever heard on his tongue, shouting all the old arguments again—Bill's dark blue eyes have become sunken, and the shadows beneath them remind Jacob just how thin the layer of flesh is that separates a man's bones from the world. If the old illness from his years in the Steel hasn't reared its head again, Jacob will eat his hat. But there's a gleam in Bill's eye that Jacob knows well of old. The satisfaction of a job in motion.

"You're planning something, Bill," Jacob says. "I haven't known you to suffer fools otherwise."

Bill grins. "Friday's a long way off. He ain't desperate yet. Twenty? Come week's end, he'll be begging me to take ninety."

The dog trots across the room and settles beneath Bill's chair, resting his shovel-broad head on his forepaws. Bill pulled Bullseye by the scruff from a coal chute where someone had been trying to suffocate him when the great brute was just a puppy. At the time, Jacob entertained a brief germ of hope that this might be a sign of Bill's better nature winning over the worse, but Bill has bent the dog so entirely to his will that Bullseye will rip out the throat of anyone Bill tells him to. That's the kind of love between them, the kind that poisons as it deepens.

"Admirable planning," Jacob says, settling back in the chair with calm he doesn't feel. "And puts my mind at ease, besides."

"What are you on about?" Bill says.

"A little bird told me you were casing a house in Chertsey, but I knew that couldn't be right. My oldest friend in the world, find a rich mark and not invite me to make a party of it? Not possible. The business with the Carmichaels explains it all."

Bill reaches down to scratch Bullseye behind the ears. The dog closes his eyes and grumbles in contentment. "Who told you about Chertsey?"

Jacob shrugs. "You know how my people are. Always whispering among ourselves, keeping our secrets."

"It's no great prize, Fagin; don't drive your greedy black heart mad. It's a rum house is all, plate easy to see from the street, and the old man's stone deaf and sleeps like a log, they say. No neighbors for half a mile any direction. And Toby's already signed on. If we can get a boy, couldn't be easier to slip in and take what's worth having."

Jacob's heart shudders at those casual words, *Toby's already signed on.* That idiot, always quick to think the glory outweighs the risk. As he's done many times before, with many people, Jacob sternly reminds himself that Toby is a man grown and in charge of his own life. And there's the second part of Bill's thought to consider.

"A boy," Jacob repeats. "Because you've always been so fond of children, Bill. That paternal streak running through your heart of hearts."

"And you," Bill fires back. "Taking in orphans you find in the gutter out of charity."

"Was what drew me to you. Never saw a more pathetic excuse for a thief."

"Never saw a mirror in those days, did you, you ugly old skeleton."

This feels, to Jacob's surprise, normal. From Nan's terror, he was certain he'd spend the conversation ducking blows and flinching away from broken glass. He came with his old knife at the ready, though he isn't so stupid he thinks he could defend himself against Bill with a three-inch blade. But Bill is positively jovial, trading insults that are more bark than bite. Maybe Nan blew the whole matter out of proportion, heard Bill threaten something in drink he'd never intend when sober. He starts to let his guard down, preparing for an easy afternoon with a bottle of gin under the increasingly slack gaze of the dog.

Then Bill shakes his head. "Don't need to go searching for a boy, though, do I? Word is there's a slimy old Hebrew in Saffron Hill who keeps them stocked by the dozens. Would sell one to the devil for the right price."

Abruptly, Bill is no longer joking. There's a barb at the end of the hook now.

"Bill," he says warily. "We've discussed this. There's our business, and then there's mine with the boys. Toby's all very well, but the children aren't ready for your sort of work yet; they're too green."

Too green, he says, because what he can't say is, *Too human, they're too human still for what you do, and if I leave them alone in your company for three nights they'll come back to me unrecognizable, up to their necks in whatever sort of darkness you've made your home in, if they come back at all. God or some devil has touched you, Bill Sikes, and I can't trust that same power to look after a boy of twelve.*

It's not altruism. It takes time and effort to train up a child until his thieving keeps food on the table. He doesn't think of himself as miserly, but he's not interested in starving, and if he loses Dodger or Charley, he understands arithmetic well enough to know he'll have to work half again as hard or they'll all have to eat one-third less. And if he sees a little of his own childhood flash-and-dagger in the boys' swaggering gait, if he sees his own ferocious ambition in Dodger's boastful retellings of his finer thefts, well, what of it? It doesn't interfere with the primary impulse for survival, and so it hardly matters whether it's real or the foolishness of a man growing old.

"Too green," Bill repeats, taking another pull of gin. "You mean to tell me that Bates boy's lived under your shriveled old wing for more than a year and still can't climb through a damned window? Don't tell me you've lost your touch."

"If Charley Bates has lived to eleven without getting nicked by the police for showing his bare arse to a magistrate, there's only me to thank for it."

"Well," Bill says, "say that's true. You're a resourceful old dog, Fagin. Find me another. Get me the boy, and you'll have the same cut as if you hauled your mangy hide down to Chertsey yourself. Can't ask fairer than that."

Bill thinks he's made a reasonable request. But Jacob's mind is whirling, grasping at a problem that has evolved beyond his ability to figure. Dodger, a prodigy and as arrogant as he is gifted, a tendency toward grandiloquent statements carried on hot air. Charley, roaring with laughter over a joke he hasn't finished telling yet, losing hand after hand of whist and wheedling Jacob for a farthing to lose on one more rubber. And how many more over the years, how many others he could still drag up by the collar and give away. For a moment, he considers telling Bill to take them all, to rid himself of the whole enterprise, wash his hands of it and starve to death in his own private den, so long as he can do so quietly, without having to make more choices.

And then he remembers. His calculus, this time, is not precisely as before.

The new boy, the workhouse castoff. No time to become anything more than a name to Jacob, a name and a quick pair of hands that can divest a house of its silver plate. That fierce look in the boy's eyes. That hunger to prove himself.

"All right," he says. "I know one who'll do. But you have to promise me something."

Bill's eyes narrow. "I have to promise *him*?" he says to no one in particular. "Damn me, how the world changes."

"Think of him as mine," Jacob says. See how he's fallen, an old man who begs for what he wants. "That's all. Something I'm lending you, as you might borrow a crowbar. Except when you're finished with the boy, I want him *back*, Bill. Please."

"You hear him?" Bill remarks to Bullseye. "Wants the boy back, he says. Same as all his lot, won't lend a friend a shilling out of his hoard to stop him starving. You're lucky I know better than to ask for your own neck."

He sees it then, the pistol in Bill's trouser pocket, right where he suspected it would be. Bill has a pistol, and his dog is sitting attentively at his heels with a steel trap of a jaw that can crush bone, and Bill is looking at Jacob with the sort of disdain that isn't unfamiliar, but cuts deeper with a weapon to back it up.

"Just be careful, my dear," he says softly. "For all our sakes."

For a beat—less than a breath—Jacob fancies he's looking back across two decades, into the dirty, determined face of the boy who nearly spat at him the first time they crossed paths. That fiery, frightened boy who still smiled and sometimes, on rare occasions, teetered on the edge of putting his teeth away. The vision only lasts a moment, like the beam of a lighthouse before the lamp circles past, warning other ships from shore.

"Go collect your boy," Bill says. "I'll come tonight, past ten, have a look myself. Not so stupid as I trust you to be a proper judge of character."

"Certainly not," Jacob says. "I invited you in that first night, didn't I?"

He's already at the door before Bill can fire off another insult. As he turns the handle, he thinks he hears Bill laugh. It could as easily be the huffing breath of the dog, the scrape of a table against the floor, a gunshot into the air from two hundred yards off. Jacob closes the door before he can determine which.

A few afternoon drinkers had trickled into the taproom while he was talking business in back: two women in heavy rouge chasing away last night's drinking with a glass of gin and water, a rangy fellow dressed as if he's only today arrived in from the country. Another man sits in the corner, resting his chin on interlaced fingers, reddish hair bound out of his face with a scrap of cord. Jacob knows without looking who the man is, and that if he asked anyone else in this tavern to number its occupants, his tally would be one higher than theirs. Barney is still behind the bar, rearranging bottles in a way that makes it obvious he's been eavesdropping.

"A groat for the glass," Jacob says, setting two coins on the bar. "And the shilling for whatever else he means to drink today. Tell him it's me who's paid. It'll do me good if he knows it."

Barney nods knowingly, whisking the money into the till. "You're in it that badly, Mr. Fagin?"

Yes and no, he thinks. It's more money than he can afford. But if Bill can drink through a shilling's worth of gin at this hour, he'll be asleep in his own rooms by ten, and the trek to Bell Court to lay eyes on a boy sprung free of the workhouse will no doubt feel like an effort unjustified by the meager reward it promises.

Jacob cannot save his boys from everything, cannot save them from most things, but he can at least give Oliver one night. Tonight, he will cook supper as best he can with what Dodger and Charley steal, and Dodger will regale them all with the embellished details of his latest theft, and Oliver will start to nod off at the table, which will send Charley into fits of hilarity every time Oliver's chin droops toward his chest. Jacob will cuff Charley on the back of the head, exhorting him to remember his manners, and with order temporarily restored he will chivvy Oliver into the basement, where the boys will bed down in the collection of blankets they've nicked over the years from the ragpickers and the abandoned homes of the dead. They'll be asleep in minutes,

Charley snoring like a man twice his size, and Jacob will sit up, watching the fire burn low, thinking of Nan's frightened eyes, and that dull rumbling laugh of Bill's, and the dog's panting breath, like the pumping of some great bellows.

"You know me, Barney," Jacob says. "I'm never in anything so badly I can't find my way out again."

The off-duty prostitutes raise their glasses at Jacob as he passes, the silent salute of a shift change at the factory gates. The red-haired man in the corner raises his glass as well. His smile is knowing, the rhythm of his gestures familiar. Jacob doesn't acknowledge him, though he feels the man's eyes follow him as he leaves.

12

1803–1807

When Jacob arrives at the room on Harrow Alley, sixteen and newly orphaned, he thinks he might live there a month. In fact, he stays more than four years.

No one is more surprised by this than he is. The tiny room houses four adults including himself, two of whom actively dislike him, which doesn't dispose him warmly to Whitechapel on the whole. Mr. Forrester was less than thrilled to return home after a long day seeking work at the docks to find an underfed thief living in the corner of his room, and his wife follows his lead in keeping her distance. Jacob, for his part, makes no effort to win them over. He sees the way Mr. Forrester looks at him, searching for proof of his theories in Jacob's voice, in his name, in his hair, in the line and curve of his nose. *Jew,* he sees the man thinking, *thief, swindler, child snatcher, miser.* It's deeply irritating that the shorthand of his face leads the man to at least two correct conclusions. Jacob leans into the role rather than away, tossing disjointed phrases of Yiddish into his conversations that have nothing to do with anything, but make Mr. Forrester whisper irritably to his wife as if the language is only suitable for hexes. Every time the color rises in the man's face, Jacob adds it to his running tally of personal victories. By the end of his first month, his list is long indeed.

The children, though—there are five, four little Forresters as well as Maggie Walpole—the children are a delight. With the guilelessness of their species, they stare at him as though he's a fantastical butterfly pinned to a card and ask him endless questions, long after the novelty of his presence has faded. *Why is your hair that color,* they ask, and *Why do you speak like a gentleman but you haven't any money,* and *Why do you never go to church with us,* and *When do you pray.* He doesn't resent these questions: there's no malice in them, and divorcing himself from sixteen years of acquaintances in a night has left him starved for conversation.

"I don't go to church because in my country, where I come from, I'm a prince," he says. "And when you and your families go to pray, that's when my advisors and ambassadors come, and we discuss matters of state. It's very important I'm here when they arrive, otherwise the entire country would fall. They can't rule it without me, you see."

And the children look at him wide-eyed, particularly little Davey Forrester, who's altogether unsure what to believe, and they ask, *Do they not pray, Jacob, in your country?*

"Oh, we do, my dears," he says. "Only there we do it differently."

They accept this explanation without question, and from then on he is not foreign but exotic, not strange but remarkable. They hound him for stories, especially Tommy, the eldest, who at eight years old is hungry for the same tales of bloodshed and scandal that enraptured Jacob as a boy. One afternoon, when the children's stomachs are growling almost loud enough to drown out the tales, he spends an irresponsible amount of money to bring back a feast for all five of them: two loaves of brown bread, a paper-wrapped package of cold chicken, half a cheese, and the crowning glory of it all, six gooseberry tarts each the size of his palm. He'll go hungry for a week after because of it, but it's worth the trouble for the way Clara's and Annie's eyes grow to the size of guineas. While they wolf down the food, he tells them the story of a feast he had once, when he was small. A feast so grand the table sagged under the weight of fine dishes, and the crisp linen tablecloth was spattered with juices and sauces and grease by the time the plates were cleared.

The feast, of course, is a lie. Jacob borrowed it from one of Leah's books, but five little faces swarm around him, hungry for a story. And he, hungry for an audience, doesn't deny them.

Jacob's first guess was right: May makes her living, such as it is, as a laundress. She works queer hours that become progressively queerer now that Jacob is on hand to mind Maggie, and more than once he sees the wrong side of four in the morning as May slips the baby into his arms before leaving for work. Fortunately, Maggie is an excellent sleeper, and Jacob can doze until seven with her contentedly drooling on his chest. May is often back by late afternoon, at which point she curls up beneath a blanket and falls asleep for an hour or two before handing Maggie to Mrs. Forrester and following Jacob out the door as they begin their respective evening shifts.

Just watching her would make Jacob swear off honest living for the rest of his days, but even May can't work constantly. On occasion, when the money is coming in well or she's on the verge of going mad without a breath of fun, she looks at Jacob with an expression that makes her seem properly her age: eighteen, not fifty.

"Come out with me," she says on these occasions, and Jacob never tells her no.

Tonight, some months after his arrival, their destination proves to be one of May's preferred cookhouses off Chamber Street—though it could be anywhere as far as he's concerned, May is very much leading the way. It's a beautiful clear night in September, not a cloud overhead, and as she guides him north, the whole blasted city almost seems beautiful. The hardest spikes of grief from Leah's death have softened over the summer. Now, if he allows his mind to wander, the warm glow of candles behind strangers' curtains sparks a proportionate warmth in his chest rather than a surge of loneliness, and the stars overhead are familiar and bright.

May is in that almost-delirious state of tiredness where she seems drunk without having touched a drop, and she hangs off his arm without shame or self-consciousness.

He wants to make her laugh, to preserve her mood and his place in it, but before he can think of anything to say, May tilts her head back to the sky and says simply, "I want to kill him."

Jacob almost trips in surprise, but he knows how to take what's handed to him. "You should," he says, ready to agree to anything. "They don't like to hang women, and you'd get three square meals a day in prison. Unless it's my head you're after, in which case, I can't approve."

She disentangles her arm from his to shove him in the shoulder. "You? You're the only one I don't mind having round. No, it's Bolton I'm going to kill. Rake his throat over the washboard and flay open his windpipe."

He should have known. The owner of May's laundry is the primary target of her hatred most days. It must help pass the time, planning a murder. "Try the lye instead," he says. "A little in his coffee every morning. Neater, and no one can pin you for that, though you've got to be patient."

They arrive at the cookhouse, a ramshackle two-story building with a door that won't close properly and the sound of raised voices spilling out to welcome them. May shoulders the stuck door all the way open and gestures with one arm, inviting him in ahead.

"You'd be frightening, if you weren't my friend," she says.

This shouldn't jolt his heart the way it does. He swallows his growing smile and ducks inside. It's busy for this hour of the evening, and after living in Whitechapel this long, Jacob recognizes a handful of the faces that occupy the main room. Calling these people friendly acquaintances, though, would overstate the case. He feels more than one darkened glance descend on him as he guides May toward a corner table, as far from company as he can manage. The cookhouse is dark, all wood paneling and thick-curtained windows, and he's most at ease where the shadows are thickest. May sits, the candle in the sconce over her head casting long shadows over her dark blond hair. The air around them is heady with sweat and brine and shared breath.

A serving-girl appears at the side of the table, but though Jacob makes an obvious attempt to catch her eye, the girl is determined only to look at May. She drops a slight curtsy, so shallow as to be offensive.

"How can I help you, miss?" the girl says.

"As many oysters as sixpence will buy," May says, passing two coins—Jacob's coins—to the girl, "and bread alongside. Beer too, if you have it."

"Right away, miss," the girl says with another quarter curtsy. The moment she turns her back, Jacob flashes a vulgar gesture in her direction. May barely stifles a laugh.

"I like coming out with you," she says. "Makes me feel terribly important."

Jacob pulls a seated bow, doffing a hat he isn't wearing. "Happy to be of service."

It took time to get used to, the instant ability of certain Whitechapel types to spot him as a Jew at forty paces. In Stepney, he grew up around as many kinds of Jews as there are stars in the sky, and if someone asked him two years ago to describe what an average member of his tribe looked like, he wouldn't have known where to begin. Be that as it may, the Whitechapel serving class has an unerring instinct for identification. Three of every four nights he spends with May, they insist on speaking only to her. The serving-girl's pointed cold shoulder makes Jacob imagine the indignant complaints such treatment would have drawn from Leah, but he doesn't let her voice linger long. He's here now, with May, a friend who cares to spend time with him. Asking for anything more would be selfish and stupid besides.

The girl returns in a twinkling with mugs of beer and a dish of oysters, which cannot be of great quality if May can secure so many for sixpence. It's another thing he had to grow used to quickly: the curious variety of slime and slop that Gentiles consider food. His days of keeping kosher died with his faith in God, and he'll eat anything that comes at a reasonable price these days, but it seems like Christians draw the line between food and garbage too charitably. The first oyster slides down his throat like he's filled his mouth with a great gulp of Thames water.

"I can't believe people eat this on purpose," he says, wiping his mouth on the back of his hand.

"You can choose the chophouse next time," May says, unbothered by his squeamishness. "Somewhere they'll open the doors to a washerwoman and a thief and serve us a rack of lamb for sixpence. If you know such a magical place."

Jacob never explained to May where his portion of the weekly rent comes from, nor has she asked, but she knows. His second week staying with her, he passed over his three shillings in rent while holding a handkerchief to his bleeding nose—a souvenir from an attempted mark who knocked Jacob to the street and snatched his own wallet back without bothering to involve the police—and she pocketed the coins without the slightest curiosity. Money is money, and it hardly matters to May whether it started its life honestly or otherwise.

"You underestimate me," he says. "Why settle for a cut-rate chophouse? I could steal us new identities out of whole cloth, couldn't I, and have us swan up to the finest place east of Hyde Park. What's class but nice clothes and pretty words?"

"And you already speak like a curate," May quips before tossing back another oyster.

"Child's play," he says, grinning. He's caught up in the story as if it's one he's telling the children, keen on anything that adds a little magic to the cookhouses of Whitechapel. He takes a sip of beer, then continues, gesturing widely with his free hand. "We'll find a posh couple moving house and lift a valise off the servants as they carry them in, couldn't be easier. I'll be..." He casts his eyes about, as if the perfect identity will emerge from the woodwork. "Lord Edgar Willoughby, of the Somerset Willoughbys. And you..."

"Lady Eliza Lamb, your betrothed," May says promptly.

Jacob snorts into the foam of his beer. He can't decide which is funnier, the name or the relation. "Lady Eliza Rack of Lamb with Roast Potatoes. Charmed, I'm sure."

"Go to hell," she says, ripping off a piece of bread. "I'm hungry."

"Well, we can see to that," he says. "Just keep your mouth closed and let me handle it, flutter a fan in front of your face. I'll have them set us up at the finest table at the Albion, linen tablecloth and all, and I'll order for us both, seeing as it's the gentlemanly thing to do."

She flicks an empty oyster shell across the table at him. "Gentlemanly?"

He tries to catch it left-handed before it skitters by and misses, but its click against the floor is lost under the noise of the shop. "Oh, because you think they'll believe a lady who speaks Cockney strong enough to make your hair stand on end?"

"And you can do better."

He wrinkles his nose, then adopts the finest tones he can manage, throws his shoulders back, even turns his nose up in a posture of studied aristocratic disdain. "Yes, I think a bottle of the ninety-eight Châteauneuf-du-Pape alongside the lamb, my good man, and do try not to decant any of that inferior swill you reserve for the lower sort, because rest assured, I shall *know*."

His French pronunciation is so bad it might kill a self-respecting Parisian, but for his current audience, it does the trick. May looks at him like he's both her prime source of delight and the most absurd creature who's ever walked on two legs. The rest of the cookhouse pointedly ignores them, but in the warmth of her attention, it hardly matters.

The night wears on pleasantly, the two of them switching from beer to gin midway through the meal upon realizing they won't get as drunk as they're hoping otherwise. It's two hours later when May arches her back in a stretch and gets to her unsteady legs. Jacob follows rather more composedly. He lets May take the lead, mostly with the intention of watching her back, listening to her muse that if they don't return soon Mrs. Forrester is liable to sell Maggie to the parish for pin-money. The moon hangs a bright half circle above them to shine on the drunks and roustabouts debating whether to stumble home or piss away sixpence more. It's coming up on Jacob's favorite time of night, the witching hour when the disreputable are newly snoring into puddles of their own drool and working people like May haven't yet begun their mornings. In the quiet of that indeterminate time, anything seems possible.

"Tell me something," he says, partly because he is tipsy but also because he is dying to know. "Maggie's father...?"

He doesn't finish the question before May scoffs and shoves him away, nearly overbalancing herself. "Don't you start that way. You're the only person left in my life who hasn't written me off as a fallen woman."

"I'm not saying that," he says, prepared to catch her mid-stumble. "I'm only curious."

"Right then," she says. "He was a sailor I met in a gin-palace one night when I was tired and looking for a bit of fun. Never did get his name. Is that what you wanted to hear?"

She's not angry, he doesn't think, but it's trending dangerously in that direction. It's the last thing he wants—new to the practice of friendship, he's forever discovering lines it's better not to cross. He smiles, lays one hand on her shoulder.

"She's a beautiful little girl," he says. "Whoever your sailor was, he wasn't worthy of you."

He means the remark as an apology, a sign he appreciates her honesty and thinks no less of her for it. So he is utterly confounded when May looks at him curiously before taking him by the lapels and pulling him in closer. There's a moment when he senses it about to happen, like watching a carriage wobble before it overturns, and he is equally powerless to stop it from taking its course.

And then May kisses him.

Her lips taste of salt and beer and something else he has no word for. She's in charge, her hands still gripping his lapels, and his mind is a raging, tempestuous blank. He kisses her back, or rather his mouth and the gin in his veins kiss her back. It cannot be enjoyable for her. It goes on another second, and the first thought that drifts by is of a child who brushed his hand against a white-hot iron, that beat before the boy realizes the sensation shooting up his arm is pain.

May's tongue brushes against his lips, and he gains sufficient control of himself to pull back an inch. However much she's had to drink, she's sober enough to feel his retreat. May springs away as though he pushed her. Her eyes are wide, her mouth half-open, and even in the moonlight he can see the flush rising in her cheeks. Realizing, he's sure, what a mad thing she's just done.

He smiles softly and shakes his head. "You don't want that," he says.

She watches him for a moment, breathing hard. Jacob is under no delusions at all about what she sees. He knows what he is: the kind of creature that belongs alone.

"Because you know what everyone wants," May says. "Don't miss a trick, you." She looks disheveled and off-balance in the semidarkness, her dark blond hair escaping its braid.

"You should go back," he says. "I'll be along."

May runs one hand along her mouth, then tilts her head up to look at the moon. In a trick of the light, her eyes look almost wet.

"You're a sad little thing, Fagin," she says.

"Go on," he says, and stands motionless until her footsteps die away.

There's a tavern he knows well, not far off. Though he'll regret it, he drinks until sunrise, conscious of his body only enough to bring the glass from the table to his lips. When he stumbles back to Harrow Alley after daybreak, squinting against the sun, Mrs. Forrester scowls at him from the doorway, not sparing a greeting before stalking off to work. Inside, the room holds five children and no one else. May has already been at work for hours.

13

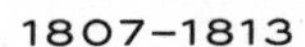

1807–1813

It's a pleasant existence as far as it goes. His friendship with May persists, though with fresh awkwardness they never quite shake, and the children continue to cling to his coattails like mothballs. But whatever tolerance the Forresters mustered for him on account of his youth and poverty grows more threadbare by the day as he becomes a man. Mr. Forrester watches him like a farmhand would eye an unbroken horse, and Mrs. Forrester quickly remembers somewhere she and her whole brood of children need to be whenever Jacob arrives with pockets freshly weighted down with coin from the dolly-shop. He bears it as best he can, preferring their familiar scorn to the unknown. But their domestic peace is so tenuous that one firm shake will displace it for good.

It's early on in the winter, and for days now the sound of enthusiastic Christmas carolers in the street has been shot through with shouts of the newspaper-boys hawking grim headlines about the two military ships capsized in Dublin Bay. Bodies have been washing up on the beach by the dozens—men, women, and children—and Jacob has never seen the newspaper-boys so joyful, fresh headlines morning and night that draw readers like flies to a corpse. The macabre images put Jacob in a lonely sort of mood, and so instead of spending the night getting drunk elsewhere as he usually would, he stays back in Harrow Alley. May is out working, but the Forresters are here, Mrs. Forrester putting her children to bed while her husband finishes a last glass of porter. Jacob himself sits cross-legged in the corner with a book, Maggie leaning against his side and pretending to follow along. Pip, the Forresters' gray cat, purrs nearby in the candlelight. Jacob has read *The Monk* easily two dozen times by now, could recite most of it from memory. Still, beginning it again makes the cold night seem a little warmer. If he focuses on the words as he listens to Mrs. Forrester singing a soft lullaby to Clara and Annie, he can almost imagine it's Leah's voice he hears.

"Darling," Mrs. Forrester says suddenly. "What is that?"

"What?" Annie says.

Jacob glances up in time to see Mrs. Forrester snatch something bright from Annie's fist. He sets aside the book. Mrs. Forrester holds the item up to the candlelight, and then he can see it clearly. A bracelet: a simple string of pink beads with a tiny gilt clasp, worth ninepence with some bargaining. He should know—he's the one who stole it in Rosemary Lane and, hearing how little he could get for it, brought it back as a trinket for Annie's seventh birthday last week. She hugged him fiercely around the waist and declared she'd never owned anything so fine. He told her to keep close hold of it. He should, he sees now, have told her to keep it out of sight of her mother.

"Annie," Mrs. Forrester says. "Where did you get this?"

Jacob is not breathing. You found it, he thinks as loudly as he can. You picked it up in the gutter. The woman down the hall offered it to you. A nice lady on the steps of the church.

"It's a gift from Mr. Fagin," Annie says.

Mr. Forrester sets his porter on the windowsill with a *clink*. Jacob scrambles to his feet. Maggie—smart girl—scurries away to hide behind the bed, closely pursued by the cat.

"You little devil," Mr. Forrester says.

Why did he choose to read in the corner? There's nowhere to go from here. Mr. Forrester stands between Jacob and the door, and all five children stare owlishly as the distance between the two men narrows. Mr. Forrester has been waiting for an excuse since the day he found Jacob occupying his flat. Jacob is only surprised it's taken him so long to find one.

"It's not bad enough you turn my home into a hiding hole for villains and criminals," Mr. Forrester goes on. "Now you want to turn my children into thieves? Make my girls into whores and have my boys creep through the streets as your minions? I tell you, I won't have it."

Mr. Forrester grabs Jacob by the shirtfront and drags him forward until he can feel the man's breath on his cheek. Smells the tang of porter. Somewhere behind him, Davey is crying. Annie is begging her father to stop. Jacob is barely himself. That unfortunate man Mr. Forrester has caught should do something, he thinks distantly, before he gets himself killed.

"You don't have children, so why would you care? Don't have parents either, I'll bet my life. Come straight from the devil without any mother or father at all, but us, we're a good Christian house, and I'll be damned if you get your dirty claws in my children."

"You've been happy to take my dirty Jewish money till now," Jacob says coldly.

He's hardly in a position to antagonize a man who currently has his throat in his hand, but something beyond sense has overtaken him. He's not the frightened youth he was when he first arrived, all raw nerves and desperation. He's a man grown, and that makes him dangerous.

"Damn your money," Mr. Forrester says. "I won't have it, I'll tell you that." And he spits in Jacob's face.

Jacob isn't a proud person, not anymore, but there's a point beyond which a man refuses to be pushed. An absolute blankness fills his mind. He is hardly aware of his own body as he wrenches free of Mr. Forrester's grip. Less so still as he punches the man in the gut with all his strength.

Mr. Forrester crumples to the ground, gasping for breath. His wife gives a strangled scream from the bed. Davey and Maggie are both weeping now. Annie is white as a sheet. But Jacob feels nothing save a faint ache in his knuckles. He's lived with these people for years, and in a moment, they are nothing to him again. Let no one in. Rely on no one but yourself. Everyone will betray you, one way or another.

He bends down to sweep his belongings into his coat pockets—the same few objects he fled Copley Street with, the candlestick, the knife, the books. When he straightens up again, Mrs. Forrester shrinks back onto the bed, as if afraid he will charge her with the knife.

Jacob chuckles lowly, shaking his head. "Not in front of the children."

Mrs. Forrester reaches for her own throat. Her husband is regaining his breath, pushing himself to his hands and knees. Paying no attention to either of them, Jacob spares one last look at the children, who stare as though they've never seen him in their lives. He's frightened them, these little ones who trailed after him like ducklings in a pond. How will they remember him, in two weeks, in a year, in ten? The storyteller? The architect of a feast? The wild-eyed man with the knife?

"Maggie," he says, with a faint smile. "Tell your mother I said goodbye?"

Maggie nods. She stopped crying, as though he might turn his anger on her if she doesn't master herself. Somehow, this hurts more than the rest put together.

Before Mr. Forrester can stagger to his feet, Jacob wraps his coat tight about him and leaves the room. Outside in Harrow Alley, it is just beginning to snow.

He passes that first night in a public-house where he has a cordial relationship with the landlord, spending a whole shilling on gin and sleeping with his head down on one of the back tables. The landlord, likely smelling desperation, leaves Jacob be until morning, wordlessly cleaning every table except the one Jacob's cheek is plastered to. He tips the man sixpence on his way out, as thanks for his discretion.

Next day, the shock has faded, and he can look about with clear eyes. He's older and more knowledgeable than the last time he sought a place to stay. By now, he knows most of the East End as well as he knew Stepney, if not better. He knows, now, where the lodging houses are so fine only a gentleman with fifteen hundred a year could pull together the weekly rent, and which landladies have unrealistic expectations for the conduct of their lodgers. He knows, too, where the rooms are so grim and crowded that he'd be better served taking his chances outdoors under the Adelphi arches with the rest of the thieves and orphans. And he knows—at least, he thinks he knows—the sort of place that will suit him.

The snow from the previous night has turned to dingy slush that stands about an inch thick in the narrow streets. There's a hole in the heel of his left shoe, and before long the whole foot is soaked and clammy. Still, he maintains an easy pace as he wanders west. Some of his most successful thefts have taken place between St. John's Gardens and Lincoln's Inn, making it as profitable a place as any for a new start. Something, he knows, will turn up.

The sun has fully set again, and the nocturnal creatures of the neighborhood returned to their rounds, by the time his wandering takes him to Saffron Hill. It's a tight, tangled corner of Clerkenwell, buildings rising so close on either side that looking at the sky feels like peering up from the bottom of a great pit. Here and there, courtyards and byways jut like crooked teeth, revealing nests of houses out of the main way, so close one atop the other that they appear to hold one another up. A pair of men make their way up the hill, one shouting and the other scowling, but neither of them spare Jacob a glance as they pass. Here, it seems, a man can keep to himself.

When he sees it, he stops dead. Stands there, hands in his coat pockets, for a full minute, just to look at it.

To anyone else, it's nothing. A half-crumbling two-story house in a minuscule court, with boards hammered over its sagging doors and not a scrap of glass left in the windows. It's clearly abandoned, and he can guess the reason: property laws have deemed it too squalid to rent, but it's still relatively stable, so knocking it down and building something new would run a significant expense. A pair of rats dart past Jacob's feet as he stands eyeing the door, chattering loudly and blatantly unafraid of him. If it's good enough for them, he thinks.

"Hello, you," Jacob says to the house.

It takes several minutes to force the door open, but the boards over it are so rotted that determination and a well-placed shoulder grant him entry. The front passage is long and narrow and dark, and he steps in with something approaching reverence, feeling his way along the corridor. Some ten feet along, he emerges into a room larger than the entire flat on Harrow Alley. His nascent smirk is a proper grin now.

The ceiling is black with dirt and age and smoke, but as he squints in the poor light, he can make out evidence of ornate crown molding, and rods on which to hang long-departed curtains. A half inch of dust on the floor takes the place of thick carpets, and he can imagine a comfortable sofa positioned in front of the ash-filled hearth on the east wall. Someone well-to-do lived here once, though decades have passed since then. Near the entrance to the front room, stairs stretch in two directions, above and below. Three stories, all to himself. The luxury of it nearly stuns him. It's an in-between space, grand and decrepit at once, and an overwhelming sense of rightness floods him as he surveys it. He removes *The Monk* and *Richard III* from his coat pocket and stands them on the dusty mantel, using Leah's candlestick as an impromptu bookend. They look good there, though lonely. With space, there's nothing to stop him from expanding the collection.

The scuffling that rises from the basement stairs absolutely does not come from a rat.

He whips around. Now that his eyes have adjusted, he can see a faint light flickering up the stairs.

Jacob had swallowed the rage from his expulsion out of Harrow Alley, but the glimpse of the light brings it all back. He's been in this house less than a minute, but already he knows in his bones that this place is *his*. His ribs squeeze his heart as he charges toward the passage and leaps down the stairs, which creak awfully beneath his weight. He feels more animal than man.

The basement room has the same dimensions as its counterpart upstairs, only without the benefit of windows. In the center of the vacant space, a beer bottle sits on the floor with the stub of a candle wedged in the neck. By its light, Jacob sees a filthy bundle, and standing beside it, a man. The fellow is some thirty years Jacob's senior, but he cowers like a child. Sandy-haired and with a long, tangled beard, the man scrambles away from the stairs, toward the shadows. His rags make Jacob's own worn shirt and trousers look like they've come from a West End tailor.

"No harm, I swear, my friend, no harm," the man pleads. "Just need a place to rest my head, I ain't got anything you'd—"

"How did you get in here?" Jacob asks. His voice has gone very low. "The door was boarded over."

"There's a passage," the man says, gesturing toward the shadows, where Jacob can see the outline of a cracked-open door. "Runs between this house and the next, no one uses it."

"Interesting," Jacob says. He folds his arms and leans against the wall, mimicking the posture he's seen the greatest swells at the pub use to frighten off weaker men. He doesn't have the physical strength of those men to back it up, but he still feels its efficacy; the beggar becomes even more servile.

"It's a grand old house, and no one comes near it. Perfect place to lie low a night or two if you need. You take the upstairs, I'll take the down, no harm."

It's as if a lifetime of anger waited until now to make itself felt—this beggar, this bundle of bones and dirt, this creature who would snatch the house away from him, this house that's his. He has taken and taken and taken everything the world has thrown at him, and today, he can carry nothing more. Today, he is going to give it back.

"Get out."

The man's face passes over anger entirely and proceeds straight to despair, a display of weakness that makes Jacob want to spit at the fellow's feet. If he had such a prize as this house, he wouldn't give it up so easily. It belongs to the person most prepared to defend it. The only law he respects: winner takes all.

"Please," the beggar says, "I've got nowhere. Been run out of three places already. Room for two, hand to God, you'll not even know I'm here, sir, I swear."

The *sir,* that pathetic sniveling word, seals it. Jacob takes the clasp-knife from his coat pocket and flicks the blade out. He holds it loosely in his left hand, considering, before taking a step toward the man.

"I told you to get out," he says.

The beggar snatches up his bundle and bolts through the passage. Jacob stands with the knife in his hand, listening until his footsteps die away. The house is perfectly silent. Waiting, it seems to him, for its true master to take possession.

"Welcome home, then," he says to himself, and closes the knife.

The den is home in an instant, and he loves it ferociously. He wastes nearly a week hauling buckets from the water pump to scrub down the floors and the interior of the hearth, until he needs to spend half an hour at the end of each day lying flat on his stomach for the pain in his arms and back to unwind. Jacob is possessed by a sort of nesting madness, and if he's going to spend his days in filth, at least it's going to be his own. His possessions wink at him from the mantel above the hearth like shabby guardians: knife, books, candle.

They aren't alone for long. He takes lascivious pleasure in outfitting the three habitable rooms with every object that catches his eye, prowling the streets for the purpose of acquiring useless treasures. The slouching house quickly takes on the feel of an antique shop blended with Ali Baba's cave, crowded and dusty and more than a little mad. Wall hangings lifted from the rag pile outside the draper's shop. A rickety tea table some society woman put out in the alley rather than pay a carpenter to mend it. Books by the dozens, some with waterlogged pages pried apart with heat and patience, others fresh from an inattentive bookseller with pages he cuts himself with a paper knife. Bird of paradise feathers freed from the confines of a fine hat and left in the necks of ginger-beer bottles, glass jars filled with foreign coins and cuff links, pocket-handkerchiefs in every conceivable color. A bed—his own, shared with no one—that he pays for outright, drags home with the assistance of one of the shop-boys, and promptly falls asleep in for a full day and a half, feeling like a god.

His possessions cannot possibly fit in the pockets of an overcoat now, however deep. They sing out from their places, each with its own niche and role. If he ever manages to claw his way into a middle-class life, the sort belonging to the people who turn up their noses at him in the street, he will never dispose of another object again. He will die buried under a mountain of treasure, like a pharaoh who commanded his slaves to stuff the hollow cavity of his chest with jewels.

The bulk of what he steals, of course, he sells. Without Leftwich siphoning off the lion's share of the money, Jacob can make ten shillings a week on average selling stolen goods to a nearby pawnbroker named Barrett, who trusts Jacob's eye for quality and never asks questions. Sometimes it's less, and those are lean and hungry weeks; sometimes it's more, and he spends the extra cash profligately on tobacco or red wine or prime cuts of beef or games of whist. His needs are liquid, shifting to match the shape of his purse, and whether his week has been flush or shabby, his pockets are always empty at the end of it. Then it's back to work, if only to silence his stomach.

The first few weeks, he finds himself wondering what May

would think of the dark passage or the creaking stairs or the strange smell of the house, and he toys with the idea of bringing her over so they might pass an evening with a bottle of gin in the old way. He spends more than one night wandering the streets of Whitechapel, stopping at cookhouses and taprooms in hopes of crossing paths with her. Nothing more than dark looks and slammed doors are offered for his trouble, and after a month, he gives up. Jacob would rather throw himself in the river than go back to the old room on Harrow Alley, and without any other means of finding May, he resolves to forget her. A clean break is easiest.

Besides, he's built a pleasant life without her. As the years pass, he gathers friends in the neighborhood to seek out when he feels like company: men and women who nod and invite him to pull up a chair in the public-house, clothes-dealers and fences and rag-and-bone men who see him coming and know they can expect clever conversation and a fine assortment of goods for their trouble, more than a few pickpockets and skittle-sharps who tip their hats in the street and laugh along as he recounts his finer victories. Companionship is there whenever he wants it, but he's never properly had solitude before, and he indulges in the luxury of a whole world and no one's will but his own to consider in it.

Until one day, when Jacob crosses paths with the boy at the church.

14

1813

The day starts unremarkably. Jacob sets up on the steps of St. Giles in the Fields, and though he arrives on the north side of noon, two ragged beggars in dented hats already lounge in front of the church to greet him. One is snoring heavily, which is an annoyance but not enough to make him give up the spot. On reflection, it might be a blessing. Next to these two conspicuous men, Jacob is invisible: a small shadow of a man with red hair and a short beard, cloaked in a stolen brown greatcoat, silently watching the world go by. If anyone casts a disapproving eye their way, these two dilapidated men will attract the brunt of the attention, leaving Jacob to his business. Besides, there's no spot in St. Giles so well suited to observing passersby as the church at its center. And to begin at least, all Jacob intends to do is watch.

He peers under the brim of his hat at a fine-looking pair strolling past, so fine he wonders whether they've gotten lost. Any respectable person who's been in London for more than ten minutes should know better than to wander St. Giles, where you're as likely to receive a cut throat as a handshake. The middle-aged woman chaperoning the pair certainly knows it, if her deep frown is any indication. She grips the handle of her umbrella like she's wringing the neck of a chicken. The pair, however, are lost in conversation, the woman laughing at one of the man's remarks. If Jacob can distract the chaperone, he'll be able to help himself to the contents of the woman's reticule, and he suspects from the quality of the pearl drops in her ears that it will be worth having.

He rises from the stairs, arching his back in a lazy stretch after a morning hunched over. There's no need to rush on these coves' account. He can tail them for half a mile if need be, and they'll never look over their shoulders. No, the movement is a signal to the other pickpockets who wait in every corner and byway that this job is spoken for. There's no honor among thieves, but there's enough common sense not to poach a dangerous man's dinner.

The shriek of a policeman's whistle chases his heart into his throat.

Run, he thinks stupidly. If he doesn't run, he's done for.

His faculties kick in before his legs can, and he stands still, scanning for the disruption like every other soul on the street. Now is no time to lose his head. They aren't after him—unless it's a crime now to sit on public stairs while poor, he's broken no laws today, and he doesn't flatter himself that the magistrate has a standing warrant out for a pickpocketing Jew of his description.

The whistle again, nearer now—and then, a beat later, its object. A bareheaded youth of perhaps fifteen with a dirty face and close-cropped dark hair that looks like it came straight from the prison governor's straight razor tears down Little Denmark Street at a dead run, weaving around its inhabitants and nearly overturning the formidable chaperone with the umbrella. A furious policeman is not far behind. The boy is obviously built for strength and not speed, besides which the policeman has six inches of height to his advantage. A heated pursuit, but it won't last long.

As Jacob watches, it's as if the stone below him begins to tilt. He wets his lips, which have suddenly gone very dry. He's been here before. The same chorus of voices roaring, *Stop, thief!*, the same sweat dripping into his eyes, the same sensation of the rope tightening around his throat. Without meaning to, Jacob raises one hand to his neck, loosening the top button of his collar. It's an eerie dream come to life, and he forces himself to inhale, feel the cold stone of the church against his palm. He's not a boy with a silk pocket-handkerchief in his fist hiding under an overturned cart. He is safe.

And even a decade ago, he knew better than to try to outrun a policeman in a head-on chase.

Hide, he wills the boy, now nearly out of sight. Hide, that's your move, can't you see that?

"One more for Tothill," remarks one of the beggars unsympathetically.

"Looks that way," Jacob agrees.

Then—in an act he will look back on as one of the most consequential of his life, and possibly the most ill-considered—he tips his hat to the beggar and saunters down the steps of the church into the alley behind it. He lingers in the cool shadows there, near the door to the rectory. He'd bolt down this alley and try to beat the policeman to New Compton Street on the other side, if he were an idiot.

He's quite right, of course. It's a matter of seconds before the footsteps ring out like cannons firing to wake the dead. A breath later, the young thief careens around the corner and crashes headlong into Jacob's chest.

"God damn you, out of the way!" the boy snarls.

Jacob catches the boy by the shoulder and places one finger over his own lips.

"Shut your mouth and come with me," he says.

The door to the rectory is unlocked. He knew it would be; he's worked this block before. The boy's eyes widen, and any other protest he intended dies on his tongue. There's little time. The policeman is already within shouting distance. With a sharp tug, Jacob pulls the boy after him into the entryway, closing the door silently after.

They stand together in a shallow vestibule, the bright afternoon light filtered through a cotton curtain draped over the pane of glass in the door. There are barely two feet between the outer door and the inner, forcing them so tight together that Jacob can feel the youth's back pressing against his own chest, the regular heaving of the boy's breath. That breathing feels impossibly loud, and he's certain the policeman will hear it. The policeman will yank open the door and find both of them, and Jacob will finish the day sharing a cell with this dirty young thief whose name he doesn't even know, all because he lacks the good sense to mind his own business.

"Quiet," he says, his voice pitched to reach the boy's ear and no farther.

He swears, for a moment, the boy holds his breath.

The policeman's movements beyond the door are impossibly loud, like a wild boar rooting through bracken. He can see the man's silhouette skid to a stop beyond the curtained window. It must seem like magic to the policeman, as if his quarry has vanished into thin air.

"Damn you," the policeman snaps, and delivers a powerful kick to the door.

Jacob feels the boy flinch against his chest, and he knows they're both picturing the way the youth's ribs would cave in against the same assault from the same boot. To say nothing of what would happen to Jacob's bones. Without meaning to, he tightens his grip on the boy's shoulder.

After what seems like an hour but cannot be more than a minute, the policeman stalks off, in pursuit—so he thinks—of the boy who gave him the slip and disappeared into the crowd. Jacob hears his footsteps fade away, and then the alley is quiet again.

They stay there a long moment, the boy still tense with the fight he just escaped. Then, when Jacob is certain they have waited long enough, he nudges the lad in the side. The boy nearly jumps out of his skin, and Jacob sees him bristle in the aftermath of it, his earlier fierceness made fiercer still by shame.

"He's gone," Jacob says, in a voice that remains low but is no longer a whisper. He reaches around the youth to open the door, and they both spill back into the alley. Other than the tail of a rat as it snakes around the corner, they are entirely alone.

No sooner are they back in the light than the youth turns to face Jacob, hands curled into fists that do not lose their threat because they're shaking. Jacob can get a proper look at him now. Dark-haired, blue-eyed, and dirty, he's unhandsome, yet striking. Looking at his face, Jacob is reminded of the busts of ancient Roman emperors in Leah's books, proud patrician noses and haughty brows. Jacob still has a head of height on the boy, but the advantage obviously won't last long. The boy is quickly outgrowing the phase of his life in which he'll still need to run.

"I didn't expect a knighthood," Jacob says, "but this does seem like an odd sort of thank-you for saving your skin."

"I won't give you a damned thing," the boy says. "And I'll cut you if you try."

In five years, in ten, these words will be threatening. Now, they're laughable. When Jacob was in this position himself, at least he knew who was asking whom for a favor.

"My dear, you don't have anything at all that I want."

The boy frowns. Jacob can see his brain working, trying and failing to understand. He doesn't blame the boy for his confusion—it's rare to offer help without expecting payment. He nods in the direction the policeman disappeared.

"You can't outrun him like that," he says. "They know all the alleys and the side streets, better than you do, like there's a map on the inside of their skulls. What they don't know is what it's like to live here. Which doors are always unlocked, which crowds are easiest to get lost in, which shopkeepers dislike the law more than they dislike your sort of trouble. If you want to escape them without a fight, and you do, make sure you know the sort of thing that's not on their maps."

The boy looks up at Jacob with newfound respect. "You're a thief?"

Jacob grins. Between two fingers, he dangles the silver watch-chain he lifted from the boy's pocket in the middle of the previous speech.

"One of the best," Jacob says cheerfully, handing the watch-chain back. The boy stuffs it into the pocket of his jacket, his anger so hot Jacob almost draws away. He's not trying to rile the boy, despite how it seems. He's trying to inspire him. "Do you have a name?"

"What's it to you?"

"Nothing," Jacob says, raising both hands, "so don't be so quick to snap. I'm the one who saved you, remember, not the other way round."

For a brief, terrible moment, he's afraid the boy is going to ask him why. He can't begin to imagine how he'll answer. Doesn't know himself, except that the memory of the children of Harrow Alley begging him for a story has somehow combined with his memory of nicking handkerchiefs while Leftwich observed from across the street, and behind both memories lives a soft voice that wonders, every so often, if he were to die, how many days it would take for someone to find his bones.

"Bill Sikes," the boy says. "And people will remember it too, before long. Can you say the same?"

Jacob can't help it—the laugh flies out in spite of himself. He leans against the wall of the rectory, his hands in his pockets. It's an absurd question. Of course the world won't remember his name. No one ever uses it. A surname is the best he can expect, if he's among friends, but more often *Jew,* more often *Thief,* more often *You there.* He's a presence, a splash of color, part of the scenery, and until now, he's been quite certain that's how he prefers it. People die. People are hurt. People are arrested, or fall ill, or abandon those they love. Background actors are left alone.

"The reason I'm alive to save your skin is that no one knows my name. You could learn a thing or two from that."

"Tell me anyway," Bill says. "God gave you a name, so give it to me."

Bill's insistence tugs like a fishhook under his ribs. He feels himself drawn to it, that refusal to accept a no. Over the years,

Jacob has learned to back away, to choose when to attack and when to bide his time. Bill treats every sentence like a fistfight. He has never met another person so stupid—nor, he thinks, so free.

"Fagin," he says, throwing half his name—the cheap half—out like a test.

The shorthand is as effective as ever. Jacob's father gave him two gifts: a reputation and an instant identifier of caste. Bill's brow lowers, and Jacob can see the machinery of associations whirring behind his eyes, putting the fuller picture together. Name. Face. Voice. Profession.

"You're a sheeny," he says.

"And you're a piss-poor thief who can't grow a beard," Jacob says, since they're trading facts.

Bill gives a barking laugh. "Difference is, I'll grow."

Jacob knows he's facing his last opportunity to walk away. He can send Bill off, hope he learns from the experience, and find another pocket to pick for his own supper. He can return to the great silent edifice of Bell Court, those three yawning rooms full of mismatched objects sitting precisely where he left them. Predictability has kept him safe since striking out on his own, but suddenly he finds himself in desperate want of a surprise.

"If you ever need me," Jacob says, "I'm living on Bell Court. Saffron Hill. It's no palace, but it does the job. Ask around, the neighbors know me."

"I won't need you."

"As you say."

Jacob remains leaning against the rectory, watching as Bill strides away. He doesn't sneak into the crowd so much as shoulder his way through it, disrupting half a dozen people as he makes his way north. There's a swagger to the boy's movement that would be ridiculous were it not for his fierce pride, which Jacob almost has to respect.

It remains to be seen whose prediction will be right, Bill's or his own.

15

Midnight has come and gone on another dull Thursday. Though Jacob is far from tired, he settles into bed simply because it's there. Nestled beneath two secondhand coverlets and his own greatcoat, he lies on his side with one arm pillowed under his head, thinking of a story Leah used to tell him as a little child. It was a fairy story he loved, about a cobbler's son and the golem he made from the clay at the riverbank to protect him from the soldiers stationed in his village. He's too old for such stories now, but he still thinks of it from time to time: the cobbler's son with his hands caked up to the wrists in clay, the golem standing sentinel at the house, its long shadow against the floor. It's been ten years since Leah's death, and only recently has he been able to think of her without feeling as though all the air has been siphoned from the room. White-hot grief has eased into something warm and blue in the pit of his stomach, which hurts like an old bruise.

He's still not used to the quiet of the building—except the constant muffled noise from outside, which is inescapable anywhere in London and so does not count. Here, it's only him and his memories, and the dust settling on the furniture, and an ever-thickening silence that sounds, in such moments, like the inside of a tomb.

His wandering thoughts are interrupted by a pounding knock that rattles the house.

He's surprised by the sound, but not frightened. Jacob doesn't make a habit of advertising his whereabouts to strangers, and while the knock is insistent, it's not the vicious demand of the law threatening to break down the door. This is the call of someone who's worried he won't be heard, or if he is, that he won't be welcome.

Jacob doesn't intend to leave his guest in that sort of suspense for long.

He heaves himself out of bed and carefully descends the darkened stairs in his bare feet, pulling his scarlet dressing-gown over his creased shirt and trousers as he goes. He left a candle burning near the bed earlier, and he brings it with him, casting a narrow circle of light over the threshold.

Bill Sikes looks up from the doorstep, ashen-faced and bleeding heavily.

Jacob blinks. "Oh," he says. "Well. I suppose you'd better come in, hadn't you?"

Bill grunts and limps inside. It's been only five days since he met the boy in St. Giles, but Bill had even worse luck than Jacob expected. The boy lists to the left, bracing himself on the wall as he traverses the passage, and a nasty cut splits his eyebrow, dripping fresh blood toward his eye. The bulk of the damage, however, seems to be to his chest. Jacob can only guess how severe the injury is, but from the way Bill presses one arm to his ribs, he gathers that whoever beat him didn't hold back. Though Bill's face is as stern as when last they met, Jacob sees the waver behind it, the lightning crackle of pain that will break if Bill isn't given a distraction. The urge to help is foreign but undeniable. God, the boy truly is a child. His smooth cheek and awkward limbs are more obvious by candlelight.

Jacob brushes past Bill into the main room and lights three more candles from the flame of the first. "You might have sent word," he says. "If I'd known to expect a visit from my young friend, I'd have prepared supper."

"I'm not so young," Bill mutters. He collapses into Jacob's chair—one of a mismatched set, this one picked up from behind a public-house and made to stand straight by hacking the three good legs to be as short as the awkward one.

Jacob sits in the other, an armchair he wrenched a muscle in his back dragging in from the street. "How old are you?" he says. "Fifteen?"

Bill tries to sit up, but the pain in his ribs draws him short. "Thirteen."

Jacob raises an eyebrow—he meant fifteen to be a facetiously low guess. "Oh, well, in that case," he says airily, "best be thinking about who will take care of you in your twilight years. Haven't any children, have you?"

"You're a cunt."

"A cunt whose door you knocked on, you ungrateful cow. Do you want me to look at your ribs, or would you rather sit there grumbling and bleeding all over my chair?"

"Hang your charity."

"I promise not to be kind about it in the slightest, if that helps. Now move your arm."

Bill's breath catches as he complies, and Jacob lifts the boy's shirt to reveal more or less what he expected: a mass of tangled bruises across his chest, clearly the result of a man's boot. He holds back a wince—pity is both too cruel and too close to kindness. Instead, he presses his palm against Bill's side, checking the curve of the boy's ribs. Even through the layer of muscle, they are still easy to trace. Clearly it's been a while since Bill's last proper meal. The boy flinches at Jacob's touch but doesn't cry out, though his breathing hitches occasionally. It makes Jacob wonder what Bill thinks will happen if he admits to pain, how weakness is usually received in his world.

"Not broken," Jacob says, with more confidence than he feels. "But it must hurt like the devil. What happened, were you kicked by a horse?"

Bill yanks his shirt back down, though the quick movement causes a grunt of pain. His scowl is deeper now. "By hell, d'you ever run out of questions?"

Jacob pours a kettle of water from the recently filled ewer on the table, setting it on the hob to warm. It seems a shame to waste his finer handkerchiefs on someone so unlikely to notice the quality, and so he riffles through a drawer for some plain linen to clean Bill's injured face.

"I can guess, if you'd rather," he says. He tosses the cloths on the table and returns to his chair, drawing one knee to his chest. "Some fellow down at the pub caught you picking his pocket and decided to save the police the trouble. You were sleeping on the king's highway and got run over by the mail coach. Your father is a good-for-nothing drunk who beats you because he can't fight anyone who might fight back."

"And what do you know about it?" Bill growls, slamming one fist onto the table so suddenly Jacob flinches. "As if you'd know what it is to have parents who'd own your ugly bones."

Jacob presses his mouth tight. Asked and answered, then. Bill thinks himself a man grown already, but there's years to go yet before he learns how to keep a secret from anyone. Without being asked, Jacob retrieves the bottle of gin from the mantelpiece and slides it across to Bill, who catches it before it topples off the far end of the table.

"Quite right," Jacob says. "My own father got himself hanged rather than look me in the eye. The one smart choice he ever made. Go on, drink. Last resort of orphans and thieves."

Bill doesn't need the invitation; the bottle is already significantly emptier than it was moments ago. He wipes his mouth and casts a searching look around the room. Jacob follows his eyes from eccentricity to eccentricity: the feathers on the mantel, the books stacked in precarious piles, the admittedly absurd tiger carved from a block of jade the length of a man's forearm that sits beside the clothes-horse. Whatever tenement Bill Sikes escaped from tonight, its occupants must have a more conventional approach to decoration.

"You live here on your own?" Bill asks.

"This is my kingdom," he says, with a wide gesture about the room. "No one to answer to, nothing to fear but the rats."

"Nothing scares me," Bill says too loudly.

The house settles on its foundation with a low groan. It does this often, as unsteady as everything in Saffron Hill, but tonight it sounds like the house has folded its arms and scoffed.

"I'm quite sure," Jacob agrees, rising to tend to the kettle. He pours the water into a porcelain basin—chipped along the rim, the pair of nothing else in the room—and swirls the rag in it, letting the water cool. "But maybe something should. Look at you."

Bill bristles immediately; Jacob is beginning to notice a pattern. "Look at me?" Bill snaps. "Look at *you.* Thin as a grasshopper, made out of matchsticks and straw. Any man you tried to fight would laugh in your face."

There's convincing Bill he's safe here, and then there's taking insults from a boy stupid enough to need saving twice in a week. Jacob likes the boy despite himself, and it's because he likes Bill that he's determined to make him learn that not all threats look the same.

Setting the handkerchiefs aside, Jacob leans both hands on the table until the fullness of his frame leaves Bill in shadow. It isn't much, the threat he's able to pose standing five and a half feet tall, but he knows how to season his appearance with a coldness behind the eyes, a sort of dark humor at the corner of his mouth. Like a cat looking at an insect, something to be batted aside and then torn to pieces. It's the look he gave the beggar squatting in the basement, the look he would give Mr. Forrester when he lacked the patience to stomach one more insult. It's the look of a man who has nothing to lose and a prize on the horizon. He sees Bill shrink back, color coming to the tips of his ears. Rethinking—as he was meant to—just how dangerous this thief might be.

"Some laugh, at first," Jacob says quietly. "But no one's ever laughed long."

Bill meets his eyes as boldly as he dares before glancing down at his feet. The effect is startling: the brazen young lion replaced by a whipped dog. "Right," he says. "Let me wash, and I'll clear off. Never stay anywhere I'm not wanted."

The darkness melts from Jacob's expression. He finds himself, to his own surprise, disappointed in the boy's fortitude. "And where will you go? Back to your father? Don't suppose you have a legion of aunts and cousins all clamoring to take you in?"

His own words stop him with a thunderclap. He clenches his fists, almost surprised to feel no rings sparkling on his knuckles. He is here, in the house on Bell Court, wrapped in his dressing-gown against the chill. And at the same time he is a boy teetering on manhood, ruins of a life scattered behind him, his mother not two days dead and a grown man looking down at him, slamming an imaginary door shut. He knows exactly what will happen to Bill Sikes if he turns him loose upon the world tonight. Bill will wander the streets just as Jacob did, sleeping in doorways and courtyards, searching for a room that will take him in. Bill will continue to steal with the subtlety of an elephant in a hothouse garden, and he'll get himself arrested or transported or hanged or all three one after the next, or he'll come to blows with one of his fellow lodgers and end up one bloodstain among many on the floor of some Clerkenwell hovel. Bill will walk out the door and, unless he is both very clever and very lucky, he will be dead before he turns sixteen. Just as Jacob should have been.

"Pass the gin back, eh?" he says, in a voice that startles him with its shakiness.

Bill complies, eyeing him warily. Jacob drinks deep. The bite of the liquor stops his spiral short, and he is himself again. A man of twenty-six, independent and secure, looking across the table at a boy in whom no one has ever taken the slightest interest. This is his house. He is the one responsible for making decisions.

"Don't trouble yourself," Bill mutters. "I'll find my own way. Always have." It doesn't escape Jacob's notice that he hasn't yet risen from the table.

"Don't be an ass," Jacob says gruffly. "Here."

He turns back to the handkerchief in the basin, dredging it out and watching the ripples as they intersect. There's more than one way to force the world to notice you. There's Bill's way, of course: with fists. But there's also a softer way, one that leaves a fingerprint rather than a bruise. He wrings out the handkerchief and leans forward to dab at the blood still streaming through Bill's eyebrow, chuckling to himself when the boy flinches.

"Damn me, would you be careful?" Bill cries.

"Excuse me if you prefer having blood in your eyeball," Jacob says. "Listen. There are some things I could teach you. If you were interested."

If Jacob is surprised to hear himself make the offer, it's nothing compared to Bill, who is visibly flabbergasted. He scowls, and Jacob wonders what man he's picturing as he considers the offer. The queer young Jew of Saffron Hill, or another, more familiar face, strong brow and deep-set eyes like his own, with fists that taught him more than he ever wanted to know. Asking for help is as foreign to Bill as the streets of Brazil, anyone can see that. But Bill bites his lower lip, and in that moment he looks even younger than thirteen. A child suddenly on his own. Wondering, not for the first time, if being cared for always leaves so much blood behind.

"What sort of things?" Bill says finally.

The agreement is already made, though neither of them would be caught dead saying so. Jacob grins, dabbing the last of the blood from Bill's brow and moving on to the mix of mud and gravel and half-formed scab embedded in his palms. It would be more effective to set Bill up with the materials for a proper wash, but that would take more water than Jacob has, and besides, he doesn't mind. "How to steal without getting spotted, for one. Your instincts are terrible."

"Nothing wrong with my bloody instincts."

"Your ribs might beg to differ," he says, and—a little cruelly—nudges Bill in the side with one finger. The boy yelps and twists away, more annoyed than in pain. "I can show you how it's done. Twenty-six and never spent a day in jail yet, and I'd defy you to find another man in Saffron Hill who can say the same."

Bill's eyes resume their interrupted wander about the room, lingering on items that might yet be worth something at the pawnshop. Jacob has been saving up his trophies for a larger trip at the end of the week, as Barrett tends to be impressed by volume and offers more for a pack of items than for a parade of them in succession. Bill spots his growing collection of pocket-watches immediately, hanging from their chains over the back of a chipped washstand.

"I could watch you work, you mean?" Bill says.

"Better than that," Jacob says. "I'll teach you proper. Stay here the night if you care to. No one will find you. And tomorrow, we can make a start of it."

Bill flexes his palm, reopening a series of shallow cuts that at least bleed cleanly now. Jacob gestures, and Bill extends the hand again, allowing Jacob to bind up each of his palms in turn. "And you?" he says. "What do you want?"

"Is it such an unthinkable idea that I might just want to help you?"

Bill scoffs. "If it's blunt you're after, I'm the wrong mark."

"Don't be ridiculous," Jacob says. "I don't want your money."

He hasn't answered the question. He's not sure what he could say that would. He realizes, with a start, that the candle burning at the center of the table juts out from Leah's silver candlestick, one he makes a point of using sparingly—generally only on the anniversary of her death. The flame draws a smile from him, then a self-reproaching shake of the head. No time to become sentimental, even if he does wonder what Leah would make of him now. He just let a wolf cub into his house. Keep one eye open at all times, and see which way the wind blows come morning.

"Go on," he says, "finish your gin, then get some sleep. You can borrow a blanket from the bed upstairs, until we get you something of your own."

"What if I took the bed, and you borrow the blanket?"

"Try it and I'll slit your throat."

16

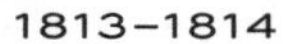

1813–1814

Jacob wakes early the next day, before the sun rises. Though the light is weak as he descends the stairs, he can still make out the vague shape of Bill Sikes on the floor near the hearth, bundled under a blanket and snoring steadily. He pauses in the doorway, watching the wave of Bill's breathing. How long, he wonders, since Bill last slept without remaining alert for what might greet him when he wakes? He remembers for himself the power of the first night that feels safe.

Later, he decides. They will make a start of it later.

He works alone that morning, unwilling to waste the time, though his mind is elsewhere and he ultimately comes home empty-handed. While he half expects Bill to think better of their agreement and run off while he's away, he returns midafternoon to see that Bill is still there, awake now and sitting at the table. His brow is no longer bleeding, though Jacob will want to clean the cut again, as infection seems a foregone conclusion. It's also easier to see the bruise along his left cheek, which deepened to a rich purple overnight. God knows what his ribs look like now. Oblivious to the fact that he's being watched, Bill keeps his eyes lowered on the knife in his hand, with which he's whittling away at a chunk of wood that broke off the mantel some two weeks prior. It's hardly artistry, simply sharpening the end to a savage point. Nevertheless, Jacob lingers in the doorway, watching Bill's broad hands cradle the knife, waiting to be noticed.

He will be waiting a long time, it seems.

Jacob clears his throat. Bill drops the knife with a clatter.

"Lesson one," Jacob says. "Listening."

"I listen," Bill mutters.

"If you say so. It's your own neck if you don't learn to catch on when somebody's coming; *I* won't be the one swinging."

Bill snatches the knife from the floor and folds it back into his pocket, though he keeps the half-sharpened chunk of wood loose in his left hand. Jacob has a sudden premonition of the shard piercing through the soft tissue of his eye, spearing his brain. But that smacks of imagination, which is a dangerous distraction. Better to focus on the possibilities that have a chance of coming true.

"Are you hungry?" he asks. "I've a meat pie from yesterday you can—"

"No, you don't."

Jacob glances to the washstand where he left the pie wrapped in brown paper the evening before. Nothing remains but the paper and a handful of crumbs.

"You really are determined to be thrown out, aren't you?"

"You offered."

"Generally one offers *before*." Jacob closes his eyes, then decides the fight isn't worth having. "All right. Let's see what we have to work with."

He's been developing the plan since the previous night. From Bill's performance in St. Giles, it's clear the Anthony Leftwich approach of "sink or swim" will see the boy hanged within a fortnight. From the vacant sconce he uses as a hatstand, Jacob takes an old dark green greatcoat, which is several inches too long for him. It does, however, have the benefit of extraordinarily deep pockets, making it well worth the coin he spent on it. He exchanges his usual coat for this one and, with Bill looking on, begins to pace round the room. Every few steps, he pauses to select an item and tuck it into the greatcoat's pockets. Ninepence in small coins. Two pocket-handkerchiefs from the clothes-horse. A sterling silver cigarette case. A pair of spectacles. On a whim, he selects a lady's brooch, an oval of gold with a spindly beetle preserved in amber at the center, and pins it to the lapel. A dare, if Bill Sikes is feeling bold.

Preparations made, he turns back to Bill and spreads his arms, letting the coat hang loose from his shoulders. "Have at it," he says.

"What are you on about?"

"What do you think? Pick my pockets."

Bill shakes his head. "You've gone mad."

"If you'd rather practice out in the street, be my guest, but I thought the object of this lesson was to keep you *out* of prison."

The jibe piques Bill's pride, which seems to be the surest way of getting him to listen. "I won't get caught."

"All right. So show me."

As if he couldn't care less one way or the other, Jacob shrugs and turns away, wandering the length of the room. Caught up in the theatricality of it, he allows his gait to take on the mincing rhythm of a high-class gentleman, pausing here and there as if to examine the fine wares for sale in a shop window, whistling to himself all the while. It takes a few beats, during which he knows Bill watches him with that same scowl on his sullen face, writing him off as a madman. Then, he hears the instant Bill changes his mind. *To hell with it,* the boy is thinking. *Fancies I can't do it? I'll show him.*

Bill Sikes is as daring and fierce as a boy of thirteen can be, but he's also loud as a herd of cattle. Jacob hears each creak of the floorboards as Bill creeps toward him, each huff of breath like the rush of a smith's bellows. He hears the soft smack as Bill's lips part. Without turning, he can see the boy's fixed expression in his mind's eye, tongue between his teeth, as he reaches for Jacob's left coat pocket.

Jacob shoots out a hand and catches Bill's wrist, hard.

"Four months in prison," he says. "Six, if you've been caught before, which after that I don't doubt."

"You're a bloody devil." Bill jerks his arm back and rubs his wrist, though Jacob knows the only injury is to his pride. "Hear an ant tiptoeing through a coal yard."

"An old bat with an ear trumpet could hear *you* coming," Jacob says. "Try again."

"Damn your daylights, I don't—"

"I said," Jacob repeats, "try again. And this time, don't stomp."

Bill keeps rubbing his wrist, looking as if he would dearly like to argue. Jacob waits. Bill can walk out, continue living by his own rules, shape his life the way he thinks best. Or he can stay here, swallow his pride, and accept that there are some things he doesn't yet know. That he does, in fact, need someone to guide him.

Jacob turns back around, wandering toward the window, and resumes his whistling.

Behind him, the floorboards creak again beneath the tread of an amateur.

Though it's all been Jacob's idea, he didn't adequately consider the loss of privacy that comes with allowing Bill to move in. Isolation is exhausting, but so is a boy of thirteen continually underfoot: toasting bread on the hob, whistling in the armchair, snoring in the basement, throwing small rocks at the occasional rat. Sometimes the proximity of Bill's breathing makes him feel as if he's returned to the cramped room on Harrow Alley. On those days, he takes increasingly long walks in no particular direction, sometimes as far west as Hyde Park. Even so, Bill never leaves, and Jacob never tells him to.

Bill is not a talented thief, but there's a doggedness to him that Jacob can't help but admire. He doesn't give up, that's certain. Each morning, sometimes for ten minutes and sometimes an hour, Jacob pulls on what he's come to think of as his training coat and puts Bill through his paces, seizing his wrist each time the boy's movements are too loud or too obvious. At first, he thinks pointing out the mistakes will be all Bill needs to correct them. If a professional thief ever said to Jacob he had a tell in the way he moved his right heel, he'd have spent the next forty-eight hours practicing in the mirror until he'd gained total control of every muscle. But as round after round of their little game ends in failure and Bill's only noticeable adjustment is to seize Jacob by the collar and threaten to throttle him after a particularly hopeless attempt, Jacob resigns himself to being more instructive.

"All right," he says sharply. "Put on your boots. We're going out."

Bill's smile is the broadest Jacob has seen yet. "I told you I was ready."

"Ready?" Jacob laughs. "You couldn't pick a dead man's pocket if you were alone in his tomb. We're trying something new today."

He leads the way into the street before Bill can argue. Trusting that he's being followed, Jacob sets a brisk pace toward Moorgate, a neighborhood he particularly likes these days thanks to the newly created Finsbury Circus. Grand new houses and solicitors' offices rise several stories high around the manicured elliptical lawn, through which the professional class strolls with all the care of a duck paddling through a lake. The pickings aren't always rich here, there being rather too many destitute clerks sprinkled among the merchants and gentlemen for Jacob's taste, but though the profits aren't vast, they are easy.

Jacob steers Bill by the arm to stand beneath an oak at the edge of the lawn, then pats him twice on both shoulders to indicate he should stay put. Bill leans against the tree with his typical scowl, compliant but not pleased.

"Watch," he says. "And while you're watching, remember what I've told you. Light tread, light fingers, gentle distraction, nothing too quickly. This is what the trick looks like."

"You're mighty confident," Bill says.

"Yes," Jacob agrees, before setting off across the green. "I am."

It's a curious feeling, stealing with an audience. The weight of Bill's eyes on his back puts him uncomfortably in mind of the law, and he must give himself an extra breath to set the fear aside before he selects his mark. A young man with a barrister's air about him, walking stick tucked neatly under his arm, is chatting eagerly with an older gentleman in a dove-gray frock coat. The partner of the firm, Jacob suspects, taking the junior member out for a stroll to bestow decades of accumulated legal wisdom. It's an ideal opportunity. They're both so enamored of the sound of the old gentleman's voice that Jacob could pick their pockets while singing all eighteen verses of "Greensleeves" and neither of them would be any the wiser.

He strolls past the young barrister with an easy spring in his step, not dissimilar from the way he first presented himself as Bill's practice mark. The barrister laughs loudly at something the gentleman has said, and Jacob finds his opening. He feigns stumbling over a rut in the grass that does not exist, catching himself on the young man's arm and muttering a curse under his breath. In the same motion, he catches the corner of the man's handkerchief between two fingers and whips it into his sleeve. The whole theft is complete by the time Jacob rights himself.

"Terribly sorry," he says, clapping the barrister chummily on the shoulder. "You'd think with all the money they spent to clear the yard, they'd at least make the damned thing level."

"Quite so," the older gentleman agrees, though he looks at Jacob with something that might, in a few moments, escalate from surprise to alarm.

No cause to linger, then. "Good afternoon," he says, tipping his hat.

"And to you, sir," says the barrister.

Jacob continues his stroll to the opposite side of the circus. Once he's confident the two men have taken their walk out of sight, he doubles back to the tree where Bill watches. Bill clearly didn't take his eyes off Jacob through the entire production. His face is very pale, though when he speaks it's as gruff as ever.

"Thought you brought me to watch you get nabbed."

"I know you did," Jacob says. He removes the handkerchief from his sleeve and deposits it in Bill's coat pocket, patting it for luck. "That's half your trouble. You're so afraid of being seen you forget about everything else, until anyone with half their senses would know they were being robbed as you came up. Don't worry so much. Sometimes they'll see you. It happens. It can even be easier when they do."

Bill's brow is furrowed with listening. Jacob can count on one hand the number of people who have ever paid such ferocious attention to him. "And how do you know when it's easier?"

"You *listen* to me, when I teach you something," Jacob says. "And you practice."

It takes so long Jacob is sure he'll die of old age before he ever witnesses it, but gradually, Bill begins to learn. As his fourteenth birthday passes, their practice with the old greatcoat becomes less exasperating, until one magnificent day Jacob turns around to see Bill with a handkerchief in his hand and a grin like a dog who's run off with a roast. Genuinely surprised, Jacob has to check the coat—sure enough, Bill picked his pocket without detection.

"Losing your touch, old man," Bill says.

Jacob makes an inarticulate sound of triumph and seizes Bill in a hug. Bill flails against the embrace as if he's fallen into the grip of a sea monster.

"You damned lunatic—"

"Let me have this," Jacob says, interrupting what has the potential to be a much-longer string of curses. Bill breaks free and adjusts his collar with dignity, still grinning. "I thought I had a better chance of teaching the rats to steal."

"I can go out on my own now," Bill declares.

"Of course you can," Jacob agrees. "Once you do that five more times and prove to me it wasn't an accident."

It takes a few more days after that, but once Bill confirms his success wasn't a fluke, Jacob sends him out to try his luck on the street. He's always at hand in case there's trouble, but Bill has at long last absorbed his teachings, and he watches with satisfaction from the shadows as Bill lifts a watch directly from a stranger's pocket. A more talented thief would have gotten the chain as well, but the victory in Bill's face as he returns with his prize makes them both feel as though they've broken into the Tower and made off with the crown jewels.

It's never quite natural, no matter how much time passes. Bill Sikes takes to pickpocketing the way a cat takes to water. Someday, Jacob doesn't doubt, he'll wake to find that Bill has grown out of the role Jacob offered him, that the fight he was born spoiling for is now ready to begin. But until then, Bill is a boy with nowhere in the world to go, and he needs to eat somehow. Like it or not, he needs Jacob.

And Jacob is very good at being needed.

17

1815

One unremarkable Sunday, Jacob wakes early—earlier than Bill, though that doesn't count for much. Bill would lie in bed every day until noon if given the chance, and take to the streets to work only when actively starving to death. Jacob knows Bill is no rich man's son—his rough manners and quick fists are a sure sign that his bringing-up was haphazard at best, and Jacob has caught him several times frowning at one of the books that line the mantel, laboriously stringing together the letters on the spine—but Bill approaches the business of staying alive like he's been named the new prince regent and has forty servants to manage it for him. It's a source of permanent irritation for Jacob, whose job it has always been to think ahead. Death, in his view, is the result of a failure to plan.

He pulls on his greatcoat—pockets empty now, as he means to work in earnest and not in jest—and passes through the darkened entryway into the street, which is just beginning to glow with the first beams of morning. He moves west through the washed-out light toward Covent Garden, taking the heaviest-trafficked paths with carelessness he only allows this early in the day or when he's in a roaring hurry. It's been some time since he's had a good take. So much effort has gone into teaching Bill that he hardly has the energy to strike out on his own anymore, and the money he now pulls in for two is less than he used to make to feed only himself. They'll survive, of course. A man and a boy can get by on five shillings a week if they have to, and if the dry spell continues he can see if Barrett will give him enough to cover a few suppers on loan. But the pit of hunger in Jacob's stomach feels sharper today than it should, and lately he sees spots like moth wings when he stands up too quickly. So it's half necessity and half ambition that makes him cross Chancery Lane with determined strides. Sunday, after all, is when London has its finery out and its guard down.

He spots his mark near Somerset House: a slight, fair-haired gentleman in a pine-colored frock coat, flipping through a volume at a bookseller's stall. Jacob scouted this particular stall before, and he knows for a fact that everything for sale here could be got for half the price elsewhere. The gentleman, however, doesn't know he's being overcharged. On the contrary, he thumbs through the book with the transparent intent of someone who came to buy. From the pocket of his frock coat, a snuffbox twinkles in the light, there and gone again as the man shifts his weight. It brings a smile to Jacob's lips. Pure silver. Of that he is absolutely certain.

He sidles closer, his shoes making no sound against the muddy street. If the finer sort populating Covent Garden notice him, it's only to frown in his direction before resuming their business. He's not welcome, but getting rid of him would require them to acknowledge his presence, and it appears to be easier for the general public to pretend he isn't there, in the hopes that soon he won't be. No one moves to head him off as he crosses the street, taking up his position beside the man in the green frock coat.

With one hand, Jacob traces the titles of the books stacked two deep on the cart. As he suspected, they're common as anything, bound in fine covers to make them look more valuable than the trash they contain. He spots three volumes of Radcliffe done up to look like a family Bible and wonders, amused, if he even needs to relieve the gentleman of his snuffbox—clearly he's being robbed already. But he came all this way, and he'd commit unspeakable crimes for an entire roast chicken. It's worth it, and he'll see it through.

With his right hand, he continues exploring the books, as though he's looking for something in particular. All the while, his left snakes behind the gentleman, dipping into his pocket, the smooth chill of silver against the pads of his fingers. He can feel the etching on the case, a latticed pattern like scales. It lifts out easily, like the snuffbox actively desires to be in Jacob's hand. His mark doesn't blink. It's perfectly executed, a dream of a theft, and he has to consciously smooth out his face to keep from giving himself away with a grin. The snuffbox drops lightly into the pocket of his greatcoat, and he lingers at the stall for another minute, feigning interest in a volume of Dr. Johnson before giving the bookseller a polite smile and wending his way back into the crowd.

He's nearly away, three-quarters to safety, when a towering man in a high cravat of black silk, passing in the opposite direction, gives him a look generally reserved for rats.

"Lost, are we?" he says, and positions himself in front of Jacob, blocking his path. "Petticoat Lane is the other way."

He's faced confrontations like this more often than he can count, the natural consequence of being visibly Jewish and visibly poor. *You don't belong here,* they all say, *go back to where you came from, keep your people in one street so we can avoid you properly.* But the snuffbox so captivated his attention that at first he doesn't realize what's happening. The smart move is to step neatly out of the way, to bow and scrape and beg pardon and help himself to the man's pocketbook as he thunders off, to teach him a lesson about civil words.

But Jacob doesn't do that. What he does instead is stand his ground, look the man in the eyes, and say, very calmly, "Get out of the way, sir."

Any child could predict what happens next. "Don't talk back to me," the man says, narrowing his eyes.

And because there isn't an ounce of sense in him, Jacob digs in his heels. "I don't want to talk to you at all. Get out of the way."

The man in the silk cravat whips back his walking stick and strikes Jacob across the knee with the silver handle.

It feels like every bone in his leg shatters. A howl of pain leaps from him, and he crumples, barely catching himself on the cobblestones with both hands and an elbow before his nose hits the street. With the force of the fall, the snuffbox skitters out of his coat pocket. The sound of silver against stone seems impossibly loud.

The gentleman at the bookseller's stall turns. He immediately understands the situation at hand.

"Thief!" he roars. "Stop him!"

Jacob's body goes white-hot with panic.

He tries to drag himself to his feet, but his leg feels like it's been left in a thousand splinters, and his vision tunnels alarmingly. He can only scramble a few inches away before the man in the silk cravat and another nearby man in a flat cap haul Jacob to his feet and pin his arms to his sides. They march him north, and Jacob realizes through a fog of pain that they're barely five minutes from Bow Street.

Animal fear turns him into someone he doesn't recognize. He thrashes against the men holding him, but another blow to his stomach knocks the wind from him, and lack of air makes terror grip his brain even tighter. He was so close, he did everything right, it had all gone perfectly, in all his years living by his hands and his wits he's never once been caught…

Never once, and now here he is. How many times has he said it to Bill? *Four months in Coldbath Fields for a first offense, six if the cove's litigious. Longer if they don't like the look of your face.* There's hardly a thief in London who hasn't done time before. Many of the men he sees at the gin-palaces and coffeehouses spend as much time in prison as they do out of it, until the guards recognize their faces and make cold jokes about reserving their places on the treadwheel. It ought to be nothing, a condition of doing business, and yet it feels to Jacob like the world is ending.

He can't go to prison. Prison is where men like him go to die. And he cannot, will not die. Not yet.

A familiar face looms out of the shadows as the men whisk him toward the Bow Street police station. Those dark eyes glinting as coldly as the manacles around his wrists, the red burn of rope along his throat. The life drains from Jacob, and he's a moment away from a scream until the policeman shoves him through the door of the station house. The familiar red-haired figure—if it exists—is left out in the street, a gruesome herald guarding the door.

The magistrate is in his chambers. Jacob can hear the dull rumble of voices through a closed door, the words indistinct but showing no sign of stopping soon. With one glance toward the chambers, the policeman on duty at the station house takes Jacob by the collar and shoves him through a different door, which promptly locks behind him. Not a word is spoken through the entire exchange.

Alone in the darkness, Jacob sinks to the floor, both hands pressed to his knee. They walked less than a quarter mile to get here, but the pain of dragging one leg behind him almost makes him faint. He focuses on his breathing, in and out, forcing himself to observe everything that isn't the flaming pain in his leg and the strengthening sense that he's going to hang. The cell smells of urine. A narrow beam of light slips under the door, just enough to see the shadows of his own feet. The rest of the room remains in darkness. Something gritty has been spread across the floor, like sawdust. There isn't much else to notice.

The sparks dancing before his eyes settle and fade, and Jacob's hold on consciousness tightens. He leans his head against the wall, exhausted. As he closes his eyes, the first image to appear through the darkness is the man in the silk cravat, wrenching Jacob to his feet with a smug smile. The satisfaction of a man who's been right all along. It's the most galling part, somehow, that the stranger got exactly what he expected.

Hours pass, or at least he assumes they do. The cell has no window, more closet than room, and though the light under the door gradually lets him see his hands in front of his face, he can't guess what's happening outside. The footsteps passing in front of his prison seem perfunctory, the murmur of voices beyond too low to make out. It doesn't seem impossible that the police forgot him and hid him away to rot. How long, he wonders, can a man live without food or water? Would it be better or worse to die here than on the gallows?

At last, the door opens. Jacob squints against the sudden rush of light. The foolish idea arises that he might run, overpower the policeman and grab his freedom with both hands, but the searing pain in his leg quickly reminds him he's going to do no such thing. The policeman leans lazily against the doorframe. Jacob's eyes haven't adjusted to make out an expression, but he can imagine it.

"Lucky for you," the policeman says, "magistrate has been called in to the high court for the afternoon. You'll be brought up first on tomorrow's docket. The gentleman you robbed has been by already. Submitted a written statement, but says he'll come back tomorrow to testify in person."

Jacob says nothing. Words have deserted him. The policeman slams the door again, and Jacob is back in darkness, more complete now than ever.

Enough time has passed that he's certain it must be nightfall now. His stomach cries out as loudly as the pain in his leg. As the hours stretch on, he has no choice but to relieve himself in the corner, the fresh smell of his own piss as vile as it is shameful. He thinks it will be impossible to sleep, but he can't remain on the bleeding edge of fear forever, and somehow he drifts in and out, the borders of his dreams blending with the blank canvas of the cell. It's the same dream in fits and starts, so real he can't be certain whether he's awake, accompanied always by that same face, those same dark eyes, that same unsurprised look from the figure that watched him enter the station house. By the sound of a noose snapping taut.

When the door opens again, he's certain he's still dreaming. He's been told he won't be seen until the next day, and when the door opens, the station house is still dark, a circle of moonlight painted on the floor beyond.

Moreover, the face now grinning at him through the open door of his cell is not a policeman, but the dirty, hatchet-broad face of Bill Sikes, who is holding a ring of keys.

Jacob stares as though an angel of the Lord has appeared in the jail, all whirling wheels and flaming eyes. "What the devil?" he says hoarsely.

Bill's grin broadens. "You'd know all about that. Get up."

There will be a time to ask questions, but it's not now. Jacob grits his teeth and uses the wall to hoist himself to his feet. It takes every bit of his will to keep from screaming, but he manages, though he must keep the bulk of his weight on his left leg. Bill swears, then slings Jacob's right arm around his shoulder, evening out the load. Bill is taller than him and more strongly built, and he bears Jacob up without strain.

"What did you do, stick your leg in a mangle?"

If he's dreaming, it's a good dream, and Jacob doesn't intend to waste it. "Later. The policeman—"

"Is getting his cock sucked in the alley by a friend of mine," Bill says with a wink. "She's good at her job, they won't be long. Hurry, old man, I'm not going to the gallows for your Christ-killing hide."

This is, oddly, the most touching thing Bill Sikes has ever said to him. Jacob doesn't push his luck asking why Bill came for him, or how he heard what happened, or what he said to convince a prostitute to help break a pickpocket out of jail. All his attention is needed to get himself through the door of the station house without howling in pain. His blood rushes in his ears like a factory whistle, but he bites his tongue and forces himself forward. He'd cut off his own leg if it meant the rest of him could walk free.

Hobbling awkwardly, he and Bill escape into the street, where the darkness swallows them up and they are lost to the sight of the law.

They are not, however, lost to the sight of Bill's friend. A tall girl of maybe sixteen, with curlpapers in her fair hair and a satisfied expression on her face, catches up before they've been free more than ten minutes. She gives Jacob an appraising glance, then shrugs, as though she hoped for better but could have found worse.

"That was quick," Bill says.

The girl laughs. "Could have told me your friend had a bum leg. I'd have taken my time. Name's Bet," she says brightly, turning to Jacob.

Still dizzy with pain and the nervous energy of their escape, Jacob can barely put one foot in front of the other, but he coughs out a response. "Fagin. And thank you."

"Right then," Bill says.

They've arrived at a hovel in St. Giles that Jacob doesn't recognize. Bill kicks open the door, which gives immediately, and the three of them troop in. It's an unremarkable rented room, a dingy bedstead in the corner, a few shabby dresses hanging from a line strung from the ceiling. Someone—Bet, Jacob realizes, for of course they must be in her room—has propped a cracked mirror on the washstand, a makeshift sort of vanity crowned with a slightly crushed carnation in a ginger-beer bottle. It's sad in almost equal proportion to its charm. Jacob sinks onto the floor, resting his back against the wall next to the washstand. They walked half a mile at most, but he's panting as if he ran for hours. His joints are on fire. For the first time since the theft in Covent Garden went sour, he takes a full, unimpeded breath of air.

"Trousers," Bet says to Jacob, businesslike once more.

Jacob blinks. He may be safe, but his brain hasn't quite caught up to his body yet.

"Give him a discount, Bet, out of charity," Bill says loudly, emerging from the cupboard with a bottle of gin. "You know how it is with Jews. Cock's only three-quarters there."

Bet turns red and averts her eyes. "Bill, honestly."

It once again strikes Jacob that Bill Sikes was never meant to be a child for long. The boy is shooting up what feels like an inch a fortnight, but he betrays none of the awkwardness of youth. How many fifteen-year-old boys could break into a station house?

What would Bill have dared to do if there'd been more than one policeman on duty?

Outwardly, Jacob grins at Bet. "Out of respect for Bill's modesty," he says, forcing his voice nonchalant in hopes the rest of him will soon follow, "let's neither of us ask how he knows how much of a cock I've got."

Bet's laugh is so contagious that even Bill, after a beat, chuckles before tearing the cork out of the gin with his teeth. With that laugh, he's the same brash young thief who followed in Jacob's shadow for weeks trying to steal a single handkerchief. Jacob does as previously instructed and rolls up the leg of his trousers, exposing the mess of bruising that splatters across his knee like pitch. Bet winces, and even Bill mutters an empathetic curse. Bet, though, is the one to take the matter in hand. She seems to have experience dealing with injuries, as she briskly washes the blood from Jacob's leg and then cups the kneecap with both hands, making a small noise of apology when he gasps in pain.

"It's a right mess, but you'll get on," she says confidently. "I'll wrap it for you to help keep it still, though you'll want a crutch if you're to move without Bill in the next week."

"A crutch," he muses. "Brilliant. Take the week off thieving and sit on the steps of St. Paul's, hat in hand. Easiest money I'll ever make."

"Better charity than the gallows," says Bet, who seems to think he's complaining. "And from what Bill tells me, you'd have a short walk to get there."

"Bill tells you a lot about me?" Jacob asks.

"Shut up," Bill mutters.

Bill Sikes would never say *I was worried about you,* would never say *I'm grateful you saved my life,* would never so much as think *I consider you a friend, and I'm glad you weren't sent to prison.* But though everyone else in Jacob's life leaves him, Bill is here. Thanks to him, Jacob is safe in a prostitute's snug little room, knee useless but likely to heal, taking a pull from a half-full bottle of gin. He doesn't know whether to be touched or suspicious. The world is studiously careful about snatching joy away from Jacob, but it gave him this moment, and tonight at least, he won't let it go.

"Pass us the gin, then, Fagin," Bet says, extending a hand.

He does, and it feels beautiful, that night, to be alive.

18

Bet is right: it's slow going for a long while after that. Not out of an excess of caution. He's rattled by his narrow escape, but he expects the police will forget about him before long, if they haven't already. They didn't even take down his name. Before the week is out, he'd feel safe slipping back into the rhythm of life as if he never darkened the station house door. No, it's the damned leg that keeps him shut up. He can move well enough to get by before long, though with a distinct limp, but the silent, effortless movement he needs to work will take much longer to regain. He's never thought about it before, the intimacy of being betrayed by your own body. Spending all his time in the armchair with a scandal paper threatens to send him over the edge into madness. Bill steals on his own now to keep them fed, though not without a hefty dose of complaining—*Bloody useless, would be dangling from a rope if it wasn't for me, ungrateful cunt*—which Jacob takes as the sign of friendship he knows Bill intends it to be.

Bet comes by from time to time, often with a loaf of bread or a meat pie to share. "Can't trust a lout like Bill to make sure you eat," she says, and it's not until the third time it happens that he realizes she must be going out of her way not to bring pork. He hasn't kept kosher in more than a decade, but he's touched nonetheless, and he comes to look forward to her visits, promising to drop by her room in St. Giles when he's well enough. It's refreshing, spending time with a person who seems to enjoy his company and knows how to show it in the usual way.

When Bet isn't with him, he drifts in and out of consciousness. Pain makes it difficult to sleep normally, and any rest he manages is an in-between type, waking into dreams from which he must wake again. So when the familiar figure of the red-haired man arrives, Jacob doesn't know whether to call him *ghost* or *spirit* or *dream*.

Circumventing the distinction, Jacob has begun to call him *Father*. A haunting or a memory, he's not taking a side for now, but it feels more natural to address him directly. After his arrest, it's foolish to pretend the man could be anyone else.

His father idles now near the table and has taken off his hat, which makes his dark brown eyes stand out prominently against his sallow skin. Jacob is twenty-eight now, well over a decade since he first saw the apparition, and his father doesn't appear a moment older. With each passing year, they come nearer to each other, like a pair of planets edging into alignment. Jacob gives it five more years until they resemble each other exactly. The similarity almost makes him turn away, but after the terror of the Bow Street cell, he forces himself to look his father in the eyes. They're on Jacob's terms now, and he must not cede control, must hoard every glimpse. Who can say when his father will come next, or what that visitation will cost.

"I thought you'd be angry I lived," he says. "Seemed so satisfied to see me arrested."

His father shakes his head, his mouth twisting, but he doesn't speak. His feet leave no marks in the dust as he paces to the hearth. The man stands with his shoulder against the mantel and sweeps the room with his eyes. Jacob flushes. As soon as he can walk without pain, he decides, he'll get the place in order. A proper scrub, even if that means three trips to the water pump. Set some money aside for a secondhand lamp, or at least a third uncracked plate. The vow is useless, broken as soon as he makes it, but it's part of his routine to make a regular pretense at growth. The same sort of empty promise he made when Leah remarked on the dirt beneath his fingernails. I can be more than this, he thinks, the words familiar and false as a prayer. I will be.

"You have her already," Jacob says. "Are you waiting until you can have me too?"

His father looks into the cold hearth. In that moment, Jacob can't decide which would be worse: that his father came for him on purpose or that the visitation has nothing to do with him, that it means nothing one way or the other whether Jacob walks the earth or vanishes from it. There's a third option, of course—that he's mad as any patient locked up in Bedlam—but contemplating madness is the first step on the rapid descent into it. If there's one thing he needs to be able to trust, it's his own mind.

"I'll tell you now," he says to his father, "if you're waiting, you'll be waiting a long time. I promised her that. They won't stop me like they did you."

His father looks at him with a half smile that exists somewhere beyond memory. All Jacob knows of his father is what Leah wrote him in her letter and the snide remarks his neighbors made out of her earshot. *A thief and a scoundrel,* they said, *conned Leah into getting with child, and then she married him, saying she loved him, but what else could she say? Only sensible thing he ever did was get himself hanged. Gone before the boy was born, but with blood like that in him, how else was the child ever going to turn out? Doesn't matter how Leah raised him, nothing's stronger than the blood.* Nothing about the man in front of him is grounded in memory or fact, and yet that half smile is so familiar. A smile that says *You're my son, whether you like it or not.*

Jacob clears his throat and reaches for a glass of gin and water, which he poured earlier before dozing off. Whatever's happening here, dream or haunting or something in between, he sees no reason to endure it sober.

"Well," he says. "Are you going to go? Or am I trapped with you all night?"

His father's gaze softens, but his body does not disappear. It's as clear an answer as is likely forthcoming.

"If you're staying," Jacob says, "tell me, then. What did it feel like?"

What would Bill think, if he wandered back in? Jacob seated at the table, one hand reflexively at his throat, asking questions to a room that would appear empty as the grave. Silent too, for of course his father doesn't answer. In all the times their paths have crossed, Jacob has never heard his father's voice.

He must frame the question differently. Play the man's game by his rules.

"Were you afraid?" he asks instead. A third of the gin is gone now, and along with it the restraint that would usually prevent him from asking. "You can answer that, surely, yes or no."

His father pauses a moment before shaking his head.

"You aren't telling me the truth, are you."

His father shakes his head again. His gaze levels at Jacob now.

There is a fresh bottle of gin across the table. Jacob leans forward to retrieve it and pours another glass.

19

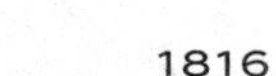

1816

Bill doesn't remember the name of the tavern Fagin brought them to tonight. The Swan, maybe, or the Star, or the Spur and Something. It's a spit of a place in St. Giles, barely worth remarking on, but it's also too fine of an autumn night to spend in the familiar pubs in Clerkenwell, where it's God's best guess whether your beer will be cut with water or piss. Here, at least, the drink's worth tasting.

By this point in the evening, a forest of empty glasses sprouts on the table around them. Bet brought a worn pack of cards, and for lack of anything better to do, they've been dealing out hands of whist for the past hour. Bill pays half attention at best to the game. The rest of his focus is on the ragged men in the taproom, who are all staring at him but try to pretend they aren't. Bill's always been big for his age, but at sixteen, he's big for any age. He towers a head over Fagin now, and fills out the frame too. Add in the shined black boots he strides through the streets wearing, and it's enough to make most cowards get out of his way. Half the men in the pub are terrified of him, and all he has to do to earn it is sit still. It's as satisfying as he always dreamed it would be.

"Now," Bet says, gathering up the cards from the sticky table, "I'll be blessed if we lose another bloody rubber, Bill, d'you hear me?"

"Good luck," Bill mutters. "Not my fault we're playing the devil."

Fagin scoffs. "My deal, Bet."

It's Bet and Bill against Fagin and the dummy hand, and even two against one it's hardly a fair contest. Fagin taught Bill how to play a year or so ago, but Bill swears the Jew held back half the rules, as he can't remember ever coming close to a win against his teacher. Besides, Bet is three sheets to the wind already, so she's no help. If Fagin had any heart at all, he'd throw a hand or two just to be sporting.

Little chance of that, as Fagin snaps the cards before dealing almost too fast to follow. Not for the first time, Bill thinks that Fagin's hands are his only attractive feature. Skinny as a drowned rat, face a mother had died rather than love, broad beak of a nose, but those hands, by God, they can do anything. Pick a pocket in broad daylight. Rig a game of cards. Slit a throat. If Fagin's hands were sewn onto a different body, Bill thinks, that bastard could rule the world.

Fagin had just turned up the queen of spades for trump when a loud voice behind them draws the room's attention.

"Well, I'll be damned."

Bill freezes. His dry mouth tastes of blood. If he doesn't move, if he's dead silent, it'll pass by, like any other dream. It won't be real if he doesn't move.

This has never been true before. He doesn't know why it would start being true now.

Bet and Fagin both watch as the man who spoke drags out the open chair at the table and slouches into it. It's been three years since Bill last saw him. Those years didn't pass without leaving a mark. The man's hair is thinner now, though his beard is thick enough to make up for it. He might be an inch shorter than Bill, though it's hard to tell sitting, and regardless Bill's brain is only capable of firing stray sparks instead of full thoughts. All he knows for certain is that his father is now sitting at the table opposite him, finishing Bet's beer.

It shouldn't be possible. Bill isn't stupid. The last time he left his father, it was in a set of rooms in Camden Town, and there's no reason George Sikes would make the hour's walk from there to a tavern so shabby half the people in it don't even know its name. But that was years ago. Bill has no way of knowing what his father decided to do with himself for the past three years. He might live anywhere, the Camden Town flat a distant memory. They might have crossed paths a hundred times before today.

Bet scowls at his father, and Bill wants to kiss her for it, spitfire Bet who's not afraid of any man. "Do you mind?" she says haughtily. "We're dealt for three and don't want another."

"Mind?" the man repeats. "Why would I mind?"

"Who've you got there, George?" the landlord calls from behind the bar. "If that one owes you money, take it outside. You've broken plenty of my property already."

His father waves a hand over his shoulder without looking. "No," he says. "What he owes me isn't money."

Fagin hasn't yet said a word. Anyone who doesn't know him might wonder if he's even paying attention. But Bill does know Fagin, known no one better since he was thirteen. He sees the way the two familiar furrows between the Jew's brows go slack. That's understanding, he's sure it is. Even their first night in Saffron Hill, Fagin understood everything he was thinking without Bill's needing to say a word. It feels like Fagin's eyes are oyster knives prizing open Bill's chest, exposing the slick heart inside. He could gouge out those eyes for seeing him like this.

His father leans forward still farther over the table. Bill can smell the reek of drink on him. "This your fine new company, William? A moneylender and a whore? That's who you abandon your flesh and blood for?"

Bet flinches. She's put the pieces together now, worked out who joined them. "Bill," she says, and she reaches for his hand.

Damn if she'll touch him. Damn if anyone will. Bill twitches his hand, almost slapping her away. Every inch of his body is alive and humming. "I'm not coming back," he says to his father. "Go to hell."

His voice breaks over the last word, and his father laughs.

Bill flinches. Last time he heard that laugh, he was thirteen. Patchwork of bruises rising across his ribs, blood streaming into his eye. He thought he might die that night. It hurt so much to be alive he hardly minded.

"Spoken like a tough old dog, eh?" His father twists sideways in his chair to look at Fagin, the group's nearest thing to an adult. "Tell the truth, Jew. How much sweat does it take to keep this boy's head out of the noose? Christ knows it was a full-time profession for his mother and me."

"Sir," Bet says sharply. "Shove off. You ain't wanted."

"Ain't wanted?" his father repeats. "I'll be blessed before a whore tells me what to do with my own." He shakes his head, then focuses the full weight of his attention on Bill. "William, you're coming home."

Bill sits statue still. He's a child again, tears on his dirty cheeks. A woman's voice, his mother, protesting his father's blows only enough so she could sleep at night with a clear conscience. He dragged himself out the door that night, every breath a sharp stabbing pain. Can see the boy he used to be like he's watching from above, that ugly stupid little rat. Nothing more hateful than weakness.

"I'm not," he says. His voice is so quiet he doesn't think anyone but Fagin, sitting at his elbow, can hear it.

"What's that?" his father says.

"I'm not," Bill says, and he pushes his chair back.

Murmurs spread from their table across the tavern. Some of their fellow drinkers know Bill by reputation, but even those who've never seen him before can sense how dangerous this can turn. Fagin knows better than to touch him, but he talks softly, like Bill's about to jump from a rooftop.

"Bill," he says. "No violence, Bill. Please."

The sound that flies from Bill's throat is half a laugh, half a sob. He snaps his head toward Fagin, and the world whirls around him as he does. "No violence?" he repeats, and gestures wildly at his father. "Tell him, Fagin, tell *him*."

"That's enough," his father says. With one hand on the table to support him, he lunges forward with the other and seizes Bill by the wrist.

Fireworks dance in front of Bill's eyes, the purple of an old bruise. Bet screams. Fagin jumps to his feet, though whether it's to intervene or bolt is anyone's guess. The grip on Bill's wrist feels hard enough to snap bone. He sees again the child he used to be. The kind of animal you drown to beat God to the punch. Bill Sikes has never killed a man, but he'll put that boy out of his misery today.

It all happens very fast.

His father starts to drag Bill toward the door, and in a moment, Bill decides he won't be moved. His body turns to iron. Just like that, he's rooted. His father stares. One heartbeat passes. He sees it in his father's eyes, the understanding that what worked in the past will not work now. It's power, dense and unyielding.

It isn't enough.

Bill's clasp-knife is in his free hand. Then the knife is buried point-first two inches in the table, in the exact spot George Sikes's hand occupied half a second before. If his father were any slower, it would have pinned his flesh to the wood like a beetle. The knife is still vibrating with the force of Bill's arm.

The room falls quiet. Bet's scream echoes like a distant ghost.

His father stands staring, cradling his nearly skewered left hand. His eyes are enormous. It seems impossible he's ever been a man to be feared and obeyed. Bill feels twice his size. His teeth could crush his father's skull like a walnut.

"Touch me one more time," Bill says, "and you'll watch that knife go up to the handle in your throat. D'you hear me?"

His father doesn't move. Nothing does but the knife quivering in the wood, and even that is beginning to still.

"D'you hear?" Bill roars.

Every person in the room flinches. His father stares for one beat more, eyes wide, lips parted in shock. Then he flees, knocking over his chair in his haste. The crowd parts wordlessly to make room for him. Bill doesn't watch him go, but the door slams to confirm it.

He's left standing, chest heaving. There's so much fire still unburned in him. His hands shake with it. Every eye has turned in his direction. They're frightened now, not impressed. Bet is frightened. Even Fagin looks frightened. Good. They should be. Would to God the knife found its mark. Not his father's hand but buried in his chest. He should have slit his father's throat and watched the blood bubble up between his lips. And even then he might not be satisfied.

Bill hardly feels himself moving. All he knows is he can't be here any longer. The back of his throat tastes like blood, and he can't think whose it is. Without a word, he turns away from Bet and Fagin and stalks off through the tavern. The crowd parts for him just as it did for his father.

The heavy air of full summer strikes Bill as he bursts through the door. It feels as if someone pressed a square of cotton over his mouth and nose. He wants to run, but he doesn't make it farther than the alley behind the pub, where ash piles and refuse send up an awful stink to mix with the sweat and shit that fill St. Giles. He braces his hands on the brick wall, letting his head hang. His legs are shaking. He might be sick.

He's gone, Bill thinks. He can't hurt you. None of them can hurt you anymore, if you don't let them.

The next thought comes loud as if someone has spoken it: You can hurt *him* now.

A power he can't control, and—worse yet—isn't sure he wants to.

He senses Fagin come up behind him, though the man is so quiet there's barely anything to give him away. Damn him. From the first, Fagin never had any idea how to mind his business. At least he knows not to speak. Bill was filled with a fury to be alone, but being watched by Fagin feels different. There's no fear of his judgment, at least not anymore.

"He's gone, Bill," Fagin says finally.

Bill shakes his head. Maybe that will rattle his brain back into place. "I'd have killed him," he says hollowly. "If he didn't run, I'd have cut his throat."

Fagin doesn't answer right away. It's silence with intent. He wants Bill to look at him. And Bill, damn him, does.

George Sikes could crush Fagin's skull under his heel, he thinks. It seems impossible the Jew has lived so long without someone flattening him like a cockroach, just because they could. With the memory of his father fresh before his eyes, Bill can see how spindly Fagin is. All bones and old clothes and red hair and those too-sharp eyes.

"But you didn't," Fagin says. "He ran, and he won't come round again."

Bill doesn't know what the implication of that promise is supposed to be, if it's *You've made sure of that* or *I'll make sure of it*. All he knows is that however dead the child in him was minutes ago, it isn't dead enough to withstand Fagin resting one hand on Bill's back, just below his shoulder. It draws a groan from Bill out of the pit of his stomach. Those damned hands. Drain a man's strength. Break him open wide. It's a kindness Bill can't afford, and there's no giving it back now.

He turns away from the wall and pulls Fagin into a brutal embrace.

Fagin flinches, but only for a second. He knows not to move. Stands there as Bill collapses into his shoulder and cries.

The tears are silent. The only thought Bill has through the pain of it is gratitude. No one can hear him, and in these shadows, no one can see him either. No one but Fagin will ever, ever know. He hasn't cried since before he was old enough to know better. He's forgotten what it feels like. He can't breathe, can't master his body, can only let the fear and shame take him.

Fagin holds him through all of it. The Jew's hands are spread wide across his back, each long finger pressing in to ground him. Bill is sixteen, and he just defeated the oldest enemy of his life, and this is the first time anyone's ever held him as he cries.

"You're safe," he hears Fagin say, over and over, as if the repetition will make it true. "You're safe."

It can't last. Bill's breath starts to come deeper, his head aching with the pressure. Still Fagin holds him. Waiting for Bill's signal. His overcoat smells of smoke and the damp of the Bell Court house. Bill allows himself one more breath before he pulls away. Fagin gently steps back without a word.

He will have to leave Fagin soon, he knows that now. The man he needs to be will never survive under the Jew's wing. Fagin lives from one day to the next by making himself so small he can burrow in the dirt below notice. Bill can't afford that. No one can make him smaller, can step over him. No man, he decides in that moment, will ever see the frightened child he used to be again.

He clears his throat, and Fagin backs off farther. Reactive as any prey animal. Bill isn't sure which of the two of them disgusts him more.

"Should get back," Bill says.

Fagin nods. Those familiar furrows are back between his brows. "You're sure?"

Bill runs his sleeve across his eyes until the stinging might as well be from the rough fabric. "Not leaving Bet," he says shortly.

Fagin is still nodding. It's like he forgot to keep control of his head. "You aren't like him," he says. "You haven't hurt anyone. And you won't. I won't let you."

The idea splits him in two. The boy who wants to grip Fagin's shoulder and hold him to that promise. And the man who wants to take this ugly little creature by the throat for dreaming he's in charge of anything.

It's easier not to answer, so he doesn't. Just grunts and nods, then turns back toward the door of the pub. Inside, Bet is still waiting, along with a roomful of strangers who must be reminded that Bill Sikes doesn't run away from anyone, ever.

There's a moment's stillness before he feels Fagin follow him, steady as a shadow.

PART THREE

20

1838

It's properly dark by the time Jacob returns home from the Cripples, his pockets newly filled. Dodger, Charley, and Oliver are waiting for him at the table, which ordinarily he'd scold them for: dusk is their prime working window, and if Jacob weren't afraid Bill might thunder through the door at any moment, he wouldn't have returned for an hour or two himself. One look at Oliver's face—as gray as if he led a charge on the battlefield—and the reprimand dries in his throat. He remembers, a little fondly, the first few days he took Charley on the streets, how the boy practically vibrated with anticipation and terror and excitement for something as simple as a handkerchief. The first time is thrilling as lightning, and leaves you charred and sparking afterward. He nods to Dodger in approval, knowing he's the one responsible, that Charley Bates would never have the foresight to stop while the taking is good.

"Anyone been by, my dears?" he asks, unloading his pockets. Oliver's eyes are wide as sovereigns, but Jacob carries on as if he doesn't notice. Dodger and Charley have no doubt spun the grisliest stories they can conjure about the dangerous old Jew who taught them the ropes, and Oliver will be as afraid of crossing him as of crossing the devil. He'll come round in the end—all the children do, once they see the arrangement suits them—but it's not a disagreeable place from which to begin a relationship. Helps remind them all who is in charge.

"Not a bleeding soul," Dodger answers, slumping down in his chair with a packed pipe. "Why? Expecting company?"

"What use would I have for company? The whole family's here."

Charley gives a sleepy hurrah, though it gains verve when he sees Jacob unload the four wrapped meat pasties he bought off the pieman. Two instincts are at war in Oliver: the starving wolf ready to tear off the hand holding the pie and the dog who's been kicked too many times to trust a stranger. Jacob gives him his supper first, managing not to lose any fingers in the exchange, and then retreats upstairs to his books and his gin. He won't sleep tonight, not when Bill might still turn up.

Soon, the voices downstairs dissolve into sleepy murmurs, followed by the steady breathing of three boys enjoying the sleep of the dead. Though he remains alert to every noise that drifts in from the street, it's the most peaceful night he's passed in a long time.

The next two days are equally uneventful. It isn't until Friday evening, when Jacob almost wonders whether Bill forgot his promise, that he hears familiar heavy footfalls in the passage. He looks up from the day-old newspaper he found near Smithfield as Bill stalks in, his tall frame taking up the entire doorway. If any fear shows in Jacob's face, it's only there a moment. He is, after all, a professional.

"Good morning," Jacob says lightly.

"It isn't a bloody social call." Bill's eyes are bloodshot, and Jacob wonders how many of the past three nights he spent up to his neck in gin. Time was, Jacob would have gestured at the open chair opposite him, would have asked if Bet and Nan planned to join them, might have made an evening among friends of the visit. That time has been past for years now. He creases the newspaper and sets it aside.

"Oliver," he calls, "come say hello to an old friend."

The pause that follows feels alive. From downstairs, he hears

Dodger hissing something that likely resembles *Go on, unless you want your hide skinned for gloves.* Sure enough, a flushed and nervous Oliver presents himself at the head of the basement stairs.

Bill and Oliver look at each other in silence. How many Olivers would it take to make up a single Bill? Four, at least. And yet the boy eyes him like he's daring Bill to raise a hand, challenging him to a bare-knuckle fight. Bill's reputation as the most fearsome housebreaker in the East End is well earned, and yet if it comes to blows, Jacob wonders whether Oliver couldn't cut Bill's throat with a penknife and sheer daring. Once, many years ago, Jacob watched a rat in the last throes of rabies charge at a spaniel and send the dog running into the night. There's a level of desperation beyond which every living creature becomes dangerous.

"Oliver, this is Bill Sikes," he says. "Dodger will have told you about him."

Oliver nods.

Bill scoffs and slouches farther down the doorframe. "Christ on the bleeding cross, Fagin, you're getting 'em younger and younger. Was this pup even weaned before you brought him in?"

"I'm ten years old, sir," Oliver says stoutly, "and I'm not afraid of anything."

Jacob could kiss Oliver for saying so. "There, you see?" he says to Bill. "Just like me, isn't he? Fiercer than he looks."

"You'd best hope he's not much like you," Bill says. "I need someone who can work, not sit in the center of his web like an ugly old spider and wait for someone else to reel in his dinner."

Jacob has half a mind to tell Bill he's mixing his metaphors, but he bites his tongue. It's going just as he hoped. Oliver had time to acclimate to life in Saffron Hill, and now he's eager for the chance to prove himself. Might even be able to do it—he's a fast learner, quick to correct his own bad habits—but that doesn't mean Jacob's nerves aren't twanging every second Bill hasn't made up his mind. *Get it done,* his heartbeat urges him, *get it done, get them gone.*

"Oliver," he says, "Bill is looking for someone trustworthy for a job across town. I told him you were new to our little gang and ready for a chance to get started, aren't you?"

"Yes, Mr. Fagin, sir."

"Well, then," he says, looking to Bill expectantly. "He's eager, he's ready, and you can't ask for a boy of ten to come smaller. What more do you want from me?"

Bill grunts. "Don't ask that, or you'll get me to answer," he says. "Right, boy. You'll come with me. We don't start till just short of dawn, but we need to be in position well before, and it's eighteen miles."

"We, sir?" Oliver asks.

Jacob taps the side of his nose and gives Oliver the brightest smile he can manage. "Another of my dear friends, one who's been working with me since he was less than your age. Nice fellow. You'll take to him like a duck to water."

He's lying wildly now—Toby Crackit may be either good or bad depending on who's asking, but by no means is he *nice*. Regardless, Bill takes Oliver by the hand, the boy's fingers small as lucifer matches in his broad palm. When Oliver looks up at Jacob, his face is ferociously set. Is Jacob the only person in this room who is afraid? The thought is unsettling. If he loses his head, there's little else keeping him alive.

"You'll be back in two days, Bill," Jacob says, a warning and not a question. "After the job's done and Toby's dealt with the take, you'll all be back."

Bill steers Oliver toward the door so swiftly the boy trips over his feet. "We'll be back when we're back," he says. "Not that you'd care, if I was bleeding out my ears in a ditch, so long as you got what you're owed."

Jacob rises from the table, realizing too late the movement looks like picking a fight. "That's not it at all, and you know it. When Nan comes, I need to know what to tell her, don't I?"

"You're not to tell her anything," Bill snaps. "Not a word, understand? It doesn't concern you what goes on with Nan and I."

He raises both hands in surrender. "As you say, Bill, as you say. Don't let me keep you."

There's not time for much more after that. Another guttural noise from Bill, a quick backward glance from Oliver, and then Jacob is alone behind the newspaper-spread table, listening to the silence they leave behind.

It lasts only a few seconds before Dodger wanders upstairs, dented hat under his arm. The boy casts an eye toward the hearth to see if anything by way of breakfast has appeared. Since it hasn't, he weaves around Jacob toward the door.

"Lucky, that Oliver Twist," he says, taking his time in going. "There's not a jailbird in London who wouldn't give his right arm to spend a night on the job with Bill Sikes."

It's a rebuke plain as anything—*Why didn't you choose me, Fagin, I could have taken that chance and become a legend*—but Jacob chooses not to hear it.

"Keep to your own profession, Dodger," he says, not quite meeting the boy's eyes. "Each to his own kind. Safest that way."

Safest it may be, but two days pass, then three, and still Bill and Oliver don't return. For the first empty day, he doesn't worry. He learned years ago that he can't govern Bill Sikes simply by telling the man what to do. Bill does what pleases him, and if he knows Jacob is anxious for his return he's liable to drag it out another half a day, just to make him sweat.

On the fourth day, Nan arrives in Bell Court, eyes red rimmed and frightened. Only then does alarm start to set in. Bill might torment him for pleasure, but if he hasn't come to Nan, then he hasn't come home at all.

"You said you would take care of it, Fagin," she says. "You said you would stop him."

"I said I would try."

And if he failed? If Bill has been caught?

Handing the boy to the police is bad enough. Oliver's smart: he won't hesitate to buy his own freedom by pouring out the tale of a hideous, villainous old Jew who ensnared him in a life of crime. And if that tale's more true than not, so much the worse for Jacob. He's already doing the math of what Oliver knows, what Dodger and Charley might have told him: Would that be a year in Millbank? Three, if Dodger was colorful? It will be three; Jack Dawkins is proud to a fault, he'll have crowed about the wicked Jew's exploits until Oliver hears the name Fagin and thinks Blackbeard on the high seas, thinks Ali Baba and the Forty Thieves. With the stories the boys tell about him, three years will be getting off lightly.

But then there's Bill. And if Bill Sikes tells the court everything he knows, well.

Bill wouldn't rat him out to escape the noose. They're beyond that now. But Jacob has known Bill twenty-five years, and never once in all that time has Bill borne a loss quietly. If Bill is taken in on charges, he'll go like a drowning man, dragging everyone within reach down with him. The stories Bill could tell, to make sure he doesn't go to the gallows alone.

"It's early days yet," he says firmly. "They'll come back. They will."

21

1818

Jacob's thirty-first birthday begins much the same as the past dozen or so have done. Each year since Leah's death, he retreats to a pub the night before his birthday as soon as the sun dips behind the rooftops and remains there until the publican turns them all out, by which point he's roaring drunk and no longer feels the January cold, let alone the dread of another year gone. This time, he chose the Three Cripples, a Saffron Hill establishment he's begun to feel something like affection for. The atmosphere is as mean and offensive as the name suggests, but he's seen two or three other Jews darken the Cripples' doorstep over the years, and the publican, a man named Travers, serves them the same watered wine and sour gin and casual insults he serves everyone else. It isn't welcome so much as lack of interest, but he feels the tension in his shoulders release each time he steps inside. At the Cripples, he is Fagin the Thief before he is Fagin the Jew, and it's a pleasant novelty, to feel the weight of those two names swap places in the scales.

All this is to say that he spent last night unthinkably drunk, and this morning he has to squint against the piercing winter sun to make his way along. Beyond him, he hears the shriek of children playing, scooping up dirty handfuls of snow and packing them into missiles to pelt shop windows with. It's as if the day declared explicit war on his headache, and he sighs before swerving off into one of the narrower byways, which at least has the benefit of overhanging roofs to block the sun. The shift in light is so abrupt that it takes a moment for his eyes to adjust, pinprick pupils widening to let the world back in, and he doesn't see the man sitting on the ground until he's practically stepped on him.

He swears and leaps back. The cardinal rule in his profession is that he must always be aware of his surroundings, must know the next move of everyone around him. It's a harmless mistake now—he's stumbled over a vagrant who poses no threat to him—but next time the stakes might be higher, and he must be prepared.

"Sorry," he says. "Find a better place to rest, my friend. Less underfoot."

He's already passed the beggar and would have continued on without a thought if not for the startled laugh that follows him. A laugh that echoes in Jacob's memory, pinning him in place.

"Christ strike me dead," the beggar says. "That can't be little Fagin?"

Jacob turns warily to meet the gaze of Anthony Leftwich.

It's been years since he thought about the dandy who taught him to steal. Leftwich must be well into his fifties now, but hard living makes him seem older: the creases in his brow look like they've been chiseled there, and there's a yellowish undertone to his skin. The formerly wheat-colored hair is thin and running toward gray. Gone are the jewels, the velvet frock coats, the walking sticks, the flash and dagger. His ragged brown greatcoat is filthy, and the uppers of his boots peel away from the soles. The shabbiness is as startling as if Leftwich had lost a hand.

"Look at you," Leftwich says. He hauls himself up using the wall for leverage. Judging from his grunt, the movement is taxing. He stoops as if there's something wrong with his back. "A grown man. And that hat! A gentleman's hat, no two ways about it."

Jacob hunches his shoulders. If he could disappear into his hat, he would. The sound of Leftwich's voice is synonymous with the last time he heard it, standing in the Copley Street flat beside his mother's shrouded body. All the old feelings of grief, fear, and anger crash over him like a bucket of cold water. Leftwich is still leaning against the wall. The man's former portliness has melted clean away. The coat hangs off his body like a set of curtains.

"You've done well, haven't you?" Leftwich doesn't seem to care that Jacob hasn't said a word. "In the old business still?" He grins as if the years separating them are minutes, a gap that can be traversed with three steps and a joke. Leftwich was his first partner, and they worked together more efficiently than he ever has with anyone else. Better than with Bill, whose loyalty has kept Jacob alive but who could never move so smoothly, so easily. This exchange is what he wanted so desperately the last time he saw Leftwich. Pride. Attention.

"Best there is," Jacob says, though his voice lands hollower than he'd like.

"And how many times in the jugs?"

"Never." It's a slight lie, but still true in the main. He is a master at what he does, and Leftwich knows he wouldn't boast without good reason.

Leftwich whistles. "That's my little viper." He claps Jacob on the shoulder. It's jarring how weakly his hand falls. Jacob still flinches under it. He can't stop thinking about Leah's skin, burning with fever. "You've time for a drink with an old friend, I hope? There's a pub not far, tell me what you've been doing, where you're staying now. I want to hear bleeding everything."

One drink. What's a drink, after fifteen years? He can't imagine a worse destination for his headache than the Three Cripples, but it's only natural that Leftwich would want to step out of the cold. The byway is buried in an unpleasant mixture of snow and mud that paints Leftwich's coat almost up to the hips, and beneath the man's somewhat forced smile, he's visibly shivering. It would be a black-hearted villain indeed who wouldn't agree to take the conversation inside. Even Leah, who begged Jacob never to see this man again, would agree with that. And how many times during his first year in Clerkenwell had Jacob wanted to sit down with his old mentor? Success cheapens without a witness.

"One drink," he says warily.

"Of course." Leftwich leans on his shoulder, and Jacob has to stop himself from recoiling. The man reeks of cheap beer and piss. "Just the one. You'll have to lend me the money, though, 'm afraid. Damn but it's been a rough month."

More than a month, Jacob thinks. He isn't sure how long it takes a man to degrade into such a creature. The descent might have already begun by the time they first met. None of his memories feel reliable.

"A rough month," Leftwich says again.

With an obvious, clumsy movement, he jerks himself round, clawing with one gnarled hand toward Jacob's pocket. It's a grotesque imitation of the maneuvers the old thief taught him, the former dance swallowed up into the near fall of a drunk with swollen, frostbitten hands. Leftwich thinks he's robbing Jacob, but there's no teeth in it, no threat.

Shock melts into disgust. Jacob cannot get far enough away from this ghost, this decrepit memory. He snatches Leftwich by the wrist and jerks his arm away. The thief yelps like a dog and skids in the slush. If Jacob didn't maintain his grip, he would surely fall. Leftwich makes another useless lunge, but Jacob twists Leftwich's arm up behind his back so viciously that the man drops to his knees. Leftwich whimpers in pain. It sounds like a child trying not to cry.

Jacob lets go, and Leftwich collapses, breathing hard and clutching his wrist. He scuffles round to look up at Jacob, not daring to stand and face him. It seems impossible that Jacob ever wanted to be like Leftwich. That as a young man—as a child—he ever asked Leftwich to look after him. Surely he knew better, even then. Everyone leaves. Everyone disappoints.

"No need for that, no need," Leftwich says. "No violence, eh? But you could spare a little, couldn't you? Someone as fine as you are. Would give me a place to sleep, if you have any heart at all, but I won't ask that."

Jacob takes a long breath. Something low and dark simmers

in him, though whether the name for it is hate or melancholy, he isn't certain. This groveling, staggering old man trying to pick a pocket he can hardly see through his own drunken fog, stockings poking through the holes in his boots, begging for a coin. Desperate for care he never showed to anyone, a starving leech grasping for absolution.

"Here," Jacob says. He takes sixpence from his pocket and throws it into the slush at Leftwich's knees. Bile coats his mouth as the thief scrambles to pick it up. "Use that to hang yourself with. Don't ever speak to me again."

"Fagin, lad—"

"You've been dead for years," he says. "Haunt someone else."

Jacob turns his back on Leftwich, who is still stammering pleas for assistance. He walks back toward Bell Court, hardly looking where he's going. It doesn't matter now. If he doesn't steal today, he doesn't eat, but what of that? His stomach is already twisted inside out. Thank God for the cold—if not for the brutal air against his face, he's sure he would be sick. He tries to dismiss the phantom of his ruined teacher by kicking a chip of cobblestone ahead of him, the sharp edges catching against the thin parts of his shoe in a regular rhythmic bruising. What happened to Leftwich, to warp him so badly that it feels dishonest to continue calling him a man? Jacob should have asked. Not that anything would change with knowing. Everything turns to death in the end. Let your guard down for a moment and the rot sets in, blackened flesh and the stink of cheap beer.

It's a reminder, and he means to heed it. Jacob hasn't relied on anyone but himself since Leah's death. He doesn't intend to start now.

But the day isn't done with its surprises yet. When he reaches the boarded-up door on Bell Court, there's a girl standing on his doorstep.

Jacob doesn't know many young girls in this part of London, and he certainly doesn't know this one. She's a fair-haired creature with too-large blue eyes and a dirty face. The girl wears what looks like a man's overcoat, but the hands extending from the rolled-up sleeves are purple with cold and bloody at the knuckles. Her shoes are at least two sizes too big, and the thought of her blisters sends a sympathetic twinge to his own feet. She has obviously been crying, but as she looks up to see Jacob, her lips part. If it weren't a mad notion, he'd think she was waiting for him.

"Move on," Jacob says, shooing her with one arm. "Nothing for you here. You want alms, beg at the church."

"Mr. Fagin?"

Jacob pulls up short. So unlike Leftwich's use of his name, the girl says it with a taste of hope. The novelty makes him curious.

"In the flesh," he says, and waits.

"I heard a man mention your name at an inn, and I asked where I could find you. I've been waiting all morning. Please don't be angry, I thought you might be able to help."

The girl clearly hopes her age and earnestness will endear her to him. On another day, they might have done. He wants to shove her aside as he did Leftwich and retreat into his house, where he will only need to look out for himself.

"And why would I do that?" He takes one feinting step toward her as if to strike. The girl shrinks but, to his annoyance, doesn't run. "I don't know a thing about you. You're nobody to me, and if—"

"You didn't know me well," the girl says, tilting up her chin. Desperation makes her bold. "I was too young then. But you knew my mother, Mr. Fagin. May Walpole."

Jacob stares. For the second time that day, it feels as if he's been struck by lightning.

Looking at the child in front of him, he's transported body and soul back to the little room on Harrow Alley, and May Walpole herself stands next to him with that smile he knew so well. Fair hair frizzing out of its knot after a long morning bent over the washtub. Winking at him behind Mr. Forrester's back, *Come out with me and do something reckless, won't you?* That kiss under the September moon. The baby secured against his chest, a whole world between his little finger and thumb.

"Maggie," he says.

"You brought home tarts for us once, I think. When I was very little. Told us stories."

"Yes," he says quietly. "I did do that. Is she well, your mother?"

Maggie's face falls, and Jacob's stomach along with it. God certainly isn't afraid of repeating a lesson. Love someone and you lose them. On impulse, he lays a hand on Maggie's shoulder. The girl leans into his touch like a dog starved of affection.

"When?" he asks.

"Six months ago," Maggie answers. "Cholera."

He nods. It's only natural, in Whitechapel, for it to be cholera. And if not cholera, then typhus, or consumption, or scarlet fever, or influenza, or any of the dozens of other diseases that pass through London's dark, close, unventilated slums, hanging as miasma in the air and floating as contagion in the water. Cholera takes as many lives as war. It's not a surprise, that one of the few people he's ever considered a friend is now rotting under the ground, and has been for half a year without his knowledge.

"I'm sorry," he says.

Maggie's stubborn bottom lip twitches. This might be the first time anyone told her they're sorry about what's happened. "She talked about you sometimes," she says. "Called you a friend, and the best thief she ever saw."

"She was being kind. I've gotten better since then."

"And I thought," Maggie presses on, "that because you knew her, and she liked you, you might. Well. Please don't be angry."

"I'm not angry," Jacob says. His smile doesn't connect to his heart, which hasn't unfrozen enough to remember that it's breaking. "You thought I might what?"

"Teach me," Maggie blurts out.

Jacob pauses. Cocks his head. "Teach you," he repeats.

The beginning of an idea glimmers in the back of his mind.

It's a dangerous notion, and it frightens him, the sharpness with which he suddenly wants it. The old overcoat with its deep pockets. A stroll through Finsbury Circus. A frail little nothing of a girl whom no one would look at twice in the street. Mother dead, standing on the doorstep, asking. People he has raised from nothing, and who will remain grateful forever. It's snowing again, thick flakes piling on his shoulders and nesting in his hair and beard. Snow that can serve the beggars of Saffron Hill equally well as a blanket or a shroud, however quick fingered a thief they were in some long-gone year.

"I've already almost been caught once," Maggie says, "and if I can't steal I'll starve, but if I'm caught again they'll arrest me. Please, I promise I'll make it worth your time. I'm a quick study. I trust you, I'll do anything you say, and I can make myself useful, however you need."

Jacob allows himself one more glance at the girl, begging him with her mother's eyes. Whenever he thought of his future, he always saw himself alone. But solitude has its dangers, and it's only prudent to hedge his bets.

"Come in," he says to Maggie, shouldering open the boarded-up door. "Let's have a cup of tea, my dear, and you can tell me where you've been."

22

Clearly the last thing Bill expects to find upon his return that night is a girl wearing two of Jacob's shirts sitting in the armchair and thawing her feet in a basin of warm water. He stands in the doorway for nearly a full minute without saying a word. His eyebrows raise until they disappear beneath his hat. Maggie meets his gaze for a few heartbeats before turning to Jacob, who nods and gives her the shadow of a smile. *Let me deal with this, my dear.*

"Fagin," Bill says, "what in blazes have you done?"

"This is Margaret," Jacob says, stepping between Bill and the girl. He rests one hand on her shoulder, squeezing it gently.

"Good evening," Maggie says, so quietly even Jacob can barely hear it. It sounds like she's greeting the parish beadle.

Bill huffs out a laugh and flings himself down in a chair opposite her, kicking his dirty boots onto the table. Maggie shrinks back until Jacob thinks she might become one with the upholstery. "Don't tell me she's yours. God pity the poor woman who'd bear your brats; she deserves a queen's pension."

It's absurd, but Jacob flinches at the accusation. Behind him, he senses rather than sees Maggie do the same.

"God, no," he says. "I'm a friend of her mother's. She's staying with us. Learning her trade."

"Hellfire," Bill mutters. He takes out his clasp-knife and flips it between his fingers, open and shut. Maggie stares as though it might bury itself in her heart. "You've gone soft. Charity doesn't suit you, not when it's taking food from my mouth."

Jacob accepts the words with a tense smile. "Maybe," he says. "But you're a man grown now, Bill. Hardly need me anymore. And you know Bet will be beside herself with joy to think there's another girl around. What wouldn't we do to keep Bet happy?"

Bill grunts, still regarding Maggie warily. "What do you say, cub? You mean to learn thieving from this old bag of bones?"

"Yes," Maggie whispers. It's the least convincing answer Jacob has ever heard.

Bill shakes his head. The knife still flips open and shut against his thumb. He's rattled, Jacob can tell. Something alarmed him, in a girl so small he could pick her up and place her on the mantel. Jacob doesn't understand it, but he trusts his own ability to work Bill out in the long run.

"Right," Bill says roughly. "On your head be it, Fagin. I'll have none of it, know that for God's truth."

Jacob's breath rushes out in relief. Not in a thousand years would he consider enlisting Bill in Maggie's education. She has no need to learn what that man can teach.

It goes on this way, their queer assortment of lives patchworked into the house. The pieces don't fit together, but then, Jacob himself has never fit anywhere, so he's accustomed to a few rough edges. Even so, it would be a lie to say Maggie settles easily into her apprenticeship. Insult to May's memory though it might be to think it, her daughter is a terrible thief. Jacob wastes many evenings imagining what he would tell her mother, if she were there to ask about Maggie's progress.

She's obvious, he'd say, and terrified of shadows, and if you look sharply at her she's liable to hide for an hour at a time for fear you're angry with her. I don't trust her taking pennies from children at the market without me watching. If a policeman shouts at her she's going to burst into tears and give the whole game away.

Every time he imagines these conversations, he pictures May's smile just the same in return and can hear the retort he knows she'd give. *She's grieving, you ass, give her time. Greatest thief I've ever known not up for a little challenge?*

Easy to goad as he is, he keeps at it.

Maggie's determined, if not talented, and under Jacob's exasperated eye she learns to make a poor living. After their lessons are finished for the day, she keeps to herself. He offers once to teach her to read, but she declines, preferring to sketch with the sticks of charcoal he brings home for her one day on a whim. She's not particularly good as an artist, but the drawings give her pleasure in an otherwise dull life, and he doesn't know what else art is supposed to achieve beyond that. She takes equal pleasure in feeding her drawings one by one into the hearth when she's finished, watching the flame swallow up the paper.

Bill, for his part, is at home less than ever. Jacob has always thought of Bill Sikes as an open book, but he sees Bill edge away from Maggie as if from a bare blade and can't work out why. Before long, it's equal odds whether Bill spends his nights asleep at home or swaggering through Clerkenwell with friends Jacob doesn't care to know, like he's determined to overshadow Maggie's weakness with louder displays of his own strength. When he does come home, he's different. Bill talks less, tells fewer stories about his thefts, but the prizes he brings home do not dwindle. On the contrary, they scale in finery beyond what Jacob can comprehend. Earrings, brooches, the sort of jewelry a lady might wear in the street but would certainly notice if someone tried to steal off her person. Bill has come a long way, but he's still nowhere near good enough to remove a diamond stud from a lady's earlobe in the middle of Snow Hill.

It's none of Jacob's business, and he shouldn't ask. So long as Bill is earning money and hasn't gotten caught, Jacob tells himself, the methods don't matter. But this is a weak lie even he doesn't believe. Everything that affects the safety of his people is his business.

"I know you're keen on that girl," Bill says one evening—a rare one he spends at home, which they're passing over a game of piquet. "What I can't follow is why. She'll never amount to anything. You're a bleeding madman, but you're not stupid. Wasting your time on charity cases, that ain't like you."

Jacob snaps the cards between his hands. Maybe he's braver than usual tonight, or maybe it's an aftereffect of having eaten nothing but two thin pieces of bread and butter from the coffee stall that morning. Bill's new spoils are gaudy enough to make the local pawnshops jumpy about buying too much too quickly, so while they're making more money now, their hungry weeks are hungrier than ever. Whatever the case, Jacob's inhibitions are down, and he makes up his mind on the spot to ask.

"No, she won't be much of anything," he says offhandedly. "But all she wants is safety and enough to eat, and that's easy to teach. Not like you, Gentleman Sikes, with whoever you're robbing to land those brass buttons."

Bill grins. "You like it?" He gestures at the bright blue waistcoat, lamplight glinting off the buttons. Jacob has been warily admiring it all evening—it bears no resemblance to what the used-clothes dealers deign to sell to people of their station. The workmanship is exquisite, the tailoring careful, though not precisely suited to Bill's frame. "It's a lark the things people think are safe just because there's a door in front of them."

Jacob nods, pressing his lips together tightly. There's confirmation, then. Eighteen years old now, Bill is over six feet tall and broad in the shoulders, moving through London like a lion come into his own. He knew that Bill's days of low-level pickpocketing were rapidly drawing to a close, if they weren't past already. Jacob wonders which gentleman will open his wardrobe the following morning to discover that London's newest housebreaker has paid his home an uninvited visit.

"Very fine," Jacob says. "The profession must suit you."

Bill laughs. "Better than yours ever did."

No doubt this is true. Bill can now take the soft movements

he learned from Jacob and couple them with his frightening strength, his daring that in the pickpocketing profession is merely recklessness but in housebreaking is called nerve. It's dangerous, but as Jacob reminds himself yet again, it's also none of his business. Bill Sikes doesn't belong to him, isn't his son or his nephew or his apprentice or any other sort of relation that would make Jacob responsible for his behavior. If Bill spends his nights in Bell Court passing the bottle between them and betting increasingly theoretical sums on successive hands of piquet, it's not out of affection so much as long habit. They owe each other nothing.

"Won't need me much longer, will you?" Jacob says. "To think there was a day I had something to teach you."

"Need *you*?" Bill scoffs. "Ain't you hearing what they say about me now? The Dick Turpin of the East End, can stroll into whatever house he likes and take what pleases him. Ladies faint in the streets at my boots coming up behind."

It would be an exaggeration, a tall tale for children, except Jacob has seen it, and it isn't. Multiple times he has seen Bill scatter a crowd of pedestrians like pigeons, from his own more circumspect position in the shadows. Bill doesn't know he's been observed on these days, which makes Jacob only more anxious on his behalf. Awareness of your surroundings is all that stops the noose from finding your neck.

"There's something to be said for fame," Jacob says. "But it never lasts, does it?"

He means it as a warning, though he doesn't have the words to say it more precisely. Doesn't know how to voice his bone-deep knowledge that the way to make a living is to chip away one day at a time, building your stores like a squirrel hoarding against winter, and to never get caught. It's all he's ever tried to impress on them, on Bill or on Maggie, the value of settling for well enough. Once, he might have been able to say it, back when Bill respected him enough to listen to him.

Bill is not listening now.

They've fought a hundred times before, but Jacob has only ever seen Bill's face so cold once, that night years ago when his father appeared at the tavern in St. Giles. Bill's anger usually flares like a house fire, half fright and half spectacle. This anger is rarer, and dark as a swift current.

"No," Bill says. "No, for you, nothing lasts, does it? That's the way you're teaching that little bitch."

Wordlessly, Jacob sets aside the deck. With his hands empty, it isn't as immediately obvious they're shaking. He darts a glance toward the basement stair, down which Maggie retreated as soon as she heard Bill's tread on the floorboards. The door to the stairs is shut now, or as near to shut as it gets with the warp of the wood. Maggie saw the confrontation coming faster than Jacob did, which is why she's now safe on the other side of a door. Perhaps Maggie is the better student after all.

"Keep your head down and hide," Bill says. "And trust the strong ones will be so disgusted by you they won't want to dirty their hands by putting you down. The rotten old Jew of Saffron Hill, hard to kill as a cockroach."

Word by word, Jacob feels the fight spiraling out of his grasp. "Bill," he begins, "my boy, I don't understand—"

"I'm not your *boy.*"

Bill stands up, and Jacob stumbles to his feet himself. It's a gut-deep instinct to draw back.

"You think I need you like she does? I could crush you. You live because I let you."

It's been true for years. Jacob never felt the weight of it until now. He could die today if Bill decides he should. This is what comes of loving a person stronger than you. They abandon you when you need them, or they stay long enough to see you as prey. Bill's voice cracked over the last words, *because I let you,* but it doesn't stop Jacob from picturing Bill's knife quivering blade-down in the table between them, inches from his hand. There was fear in Bill's voice that night too.

"I know, Bill," he says. He hates the small, frightened person he becomes when faced with a threat. "And I'm grateful. People let me be because they know I know you. I helped you once, when you were small. And now I'm getting old, and you're helping me, and I'm grateful."

The words jump out without thinking—*old*, he's thirty-one, God willing he's not half done yet—but they feel true as he says them. He's already outlived so many of the people he used to depend on. Each of his years must count for two of a rich man's.

Without warning, Bill hurls a teacup against the wall. Porcelain shards spatter like a man's brains. Jacob flinches. It's followed by a scuffle against the basement door, as though a small person until recently listening at the keyhole decided to retreat to safer quarters. The buttons of Bill's waistcoat wink like the teeth of a dead man in a polished skull. Like Jacob's father's bright eyes in the shadows, as constant as prophecy. He closes his own, but the vision of the two men before him, one flesh and the other blood, does not fade with the darkness. If anything, he sees them more clearly.

"A rat," Bill shouts. "A maggot eating through the coffin-lid, that's all you've ever been. What kind of a man do you call that?"

What kind of a man indeed.

"One that's alive, my dear," he says quietly. "I don't ask better than that."

Bill's mouth twitches, as if he's about to say something. Then, roughly, he turns away. Yanks on the coat he's thrown over the armchair. Jacob hears the dull thud of the knife in the inside pocket bumping against Bill's ribs. Then he's gone, the door slamming shut behind him against the night. Jacob doesn't have to be told not to follow.

Alone, he sinks back into his chair. He reaches for the bottle before remembering that it's empty, that Bill has already taken that comfort from him too.

"Maggie," he calls out, a little hoarsely.

The girl appears after a moment, wide-eyed and pale, hanging back in the doorway. "Is he gone, Fagin?" she says—Jacob trained her out of the preceding *mister,* though it took weeks.

"He'll be back," he says, and it isn't until he says it that he wonders whether it's true. "Meantime, do me a favor?"

"Now?" Maggie says, alarmed. They haven't evolved to evening work yet, when the pickings are richer and the police correspondingly more alert. Maggie doesn't have the skill for it, and besides, Jacob knows the kind of people who come out after the sun goes down, knows Maggie has a long way to go before she's strong and fast and brave enough to knife a man who gets too fresh. No, he's not sending her far.

"Not that," Jacob says. "Take ninepence to the Cripples and come back with a bottle of gin. And tell Travers that since I'm doing him the rare honor of paying, I won't be cheated out of the pure, understand?"

Maggie nods silently and takes a palmful of coins from the nearly empty box on the mantel.

"And if *you* run off with it, mind..." Jacob begins, though more for show than out of suspicion. Maggie's more likely to die of fright than she is to rob her teacher.

"I'll be back quick as lightning," Maggie vows, and like that, she's off.

Nearly a fortnight goes by before Bill strides back through the house's shadowy passage again, that familiar swagger in his step. It's all Jacob can do to keep himself from retreating to the basement as he hears Bill approach. Until their last conversation, he was confident in Bill's limits, knew exactly how far he could afford to push. Now, some invisible hand has erased the lines, and he must feel them out for himself again.

Bill arrives when Jacob and Maggie are midway through breakfast and sits at the table without being invited. Though he looks a little less well kempt than usual and his beard has come in unevenly, he's not the kind of disheveled that comes from two weeks' sleeping in the gutter, which supports Jacob's theory that he's found a new room to lay his head in. Maggie looks warily at

Jacob for instruction. She thinks too highly of him if she believes he knows what to do.

"That's all right," Bill says loudly. "Go on and eat. I'll starve."

"No need for that, Bill," Jacob says. "You're welcome here as ever." Bill's absence, paradoxically, made work easier these past two weeks—none of the dolly-shops are afraid of Jacob on his own, and he's been winning back their favor by selling them low-risk, untraceable prizes and accepting less than they're worth. While it's no great fortune, it's enough to restock their store of provisions, and so he tosses two more pieces of bread into the pan to toast as a peace offering.

Bill stretches in his chair and grins, and with the movement Jacob catches sight of something silver glittering at his wrists. Jacob's mouth tightens, though he says nothing about the cuff links, or about how any policeman with an ounce of brains would look at a man like Bill walking around with someone else's monogram on his cuffs and think to ask a few questions. It's Bill's signal that he won and Jacob lost, that Bill will be the one to chart his own course.

"Good week?" Jacob says.

"Brilliant," Bill replies. "If Bet weren't busy every night and leaving my bed cold, it'd be the best week I've had in ages."

Jacob supposes Bill is aiming for easy conversation and responds with rolled eyes. "Flattered I'm sure, Bill, but you aren't my notion of a good match."

It's a test of sorts, and Bill's loud laugh reassures him that his friend's simmering hatred has dulled since their last meeting. He should be grateful. It feels like an icicle gored him through the ribs.

"As if you can afford to wait for a good match," Bill fires back. "You'd take whatever man, woman, or devil would be brave enough to fuck someone as ugly as you, and you'd thank them for the charity."

Jacob swallows the insult and hides his tension with a smile. "Manners, Bill. There's a child present."

If Bill wants him at a distance, he can maintain the arm's length with the best of them. There's hardly a person in London better prepared to bear offense than he is. When he's pushed too far, he'll snap, and to hell with the risk. But until then, he'll hold his tongue, and he'll wait.

23

1818–1825

It should be quiet after Bill moves out, but that wouldn't be London. Bill's new lodgings are half a mile west in Bethnal Green—not nearly so spacious or well ventilated as the Bell Court house, but independence, not comfort, seems to be the attraction. Jacob makes the trek at least one night a week to stroll with Bill past the brothels in St. Giles for an evening's entertainment, or to stay in with as much porter as the potboy can carry in a single trip while Bet regales them with stories of the well-to-do customers she's had that week. Both Jacob and Bill know she's lying through her teeth—the odds she's fucked Lord Melbourne are so long not even the most unrepentant gambler would take them—but she spins a good tale and keeps the peace besides, so they let her elevate the gentility of her clientele. Other nights they haunt the alleys behind the chophouses, Jacob cheating one man after another in rigged games of skittles while Bill leans against the alley wall and watches the con lazily. If Bill thinks it's beneath their dignity to sharp a poor man's game at threepence a throw, he doesn't say so—and though Jacob is increasingly aware of the anxious looks his marks give Bill even when he keeps to the shadows, as if catching sight of Bill Sikes is an omen of death, he says nothing about that either.

There seem to be more subjects they can't talk about, these days, than those they can.

Other than these evenings, Jacob is back in Bell Court, which—to his surprise—has established something of a reputation in Saffron Hill. Maggie Walpole is a young woman now, and as able a thief as Jacob could have hoped for given her unpromising beginnings. She stayed with Jacob for a few years before taking up with a young fellow who lived near Seven Dials, though she drops by now and again for a supper she knows he'll provide for free. But word spreads, and even before Maggie left, two more youths had turned up at his door, one after the other. Boys, these, thin and shivering, battered hats in hand. He doesn't turn them away, though he considers it—it's a liability, having children so green under his roof, but there's mutual benefit to be had.

The younger boy, a pistol of a six-year-old named Toby, has a fire in him that's unpredictable but more useful than it is dangerous. The child understands the game straightaway, before Jacob has even invited the boy inside. Simply stands there on the doorstep, light brown hair flopping into heavy-lidded eyes, and states his case with the confidence of a three-foot-tall justice of the peace.

"I want you to teach me," the boy says, before even a hello. "Teach me everything you know, the way they say you did Bill Sikes. Teach me and I won't never rat you out, and I'll make you enough money you won't never want to rat me out neither."

Jacob leans against the doorframe, considering. It feels peculiar to hear the case put so bluntly. These are the sorts of bonds built in London's rookeries. Loyalty by co-creation, each tangled so deeply in the making of the other that turning your back on them means driving the knife into your own heart. At least he won't need to teach that lesson to Toby.

"All right then," he says, and gestures down the corridor. "Let's see if you have the makings of another Bill Sikes. Though if you're hopeless, I reserve the right to turn you out."

Toby grins and darts inside before Jacob can change his mind.

The other boy, comparatively mature at thirteen, turns up three weeks after Toby, and he doesn't even wait to be invited in. Jacob returns from Petticoat Lane in high spirits, having sold a particularly fine batch of silk handkerchiefs for five whole shillings, to find Maggie at the table across from a wiry, dark-skinned boy in a coat four inches too long for him. The boy must have walked the length and breadth of London without shoes, from the look of his shredded feet. Maggie filled a chipped basin with water and is washing the mud and gravel out of the cuts. It has to sting like the devil—the basin water is brownish red, and Jacob doesn't think it's dirt—but the boy doesn't flinch. He simply looks up with sharp eyes as Jacob enters and says, "You're going to teach me, Mr. Fagin."

Jacob pulls off his coat and glances at Maggie, who shrugs as if to say *Don't ask me* and continues tending the boy's ruined feet. "Am I?"

"Yes," the boy says.

He sits opposite the boy at the table, and the boy stares him down. There's steel in his eyes, and something else, something Jacob doesn't know the word for. Later, he'll come to know it as the same sort of spite that drives him, the desire to stick two fingers in the eyes of a world that's wronged you. Five shillings don't stretch so far with four mouths to feed, but he's handled sums more dire than that before.

"All right," he says. "Looks like I am."

And that, as far as Ned Brooks is concerned, is that.

The new boys couldn't be more different. Both of them are quick studies, but Toby thinks he's learned everything before he's properly begun, while Ned is methodical, takes to the profession with the sobriety of a cleric and runs no risks until he's assessed them from every angle. Jacob adapts his approach without thinking about it, molding himself into the instructor each of them needs. He's done it both ways now, showing an overconfident protégé how exposed they are, helping a cautious neophyte determine when a risk's worth taking. Showing them both how much they still need him.

Maybe he is a good teacher after all.

When Bill turns up one October evening some years later, early enough that the boys are still at work, Jacob is instantly suspicious. As Bill's fame as a housebreaker grows, Jacob's increasingly the one to make the trek to him, and seldom the other way around. If Bill's giving up that petty form of power and seeking him out, it's because he has something to say. Besides, Bill hasn't come empty-handed; he's holding the evening *Times*. Bill Sikes is not theatrical. He doesn't bring props unless he intends to use them.

"Never took you for a literary man," Jacob says, gesturing.

Bill pushes the paper into Jacob's hand. "Not for me," he says. "For you."

Jacob glances down and reads the headline Bill folded the paper to display, frowning as he does.

JEWISH DISABILITIES BILL ENTERS SECOND WEEK OF DEBATE IN HOUSE OF LORDS; INITIAL VOTE ON ROTHSCHILD SWEARING-IN TO BE CALLED

There's no need to read further; he creases the paper sharply. Unlike Bill, who never spares a thought for anything that doesn't directly concern him, Jacob uses his time between thefts to listen, and he's well aware of the genteel debate currently underway in Westminster. Baron Lionel de Rothschild was elected to represent the City of London in the House of Commons months ago, and ever since, Parliament has been thrown into a bureaucratic storm over whether a Jew must take the oath of office on a Christian Bible or the Old Testament might be equally binding. The caustically polite tenor of the debate gives the whole matter the air of a farce.

"Fascinating," Jacob says dryly. "Anything else?"

"Don't be that way," Bill says. He's jovial today, leaning back in his chair with one arm dangling toward the floor. Bullseye trots up to his extended hand, the fool of a dog still expecting a friendly pat between the ears. The white bull terrier is a new addition, only five months old, but already he's been incorporated into Bill's mythos, though the dog is too young and ill-behaved to live up to the legend yet. Stories in the pubs talk about Bill Sikes and his hellhound; in person, it's more like Bill Sikes and his untrained puppy prone to piddling on the floor. Bill twitches his wrist, not quite a slap, and the dog flinches back but doesn't go far. "All those swells in Parliament, paying you lot such bloody compliments."

Jacob snorts and swipes the paper off the table. He considers throwing it into the fire, but that would show Bill his needling was successful, and he doesn't want to give that satisfaction. "Leave it alone, Bill."

Bill laughs. "Oh, come off it. You think the MPs are smoking their cigars and going on about how noble a race I come from? The way you Jews have the lot of them twisted round your finger, they'll slit their own throats to keep you happy. Could swear the oath on a murdered child if it meant they could stay in your pocket."

He sighs. For what reason Jacob can't guess—a disappointing day, a dark memory, the boredom and quiet that torment a loud man living alone—Bill came today expressly to fight Jacob and beat him. Cruelty is something to fill the hours, hate an easy emotion to summon. He's seen Bill do it a thousand times before to the skittle players, the policemen, the poorly dressed women trying to waylay men headed to the brothel. Bill knows the most painful places to aim his claws with Jacob, and he can knock him down a peg and walk away knowing he's still the strongest man in the room. Well, if it's a fight Bill wants, Jacob decides, against his better judgment, to give him one. It's been a while since he taught Bill anything useful.

"You aren't stupid, Bill," he says coldly. "So don't act like it."

Bill frowns. Jacob has to tamp down an urge to kick the dog as the only creature in the world he currently feels stronger than.

"You don't have the right to call me stupid."

"Then think, and prove it," Jacob presses on—he's turned the tables, and the more urgently he talks, the more Bill will listen. "Papers print what politicians say in the House. Maybe some of them even mean it, in the moment they're saying it. But what do you think they say after?" He stands up, running both hands down the length of his face. "When they tuck their walking sticks under their arms and hide away in their offices, and the papers aren't there to hear them? Or when they see a clothes-dealer with his cart in Petticoat Lane, or a pawnbroker in Houndsditch? Change their damned tune then."

"Don't see Rothschild complaining, though, do you," Bill says.

"Rothschild has money," Jacob reminds him less than patiently.

"So you think it's just poor sheenies like you they hate. Poor old Fagin, can't even be the right kind of Jew."

The kettle on the hob has begun to boil, and Jacob removes it before the water can bubble over. Everything in the room seems fragile, like one piercing noise could send the lot of it shattering. It's gin he needs now, not tea, but at least brewing the pot gives him something to do with his hands.

"You aren't listening," he says to the tea leaves, trying not to feel Bill's eyes on him. "They can't close the doors on Rothschild because he's got enough to buy half the world. They'll say what they need to so they can work their way into his pockets, so they can call on him for favors, use what he has and know who he knows. But it's just the same. As soon as he turns his back? They start talking the way they always talk. Don't even wait for him to leave the room, I'll bet my life on it. Better a rich Jew than a poor Jew, but better a dead one than either."

Bill slouches down farther in his chair and stretches out his legs, crossed at the ankles. He obviously stopped listening partway through Jacob's speech—a cheap way to win the fight. A flash of irritation sears through Jacob, there and gone in an instant. Of all the things in the world it's useful to be angry about, Bill Sikes not listening when he has something serious to say must be close to the bottom of the list.

"Typical, ain't it," Bill says. "Want the world handed to you, then get all up in arms when it is."

"Do you expect me to stand for the House of Commons?"

"If it was on offer? You wouldn't take it, greedy as you are? I'd rather have Rothschild's lot in life than yours."

"Would you?" Jacob says. He returns to the table with his cup of tea; Bullseye grumbles at his presence. The dog, despite his stubborn good nature, has never liked Jacob, which is just as well; Jacob doesn't like him either, head like a sledgehammer, the wet piles of drool he leaves under the table. "Sometimes I wonder. Seems to me being poor and hated is more honest than being rich and hated."

Bill throws back his head and laughs, and Jacob nearly shivers with relief. The threat has resumed its usual proportions. So long as Bill can still laugh, he's not lost yet.

"Oh, go to hell," Bill says. "You wouldn't know honest if it bit off your cock. And I know you, you miserly old rat. You'd rather have the money."

Jacob lets the silence hang just long enough to sip his scalding tea. Somewhere on the other side of the city, Baron Rothschild is no doubt sitting down to a tea of his own, served on glittering silver with pristine white cloths draping the tables. The tea the finest that can be procured. His pocket-handkerchief of exquisite green silk, embroidered with the great man's initials and creased to a square edge. A valet brushes his dinner jacket every evening with a soft horsehair brush before he descends to the dining room. He travels by carriage from Mayfair to Westminster, the clean soles of his leather shoes scarcely brushing the streets. Into the Houses of Parliament, where a thousand voices whisper in every shadow, hiding sharp teeth behind politic smiles. Surely Bill Sikes knows what it feels like to hear wary murmurs as you turn your back.

"Yes," Jacob says, "I'd rather have the money."

24

1826

One beautiful clear night at the end of May, when Bill is unaccounted for and the streets are alive with the giddiness of impending summer, Jacob decides it's time to enjoy himself a little. Lately, he's been sticking to the sure business, the regular crowds, neighborhoods where green policemen hesitate to patrol and experienced ones have bigger problems than petty thieves. But it's been an exhausting week, the dull grind of two-a-penny thefts beginning to wear on him, and he's in the mood to indulge himself with something flashy and impractical.

Ned has promised to keep track of Toby, who at ten is a greater terror than many seasoned criminals of thirty, and to manage the exchange with the pawnbroker that evening, assuming he can get a good price for the week's take. Jacob wouldn't ordinarily trust anyone but himself fencing anything worth more than a farthing, but he likes Ned, who is an exceptionally practical thief and good company besides. Now going on seventeen, Ned Brooks arrived in London at twelve, stowed away alone on a ship from Jamaica and determined to make something of himself in a world that didn't want him. He disappears into a crowd more effectively than Jacob has ever seen anyone but himself manage, and though the boy's quiet by nature, it's obvious how desperately he wants to prove himself worthy of Jacob's trust.

Jacob combs back his hair, trims his beard a little, and puts on the clothes he's picked up from a dealer in Petticoat Lane, a black linen frock coat and trousers he's pressed for the occasion, a little color via a bottle-green waistcoat and one of his favorite pocket-handkerchiefs from the collection on the clothes-horse. The ruse won't fool anyone into thinking he's well-to-do—that trick would require silk and velvet and oiled leather and an equipage to tie it all together, he's a good liar but he's not a magician—but it will do if no one looks closely, and he doesn't intend to let anyone observe him for long.

A night at the opera, he thinks, is just what his mood calls for.

The Covent Garden Theatre is already crowded when he arrives. They check tickets at the entrance to the great hall, the fools, not at the foyer. He plunges into the crush of people, feeling the familiar buzz of excitement at an unnecessarily daring trick. The operagoers' finest jewels will have to stay where they are for now, as their owners are rabidly conscious of them, preening like turtledoves. But the lesser wares are still worth the effort, and he browses like a gentleman in a shop until something takes his fancy. A watch-chain. A pair of cuff links, loosely attached. A lady's lace fan, because why on earth not? Ladies drop such things all the time.

He carries on untroubled until he feels the brush of another hand trying to insert itself into his pocket.

Without thinking, he shoots out a hand to catch the thief by the wrist and registers only faint surprise when his grip closes on a woman's arm.

Jacob turns to see an unremarkable face looking at him in horror from beneath a slightly crushed bonnet. His would-be robber is young, roughly Ned's age, with thick dark hair that has been brushed and set nicely but looks unaccustomed to being made presentable. No doubt the girl also costumed herself with the help of a secondhand dealer, though his own disguise is more successful than hers. Her dress is a pretty lilac creation that does not suit her figure, tailored for someone with larger breasts and wider hips, and the cut is several years out of fashion. It's not so bad that anyone would notice unless they're paying close attention, though, and few people here will do that. The girl's face, from its large brown eyes to its broad nose and wide mouth, is neither ugly nor beautiful, noteworthy only for its utter lack of interesting features. He has seen a thousand faces that look just like hers.

It is, he thinks suddenly, one of the greatest assets a thief could ask for, a face like that.

"Don't shout, sir, please," the girl says in a low voice. She looks at him with the frantic deference Jacob has seen the boys use to talk their way out of any number of scrapes. He almost laughs at the thought of the girl trying to flatter him into mercy, like he's any other gentleman prone to calling in the law. "I'll go, I swear it, only don't—"

"I'm not going to *shout,*" he says, only loud enough for her ears. "I've got three men's watches in my coat pocket, how would it look if I shouted?"

Her alarm melts away so transparently Jacob can't hold back the laugh anymore, though he disguises it as part of an ordinary bourgeois conversation. He shifts his grip so he's holding her hand instead of grasping her wrist. With a bow, he presses a kiss to her knuckles as though they're old acquaintances and he's overjoyed at the surprise of their paths crossing. She leaps into the fiction, lowering her eyes and giving a delicate curtsy. When she looks up again, her wicked eyes send a spark of delight flashing through him. It's been so long since he worked with anyone he didn't train from the ground up, someone whose tricks he doesn't know to be a watered-down version of his own.

"Tell you what, my dear," he says. "I've always found the opera to be more enjoyable when you see it with a companion."

"And it's so dangerous these days for a young lady without a chaperone," she agrees.

There's no need for additional talk; just like that, they are at it.

It's an easy partnership, preternaturally so. Jacob and the girl fall into a shared rhythm as though they've been working together for years, each covering for the other and opening the possibility for yet more daring exploits. If he came here tonight for artistry, he found it. Each movement is light as a dancer's gesture, the risk barely even a flutter before they're off again to the next target, undetected and that much the richer.

They know, though, not to push their luck too far. Before long, the orchestra settles into its tuning notes. As the crowd departs the foyer for their seats, the girl touches the brim of her bonnet toward him before heading for the south door. His heart swells with satisfaction as he sets off for the north. It's a hard skill to teach, when to stop. The fact that she already knows it confirms what he suspected: that though she's young, they have more in common than it might seem.

A few minutes later, he sees the girl waiting for him in a narrow court near the theater, safely away from the lines of carriages and cabmen prepared to pick up a bored fare walking out mid-aria. The girl's face is flushed with excitement, but she clearly knows the trick isn't complete until they've transformed every prize in their pockets into ready cash.

"You have a fellow you trust?" she asks.

Jacob nods. She doesn't, which means she's either new to the neighborhood, new to the trade—unlikely, given tonight's performance—or in the habit of working for others. In any case, he doesn't hesitate to introduce her to Barrett. It's not as if she threatens his standing in Clerkenwell, and then she'll owe him twice over, which is a pleasant way to start a new acquaintance.

"Follow me," he says. "Bit of a walk, but best not to keep hold of this any longer than needs must."

They leave the West End in relative silence, though the streets around them are as lively as ever with traffic and shouts and barking dogs and the bellow of drivers. The cab traffic thins as they move farther east, and it becomes feasible again to speak without shouting.

"You're good, you know," she says cheerfully. "Very. I've been working with a man in St. Giles and he ain't half as neat as you are, I can tell you that."

She may be trying to flatter him, with the goal of getting a more favorable cut of the profits. If so, he lets her—flattery is a rare treat.

"You have a name, I suppose?" she says.

"Fagin. And you?"

"Nancy Reed," she says. He expects the usual remarks on his parentage, but there's nothing of the kind. She juts out her chin in a way that makes her look even younger than he suspects she is, a kind of defiance that invites trouble. "Friends call me Nan."

"Are we friends?"

"I don't know," she answers. "Call me something and we'll see."

He gestures, indicating a turn toward Clerkenwell. The city's love affair with gas lighting has not yet penetrated so far from the genteel corners of the West End, and soon the only illumination comes from what residents have rigged up themselves against the night: candles tucked into dirty lanterns, an oil lamp that spits and threatens to burn down half the street. Jacob takes a perfunctory lap around the building to ensure no policemen are about before beckoning Nan into Barrett's pawnshop, indicating wordlessly that he'll handle the negotiations. Nan hangs back, watching the business with her eyebrows lightly raised. She's not impressed, not yet, but she's ready to be.

Either Barrett is in a good mood tonight, or they've truly pulled off a triumph in Covent Garden, or both. Jacob talks his way into a sum that even when split is enough to cover his most pressing debts and still make some irresponsible decisions to finish out the night. He shakes hands with Barrett and divides the money—a little in his favor—before following Nan into the street.

"Early yet," Nan says, then frowns. "I think. Ought to have kept one of the watches, to tell time with."

"Not yet eleven," Jacob agrees. He knows the rhythms of Clerkenwell like the beating of his heart, could tell the time to the quarter hour based on the traffic in its streets. "Come for a drink?"

It's a friendly offer, made on a whim, but Nan interprets it differently. She scowls and draws away, those expressive brows low.

"I'm not in that business," she says, and she pulls her shoulders back with great dignity. "And I'll thank you not to flatter yourself I'd do it for free."

Jacob raises both hands. "I mean it," he says. His voice is placating. Not so many days ago, he used a similar tone on Bill, talking him down from a ledge, coaxing him back into his chair when he seemed ready to storm out. He can barely remember the subject of that argument anymore. They come too close together these days to separate them. "I'm too old and ugly for you, girl. It's an honest drink I'm offering, nothing more."

She looks at him askance. "When's the last time you've had an honest anything, I wonder, Mr. Fagin?"

He grins. "A dishonest drink, then."

Nan lets another beat go by, considering. On balance, she must decide he's more harmless than in fact he is, because she makes up her mind with a shrug.

"All right," she says. "But anything funny and I'll poke out your eyes."

It's a free-and-easy night at the Three Cripples, he discovers, as they round the corner to a wave of drunken singing. As a rule he tries to avoid these nights: the room tends to be too full of friendly faces that goad him to lead a song, and though he can carry a tune as well as any drunk in Saffron Hill, he knows the reluctant tolerance he enjoys at the pub doesn't extend to a real welcome. The more eyes on him, the more likely he is to be suspected, mistrusted, thrown out, even in the places he considers safe. No, he prefers the anonymity of an ordinary night, when the only ones paying attention to him are his immediate neighbors and the people he's brought with him, and he can manage any trouble with a well-placed word and an offer to buy the next round. There are dozens of public-houses in Saffron Hill, half of them a stone's throw from where they stand. It would be the work of a minute to find somewhere quieter.

But Nan finds the music as welcome as a fire in the dead of winter. All the flash and bravado from their night's work leaves her, and she looks like any other young woman as she tilts her face up toward the second-story window, letting the light paint her warmer than rouge. It's the look of a hungry child at the edge of Spitalfields Market, of a shoeless matchstick seller watching a carriage rattle through St. James's Park. She's nothing to him, and he nothing to her, but he doesn't feel capable of tearing her away from something she clearly wants so desperately. Bracing himself for the worst, he ushers her into the pub.

Travers is in his habitual role as master of ceremonies, bustling through the taproom refilling mugs and whipping up good cheer. He beams as Jacob enters with Nan at his side, and though Jacob isn't sure whether the smile connotes welcome or amusement, he doesn't press the point.

"Mr. Fagin!" Travers says—a proclamation that draws several shouts and more than one raised glass from across the taproom. "Can't say I thought we'd see you tonight. And with a pretty little friend, no less."

"A drink for Miss Reed," Jacob says. "She came for music, and I came to see you don't charge her double for your piss-poor ale."

Travers presses one hand to his chest theatrically. "You see how the old Hebrew slanders me? As if I'd cheat a fine young lady such as yourself. Keep your eye on him. He's good company but not to be trusted."

Not to be trusted is a weak insult coming from Travers, who has personally sheltered most of the rogues and convicts in Saffron Hill, but Nan is unbothered. She draws Jacob to a table in the heart of the crowd, turning a bright smile on the publican.

"I've got good instincts for men," she says. "I'll take my chances with this fellow, wicked though he is."

Travers rolls his eyes but draws them each a pint of porter. Nan's smile doesn't dim as she takes a healthy swig. As one song closes and the crowd sets up a call for another, she's already clambering to stand atop her chair, toasting the room with the pint.

"All right then, my good friends!" she roars, and instantly each person in the room is enamored with her. "Do any of you ne'er-do-wells know the words to a little tune called 'Jack Hall'?"

Voices and glasses rise in agreement. Her grin broadens farther. Before Jacob's startled eyes, she leads the room in a lively song about a chimney sweep hanged for thievery, her warm alto carrying the verses to each corner of the room while her infectious enthusiasm brings everyone into the chorus. He even finds himself singing along, swept up in the pure joy that makes Nan Reed look her age. It reminds him of how Toby laughed, the week before, at a sleight-of-hand magician who paused at the corner of Snow Hill to show off his talent—the laugh not of a sly street thief but of a boy happy to be entertained. In a different world, a better world, Nan might have spent every evening like this.

In the only world they have, he pays for her drink and allows himself the pleasure of listening to her sing.

25

He leaves Nan that night with instructions to find his house should she care to, and they each stumble their separate ways from the pub, humming bits of the final song as they go. He expects she'll use the information only to know which street to avoid in the future, but too much ale and an unfamiliar hope empower the part of him that makes foolish decisions, and he leaves that for her to decide. Next day, as he emerges into the street at a quarter past ten in search of something to eat that will curb his raging headache, she's already waiting for him. More surprising, she's knelt down in the filthy courtyard to scratch Bill's white bull terrier behind the ears. A thing Jacob has never seen anyone but Bill do, because no one else with sense would try it.

His heart catches, and he sprints to warn her away. Neglected from birth, Bullseye has only ever known Bill's affection, and in exchange the dog loves him to the total exclusion of all other creatures. Bullseye is a companion to Bill and a hellhound to the rest of the world, and if he bites off Nan's hand at the wrist Jacob won't be at all surprised. But the dog sits neatly in front of Nan with his ears perked up and nudges his head into her hand, insisting to be petted. His tail is even wagging.

"Either this is witchcraft or you have a leg of mutton in your pocket," Jacob says.

Nan looks up. To his further surprise, she's pleased to see him. "Animals like me."

"And demons too, apparently. I'm off to find breakfast. Join us?"

She hesitates. "Don't want to be a bother."

"You wouldn't be. Toby and Ned will piss themselves with joy to have someone to talk to who isn't me."

She grins, and he knows she doesn't need more convincing. "I forgot you're headmaster of a school for degenerates."

"Something like it. Come on."

They head a few streets over, to a corner with a coffee stall and a woman who sells jacket potatoes two for a penny. Not a glamorous meal, but an effective way to counterbalance too much porter. Bullseye trots along amiably after them, as though pleased to be included. Bill himself is nowhere to be seen, though he'll show up before the day is out; the dog is a sure sign of it. But for the moment, it's only him and Nan, a partnership that already feels more natural than it has any right to. It seems foolish to seek someone out because they make him happy, but there it is: he'd like having her around even if it weren't profitable.

Shopping done, they return to the house, where Toby and Ned sit at the table. They've been irritably waiting for breakfast, but breakfast hasn't come alone. Ned scrambles to his feet as he spots Nan, and Jacob could laugh at how eager he is to sweep off a hat he isn't wearing. Ned is a man now, he realizes. The perfect age to behave like an idiot in front of a woman.

"Boys, this is Miss Nancy," he says; Nan pulls a playful curtsy. "A better thief than either of you will ever be. Show some manners and draw up another place."

Ned nearly trips in his haste to offer Nan the room's only spare chair. Jacob settles in at the table, smirking.

"Miss Nancy!" Toby exclaims. "Do you want to see what I found yesterday?"

Found isn't the most accurate word for whatever Toby has, but the boy bounds down the stairs in search of it before Jacob can say so. He gives an apologetic look to Nan, who puts on what seems to be a sincere smile as Toby barrels back with a garnet brooch on a gold-leaf backing. It's without a doubt the finest prize Toby's managed to steal during his time as Jacob's student, so Jacob doesn't make fun the way he usually would as Toby drops the gem into Nan's outstretched hands.

"Well, aren't you a fine little thief!" she says. "It's beautiful, this is."

She starts to give it back, but Toby shakes his head and presses her hand closed over the brooch. "It's for you," he says. "Pretty jewel for a pretty lady."

Ned cringes with such embarrassment anyone would be forgiven for thinking he'd tried the line himself. But Toby glows with pride as he pins the brooch on the upper left of Nan's dress, the gem sparkling against the faded linen. Jacob shakes his head—Toby's learned plenty about pickpocketing since his arrival, but it seems unlikely he'll ever learn how to be subtle with women—but Nan seems charmed and kisses the boy on the cheek.

"What a dear," she says. "Now sit down, love. You must be hungry."

With the four of them crowded around the table and Bullseye settled in the corner with his bright black eyes fixed on Nan, they feel almost like a little family, dividing up the food and passing the two tin mugs of coffee around to drink from in turn. Nan's laugh fills the room at Toby's jokes, which become more ribald to impress his new audience. Ned is quieter even than usual, and Nan invites him into the conversation with kindness that makes him even less able to speak. For the first time since Bill moved out years ago, the room feels properly full again.

He and Nan work together so well that by week's end they decide to test their joint powers on a greater prize: the Epsom Derby. Ned is itching to join them, maybe to impress Nan, but Jacob dissuades him. There are equally grand prizes to be had locally, he claims, and too many of them gathered in one place will draw attention and ruin their chances of bleeding the racetrack dry. Ned's talented, and someday he could give Jacob a run for his money, but not yet. Certainly not if he's still mooning after Nan:

a lovesick youth is hardly the most reliable partner in crime. Besides, Jacob has worked the races before, and while he can blend into this crowd with a little effort, as a Black man Ned cannot. The only ruse he can think of that might work is for Ned to pose as his servant, a thought so distasteful he sets it aside. Two will be more than enough today.

He and Nan follow the early crowd southeast from the city, the roads already packed with carriages and dogcarts and people eager to be entertained. Jacob had stopped off at his usual dealer and secured a cream-colored waistcoat and brown linen breeches for a shilling and six, which makes him walk with his shoulders back and a little extra swagger in his step. He slicked back his hair with pomade and donned a dark blue frock coat with the added benefit of especially deep pockets. Nan, on his arm, looks smart as anything in a pale pink muslin he helped her select, a straw bonnet over her usually unruly hair. They are posing as father and daughter for the day—she suggested they go as sweethearts, which is apparently how she usually plays the trick, but Jacob laughed for a full minute before assuring her there's no need to try such an implausible lie as that.

"You aren't so terribly old," she said, as she adjusted his cravat. "What are you, forty?"

He is thirty-nine—older, he realized with a jolt, than he ever expected to be, older than either of his parents ever were—but he brushed off the question. "It's not only the age that works against me, my dear," he said. "No one in their right mind would believe a girl like you would choose a man like me. Besides, can't a father take his favorite girl to the races?"

"Oh, Papa," Nan said with a wink. "You always did love me better than my brothers."

"The rascals your brothers were at breakfast, can you blame me?"

Surely no one can, when Nan looks the way she does today, her eyes sparkling, tugging on Jacob's sleeve every few minutes to point out some idle amusement. Jacob only rarely goes to Epsom, but he spends time at enough gin-palaces and gambling dens of Southwark and the Borough to recognize the energy. It's a brilliant sunny day, one of the few England gets a year, and every gentleman and lady has turned out to make the most of the festive atmosphere. Linen and silk and fine shawls and parasols whirl around Jacob and Nan like the inside of a kaleidoscope, and everyone presses in toward the track, eager to catch sight of the jockeys and their horses before the first race. There's a contagious sense of daring, of money to be made or lost, and a high time to be had either way.

Of course, fine society isn't the only type that comes out for Derby Day. Jacob spots several of his and Nan's peers among the crowd, though a less-educated onlooker might miss them. In the fierce-looking youth in the peaked cap, he sees the nervous caution of the untrained pickpocket; in the two girls wearing patterned cotton dresses and spencer jackets, there's the confident movements of the practiced thieves who prey on the riders of London omnibuses, long shawls draping over their hands to conceal quick dips into other people's pockets. Everyone came here for the same reason: for a chance to make a fortune, either on the Derby grounds or at the betting window, and to spend an afternoon under the open sky. There are worse things, he supposes, for mankind to have in common.

"Come on, Papa," Nan says, and he realizes he's been standing near the promenade staring like a rustic who's never seen a crowd before.

"Anything you like, darling," he says, rather theatrically. If he ever loses his touch at picking pockets, there's always the stage to consider. "Shall we find you a lemonade, somewhere to sit?"

"That sounds lovely," she replies, and with that, they're off.

Other than when he's teaching the boys, Jacob always works alone. It isn't the norm among pickpockets: usually it's advantageous to have a partner who can cause a distraction or shield your hands from view. Most people in his circle these days are still too green to be useful, and besides, he's grown used to it, not consulting anyone but himself. Long enough looking out for your own back and it starts to feel natural.

Working with Nan, though, is like magic. It's as if she found her way into his brain and can follow every movement three beats before he makes it. Without a word, she'll linger in front of the slate listing the odds, asking the man beside them some inconsequential question about horse racing while Jacob divests the fellow of tenpence and a tiepin. And then quick as a step change in time to music they flit off again, and he positions himself between a pillar and a lady's back so no one notices Nan snip the drawstring of her reticule and catch the purse before the money inside can clank against the ground. Nan tips the money into her own pocket and tosses the maimed reticule discreetly aside, and Jacob continues their conversation about the finer points of horse breeding easy as anything, as if there's nothing else on his mind—he's lying more freely than he's ever lied in his life, all he knows about horses is that they're tall as mountains and shit like thunder, but with his and Nan's pockets newly weighted down with coin, it feels as if he could manage the king's stables with ease.

After an hour or so, he loses track of the value of their take. Usually he's good at tallying figures in his head while the game's afoot, but they're moving in such perfect synchronicity and the smell of horse and beer and summer sunshine is making him careless. There's amusement to be had of the ordinary sort as well, and he'd rather keep what they have than lose it all aiming for more. He rests one hand on Nan's shoulder. She looks back, called away from appraising the pocket-watch of a gentleman some ten yards off.

"Have a seat, my dear?" he says, nodding toward the stands. "The races will start soon, and I don't want to overtire you."

She looks at him in surprise, almost shame, which baffles him. He can't think what would make the color rise in her cheeks like that. Maybe in the end she chalks it up to the role he's playing of the indulgent father, one who wouldn't let his respectable daughter stand in the sun without worrying for her delicate constitution.

Whatever she's thinking, she masks it with a smile and allows him to lead her to a secluded corner near the back of the grandstands, where a few overeager spectators wait for the race to begin.

"Did I do something wrong?" she asks.

She has her hands in her lap and steadily twists the fabric of her skirt, looking at the ragged edges of her nails and not at him. She's frightened. He doesn't understand why, but he recognizes a person plotting an escape when he sees one. He takes both her hands in one of his. She flinches and looks up, uncertain what to make of the fact that he is smiling.

"The opposite," he says. "We've done what we came for, haven't we? Surest way to lose a good day's work is to try your luck once too often. That's what I always tell the boys: the better part of valor, in our business, is discretion."

The source of the quotation goes over her head; well, she and the boys have that in common. "So you don't think I've ruined it?"

Jacob can't decide whether the proper response is to laugh or to show her that his heart is breaking. "Nan, I haven't had such a brilliant day of it since I was half your age. You're better than Ned and Toby put together. God's sake, do I think *you* ruined it? You'll be begging my old bones to leave you be before I've tired of you."

Nan smiles, pleased at the praise, though he can't imagine she needs to hear it. She must know their partnership isn't the sort that comes about every day. Even so, hearing that he's not angry seems to have done the trick, and when a vendor passes them with a tray bearing glasses of lemonade, she waves him over and purchases one with sixpence and a wink the young man won't soon forget. It's hot, but he doubts this is why the pink still hasn't left her cheeks. Nan isn't the sort who lets emotions pass over like clouds, leaving nothing behind. Her next words confirm his suspicion.

"I've run this circuit with a half dozen men before," she says, keeping her voice low. "I thought you'd do the job the same as they did."

"What do you mean?"

She looks at the half-empty glass of lemonade as she answers. "You know. There's no leaving off while it still feels good. They're the ones who say when we're finished."

Her hand clenches around the glass, and Jacob struggles with an urge to lay his hand on her knee. He doesn't, of course. Isn't naïve. Her initial proposal that they pose as sweethearts returns to him with new, awkward weight. He swallows hard before continuing, but when he speaks, he is full master of his voice again, and his tone is as light as ever.

"Young men can afford to be reckless. Me, I need to watch my back, you see. And I do. Thirty-nine years I've been alive, and not spent a day in prison."

It shouldn't be funny, but the absolute disbelief with which she receives this information is hilarious. It's not a strong vote in favor of the company she keeps, if all a man needs to do to amaze a woman is refrain from darkening the doorstep of Coldbath Fields.

"Not at all? You've never been nabbed?"

"Only once," he says, "but they couldn't keep me long." He taps the side of his nose, then points with the same finger over her shoulder. She composes her face into a sunny expression as a married couple settles into the stands two rows in front of them, the wife pointing out one of the jockeys taking the horse for a final walk around the track. The time to speak openly has passed, but they both adapt easily to the need for double meanings. "I imagine it's my face that frightens them off. Don't want my ugly old mask looming at them, do they?"

"Now don't do that, Papa," Nan says, and though her voice is light, she's looking at him intensely. Jacob isn't attracted to her—she's less than half his age, and he's not going to swap a good working partnership for something so pathetic—but it's obvious why another man would be. She is a shooting star come to earth, and if you treat her roughly she'll burn down everything for miles around. "You're not hideous, and there's a dozen handsome widows in London who would be delighted to have you call. You mustn't think of yourself as a monstrous old creature just because Mama has passed on."

Fictitious dead wife aside, Nan seems to be in earnest. Briefly, he tries to see himself the way she evidently sees him. A clever, capable man of nearly forty, well-dressed and well-spoken, outsmarting the police so thoroughly they don't even know his name, let alone the hundreds of crimes they should want him for. The kind of man who could sit across from a good-looking woman at a public-house and pay for her gin, laugh at her stories, court her and not find his advances unwanted. It's an incomprehensible picture she's painting, and he hardly knows what to do with the idea. He's spent so long accepting the story of himself as a devil as ugly inside as out, anything more complimentary feels hollow. It's not as if romance is something he's been actively denying himself. He never thinks about it, considers it irrelevant. But more than the idea of having a woman fall in love with him, he finds himself charmed by the notion that Nan thinks it's possible. That she thinks others could want him. That he's a person, the same as all the rest.

"You're very kind to flatter your papa," he says, and pats Nan on the shoulder. "But you needn't worry about me. We've a fine life together, you and I, haven't we?"

They lean forward, Nan on the edge of her seat, as the horses take their places in the starting gate. And then the trumpet sounds, and the warm peace of the afternoon is lost under shouts and hoofbeats and clouds of hot dust.

They wander back late from Epsom, both a little drunk and more than a little pleased with themselves. The golden sun of the afternoon didn't last much longer than the final race, and thick clouds roll in as they walk back to London. By the time they reach the familiar streets of Saffron Hill, the skies have opened to a steady rain. Soon their secondhand clothes are soaked through. Nan takes off her bonnet, and her hair looks black as ink as it sticks to her face in tendrils. It's glorious after the hot day at the track. The people they pass shield their heads with parasols and newspapers, throwing dirty looks as they hurry by, but the afterglow of their success is more powerful than the city's scorn. Nan stumbles on a loose cobblestone and catches herself on Jacob's shoulder, both of them laughing like fools.

With each step, Jacob expects her to pull off and turn toward her own lodgings, but either she's making for the house directly opposite his own or she's simply following wherever he leads. He stops and steadies her, taking in her face through the rain. She looks younger in London than she did in Epsom. No less in control, but more violent, like a small bird of prey turned loose somewhere unfriendly.

"You haven't got anywhere to go tonight, have you?" he says.

Nan brushes a rivulet of water from her eyes. "World's wide, isn't it? I'll find a haunt. Wanted to be sure you weren't nabbed before you were safe inside. Seems a shame to break a record of forty years." She seems unbothered, but Jacob shakes his head.

"Come stay at mine," he says.

"Don't be daft. You've had enough of me."

"Really," Jacob says, driving over her protest. "You've seen how it is, it's only me and the boys, we've room. Friends come by now and again, when it gets too hot elsewhere. Come stay."

"Oh, friends come by, do they, Fagin?" Nan shoves him into a nearby puddle, playful and brutal with drink. "Could have said as much when I asked you to pose as my fellow, didn't need to cook up some story about being too old—"

"Not that sort of friend," Jacob says, shaking out his trouser leg, which has now surpassed wet and is positively sodden. "Call me a fool, Nan, but I like you. And I'd rather have you live to morning, if it's all the same to you."

If he has an additional motive—he's never made as much in a day as they just achieved at Epsom—it doesn't make his good intentions any less real. All the strongest friendships are built on mutual benefit. It's good sense, is all, and good sense and a kind act needn't always be at odds.

"All right then," Nan says, and loops her arm through his. "Lead the way, will you? If you haven't noticed, it's bloody raining."

When they reach Bell Court, he unlocks the door to discover a light burning in the basement. He peels off his coat and lets it pool on the floorboards, leading her downstairs toward the light. Only the boys, he reasons: Ned and Toby up late to see the results of a merry day at the races. But Toby is never this quiet, even when he's asleep he makes more noise than this, and if the person sitting up with the lamp were one of the boys, he'd already hear an onslaught of rude remarks and insults drifting up the stairs to greet him. It is, therefore, not a surprise when they step out into the room, Nan reaching the bottom of the stairs a beat before he does, to catch sight of Bill Sikes, slumped at the table with a bloodied handkerchief at his brow.

What happens next, however, is.

It's as if they've all been jolted by lightning. Jacob is rooted to the doorway, left to watch as Nan rushes forward and kneels in front of Bill, her quick hands easing the handkerchief away from the wound to gauge the depth of the cut. He can't see Bill's face clearly from here, but he can see the wideness of Nan's eyes, the slight part of her lips, and he knows at once that if Nancy Reed comes back to Bell Court in the future, it will not be for Jacob Fagin's company.

"Lord alive, what happened?" she breathes. "You poor fellow, here—Fagin, you've got water, haven't you?"

Bill glances over his shoulder at Jacob, looking like an angel has just descended from the heavens—awestruck, and not a little frightened.

"A friend from the races, Bill," Jacob says weakly, turning away from Nan's skirts dripping water, Bill's brow wet with blood, some awful statue terrifying in its loveliness. "Here, my dear." He brings the ewer and the basin to the table, setting them down before backing toward the stairs. Neither Bill nor Nan spares him a second glance. His participation is purely incidental, the mechanism of bringing together these two beings for whom foolish, dangerous things like love at first sight are possible.

"What happened, in the Lord's name?" Nan asks. She takes a damp handkerchief from her pocket and swirls it in the basin, for while the pump water is likely no cleaner than the rain, it's easier to pretend it might be.

Jacob sinks into an armchair and folds his hands between his knees, gripping his own fingers until the knuckles ache. From here, he can see Bill's sunken eyes soften, the deep furrows in his brow almost smoothed over. It's like watching a wolf tamed by the piping song of a shepherd.

"Trouble on the job," Bill says gruffly. He flinches as Nan touches the cloth to his cut forehead. Nan clicks her tongue and continues on with her task undisturbed. She just met Bill this minute, but she already knows how to manage him as well as Jacob ever has, if not better. Tends to his hurts without ever acknowledging them as a weakness, soothing both his body and his pride. "Servant caught us leaving a house off Regent Street and got one good blow in before I bowled him over and ran."

"Bill, sometimes I think you want to be hanged," Jacob mutters. "Regent Street. Honestly."

He may as well have held his tongue. Nan looks at Bill as though an ancient hero of legend has materialized in the house, King Arthur in fustian breeches and a ragged cravat. "Regent Street," she repeats. "Think of that! The crown jewels you could've made off with, if you hadn't been surprised."

The glint that dances in Bill's eyes then is an all-too-familiar one. It plays out in front of Jacob like a cut-rate theatrical, the way Bill winks and reaches into his jacket pocket for a lady's brush and comb set that looks to be made of pure gold, tiny gemstones set into the inlay. Every step of what comes next is predictable as if it's been written down, and from where he sits, Jacob can see it all.

"I'm hard to scare, little bird," Bill says.

Nan laughs with delight, and Bill—twenty-five now, long

past the age when he would have tolerated Jacob tending to his injuries—closes his eyes and allows her to finish bathing his wound. The gold of the lamp makes them both look sun-drenched and rich, sanctifying the rough line of Bill's beard, the dark, stringy curls of Nan's wet hair. Jacob sits in the shadows and watches Nan's fingers trace the length of Bill's throat, watches the working muscles as Bill swallows. King David, once, watched a woman bathing from his roof and felt something unholy and determined flame within him. David only had to kill one man to get what he wanted. Jacob, tonight, isn't sure who must die to sate what's stirring in his chest.

"Don't fuss," Bill says gruffly after a moment. "The other fellow got the worse of it, I can promise you that."

"Even so," Nan says. "You deserve to have someone take care of you now and again, surely. It's a hard heart that would leave a man bleeding and not fuss a little. You're a friend of Fagin's?"

Bill's chuckle rises from somewhere low. "Manner of speaking. Good to have the old man around if you want to get rid of something quick. Speaking of," he adds, tossing his voice back toward Jacob without turning his head, "what kind of friend from the races?"

"The kind you can speak freely in front of," Nan says firmly. "Thief same as you."

"*Thief*," Jacob says to no one in particular, "is a weak sort of word for what Bill is."

"Rest of the plate's upstairs," Bill says. "Streets were swarming, I barely made it here. Melt it down and deal with it in the morning, would you? No one saw my face but the servant, and he won't remember it after the knock I gave him, but it was damned close."

It is something, to be needed.

"I'll take care of it," Jacob says. "Make yourself at home, Nan. There isn't much here, but what there is, you're welcome to it."

She smiles at him, friendly but distracted. He doesn't wait for more. The room upstairs isn't empty, to his dull surprise: Toby adjusted to Bill's unexpected arrival by falling asleep in Jacob's bed, though he's bundled so tightly in the blanket there's little sign of him but a tuft of unruly hair and a steady snore. On another night, Jacob would drag Toby out by his ear and shout himself hoarse before sending the boy back downstairs, but just now his mind is elsewhere. So is Ned—two stories' distance from Bill must not have been enough for him. Who knows where the older boy found to lay his head tonight.

In a few minutes, Jacob has a bright fire in the hearth and the silver pot heating on the flames. Bill was practical, for a change: the bulk of his take came in the form of tableware. Spoons, saucers, a fine pair of sugar tongs, all items he can melt down easily into simple, anonymous silver anyone might buy. Jacob has done it a thousand times before. As Toby sleeps, Jacob crouches over the fire, watching the silver soften and spill into the pot, feeling each flame dance across his face like a phantom hand. The church bells nearby clang midnight as though they're striking against his own ribs. From downstairs, Nan's laugh rises bright as a songbird.

26

1826–1831

After that, Nan is no longer Jacob's—she belongs to all of them, and they to her. Bet was skeptical at first, not jealous of Bill but nonetheless protective of him, until Jacob arranged for the two women to spend an evening together with him at the pub, and after an hour it was like they'd known each other since childhood. "I tell you this, love," Bet had said, kissing Nan on the cheek. "I don't know how you turned that brute into a sighing schoolboy, but I need you to teach me the trick. I'll make a thousand pounds a week." Nan laughed and solemnly promised to offer lessons. From then on Jacob finds them together more often than not, putting away porter in Bet's room like ruffians twice their size and trading the kind of jokes familiar to two women who spend most of their time with men. There's no possessiveness between them, no competition. King George and his late wife, Jacob thinks, could have learned a thing or two from them.

Ned, too, keeps his jealousy under cover, though Jacob suspects it's out of self-preservation more than Bet's flavor of selflessness. He's still tongue-tied around Nan, but unfailingly polite, a long-suffering Saffron Hill Lancelot pining after his Guinevere and her dusty boots. Toby is harder than ever to rein in as he grows up, spending nights drinking with friends in skiffs on the Thames or holding court in the chocolate houses with a dozen girls, but a pointed word from Nan always brings him back to his senses. Jacob, for his part, falls into an easy thieving rhythm in her company, skimming off the top of London's most profitable sources of entertainment. Street fairs, market days, charity balls, the king's birthday celebration: there's not a public assembly they don't dart through, only to emerge an hour later with pockets heavier than before.

Each of them is richer for knowing her. But no one feels the arrival of Nancy Reed more powerfully than Bill.

They step into each other's lives like a clap of thunder. Jacob hardly sees Bill anymore without Nan leaning against him, Bullseye trotting at their ankles, her laugh rising like a cloud. Bill in these moments is barely recognizable. He reminds Jacob of the awkward young thief he used to know, lit up from within that anyone considers him worth paying attention to.

"She's a damn fine girl, Nancy," Bill says one night, apropos of nothing. He spread the spoils of the night's theft across the table, and Jacob keeps his eyes on a pair of silver teaspoons rather than look him in the face. Jacob can't quite keep himself from smiling, and if Bill were to see it, his hurt pride could lead to something dangerous.

"Right enough," he says.

"They don't make many of 'em like that," Bill goes on. "Clever, I mean. Knows the game before anyone's said a word. And Christ but I've never met a girl half as fun as she is."

"I won't tell Bet," Jacob says.

It's as close to a jibe as he allows himself. Jacob has never heard Bill express the least interest in *fun*. Before Nan, it's doubtful he ever used the word properly. But it's the next sentence that makes Jacob set the teaspoons aside and stare at Bill.

"You know her. Help me. I want to do something nice."

Jacob's mouth is half-open to say something incredulous—Bill Sikes, all storm and terror, grasping for a romantic gesture? But that storm and terror is on full display at present, so Jacob shuts his mouth again. Bill's brow is lowered, his arms folded, and he might knock Jacob down if he gives the wrong answer. Still, he asked the question. It shouldn't tug at Jacob the way it does, not with this warm ache under his breastbone. Bill is happy, probably for the first time in his life, and the full weight of his attention is turning elsewhere. Nan will be the world to him, a world that Jacob once opened.

"Take her out, my dear," he says, returning to the teaspoons. "Show her off a little. She likes music and gin and a fast time, but more than anything, she wants people to see her with you."

"With me," Bill repeats, skeptical.

"She wants to be *yours*. Show her you're proud of her."

"Proud? To have the best damn girl in London on my arm? She knows."

"I wouldn't be so sure," Jacob says. "And even so, show her anyway."

Bill stands there another moment, considering. Then he shakes his head with a low laugh. "Send Toby round to mine when you have the money," he says, gesturing at the stolen goods on the table. "I'll need it soon."

He goes without waiting for an answer. Maybe this is what soldiers feel like when they come home from war, Jacob thinks. A little sad, now all that's left to do is breathe easy.

Not two days later, Nan turns up for tea with stars in her eyes, telling him about the evening she and Bill just passed together. They spent hours at the Eagle, the premier East London tavern for nightly music, and after Nan finished leading the room in a song, Bill joined her standing on a chair, and he hooked his arm around her waist and kissed her until the whole room erupted in cheers. And, she tells him further, Bill said there was a surprise waiting for them after, and as the bells struck eleven he led her to a chophouse in Deptford where he had rented out the entire top floor, treating her to a private meal like she was the queen herself. They're going to St. James's Park on Friday, she tells Jacob—who is still listening, can only listen, and hope to steady her as she comes back to earth—and she's determined to get money before then for a new bonnet, a proper one, so she and Bill can look as fine as any of the couples out for an afternoon stroll.

It's all as lovely and fragile as spun sugar, and he only nods as she speaks. Bill can be charming when he wants to, and he has always wanted the world to envy him. Until now he drew eyes with a crowbar in his hand, but it can also be done by making his girl shine bright for all London to admire. They are happy, both of them, and that should be enough to satisfy him. Love is none of his business.

Time goes on, during which Bill and Nancy cement their reputation as a single entity joined at the seam. On occasion, they pull others into their orbit, largely by the gravitational force of her enthusiasm. Today, they—or rather Nan—coaxed Jacob and Bet out to watch the regatta on the Thames. He has no interest in the spectacle personally, all the discomfort of being surrounded by crowds without even the practicality of work to make it worthwhile. But Nan is in one of those moods where only a pillar of salt could say no to her. Besides, Jacob has been trying to catch Bill alone for days now. Bill promised to bring the spoils from a robbery near Hyde Park to divide and dispose of three days ago, and still nothing has turned up. It's as good an opportunity as any for catching Bill in an approachable mood.

They arrive at the Dolphin in Hungerford near midafternoon and make their way to the tavern's rooftop terrace, already packed with spectators looking for a clear view of the river churning three stories below. The sky threatens rain, but the Thames watermen carry on in defiance of the weather. Races have been underway for hours—punctuality is a foreign concept to Nan—and shallow boats crewed by six ferrymen each skim along the surface of the water like great insects. Both Nan and Bet lean over the railing to get as close as possible to the action, eager and heedless of danger as children.

"If you fall," Bill says, "I'm not wetting my boots to fish you out."

He and Jacob slouch in chairs well away from the edge. Bill

stuffed his pipe with a foul-smelling tobacco that sends up gouts of smoke to blend with the humid mist. Bullseye settled beneath Bill's chair, gnawing on an old ham bone Bill paid twopence for to keep him entertained.

Nan laughs loudly. Her hair whips into her eyes from the growing wind, and though she rakes it away with one hand it's as unruly as before within seconds. "Don't you listen to him, Bet," she says, bracing herself on the railing and leaning over still farther. "He's all bark and no bite."

"You know I'm more than talk," Bill drawls.

"Say I've forgotten," Nan says. "You'll show me, will you, when we're back at home? We've all night."

"Shouldn't take long," Bet quips. "Unless it's gotten better since my time, you'll see everything you're going to see in three minutes flat."

Nan erupts into peals of laughter as Bill glowers into his cloud of pipe smoke. Jacob has a sense of what Bill will tolerate as a joke and what will set him off, but for the ladies, the rules are different. Unsure whether he should be concerned or amused, Jacob settles for finishing his beer and sending the potboy for another. Even the straggling boats have by now passed out of sight, but the crowd assembled on the roof and in the streets will not let a simple lull between races curtail their enjoyment. At least three women at street level yowl their way through a song like cats in heat, and Nan and Bet lend their voices as well, each choosing her own key without regard for the other.

"Now, Bill," Jacob says, "you can tell me, can't you? What's happened with the house?"

Bill emits an annoyed gust of smoke. "Christ. Can't you think of anything but your money?"

"I don't mean anything by it, it's just—"

"Look at them," Bill says, gesturing sharply with the pipe at Bet and Nan. "They know some days a man just has to live. Ask me about it again and you'll get a broken skull for your trouble."

He might be joking, but Jacob doesn't care to take the chance.

Nan, who reads Bill's moods like augurs do birds, detaches herself from the rail and takes Jacob by the arm, pulling him to his feet.

"Come on, Fagin," she says. "You can just see the next boats about to start. Stand here, look."

She drags him to where she and Bet were standing and points downriver with all the joy of a captain sighting land. He isn't fooled for a second. Nan pulled him out of harm's way, letting Bill's mood settle. Once, Jacob guided others on the best way to handle Bill gently. God help him if he's losing his touch. He follows Nan's finger with his eyes. Sure enough, the boatmen are readying their oars for the next heat. Brightly colored flags whip in the wind at the back of each boat, some tossed about so roughly that the hem of the fabric frays.

"By God," says a voice from behind them. "Surely not."

It's a voice Jacob has never heard before, and no surprise. Men who speak that way don't consort with men who squat in abandoned houses in Clerkenwell. He turns away from the railing. Two young men in linen tailcoats and fawn-colored trousers have arrived, one holding a walking stick that reeks of affectation, the other distinguishing himself with what might be the tallest hat Jacob has ever seen. Both of them are clean-shaven, trim waisted, and as out of place in Hungerford as peacocks in a henhouse. They stare at Bill with wide eyes and dawning smiles. Bet reaches to take Jacob by the wrist. They share the same thought, he knows: whatever these two want from Bill, it can only end badly.

"They told us downstairs there was a legend in the place, but I hardly believed them," says the fellow with the walking stick.

"It is you, isn't it?" asks the one in the hat. "Bill Sikes? I thought so, from the dog."

It's debatable whether Bill or Bullseye most wants to tear out the man's throat. Even so, Bill scarcely looks up. The muscles in his jaw twitch as he swallows a response Jacob can only imagine.

"You know my name," Bill says in the end. "I reckon you also know I don't like being bothered."

The man in the hat laughs as though he just witnessed a daring trick at the circus. "He's exactly as the stories say, isn't he?" he says to his companion. "A regular Ajax. When I tell Fanny about this, she'll faint."

"Is there something we can help you with, gentlemen?" Jacob says.

He's as polite as he can manage, for he knows there's no chance of Bill taking the politic way out. Jacob can put his anger in a cupboard and close the door on it better than anyone he knows. But just because the anger is hidden doesn't mean it's gone. Jacob is so angry he is trembling with it. Taking insult for himself is easy. He's always found ways of getting even, by one means or another. But to watch these two dandies preen and gawk at Bill as if he's a tame beast devoid of understanding is almost more than Jacob can bear.

"Nose out," says the man with the walking stick, dismissing Jacob with a wave. "We only want a friendly conversation, that's all."

"It's not every day you get to speak to the condemned before he gets up on the scaffold," says the other.

Jacob can almost hear Bill's teeth grinding. Bullseye lets out a low growl. Any moment, Bill will stand up, will say something, will release that storm cloud brewing in his chest and send these two skittering for cover. It must happen; Bill is stronger and more frightening than five of these young blades combined. They'll see, then, a kind of strength that money can't buy.

A moment later, someone is speaking, their voice pitched to cut throats.

Except that person is not Bill.

"How dare you," Nan says.

Jacob's body rushes cold. Beside him, Bet grips his arm so tightly he's sure it will bruise. Nan is closer to Bill than any of them these days. She of all people should know the one sin Bill Sikes will not allow is someone fighting his battles for him. But Nan charges ahead.

"He's a man, the same as either of you. Better—you're tadpoles next to him, little creeping snails."

Where she kept it Jacob isn't sure, but there's a knife in her hand now. The man in the tall hat looks at her with a flash of terror. For all Jacob cares, Nan might bleed the man like a pig. All he can look at is Bill. Bill, seated at the very edge of his chair now, back straight as an iron bar. His hands clench so tight the bones of his knuckles gleam. He watches Nan defend him, watches her shout down two men with a knife in her hand, and Jacob expects at any moment for Bill to lunge to his feet. A mad impulse urges him to throw himself between Bill and Nan, to absorb whatever blows are meant for her, now that she broke this one dreadful rule.

But somehow Bill does not move, and Nan advances farther on the two men, who by now are in visible retreat.

"Clear out," she says, "or I've a mind to make you."

The men turn tail and bolt without a shred of dignity between them. It feels as though someone has put a pistol to Jacob's temple and pulled the trigger, only to discover the chamber is empty. Below, the next heat of the race glides by along the rippling Thames. The cheers of the crowd reach him as if through three feet of water.

Slowly, Nan pockets the knife again, then lays a hand on Bill's shoulder. All three—Bet, Jacob, and Bill—flinch at the touch.

"Let me get you a drink," she says softly.

"Damn your drink." Bill does not push her hand aside. For a moment, Jacob isn't certain whether Bill will strike Nan or begin to cry. Difficult to say which would be more unnerving.

In the end, Bill does neither. He clears his throat and stands. Bullseye is already sitting upright at his heels, the picture of obedience.

"Come on," he says sharply. "All this, it's games for children."

"Bill—" Nan begins.

"Come on, Nancy, I said."

Bill is already striding toward the doors that will lead them downstairs. Nan hesitates only a moment before following, steps behind the dog. Jacob and Bet are left alone by the railing. The pennants on the passing boats snap like wild animals below.

"You can let them go," Jacob tells Bet softly. "He's not yours to mind anymore."

Bet winces. "Not yours either."

There's no need to say anything more. One of them will heed this advice, and the other has never learned how.

Jacob waits another few seconds for them to pass out of earshot, then crosses the terrace toward the stairs. He allows one last glance back as he descends, to see Bet leaning over the rail. She looks like the figurehead on a ship, watching the little shapes of people in the street below.

Bill and Nancy are an easy pair to tail. They make no effort to conceal their direction, and Jacob is able to slip neatly into their wake, keeping to the corners and the shadows of the narrow laneways in case they turn around. Bill stays several steps ahead, and not only because his strides are naturally longer—he seems simultaneously to want Nan close at his heels and to leave her a mile behind.

At last, tired of being ignored, Nan catches Bill by the forearm. Bill whips around so quickly Jacob scarcely has time to fling himself into an alley and out of sight before he's spotted. He cannot see them from here, but he can hear them. His back is flattened against the wall as if he can melt into the brick.

"Don't touch me," Bill says.

"What's wrong? Why in God's name are you angry with *me*?"

Bill's laugh is almost wild. It sends Jacob's skin crawling. "You want me to thank you for making me into a boy hiding behind his mother's apron?"

"Bill," Nan says, with lightness Jacob yearns to warn her away from, "if you don't drop your pride and let me in, you're going to go mad."

The next sound is indistinct. A scuffle, or merely a step forward. Nan gasps. Jacob presses his palms against the brick until the rough surface nicks his skin. There is no line he's waiting for Bill to cross, no sign that it's time for him to intervene. Perhaps his only role has ever been as witness.

"Mad? I'm half mad with you already, girl. You're in me, all the way to the bottom, and damn me if I know how to get you out again."

Bill's voice breaks before the words are done. Jacob has never been so aware of the thin line between anguish and anger.

"Then don't," Nan says. "Don't get me out. Let me stay, Bill. All you have to do is let me."

"Hellfire," Bill says, "I don't know how to *stop* you."

The far end of the alleyway opens on a dim courtyard, where there's a tavern with a coach house that empties into the main road beyond. Jacob's feet guide him through the dark and the dirt and the stink, each step carrying him farther from the laneway where Bill and Nan remain. Whatever's to come next between them, whether love or hate, Jacob is sure it's not meant for his ears.

27

1834

Jacob and Ned are playing a lackadaisical game of hazard to unwind after a particularly productive morning when Bill lets himself into the house uninvited. The housebreaker looms in the doorway, watching the dice skitter across the table in a roll that would have cost Jacob a considerable sum if they'd been playing for real money. Bill hasn't said a word yet, but Jacob flushes and sweeps the dice away into his pocket as quickly as he can. It seems disrespectful, somehow, to be doing anything light-hearted in front of Bill these days. Ned's posture stiffens as he sees who's joined them.

"Now this is a surprise," Jacob says as pleasantly as he can.

"Don't pretend to be happy to see me," Bill says. "Come for a walk."

The words themselves aren't threatening, but Jacob leaps to the conclusion that Bill is going to take him into the alley and shoot him between the eyes like a lamed horse. It's an absurd thought, and one he doesn't allow to linger. It's Bill, not the devil himself. They'll use words first, whatever happens. Ned, however, requires more reassurance. He stands, reaching for his coat.

"I'll come with you, Mr. Fagin," he says. "Just to be certain."

"Certain of what?" Bill says. "Of me?"

Ned lowers his eyes, paying sharp attention to the buttons of his jacket. He's terrified, but more than that, he's angry that he's terrified, and the anger is turning into stubbornness. After so many years instructing him, Jacob hoped Ned would develop something resembling self-preservation, but that seems to be too much to hope for. Ned's instincts are starting to look dangerously like chivalry, which is a sure way to end up with your eyes cut out.

"It's only a walk, Ned," Jacob says. "Don't trouble yourself. Let Toby know I'm out when he comes back, won't you?"

Ned says nothing, but his mouth goes very thin.

Bill heaves a sigh. "If I swear to bring his filthy hide back in one piece, boy, will that satisfy you?"

For what it's worth, Jacob doesn't feel particularly satisfied by Bill's wording, but at least Ned backs down. "Just be careful," he says.

Jacob gives him an encouraging smile, but there isn't time for more—Bill has already turned on his heel, and Jacob must hurry to keep up. Bill waits in the courtyard by the time Jacob navigates the passage. He shifts his weight from leg to leg, like an animal leashed but preparing to run.

"You're in a roaring hurry, Bill," Jacob says.

Bill grins. "It's the perfect time; it'll be mobbed as Noah's bloody ark out there. Move your bones, old man."

It's a damp afternoon in mid-October, the sun trying and failing to penetrate a sheen of fog, and Jacob's footsteps are muffled in the soupy air as he trots after Bill. He's never felt more like Bullseye. He's even panting for breath. He isn't as old as Bill makes out—forty-seven isn't young, but there's some distance between himself and the grave yet—but his days of sprinting the length of London at the drop of a hat are well behind him. Fortunately, Bill seems to have a plan. His strides are long and agitated but they are purposeful, steering them steadily westward. At intervals, he glances over his shoulder to be sure Jacob is still following before lunging off again through the streets.

At long last, Bill slows his pace near Golden Square in Westminster, a posh, sedate neighborhood neither of them belongs anywhere near. Jacob feels the distrusting glances tossed their way from the well-to-do, the way strangers cross the street to avoid them. Has Bill lost his mind after all? Hard enough doing their work when they don't stick out like two wolves among sheep. But Bill thought of that too, it seems: he leads Jacob into an alleyway behind a milliner's shop where they are able to lose themselves in the shadows, and passersby continue on unawares. Immediately, Jacob breathes easier.

Bill positions himself behind Jacob and points over his shoulder, directing his gaze. "There."

It's a fine three-story house on the north side of Golden Square. Not that Jacob can see much from here beyond the neoclassical facade: a cluster of carts and low wagons idle in front, and thick damask curtains hide any activity within. The life of the house's inhabitants, however, is not left entirely to his imagination. The front door is flung wide, and through it flows a flood of servants, carrying in a dizzying array of possessions. From his position behind the milliner's, Jacob can see it all, the plush carpets, the high-backed chairs, the dozens of brass-bound trunks, the spinet maneuvered delicately up the stairs by two strong men in white gloves. A bronze peacock some three feet high, with what seem from the street to be real diamonds and amethysts studding its fanned tail—a ludicrous ornament, what purpose it serves Jacob cannot begin to guess, and yet his palms are itching with the insatiable need to own it.

"Well, I'll be damned," he murmurs.

Bill's sharp laugh makes him flinch. Surrounded by such glittering wonder, Jacob forgot he isn't alone.

"Don't ever say I don't look after you, eh?" Bill says.

With effort, Jacob tears his eyes from the house. Bill leans against the wall, watching. For him, Jacob is the spectacle, not the riches on display.

"What do you mean?" Jacob asks.

"I'm going to sting the crib, Fagin. And you're going to help me."

Jacob stares. He wants to laugh, but Bill is not smiling. "What?"

"Couldn't be easier. I've been asking around; all these swells have on as staff is a steward, and God knows he's nothing to worry about; he must be eighty. Or ain't it a rich-enough stake for your foul old heart? Is it Kew Palace or nothing for you?"

Jacob glances back toward Golden Square. Another man has arrived, this one carrying a framed oil painting that looks distinctly Dutch. A series of images flash through his mind: kid-leather gloves and silk waistcoats, a fleet of carriages, heaping platters of roast duck. With one-quarter of the wealth he's imagining, he could purchase outright a house in Soho and never work another day in his life. Pay a servant to do the bloody washing and cooking.

"You see," Bill says; he's still not smiling, but his eyes glitter like twin piles of gold. "It's the grandest yet. And one servant? All I need's a distraction. Turn up at the back door when the lord's out, bring your bag of baubles and pretend to be a peddler. However you want to play it. The more time you get me, the more you'll have for your cut."

Bill has thought through every move. He must have paced these streets for weeks, whispering to the neighborhood's sneaks and gossips, gathering information, scouting routes. Biding his time for his crowning glory. Bill Sikes, the famous robber of Golden Square.

Say that it falls out as Bill describes. The lord of the house out at some supper club or drawing room, and once the carriage has trundled away for the evening, Jacob, dressed in his rattiest greatcoat, hair tangled, carpetbag hiked over his shoulder, arriving at the back door. The elderly steward frowning at the vagrant Jew on the threshold, until Jacob turns on his most wheedling voice and begins to unpack treasures every new household will need in bulk: lye, beeswax, pins, plaster, he hasn't decided yet what will serve best, but whatever it is, Jacob knows someone in Holborn who can help him get it. And the longer they speak, the longer Bill will have to nip across the roof opposite, duck in through the skylight, taking everything he can carry and then some. It would set them up for years.

Why, then, the feeling in the pit of his stomach, as though Bill has handed him not a chance for riches but the means to hang himself?

He wets his lips. "And why do you want me?" he says. "Surely Nan would be better for this sort of job. A friendly, trustworthy face."

Bill shakes his head. "You'd have me put my best girl in danger? I take care of her, Fagin. She don't need to steal while she's got me."

He says this with such certainty. Does he not know, then, about Jacob and Nan's continued partnership? Just yesterday evening, they picked the pockets of three country gentlemen descending the steps of St. Paul's. If Nan is keeping that a secret, if she wants the independence of her own income without the violence of Bill's disapproval, Jacob won't be the one to betray her, though she's playing a dangerous game. Regardless, none of this answers the question he asked.

"But why *me,* Bill?"

There's no time to react before Bill grabs Jacob by the collar. It's not a tight grip. Jacob could detach himself if he wanted to. It's not Bill's hand that freezes him so much as Bill's eyes, which are still glittering like poisoned gold. Pinned like this, Jacob finds it easy to see why Nan keeps her secrets.

"Because you're forgetting how the trick is done, old man," Bill says.

He starts to protest, but there's no arguing with Bill Sikes in such a mood. This Bill has the power of a god, one who will not be disagreed with or interrupted.

"When's the last time you ran a risk? Done anything more dangerous than send children out to do your work? Be a man, Fagin. Live. Or go hang yourself and save us the trouble of looking after you. But don't be what you've become, a damned ghost in your dusty cave. Do you understand?"

Bill Sikes has never known how to say *I care about you.* Both a smile and a snarl begin with the teeth bared.

"Of course," Jacob answers, because what else can he say? "Of course I understand. You can count on me."

The appointed day for the robbery slouches nearer. Jacob has always acted on impulse and opportunity; pickpocketing never gives him so much time to think before a job, so much time to imagine everything that might possibly go wrong. He itches all over with it. Bill wants him to prove himself, to show he's still a person worth knowing. By Bill's standards, he sees now, he's no such thing. He wakes each night in a cold sweat from dreams of discovery in a thousand forms, a flood of blinding light, a knife between the ribs, the twining embrace of the noose. There are a thousand ways to fail, and only two to live: summon the courage to charge into the fray, or trust that another path forward will reveal itself in time. Bill will choose the first way, he knows, and Jacob will rely on the other.

It's Bonfire Night, and Jacob and Nan are returning late from a fireworks display off London Bridge, where the colored flames lit up the staid water in blues and pinks and whites more vibrant than any flowers. London loves a visual spectacle as much as it loves a human one, and as the explosions danced overhead and the crowd craned its necks back to watch, Jacob and Nan filled their own pockets with sparkling treasures of a more earthly variety. It's not enough to shake his unease, but it's the sort of work he knows, and he can take comfort in that.

"Bill's told you about Golden Square," he says under his breath.

Nan takes him by the arm as though he really is her elderly and infirm father. "Bill tells me everything."

And you don't return the favor, he thinks, but doesn't say. They're lying to him right now, by being here together. Coward that he is, he wants no part of that fight.

"He isn't worried, is he?" If Bill is having second thoughts, Jacob might have found a third way, the perfect way—say nothing, do nothing, the problem dies away and all goes on as it was before. Yes, the specter of endless wealth has appeared before him every night, but a man can't spend money if he's dead. He's never worked out whether he's more afraid of Bill Sikes or of death. The two threats seem to be constantly changing places.

Nan shakes her head. Her collar, he notes, is higher than she usually wears, higher than what's fashionable. It doesn't suit her, but it's not his place to say so. "He's only worried about you."

"Me?"

"That you'll lose your nerve," Nan says. "I keep telling him you won't, but you know how he is when he gets an idea."

There's something wrong with her voice too. She's talking about his life, his reputation, but for all the expression in her words she could be telling a stranger about the weather.

He stops walking, and she, still holding his arm, jerks to a surprised halt. He turns her to face him, unsettled by how easily she gives in to the direction. Nan's face looks paler than he remembers. The longer he looks, the more he thinks he sees the shade of bruising in the half inch of skin her high collar leaves exposed, though it could just as easily be the false shadows of the fireworks, red and purple and blue.

"Nancy," he says. "You'd tell me if you weren't all right?"

She releases his arm. "Of course I would, but I am."

Jacob has survived nearly five decades thanks to a particular set of skills, one of which is his ability to tell when someone's lying. With the merry crowd whirling around them, he folds his arms, becoming a fixed object before her. "Roll up your sleeves, my dear."

"Fagin," she says, exasperated.

"Do as I say."

She presses her eyes closed, then sighs. The bruises she reveals on her left arm are no trick of the light. They stay visible only a moment, before Nan whips the fabric down again. Another of her secrets. His now too.

"I know you think he's frightening," Nan says—and it should be a sign of something, that neither of them needs to say his name, to clarify where these bruises have come from—"but I'm not afraid of him, Fagin. I've never been. He's strong, and I love him for it. Nothing will ever scare him or make him stop. No one's ever cared about me enough to keep me safe, but he wants to protect me from the whole world. Wants me to be only his. He loves me."

He does not say *I know that.* He does not say *That's why I am afraid.*

"He adores you," he says instead.

This, he realizes almost at once, may be the worst thing he could have said to her. Bill has never known how to love anything that can love him back. Care is weakness. Fear is failure. He and Nan will continue to give Bill their love and care and weakness, and Bill will bash his own fear against it until one or both of them breaks. Bill is afraid that Jacob's losing his touch, but tonight, looking at Nan under the fireworks, he is certain it's already lost.

He can't do this. Nan may value love more than safety, but he can't. Let Bill hate him for it, very well, but he cannot become the person he's looking at now, this unselfish creature for whom pain feels like home.

"Tell him I'm out," he says.

Nan stares. "Fagin. Think first."

"I am thinking. He can do it just as well with someone else. Or alone, that's how he likes it now. But not with me."

His greatest act of cowardice: that he doesn't wait to hear her response before turning aside and disappearing. He's walking so slowly that Nan could overtake him if she tried, but he crosses the full distance home without encountering another living soul he knows.

28

The next night, Jacob wakes from a deep sleep to someone hammering on the door fit to wake the dead.

No one he knows would knock like that unless they were in immediate danger for their lives, and the only strangers he can imagine turning up at this hour are policemen. In either case, he has to act quickly. He's already halfway to the door before his panicked heart gives him a chance to realize he's moving. He's done nothing exceptionally illegal tonight, other than sleeping in a place he doesn't pay for, but crimes compound like a bankrupt's debts, and if a policeman has arrived to investigate, there are decades' worth of broken laws for them to collect on. Jacob stands on tiptoe to peer through the hole in the boarded-up window.

It's Bill on the threshold.

He must have tried Golden Square tonight.

Not at all reassured, Jacob draws back the bolt.

Bill's dark blue eyes are wide and burning. They remind Jacob of a stoker shoveling coal at the mouth of a speeding train. There is nothing in Bill's hands, and yet his fingers grasp the air, curling around the absence of a weapon. This man is dangerous, Jacob thinks, and I should be afraid of him. He stands mute a second more, watching Bill's chest rise and fall.

"What are you waiting for?" Bill says hoarsely. "Let me in, before they find me."

And Jacob moves, not because he's suddenly unafraid but because it's Bill who's asking.

Bill darts down the passage, and Jacob can picture him as he must have appeared during the burglary, a vast broad-shouldered shadow creeping along the rooftops of Westminster. Bill ignores the table and sinks to the floor instead, taking his head in his hands. There's something staining his palms. The light is poor, though, and Jacob can't make it out. Without being asked, Jacob opens a bottle of gin, pours some into a glass for himself, and then passes the bottle to Bill. He watches the movement of Bill's throat as he swallows and thinks about the gulls that swarm near the docks at Rotherhithe, throwing back their heads to choke down fish still alive and wriggling. Only then does he reach for the lamp.

The addition of the light seems to bring more shadows than it does brightness. The hollows of Bill's face are deep as caverns, and his chest heaves with irregular breath. Jacob wants to draw back, but he sits on the floor cross-legged opposite Bill and keeps his fear to himself. The seams of Jacob's trousers strain as he moves, the knees shiny with heavy wear. He needs a new pair soon, before these tear beyond use. He could mend them, but it's never seemed worth the effort to extend the life of something so clearly ready to disintegrate.

"What happened?"

Bill doesn't respond. His pockets are empty. This is unusual. Even if he leaves the greater prizes with a fence or at a hiding place, he always brings one trophy at least to Bell Court to crow over. His left hand, nested in his hair, seems to be trembling, or else that's a trick of the weak lamp.

"You're hurt?"

"No. Let me stay here, Fagin. Till the Runners lose the trail."

Jacob shivers. Bill's had close shaves before, messy burglaries that ended with screams and barking dogs. He's never had the Bow Street Runners nipping at his heels. Whatever's happened, it's worse than it's ever been.

"I'm not turning you out," he says. "But tell me what happened. You tried it alone?"

Bill's head falls back in relief. As if Jacob could have sent him away. As if the years haven't braided their existences together, Jacob's and Bill's and London's, until it's impossible for Jacob to tell what is their own history and what is the city's, these streets that have always been home to them both. They are their own world and all the people in it too.

"I'm the best there is," Bill says. "Don't need help, never have. And you said no."

Jacob finds his eyes drifting back to Bill's hands. Those broad strong hands that hold their own in every fight London thinks to give them, and in every one he chooses to pick himself. Those hands, rusty looking in the darkness.

"That's blood, Bill," Jacob says. "Isn't it?"

"Must be."

The confession has all the sentimentality of a newspaper headline. Jacob inches back from him.

"Wasn't meant to be anyone there." Bill keeps his eyes lowered, his voice lower still. "Only the steward, old as sin. I could have managed the damned steward. But they hired a manservant too, since I cased it. I didn't know."

Jacob can't help picturing the back door of the Golden Square house, himself dressed in his ragged greatcoat, drawing off the attention of the manservant with a carpetbag of wares. As Bill had asked him to do. *Tell him I'm out.* Bill's rust-colored hands.

"I only hit him to stop him shouting," Bill says. "All I meant was to keep him quiet."

Truth or lies, it doesn't matter. Jacob can picture it as though he were there, a startled servant, a panicked thief, a body falling, a temple catching on a wooden table, a pool of blood on the parquet. He can picture it another way just as easily, a purposeful blow out of the darkness, a strong one to ensure silence, and only a dull realization after the fact. He knows Bill like he knows himself, knows the anger he keeps leashed, knows who will always come out first in Bill Sikes's calculation of himself against others.

A man is dead. Bill Sikes killed someone, the blood still wet on his hands, the Runners in hot pursuit.

A man is dead, and if Bill doesn't get well clear of the city limits, he'll be responsible for two more corpses before sunrise.

"You came here?" Jacob says. He's angry. It surprises him, that he moved past fear so quickly. "Of all the places on God's earth, you came here."

Bill flinches. "Where else? It's your fault, you coward."

It's far from the first time Bill has been cruel to him. They've always traded insults in friendship that would be cause for a fistfight among strangers. Jacob has generally been able to hear the difference, the thin but distinct line between *I take pleasure in hurting you* and *No one is allowed to hurt you but me.* He does not hear the difference tonight.

"Mine?" His voice is rising now, buoyed by the rage he rarely allows himself to feel. A base, animal panic has set in, and he can hardly see Bill in front of him, can only hear the thundering of jackboots in the alley, the slam of Newgate's doors. He said no to protect his own life, but Bill brought death to his doorstep anyway. "Because I wouldn't put my neck in the noose for you?"

"Servants were your part," Bill snarls. "If you had the guts to do as you were told, we'd both be rich."

"I told you *no.*"

"And look what's come of that!"

Bill pushes himself to his feet, towering over Jacob now. His pistol must be near at hand. He wouldn't be so thoughtless as to leave it at the site of the botched burglary. Jacob tastes blood on his tongue. He stands, only because it seems foolish to die sitting down in his own home.

The anger rushes out of Bill like a great bellows. "Please," he murmurs. Jacob wonders whether he's ever heard Bill say the word before. "Let me stay tonight. Just for tonight, till the Runners move on. People die every day, Fagin."

The carelessness, somehow, is what breaks him.

He understands perfectly well what Bill is asking. They're far from the scene of the burglary, and if the Runners aren't already at the door, there's a chance they've lost the scent. Maybe it's all over already, and all Bill has to do is sit here quietly another hour to be sure. And even if it isn't, Jacob knows how to turn the police away. Bill could hide in the basement while Jacob meets them at the door, rubbing his eyes as if he's just woken—could pretend to speak only Yiddish, a lonely cantankerous old Jew who's not worth the trouble of interrogating. It's what Bill wants him to do, one more plan handed over fully formed for Jacob to accept without question. But there are limits. There have to be. It doesn't matter how much Jacob loves the man standing in front of him. It's the first lesson he taught Bill: don't ever love anyone more than you love yourself.

"I'm leaving," Jacob says. "And when I come back, I don't want to see you here. Don't want to see you in the city for a fortnight, do you hear me? I'll tell Nan what's happened. Make for the suburbs, the country, find a barn somewhere and lie low. You dug this grave, Bill, now get yourself out. I told you I wouldn't be a part of it."

"Fagin," Bill says, one last time. "You turn me out, they'll kill me."

"Then don't get caught," Jacob says, and leaves.

Saffron Hill is the pale lavender gray of a bruise as he emerges from the house. It's fully night still, but the moon glimmers so brightly overhead it feels as though dawn is just around the corner, and lamps and candles flicker in windows, the neighborhood taking advantage of the clear night to put off giving up the ghost a little longer. He wanders south, past the viaduct, until he crosses Fleet Street. It's been a long time since he walked like this, to escape rather than to hunt. Rabbi Singer used to taunt him for it, call him Moses and mean it as an insult that didn't seem fitting from a holy man. He takes the thought of the rabbi and places it deep in his pocket, beneath his closed fist, beside the memory of Bill's rust-colored hands, of a blow meant only to keep quiet.

He was right to leave. It isn't his crime. He isn't to blame.

The tide is out when he reaches the wharf, leaving only a few sailors milling for work or unloading their cargo, but the river has its own rhythm that continues regardless of the moon and sea, and the streets are far from empty. There are always transactions to be made here, at the intersection of those eager to buy and those desperate to sell. In a few hours, the dockworkers will throng the streets, brandishing their caps like flags, shouting their own names or the foreman's, fighting to be chosen for a day's paying work. Those passed over will skulk away to drink their frustration under the table and try again tomorrow.

A young girl sings in the shadow of a sailors' tavern. Fourteen at the oldest, maybe as young as twelve. She doesn't have a good voice, as far as he's qualified to judge. Most likely it will gain richness in time, but now it's weak as too-new wine. She pipes away of true loves and sweethearts, of loyal sailors sunk with their ships into the dark sand, and though there's sadness in her voice, he can't imagine she's old enough to have felt the sting of lost love and loneliness. Perhaps that's part of the attraction, for the men she's attempting to coax toward her. The allure of being the one to teach her something she doesn't yet know. Jacob can understand the logic, though as with so much he can logically understand, the feeling doesn't reach his heart. He's spent decades learning that people are cruel and the world indifferent, and he has no desire to guide someone else to the same conclusion.

Still, he lingers, and he listens. As the girl finishes her song and looks up to gauge the results of her efforts, she sees him watching. Sees him with reddish hair and beard going gray, sees dull brown eyes, sees long neck and thick brows and nails that never stay clean. A man who took in children as old as her, as ragged as her, and transformed them into the kind of murderers who turn up in the darkness of November with blood shadowing their open palms. Who then sent those same children to the gallows to save his own skin. The girl sees him and her eyes widen, and she snatches up her overturned hat littered with pennies, and she darts away into the night.

Jacob would like to carve off his own face with the side of a straight razor until only his bare skull is left to grin at the world, sea air against bone.

The image of the bludgeoned servant will not leave him. He tries to outrun it, but it follows at his heels, along the banks of the Thames, away from the ghosts of the dockworkers. Temple Gardens to his back, black water twisting at his feet. Blackfriars Bridge is not far off, its arches diving into the river and darting back out again like needle and thread through fabric. Nearly every month, at least one Londoner plunges into the river from atop that bridge, and the water closes over their head and does not open again. There's a ballad about one of them, a ruined prostitute who flings herself into the abyss to escape the doom of living her own life for the space of another day. It seems like a failure of poetic imagination to think the division is that simple, a great rupture between what cannot be borne and what is simply accepted, felt, known, day in and day out. He looks at the bridge against the black sky, considering.

Without making up his mind, he wanders toward the bridge. His fingers worry the loose thread in the cuff of his sleeve. At this rate, he will unravel the entire shirt by the time he decides. He didn't think to take his coat when he left the house, but he doesn't feel the cold.

You've got the courage to kill me, Bill's voice says, *now try it yourself; no one's piss-poor life is an inch the better for having vermin like you in it. Jump, and see if anyone will notice, let alone miss you.*

The Bill Sikes he knew before tonight would have said so, and the person he'd been before tonight would have brushed it off, and the brief spasm of melancholy would pass. After tonight, he's no longer sure what anyone is capable of.

When they hang two nooses from the gallows at Newgate, one for Jacob and one for Bill, it will be nothing more than either of them deserves. He's earned it, this creeping cancer he called a friendship. It's all he's worth. A weed growing between the cracks of two cobblestones, neither of which will claim him. Bill Sikes killed a man. Bill would kill *him,* if Jacob gave him the chance. Already has. It's his skull Bill cracked open with a crowbar, his brains splashed across an entrance hall in Golden Square. Jacob created a monster out of clay, raised him by hand like a dog scrubbed out of a coal scuttle, and tonight that monster kicked the stool out from under his feet for the final drop. He told himself when Leah died that he would never care for anyone again. Look what came from letting his guard down.

At least drowning seems a peaceful way to die, he thinks, mounting the stairs from the bank to the bridge. Quiet. In Saffron Hill, he can never seem to get his hands on quiet. Always someone raising hell on the other side of the wall, someone screaming, someone fucking, someone giving birth, someone dying. The last time he knew true quiet was in Rabbi Singer's flat in Copley Street, when a dozen boys sat crowded around a single copy of a text they barely understood and studied laws and prophets that seemed a thousand miles removed from their own sunken cheeks and dirty feet. Maybe the others found something in the holy books that connected them to the divine. For him, it was the silence that felt blessed.

Now, watching the river flow beneath him, he's less sure. He knows without looking that his father is on the bridge behind him, close at his back. Knows the smile at the edge of his father's mouth, the way he'll tilt his head as if to say *Surely there are worse ways,* as if to remind him *You said you would outlive me but you never said by how much.*

The servant at Golden Square is dead, and at the deep, rotten core of himself, Jacob doesn't care. He didn't know the servant. The man is nothing to him. What is something to him is Bill, who will have blood on his hands until the day he dies. Is Nan, who's living with a murderer and will never convince herself to leave him. Is himself, who has suddenly looked ten, twenty years ahead as if someone ripped away a curtain into the perfect blankness of his own future, which whips away in front of him on the current of the Thames. Nothing is going to change. He will always be what he is. He will continue waking and stealing and selling and eating and drinking and sleeping and waking and stealing, until one day he is jolted off the dreadful round altogether, and despite more than four decades of effort not a single person will remember him, except to remember the ways he wronged them. Some might think back fondly the first day or two after his death, though that number will dwindle by the hour. But by daybreak on the third day, even the memory of him will be a ghost story brought out over a bottle of gin: *Do you remember that skinny red-haired Jew who used to live in the old house on Bell Court? Took in street children, taught them to steal. I swear, I'm not telling tales; he was real. As foul a devil as you ever saw. No, I don't know what happened to him. Hanged, like as not. Like his father.*

If he steps off this bridge tonight, the voices will be gone, and so will the stories.

He hasn't made up his mind, but in the next beat, it's made up for him. A pattering of feet on the bridge, and then there's a hand on his shoulder, a warm hand, a living one. It startles him so badly he nearly topples off the bridge after all, bringing his visitor into the waves with him.

"Look sharp, Fagin," says one of the young men at his side.

It's Ned, somehow. And Toby at his heels, face flushed, that familiar slanted grin. Ned's face is impassive as ever, but Toby's makes it obvious where they're coming from; they've sunk their spare coins into one of the dozens of brothels lining the river and have topped off their evening with one more drink than necessary. Jacob doesn't believe in coincidence, nor does he have patience for miracles, but whatever made the boys cross his path seems to have declared that now is not the time for him to die.

"You're out late," he says to the water.

"Early yet," Toby says, "but Ned's an old man, ain't he? Already tired."

"Heard you and Bill shouting at the house," Ned says, ignoring him. "Thought it might not be a terrible idea to take our time going home."

Jacob nods. Ned is a smart lad. Jacob never needs to worry about him the way he worries about Toby, who would lock eyes with some flower seller in the street and in trying to catch her attention saunter directly into traffic. Ned knows what's good for him, and when he sees danger on the horizon he swerves left and keeps his nose out. It's a lesson Jacob could stand to learn.

"But if you're going back," Toby says, and he stifles a yawn in the crook of his elbow, for all his brave words about Ned being the more tired of the two, "I wouldn't half mind keeping you company."

"No one would dare cross three men at night," Ned adds. It's not clear which of them Ned thinks needs protecting.

He sighs, but when he turns to face Ned, it's with a smile he dragged up out of some forgotten corner, and Ned's discomfort melts away until it resembles Toby's familiar, cocksure ease.

"No call to fear Bill, my dears," he says. "I taught him everything he knows, remember."

"Like you taught us," Toby says brightly, and they walk north from the bridge, back into Blackfriars proper, the river lapping against stone behind them.

As it happens, all their precautious are for nothing. Nobody so much as looks at them on their return journey, and when they reach the house, Bill is already gone.

Ned and Toby sleep easily that night, but Jacob doesn't close his eyes for a moment. He lies in the dark, staring at the ceiling, feeling the whistling breath of his father's ghost, only air, never words. At last, near five, the street begins to come to life again. Costermongers and butchers drag their carts toward Smithfield Market, the calls hawking goods for sale mingling with the rough greetings and insults that make up the native language of the neighborhood. The coffee stalls are setting up to catch the first shift of factory workers and law clerks on their way in, providing something to cup between two palms against the November chill. It all sounds so perfectly banal that he wants to cry. Had he thrown himself into the Thames the night before, these people would rend the air this morning just the same with their cries selling watercress and oysters and coffee and lucifer matches. It could take a man's breath away, how little any of it matters.

The boys are awake when he comes downstairs, and though they go very quiet as he arrives, they don't comment that he missed one of the buttons on his jacket, nor do they invite him to pour a cup of tea from the pot on the table. They nod and let him go without a word. They're smart fellows, and they'll make a name for themselves one way or another. He's not sure whether he's to thank for that or if they've managed it in spite of him.

It's long before his usual hour, but he makes his way toward the market nonetheless. He slips between the stalls and the carts, brushes off every acquaintance who tries to engage him in conversation. The boy with the day's *Times* is precisely where Jacob knew he would be. He takes the exorbitant price of a groat and threepence without a word and hands Jacob the paper, sensing his dramatic headlines of murder and arson and scandal aren't needed to make the sale. Once Jacob is out of sight of the boy, he tears open the paper and scans it for the story he is both expecting and dreading. It takes him several minutes to find it, a small item on the very bottom of the third page.

BETHNAL GREEN HOUSEBREAKER ARRESTED in the early hours in connection with the brazen robbery of Lord Eldridge and the assault of his valet in Golden Square, Westminster. The serving-man was brought to St. Bartholomew's for immediate assistance and remains in critical condition, though medical professionals are of the opinion that he is like to live. The housebreaker,

> who gave his name to the magistrate as William Sikes, wanted in connection with a string of burglaries across the city, was apprehended with the majority of the stolen goods still in tow, owing to the exceptional policemanship of Officer Alastair Fang, who will give evidence at the criminal's arraignment before the Old Bailey sessions on Wednesday at nine.

There are no thoughts in Jacob's head as he folds the paper and tucks it into his coat pocket. There are only facts, and these drift as disjointedly as the few chill raindrops that fall ever faster on the market, sending shoppers scurrying for umbrellas and shelter. The facts, as he sees them, are these:

Bill Sikes did not kill a man.

Bill Sikes will go to prison for this crime, but he will not hang.

Bill will go to prison, and Jacob will not.

The rain is becoming heavier by the moment, and soon the paper will be too wet to read.

If he wants to eat today, he has work to do.

29

1834–1835

Word spreads through Clerkenwell of the sentence handed down at the sessions-house. Bill Sikes, they say, loomed in the dock like a statue and said almost nothing for the length of his trial. Gave his name to the judge and then sat silent while the barrister brought forward witnesses to testify. When the jury foreman stood, the room hummed with uncertainty—wondering whether the jurors would be too frightened to levy a sentence against someone with such a reputation. But the inevitable came to pass, and Bill was condemned to two years in Coldbath Fields for burglary and assault. Nan, who was there, says he took the sentence without blinking. Says he walked out of the sessions-house and didn't say a word, as if a sentence of two years troubled him no more than one of fourteen days would have done.

Jacob wouldn't know. He didn't join Nan in the gallery, didn't ask anyone who'd attended what they saw. He already knows more than he wants to.

Not long after, Jacob is woken in the dead of night by scratching against the front door and a plaintive whine that he, still half asleep, first assumes to be the product of some nightmare strolled out of his mind and made real. When it persists, he curses and throws on his dressing-gown, making his way down the darkened stairs and to the door. The house is silent, both Ned and Toby fast asleep, which only makes the soft whine cut more piercingly. He presses one palm against the door, feeling the vibrations as the scratching comes again.

"Damn you," he mutters, realizing what it must be, and opens the door.

Bullseye sits on the doorstep, glowing white as moonlight through the shadow. It's not a surprise, but the eeriness of seeing the dog makes Jacob flinch back and almost slam the door in his face. He's never seen Bill's bull terrier sit so still before, jaws closed, ears perked, as though he expects Jacob to say something. It's a look Jacob's come to know well, that of a creature with nowhere else to go.

"All right," he says coldly, and steps aside. "Get in."

Jacob following close behind, Bullseye moves into the main room and curls up beneath the table, which at present is loaded with a packet of pocket-handkerchiefs Jacob will take to Barrett in the morning. The dog settles his great blunt head on his paws and goes directly to sleep, without waiting to see if he might have any success begging for food. He wouldn't, but Jacob respects the animal a little more for not trying. Jacob fills the washbasin with water and leaves it on the floor by the window before returning upstairs to bed.

When he comes back the next morning, Toby is sitting on the floor with his long legs crossed and his head cocked, grinning as if at a great joke. Beside him, Bullseye crouches over a rasher of bacon, which the dog devours in a gulp before licking the grease from Toby's hands.

"Is he staying?" Toby asks eagerly. "Oh, let him stay, Fagin, it'll be such a lark, and the old bruiser likes me. Can you imagine, me strolling up Thames Street with this bleeding monster beside me? Christ, they'd talk of nothing else for weeks."

Jacob sighs and eases himself into the chair. Bullseye licks his chops and watches him with the sort of attention that promises judgment.

"It'll stay if it wants to stay, Toby. Don't *feed* it."

The dog, of course, stays. It's not the first time Jacob has felt haunted, but it is the first haunting that's come with a hungry belly. He resents every scrap he hands over, but before the week is out, Bullseye follows at his heels when he works, utterly indifferent to his feelings on the matter. A shadow so familiar that soon, he doesn't even notice it.

Ned strikes out on his own not long after, which has been a long time coming. He is well past the age when living under another man's roof, even free of charge, becomes more imposition than convenience. Still, Jacob knows what's really to blame. Ned and the dog cohabitate uneasily for a week or two, Ned shooting wary looks as Bullseye prowls the house, eats the scraps Toby leaves for him despite Jacob's exhortations, barks late at night at nothing at all. Then Ned comes down to breakfast one morning with a carpetbag and the news that he's taken his own room in Southwark, and that proves to be that.

Jacob doesn't waste his breath arguing for Ned to stay. Instead, he dips into the vase atop the mantel and counts out ten shillings, which he pours into Ned's hand as a farewell gift. Toby's eyes nearly bulge out of his head at the sum.

"Manners," Jacob says, and Toby darts away, embarrassed as any self-respecting pickpocket to be caught ogling. True, it's all the money he planned to spend on food for the next two weeks, but he allows himself the indulgence, knowing that the gesture marks the end of an era and Ned won't refuse him. The lad has a good head on his shoulders, and while he'll miss Ned's practicality as a counterbalance to Toby's relentless stream of nonsense, he doesn't begrudge him going. Each must shift for himself as best he can.

"You can come back, you know," he says, as he sees Ned off at the door. "If it gets bad. There's always room for you here."

"I know that," Ned says, and they shake hands briskly, man to man now. "If we're being honest, Mr. Fagin, that's what worries me."

Jacob doesn't believe in fate or destiny, but he does believe in the natural propensity of people to talk. It will only be a matter of time before the right person hears the thief trainer of Saffron Hill has an extra place in his den. He's never gone more than a few years without a new face turning up, and it occurs to him with Ned's departure that if he were to go out recruiting, he could make a true enterprise of it. Catch the matchstick sellers and the crossing sweeps and the beggars' boys at their usual stations on the pavement, win them over with a penny-loaf and the promise of somewhere warm to sleep. It would be laughably easy, and profitable too. By New Year, he could have himself an army of boys and girls hanging on his coattails, giving him fifty percent of their take for the privilege of bed and board and a chance to learn the ropes from a professional.

If he were a more ambitious sort, he might do it, but something stops him. Not scruples, exactly, but a sense that if he brought them in through tricks and persuasion, it would be different, in some nameless way that would sour everything. The children who come now need him. They choose him, they seek him out, and were it the other way round, he would no longer quite know himself.

As it happens, there's no need to go searching, because he's right. They always come, sooner or later.

It's the dog that alerts him. Toby—eighteen now, and still as reckless and overconfident as he was at six—left to work his usual routes hours ago, though the odds are good he stopped working after the first thirty minutes and spent the rest of the day idling somewhere. At first, Jacob thinks that must be why the dog's barking, that Toby came home whistling a tune he picked up at the brothels and Bullseye, not to be outdone in the business of behaving recklessly enough to give Jacob fits, decided to add to the noise.

"Quiet!" he yells, throwing a shoe down the corridor.

Ordinarily, when it's only Toby at the door, such a display will hush Bullseye, confirming Jacob's suspicion that the dog only does it to annoy him. But Bullseye carries on as though every member of the Bow Street Runners has taken up residence in the courtyard. While he isn't truly afraid, the situation needs to be investigated. Standing on tiptoe, he peers through the knothole in the boards that block out the window, a small peephole that lets him see the street without risk of being seen. He can't spy anyone, but the dog is barking fit to wake the dead, and he's already thrown a shoe and shouted, so it seems rather late in the game to pretend there's no one at home. He nudges Bullseye aside with his foot and opens the door.

For a beat, he's alone there on the threshold. Then he remembers to look down.

The boy on his doorstep is no younger nor any more ragged than the rest were. He's almost certainly older than Toby was when he turned up, so small Jacob couldn't always see him over the table. Nor is he the poorest dressed—he has shoes, though they don't fit, which makes Jacob recall the two weeks Ned spent in the armchair healing his cut and frozen feet before he could stand without wincing, Maggie hovering nearby changing his bandages. It's clear what the boy wants. Toby, or Nan, or Ned, one of them told this boy about him, or someone else told someone else and the boy overheard. Finding a child on his doorstep is as natural as a sunrise.

But what the dark-haired boy in the crushed hat and the rolled-up jacket makes Jacob realize is that while the boys aren't getting any older, he is.

He's forty-eight years old now. This boy is eight or nine, because the boys who come hungry to learn are always eight or nine, old enough to need a profession but too young to be taken seriously. There will always be boys of eight or nine knocking on his door, and he will always let them in, and they will always grow up to leave him, and he will remain here to open the door at the next knock. He will be living this moment over again for the rest of his life.

The boy cranes his neck up at Jacob. "I thought you'd be uglier," he says.

Jacob laughs. Just like that, the grand cycle of the future no longer matters—there is only the present moment, and in it he is himself again. "A charmer as well as a mobsman, eh?" he says. "Who sent you?"

"No one sent me," the boy says, drawing himself up to the entirety of his four feet in height. "Heard a bloke down at the Cripples saying he knew the hook-nosed old Jew that trained Bill Sikes, and seeing as I mean to be the best, thought I might as well start there. But if you ain't him, and there's a worse-looking, ancienter Jew whose door I should be knocking on, tell me and I'll leave you be."

Jacob isn't sure he believes in God anymore—he stopped thinking of God as a benevolent force at Leah's death, and what remains of his faith are the stray sparks that aren't worth the trouble of extinguishing. But it almost rekindles some belief in him, that this is the kind of boy to turn up just now. His little speech reminds Jacob of his own introduction to Leftwich nearly forty years ago.

"No, I know Bill," he says. "Knew him since he was near your age. Do you have a name?"

"Jack Dawkins," the boy says. "Mates call me the Artful Dodger, on account of—"

"Yes, I can imagine on account of what."

"If you don't want me, say so," the boy says, his brashness not hiding his fear. "I don't go where I'm not wanted."

There's fondness as well as regret in Jacob's smile as he steps aside, shooing Bullseye farther down the passage to make room. "Stop wagging your tongue and come in, before the police take us both for some common thieves. And mind you don't let the dog out."

The boy's face lights up, and he follows Jacob in. It all unfolds the only way it could, the two of them acting out the old pattern.

This life has begun to scare him, though not for one day has he ever tried to choose a different one. He catches a brief flash of confusion in the boy's eyes before the door closes and they're plunged into darkness.

"Ain't we thieves, though?"

"Of course," Jacob says, leading the boy deeper into the house, where the light from the lamp still glimmers. "But once you're through learning from me, my dear, there won't be anything common about you."

It comes as no surprise that Jack Dawkins and Toby are soon inseparable. Dodger, as he continues to insist on being called, has all the self-importance of a man of thirty and all the self-control of the child he is, and Toby, always passionately ready for a lark, finds the lad to be a source of never-ending amusement.

"Christ on the bleeding cross, Fagin, this one's a regular Bill Sikes in miniature, ain't he?" Toby says with a laugh one afternoon, as Dodger puffs away on a stolen cigar and beats the older boy handily at whist for the third rubber in a row. Dodger preens, not a little pleased with the praise.

"More than you ever were," Jacob says from his armchair, where he's been feigning absorption in a book, "if you think it's such a great laugh you've lost a week's take to a nine-year-old."

Toby colors and occupies himself with shuffling the deck.

It's true, though: before Dodger turns ten, he's identifying coves on his own, coming home from a trip to the pawnbroker's with a take Toby would need a month to match. With Bill, Jacob knew the profession he was teaching would never be more than temporary, cast aside as soon as the student came into his own. With Dodger, he feels as though he's the painting tutor to a Michelangelo, that if people remember Jacob Fagin's name in the future, it will be because he taught the Artful Dodger, the greatest pickpocket London ever saw.

Dodger brings a sunshine to the house that Jacob hadn't realized was missing, casting out the cobwebs and dust that settled on everything since Bill's arrest and Ned's departure. The boy makes it his mission to coax a smile out of everyone. He even manages to charm a melancholy Nan, kissing the back of her hand with the solemnity of a lord until she laughs and gives him one of the ribbons from her bonnet as a token.

Even so, after the boy falls asleep in the evenings, Jacob is left alone with the light of a candle and the dog's snuffling breath and his own thoughts. One night, lost for another way to distract himself, he riffles through the chest of drawers in the central room, from which he takes a pen and a few handbills advertising an exhibition that are blank on the verso. Strengthened either by gin or by foreboding, he sits back at the table, and before he can tell himself to see sense, he begins to write.

Bill,

Near on six months and I haven't written yet, so you'd think I'd have enough saved up to say. The truth is, I can't think the last time when I've had something true to tell you. I used to, once, when you were young. Told you everything I thought, everything I wanted, and you hung on my every word. I loved the way you listened. It made me feel like a prophet.

I'm not certain what it says about me, that I only have something to say to people when I'm teaching them, when they need something from me.

There are a great many things I'm not certain about, when it comes to it.

This is all wrong. He tries again.

I've thought about you every day you've been locked up. It's impossible not to. Every inch of this house has your fingerprints on it. Everything I've made for myself you've taken your share of, or you've been there to witness, or you've remarked on in that cutting way, reminding me how small and useless it all is. The past six months hardly seem to have happened at all, because you weren't there to see them.

I've slept better than I have in ages, these six months you've been gone.

He scowls at the page, sets it aside, begins again.

Yesterday I told Nan I thought you'd never forgive me. She says I'm wrong, but she doesn't know you the way I do. I know what I've done. You'll need more than a few drops of ink before you can see me as a friend again, not the man who failed you and left you to die. I know that.

You'll have to give me a chance, though, for me to manage it. Write to me. Tell me what you need. I'll deliver. I always have, except for that once. Whatever else you might believe about me, you have to admit that's so.

He's rapidly running out of handbills. Surely there are other sheets of paper somewhere in the house. He never throws anything away. Half the flat surfaces are stacked with books; he can start tearing out pages if it comes to it.

You should hate me, but I hope you don't. I don't hate you.

Now he's lying. The point of this was not to lie.

I miss you. Come by when you're out. I still have your bloody dog.

He crumples the page along with the rest and tosses them into the fire. He'll see Bill face-to-face, one way or another, when it's all over. God willing, he'll know what to say then.

30

1836

A quarter past seven one November morning, Nan stands on the pavement outside Coldbath Fields. It'll be hours yet before anything happens, she knows that. Nan did time herself once, four months in Tothill Prison, and before she met Bill she ran with a crowd of thieves who all did more. Releases involve mountains of paperwork and never finish until at least ten o'clock, and the governor sends all the day's prisoners out at once as if it's the Tyburn Turnpike and they have to pay a toll each time the gate opens. But Nan will be damned if she's not there when it happens. She didn't sleep a wink all night. Might as well be worried half to death here as at home.

It's a thickly overcast day, fog descending low over the streets. Nan can't see much of the prison in front of her but the blurry glow of its windows, lamps well tended in the governor's office. There's barely enough sun to know whether it's morning or night. Dimly, she sees the shapes of a few other bodies, mostly women, waiting in the fog nearby. Silent ghosts each charged with their own hauntings. No one standing on this corner is ever in the mood for conversation, and they leave one another be.

She hears the prison door open before she sees it. Clutching her hat to her head, Nan rushes forward, peering through the fog to see five men stumble through the prison gate and into the street. For an awful moment, none of them look familiar. Have they extended his sentence? It's possible. One misstep inside and it could be another six weeks or more.

"Bill!" she cries.

One of the men looks up.

On all of her trips to the prison these past two years, Nan only saw Bill through the small, barred window of the visitation cell. His skin was yellow like old paper from prison sickness, and the ridges of his cheekbones sharpened week by week under the warden's close shave, but his face still looked like him. Now, she can see his body too. Bill is haggard and bent, and he's lost weight, his overcoat hanging off his shoulders. He looks both younger and older than she knows he is, aged ten years in both directions. The eyes, though, are the same. She'd recognize that face even at the gates of hell.

Nan charges across the street, the loose sole of her shoe slapping after her. She throws her arms around him like someone might take him away again if she isn't quick. Two years behind bars have weakened Bill, but he's still strong enough to lift her off her feet and swing her round. Nan laughs, imagining her skirt cutting a clear path through the fog. When he sets her down and she can see him properly, he's beaming. His dark blue eyes are wide and bright. He's himself again, and for the first time in years, she is whole.

"My girl," he says. "Been waiting two years for this."

And he takes her face in both his broad hands and kisses her until her blood turns to stars.

He's always kissed her like she's the only person living, whether it's in the middle of a crowded tavern or in their own bed. But with two years separating them from their last embrace, two years and a set of iron bars, this kiss turns Nan's head entirely. By the time they break apart, there are tears on her cheeks. She hopes he won't notice, but it isn't to be. He brushes her tears away with the pad of his thumb. Gentle, like a wolf grooming a pup.

"I swore I wouldn't be a silly girl about it," she says with a watery laugh.

Bill shakes his head. "You couldn't be silly if you tried your damnedest. Cleverest girl in London, you are."

She's woefully out of practice at taking compliments. "Come on, now," she says. "You need a meal and a proper rest, is what you need."

There's a new spark in Bill's eyes. She missed this expression of his too. Missed what it promises even more. "Have we still got the room in Bethnal Green?"

"Just as you left it."

"Then I need something else first, pretty lady, before any of that."

The part she longed for more than anything comes after. Bill's arm circles her waist like the fog circles the little room, his breath steadily rising and falling. His bare skin against hers is white-hot, and his body feels different now. Strong still, but unsteady. Bill traces his thumb between her breasts as though he's never touched her before. It makes her think of the caged lion in the menagerie at Exeter Change, cowed but bitterly aware of its former glory.

"I missed that," Nan says.

Bill hums. She feels it as a low rumble in her bones. "Did you? Didn't have anyone filling my place, little bird?"

"No one could fill your place."

"Damn right," Bill says. "I hope they paid you well, if they couldn't give you anything else."

She flinches. No surprise that his mind goes there. People talk, more cruelly when they think there aren't any consequences, and Bet told her about the rumors that Nan had found new ways to make ends meet in Bill's absence. There's no truth to it, but that doesn't mean she likes hearing the accusation in his voice.

"I haven't so much as touched a man since you've been away," she says. "God as my witness I haven't."

Nan can't tell if he believes her. She's afraid to turn around, because if she sees his face, she'll know one way or the other. But he doesn't take his arm away from her waist. When he speaks, it's very low, and not at all angry.

"They had me in the dark cells once. Four days alone, couldn't see my hand in front of my nose."

It should be impossible to feel so much relief and sorrow at the same time. Nan shifts in his arms until they face each other and kisses him near the collarbone. He believes her, or he's going to try to. He would never show his pain to her so honestly if he didn't trust her. Bill doesn't want the words another woman could offer him now, *I'm sorry* or *It's all over now* or *I love you.* He wants her touch and her silence and nothing else. No one, she thinks with fierce pride, could care for him in this moment as well as she's doing.

"Do you know what I thought about all that time?" he says.

"Beefsteak and gravy," she guesses.

Bill laughs and kisses her forehead, then her nose, then her lips, where he lingers. "You, little bird," he says. "I thought about you. How if I had you waiting, what did any of it matter? What could they do to me, if I had you waiting?"

What else would she have done but wait? Nan could have left London, left England, traveled in a mail ship to Boston or Barbados, and still the core of her would be in the street outside Coldbath Fields, waiting for Bill. She's as likely to stop waiting for him as she is to leave her own heart behind.

"You have me, Bill," she says. "Body and soul, you do."

"And don't I thank God every day."

Nan takes the lead in their next kiss, winding her way from his lips to his neck, behind the curve of his ear. Bill's firm, satisfied exhale is as familiar as a favorite song. He loves her. Not for what she can steal or for what money she can bring, but for who she is. His clever little bird. No man ever wanted to possess the cracked gem of her heart before. Here in his bed, it's his. If it's more cracked now than it was before, so be it.

The kiss trails off. Ordinarily, both of them would be ready for another round by now, but Bill hasn't yet eaten anything but prison fare, and she senses him tiring. To spare him the shame of having to say it, she smiles softly, then rises and begins to dress.

"I'll find us something to eat," she says. "Stay there. Rest."

Bill sits up, looking as if he'd like to argue about going with her for protection. But he's aware of his own weakness, and he holds his tongue. Besides, there's no need. Word will be out by now that Bill Sikes is sprung from prison, and no one's mad enough to bother Bill's girl now he's back on the streets. The rumors will take care of themselves, by the end of the day.

"Take the dog, at least," he begins, then winces. "Damn me. The dog."

"It's all right," Nan says. She's dressed now, though she can't quite reach the last button in the back of her dress. She wrinkles her nose and stretches both arms first up her back, then over her shoulders. It's no good either way. "Fagin's got him. You'll laugh yourself sick, when you see how Bullseye follows him about."

The softness in Bill's eyes goes out. His hand wrings the blanket like it's a man's neck. "Surprised the old devil has that much heart left in him," he says. "Or that much conscience, after he left me to die."

Nan knows that look. She'll visit Bell Court that night after Bill's asleep, tell Fagin to lie low for a week until Bill calms himself. She doesn't have so many friends she can afford to send any of them to the grave.

"He loves you too, Bill, you know," she says. "In his way."

"Two years," Bill says. There's a new note of roughness in his voice, one Nan doesn't associate wholly with anger. "He knew I was there for two years, grinding the wind, locked up for a job he sent wrong himself, a job I could've been hanged for, and he never came."

Bill is a clever man, but when it comes to Fagin, he's bafflingly shortsighted. Nan knows, clearly better than Bill does, that no one ought to count on Fagin to do anything that puts himself at risk. It's every man for himself, but Fagin for Fagin most of all.

"He didn't know what to do," she says. "You know him. He's not as strong as you. He'd die of fright just thinking about what you've been through."

Bill lets his head hang, anger spent already. He seems so young without his usual stamina. "Too right he would."

Dinner can wait. Nan sits beside Bill, leaning her head on his bare shoulder. He melts under her touch, twining one arm back around her waist. After so long apart, she doesn't think they could keep space between them if they tried.

"You don't have to tell me about it, Bill," she says. "But you can."

"It wasn't even hard labor," Bill says hollowly. "They couldn't find anything too much for me, and if a fellow in there got the notion to cross me, I could send him packing again, you know that."

Nan nods against his shoulder. She can see it clear as if she was there, Bill dragged off to the dark cells after breaking the nose of some convict foolhardy enough to challenge him in the prison yard or whisper some insult in his ear as the prisoners file out of the chapel. The Bill she knows would take strength from that kind of fight. That doesn't explain the man in front of her.

"Then what?" she says.

"You're not—" Bill begins. He coughs. Other men have coughed that way to hide tears. Not her Bill, but others. "You're not a man, inside," he says. "No one speaks to you. No one looks you in the eyes. After two months, damn if I didn't start to think I'd got it wrong. That it was me what had died at Golden Square, and I the only one who didn't know it."

Nan pulls back and fixes him with a glare. "Now, none of that," she says. "You're Bill Sikes, and you're free, and you're mine. That's all there is."

"An animal turned loose," Bill says bitterly. He doesn't meet her eyes. "That's how they looked at me when they let me go. Like they knew they'd see me back again, and next time it would be to stay. On God, Nan, I won't get taken again. The next time they come for me, I'll take a pistol and put an end to it myself."

She loves him. Loves him and pities him, for while the world knows Bill Sikes the lion, she knows him better, and she's never met a man more frightened. He doesn't have the courage or the imagination to tell them they're wrong, that he isn't what they think of him. Well, that will have to be all right. She can be brave enough to dream for the both of them.

"None of that," she says again, and stands. "I've waited two years to have you all to myself, and I won't have you spoil it by moping. Now. Do up my damned button, you, and then rest. I'll be back in a flash with supper. Can I trust you not to shoot yourself for a quarter of an hour?"

She wouldn't joke about it with anyone else, but he responds exactly how she knows he will, with that barking laugh that says he agrees to put an end to self-pity.

"If you're quick," he says, and slips the button through.

She wrinkles her nose at him, then lingers for one more kiss before setting off. The cookhouse on the corner isn't high-quality, its wares barely even edible, but Bill will be able to eat that food in his own house off his own plate, and talk while he does it, and no one will discipline him for anything. But as she walks, drawing her shawl about her against the fog, it isn't the food she thinks about.

It's an old dream, the one she welcomes back. Sharper now, though, as if it's finally close enough to see properly. It's not London, wherever it is. The sky is vast and open above her in this unreal place she dreamed up, and Dream-Nan stands in the yard of a little house at the edge of a wood, smoke curling cheerfully from the chimney. A chicken pecks about her feet, searching for grain—until she remembers the mess a chicken can leave on the floors, the cocks crowing at ungodly hours, and upon reflection she erases the chicken from her imagination.

Dream-Bill comes back from the woodpile at the side of the house with an axe over his shoulder. His sleeves are rolled to his elbows, and there's sweat on his brow, but he smiles at her, and kisses her as he leaves the axe leaning against the house. He's tired but happy, and he smells of sweat and smoke and sawdust. Later that night, he'll wander down to the village pub, where he'll drink with the other men. Maybe he'll knock one of them down in a fistfight—it's a dream, not a delusion, and he's still Bill. Whatever happens, he'll be home before midnight and in one piece. She'll have friends, and a house that's small but as clean as she cares to make it. On Sundays—not every Sunday, but some—she'll go to the local church on Bill's arm, and the farmers for miles around will tip their hats in welcome as they take their pew. The image is so clear that for the first time, she feels almost able to put it into words.

Not yet, she thinks, as she opens the door to the cookhouse. He's not ready to hear it yet, and she has to tread carefully. It's a new life, an end that isn't the mouth of a pistol, but his pride won't bear it unless he thinks it's his idea. Still, she can work on him. Now that he's afraid, he might be open to suggestion. And she's always been the only one able to change his mind.

"Miss Nancy!" one of the waiters says as she enters. "The usual for you?"

All thoughts are neatly locked behind her eyes again, and Nan is smiling, the same carefree woman these people have come to know. "Not tonight, Richard," she says. "Finest you've got tonight. It's a celebration."

Remembrance darts across Richard's face, almost fear but not quite. "Christ alive, it's today!" he says, and claps his hands. "On the house, then, with my compliments."

"Oh, don't—" she begins. She already has a handful of shillings at the ready. She saved for this occasion going on a month.

"With my compliments," Richard says firmly. "You tell Mr. Sikes that Dick Graceling at the Black Dragon is right glad he's back in the neighborhood, eh? You tell him that from me."

Nan pockets her money again, nodding. She's buying dinner with the promise of future goodwill, which can go just as far as sterling.

Richard is gone in a flash, off to package up whatever has gone unclaimed in the kitchen. Nan almost laughs, imagining him sweeping up an entire roast chicken from the counter, informing the man who already paid for it that in this house, Bill Sikes takes precedence.

"He's well, Bill is?" asks another man at a nearby table, his fork deep in the filling of an eel pie.

"Just the same as ever," she says.

Thinking still of the smoke curling up from a far-off chimney, Nan privately hopes she's lying.

PART FOUR

31

1838

Just past dawn, six days after the robbery in Chertsey was meant to go off, Jacob sits with Nan at the table, both trying to pretend they aren't waiting. She's barely left his side since Bill set out with Oliver and Toby, haunting the house with an expression so grim he long since gave up trying to reassure her all will be well. They're not speaking so much as occasionally making sounds to fill the silence: both ran out of meaningful things to say days ago.

When the door opens, Jacob folds the paper he was holding but not reading. He looks up but forces himself not to move. More than likely it's only Charley. He expected the boy home by midnight, and while it hasn't been long enough to worry, it's long enough that Charley will deserve a good raking over the coals when he does get back, to keep him from making it a habit.

But the tall shadow standing on the threshold isn't Charley. It's Bill. And he's alone.

Bill doesn't knock, of course. He's had right of entry since he lived here himself, and besides, if anyone knows about opening doors that don't belong to him, it's Bill Sikes. But even though this moment has been nearly a week in the making, seeing the looming shadow of his oldest friend nearly makes Jacob cry out in fright. Bullseye appears at Bill's heels a moment later, ears lowered, white coat dirty.

The moment Nan claps eyes on Bill, she shouts in relief and rushes to throw her arms around him, heedless of the mud that coats his trousers up to his knees, the ash and dirt smeared across his brow. Bill stands stiff as the embrace happens around him. He flinches in anticipation of a blow that must seem more likely than Nan's affection. Only when he's frightened does it seem possible that East London's most notorious housebreaker was once a filthy child hiding from a policeman in the shadow of St. Giles in the Fields. The memory wavers, and Bill pushes Nan off with such force that she stumbles back and might have fallen if Jacob didn't rise to catch her.

"None of that," Bill says. "I'm alive, you've seen it, so quit your pawing at me like you think I'm a ghost."

"I thought—" Nan says. "Oh, Bill, I don't know what I thought."

"Well, don't think it," Bill snaps. "Get us a drink, Fagin, unless a man needs to be spitting blood first."

Jacob pours the gin and pushes it across the table toward Bill's outstretched hand—filthy, black around the nails, and trembling too, though they all pretend not to notice. Jacob's hand shakes as well, he's not too proud to admit it. Every day he waited for Bill to return, there's been a universe of potential reasons for the delay. Bill and Oliver and Toby got away with a thousand pounds and spent the week disposing of the goods. They decided not to try the job at all, thinking better of the risk. But now Bill arrived alone, and the expanse of possibilities is rapidly narrowing. Whatever it is, soon he'll know.

"The boys, Bill?" he asks quietly. "What happened to the boys?"

Bill curses. Nan draws back, but Bill doesn't care. Wherever he's been for the past week, it wore away at the shrinking part of him that cares what others feel. Today, the only pain that interests him is his own.

"I might have known," Bill says. "Same as before. Don't give a damn for me so long as you know what's happened to your property. Well, it's too late for that, ain't it?"

"What do you mean?" Nan says.

Bill bolts down the gin and wipes his mouth. "Job was a bleeding disaster. I'm all right, though a great lot you care. The valet fired off three shots as soon as we got in through the window, and one of them hit the boy. Toby and I had to dump him in a ditch, else we'd never have made our own way away."

The hand holding the glass is still shaking. Bill will not meet Jacob's eyes. It's by these signs he knows his old friend isn't lying. Toby is on the run somewhere, and Oliver is alone, on the outskirts of the city, torn up by a valet's bullet. Either he's dead or he's bleeding out in a ditch, but whatever fate found him, Jacob sent him there.

"Which is what you wanted, isn't it?" Bill says. "Rather have me off dead somewhere and your little trained monkeys back in hand?"

"I've never wanted anything ill to befall you, Bill," Jacob says. "You know that."

"Maybe once I did. These days, you don't do much to prove it, do you? Going to send me away again? Call the bloody police yourself this time?"

Jacob knows the moment has come. For decades, he allowed himself to be a coward. Fifty-one years he closed his eyes and told himself it's none of his business, that nobody ever tried to protect him and so what debt does he owe the world? And maybe it's not even now a question of debt. Maybe it has more to do with the fear in Nan's eyes. Maybe he's curious what it would feel like, for a change, not to be the cause of alarm or disappointment but of relief. Maybe it's a crossroads he hadn't realized he was approaching: whether he's going to be the man who taught Bill Sikes, or he's going to become someone else.

"We have to go back for him," he says, and the suggestion doesn't sound like him at all, but he presses forward. "If he's still there. If something's happened. We can't just leave him."

"Like hell," Bill says. He slams the glass down. Nan flinches.

"But if they pick him up, Bill," Jacob says, wheedling now, reaching for the second reason—arguably more urgent than the first, and one he knows Bill will understand—"if he's not dead and they take him in, he'll tell them everything. You've already done two years, what do you think they'll give you the second time?"

It's not anger that lights Bill now. Jacob knows Bill's anger like a dog that nipped at his heels for years. This is terror. Bill Sikes never learned how to be afraid, and the fear spills out of him in every direction, soaking them all like rain. Jacob taught Bill so many lessons, but the one neither of them ever learned, from each other or anyone else, is what to do with fear.

"You devil," Bill says, and he's on his feet now, looming like the golem in Leah's story, great clay hands that can crush bone. "Whose fault is it I've done two years? And you think I'll let you do it again? Every time you get the chance, it's my neck in the halter to save your own."

"Bill—" Nan begins, but he swats her aside as though she's a sparrow. She stumbles into the clothes-horse, and it topples with a crash that sets the dog to barking. She edges back toward the wall, and Jacob wills her to stay where she is, not to divert this storm that will strike hard, when it strikes, which will be soon.

"Place will be bloody swarming with police, you know it. You'd have me walk into their trap? Go back for the boy and hand myself over? Faster to have you cut my throat yourself, if you had the nerve to dirty your hands anymore."

Jacob steps nearer, laying a hand on Bill's forearm, but Bill takes his wrist and drags them together until their faces are inches apart. Bill is still thinner than he should be after Coldbath Fields, though he's been out for more than a year now. Something he picked up there has dogged him ever since. The yellowish tinge to his skin reminds Jacob of turned meat.

"I'm trying to keep you safe," Jacob says. "I want us both to live."

"Bill, listen to him," Nan says. Around her, handkerchiefs litter the ground like autumn leaves. "I love you, he loves you, don't you see, let us—"

"Like hell," Bill says again, and the grip on Jacob's wrist tightens until he cries out. The cry is so sharp it even seems to surprise Bill. He lets go, and Jacob sinks to the floor, cradling his injured wrist. "If you try to turn me in, Fagin, I'll kill you first this time, I swear I will."

Death has stalked Jacob all these years, ever since he was a boy, but it's never been closer than it is now. He crumbles, as he always crumbles, in the face of it. His life is worth nothing, is hunger and lies and danger and every single day a fight to make it to the next, but it is *his* life, and he grasps for it with a desperate and single-minded avarice. He will not die. He will give up every last principle, will send everyone else he knows to the gallows in a single-file line, if only it means this useless wreck of a life he calls his own stays where it is, firmly clenched in the palm of his hand.

"I know," he says. "You're right. I failed you once, Bill. I won't do it again. Forget I said anything."

Nan steps forward. He wants to tell her to stay back. Wants to tell her that heroics are not for people like them, that there's no shame in cringing and hiding when you're so badly outmatched. But Nan has never been a coward.

"No." She sounds like a commander now, her voice ringing as she bears down on Bill. "No, maybe he failed you, Bill, but I never have. I've been there always, through all of it, and you know that's so. So you'll listen to me, and you'll let me have my say. Haven't I earned that by now, the chance to have my say?"

Nan will not be silenced now, and even Bill can only keep quiet and let her finish. Jacob wonders, distantly, how long she spent preparing the speech she's about to deliver. If she even thought about what might happen once she's done giving it.

"He's a boy," she says. "The same as you were a boy, the one Fagin brought in and looked after. A boy who doesn't deserve to die alone, and if he has, he deserves the safety of a grave."

"Woman, enough," Bill says, but there's panic to it now, and Nan talks straight through him.

"You pretend none of it troubles you, but I've heard you cry out in the night since the Steel, and I know it does. I know you, Bill Sikes, in my heart and my blood I know you, and you're not afraid of anything on this cruel earth but yourself. It's what makes me love you, through it all. Go back for the boy, leave him on a doorstep somewhere they'll look after him, and then let's go, you and I. Out of here, as far as we can, and let's start again. You'll have me always, you know that. But don't make a murderer out of the man I love."

These last words break something in all of them. The break separates the possibilities of *before* from the certainty of *after*. Jacob flinches as he hears it. The sound must reach his ears before it reaches Bill's, for there's one awful moment in which he knows what's going to happen before either Bill or Nan. A terrible gift of prophecy, gazing into a ruin he's about to watch collapse.

And then the words fit together in Bill's mind.

"Make a murderer of myself," he says, slowly at first. "You think I made myself any of this? The boy Fagin looked after, you said, and see how he's looked after me. See how he's doing it still."

The words to save himself are there, on Jacob's tongue. Something made you the way you are, he should say, but it wasn't only me, any more than I made myself into what I am. It's the world, my friend, my dear boy, it's the world that takes us by the collar and drags us forward, because what use is an honest man, Bill, when that honest man is dead in a ditch, the point of life is to *live it,* that's all I ever tried to teach you.

But the words won't come. There's nothing to interrupt Bill when he says, hands shaking as badly as his voice, "I won't let you take me down, Fagin. If I'm a murderer already, let me take a life worth taking."

And as he draws the pistol from his coat pocket Jacob suddenly no longer sees Bill's anguished face. Instead, he stares into the familiar eyes of a man now standing between the two of them, in a dark brown overcoat and a flat-brimmed hat covering his red hair. A young man, the figure seems now. Barely thirty. Devoid of knowledge, of judgment, of power. Just the sad, unsurprised face of a man dead before his time, who gives Jacob the smallest of smiles and says, softly, in a voice Jacob has never heard before, "Here we are, then."

He doesn't flinch. Doesn't try to run. Jacob Fagin looks into his father's eyes, and he nods, and the gun goes off in Bill Sikes's shaking hands.

32

They're no longer people at all, then. Reduced to figures in a painting, brushstrokes and shadow. They are set pieces, frozen where they stand.

Bill stays fixed in place, the gun hot in his hand.

Jacob can't feel his body. Drifted away from the pain, he can no longer track the beating of his heart.

Dodger hovers in the doorway, eyes wide and shining, looking every day of twelve years old. Charley peeks out from behind him. Both boys drawn in from the street by the shouting, by the inescapable human drive to witness.

Nan falls to the ground as if through water. Blood slips between her fingers where the bullet struck her chest. Each muscle unspools and settles as she falls. The most profound weariness Jacob has ever seen in a body, a life's worth of fear and love and hope and hate purged with each drop of blood. Jacob has seen many dead people—two weeks in Saffron Hill would introduce any man to half a dozen—but only one other in the act of dying, and it was nothing like this. Leah vanished into silence, eyes closed like a child preparing to swim in a cold river, as though blunting one sense would numb all the rest. Nan is different. There is so much life in Nan Reed's dying.

She laughs once as she catches herself on the floor with one hand. The laugh hasn't finished ringing before she sinks fully down, and the blood continues to run, but she's gone so still.

How can blood continue to flow when the heart pumping it has stopped? It seems like there should be a natural law against it.

The thoughts flood his brain to drown out the sound of that disbelieving laugh, Nan Reed's final goodbye. He will hear that laugh every day for the rest of his life.

"Bill," he says, because he's a fool, and to the end he persists in saying the wrong name.

The gun falls to the floor but does not go off again.

"I didn't," Bill says to no one.

Charley stands silent in the doorway. Jacob looks at him because he can't bring himself to look anywhere else, because everywhere else in this blasted house is blood or death or murder, but Charley, Charley's and Dodger's hands are still clean.

"Monsters," Charley says.

Before anyone can stop him, he bolts out the door, screaming to raise the whole of Saffron Hill.

"Stop him," Bill says hoarsely, though he makes no move to do so, doesn't look away from the body. "For God's sake, Fagin, stop him."

The red-haired man in the wide-brimmed hat looks down at Nan's blood staining the floor and shakes his head.

"Murder!" Charley shouts from the street.

33

Charley's voice shakes them all back to life. Dodger runs forward to cradle Nan's head in his lap. Blood coats the boy's hands. Bill doesn't look at Jacob. Locks eyes on Nan's body instead. Jacob can't name what he sees in Bill, whether it's horror or hatred and, if the latter, who the target is. Bill sways on his feet, and Jacob feels the suicidal urge to step forward, to steady Bill with one hand on his shoulder. It's anyone's guess what will happen if he tries, whether Bill will collapse into his arms or rip out his heart with his fingernails.

"You have to go," Jacob says. "Run, Bill, don't just stand there."

It's vile and cowardly, but forty years of habit can't disappear in an instant. The case, in his current state of hollow shock, appears very simple. One of his friends has died today. If Bill doesn't move fast, it will be two. Bill needs to get away, or the law will catch him, and it takes no imagination to work out what will happen then.

But there's no self-preservation left in Bill. He stands silent with his arms loose by his sides, and he looks down at Nan's body with that same illegible expression, and he does not move. He reminds Jacob of a child who played too roughly with his toy and smashed it to pieces, caught in the empty moment between violence and consequence.

"Nancy," Bill says.

The sound of her name in Bill's voice, her body not yet cold, head in Dodger's lap—it shakes Jacob back into motion. Anger, cruelty, these are things he's felt before, but he has never felt this.

A lifetime of anger sears through him like a pillar of fire. He steps forward, and Bill draws back from his approach. If his rage is to have consequences at last, it seems right that it should be today.

"Yes, Nancy," Jacob says, and his voice is low and deadly. He no longer knows if he wants to urge Bill to run or drive a stake through his chest. "Nan, Bill, your girl. The one who loved you so much she wouldn't leave, thought you couldn't bear the pain of being yourself on your own. And now look. Look what's come of someone loving you."

He can't remember the last time he cried. Can't be sure whether he's crying now. The room might be shimmering at the edges from the purity of his anger. The balance of power, inverting steadily day by day for years, suddenly swings back in his favor, like some great angel turned the world upside down. Bill is nothing but a frightened boy in front of him now, and he the voice of God.

"Shoot me too, then, Bill," he says, and he spreads his arms wide, baring his chest. "It's what you meant, isn't it? Thought putting me in my grave would take it all back. Well, try it, then!" He's shouting now; something has snapped, and he cannot put it back together. "Try it! See if putting a bullet in my heart will change you. Would to God we both spent our whole lives alone, where we couldn't hurt anyone."

"Please," Bill says.

If he means anything to follow that word, there's no time for it.

The front door flings open, slamming against the wall and flooding the passage with light. The first people to enter are not in uniform—workmen, roustabouts, the type lounging against the wall of any public-house in London, waiting for an excuse to break up or start a fight as the case demands. The police aren't far off if this makeshift vanguard already heard the commotion, but London loves an arrest the way it loves a fire, and these strangers came to make sure the city isn't denied its spectacle.

There's no time left to run, but coward that he is, Jacob still tries. He dives toward the basement stair, where the panel behind the table will lift away to reveal the door connecting to the cellar of the house opposite, a secret only he and one other person have ever known, that nameless beggar, doubtless long dead. No use. The men are younger than he is, and stronger, and better fed. He doesn't make it to the stairs. One catches him by the collar and yanks him back, throws him to the floor. His yelp gives way to a howl of helpless rage as they are on him en masse, one pinning his arms behind his back, paying no heed to his injured wrist.

They force his cheek into the floor, and from here all he can see is Nan's face, Nan's eyes, Nan's lips still parted with that final laugh.

He doesn't hear the mob apprehend Bill. Perhaps they don't need to. That motionless, frightened wreck didn't seem like a man capable of defending himself.

The police are there in moments, pouring through the door one after another. Two of them seize Jacob by his upper arms and haul him to his feet, drag him from his den still kicking and fighting. He cannot turn around, cannot see Bill's last ferocious stand—what he hopes will be a stand, because somehow it's more awful to imagine Bill Sikes going quietly. Will they fall on Dodger as well? He's a boy, but his hands are drenched with Nan's blood, and half the policemen in the neighborhood will recognize his face from one picked pocket or another. No doubt they'll take him too. And then there will be no one in the room but—no, he won't think of that. Won't think of the body they have left behind, of those sightless eyes staring.

The police pull him into the street, the air misty with dawn. London's morning shift of vendors are already out for work. The costermongers and their barrows, the coffee-cart men, the watercress girls with their baskets tucked under their arms. All of them where they always are, gaunt and shadowed with lack of sleep, halted on their usual rounds by the best entertainment London has to offer the poor: a commotion. He scans their faces, searching for one of them to look dismayed, for one to extend a hand—if not in help, then at least in sympathy. Saffron Hill has been his home for thirty years. He's known these people the entirety of his adult life. They poured him gin, served him meals, bought his goods, told jokes for his benefit and at his expense. One of them, he thinks—surely, one of them—will be sorry to see him go.

It's a sign he's growing old, that he's foolish enough to look for pity.

He doesn't see which of his neighbors spits at him, only feels it land against his shoe. The silence that ushered in his arrest is fracturing, first in murmurs and then with a girl's voice, high and clear and nothing at all like Nan's, and yet it's her face he sees as the cry grows across the neighborhood into a full chorus.

"Murderer!"

At the word, his ribs burst open. There's nothing now where his heart should be. He is bones and skin and teeth, something feral and unchained, and he fights against the policemen with the strength of a man twice his size or half his age. For a moment, he frees his left wrist, reaches for the clasp-knife in his pocket, the same one he lifted from a sailor as a child—though what he intends to do with it, he has no idea—but a policeman catches his arm before he can manage it and lifts the knife from him with the cool precision of a watchmaker removing a cog for repair. He is shouting now, screaming, and the crowd jeers back, pleased to see him dragged away, but he can't hate them for it, can't hate anyone, because his heart fell from the open cage of his ribs when he heard the word he will never stop thinking of for the rest of his life, *murderer,* because Nan Reed is dead.

They aren't wrong. He did kill her. It's what enraged him about the surprise in Bill's face, as though he still didn't know what he did. They killed her, Bill and Jacob, each of them the same. Bill pulled the trigger, but Nan is dead because she tried to pick Jacob's pocket that long-ago night at the Covent Garden Theatre, and he has been drawing the blade across her throat ever since simply by knowing her.

The policemen bundle him into the back of a wagon, shoving him forward onto his belly and cuffing his wrists behind his back as the wagon doors slam shut. The pain is sharp but not as sharp as it might be, suggesting that his wrist is only badly bruised, not broken. For a moment, he thinks there's been a mistake, that they can't take him away without Bill, but of course they'd split up a pair of murderers as soon as they can. No doubt there's a second wagon already on its way for Bill. Jacob is still shouting, though he hardly realizes it until one policeman threatens to gag him if he doesn't stop, to which he responds by trying to bite the other's thumb off his hand. Eventually the weight of the policeman's knee on his back pushes the breath from him, and he leaves off, panting but otherwise quiet.

His father's ghost still sits beside him. He can't turn to look, not with the policeman's knee in the small of his back, but he feels himself being watched, and there are no prizes for guessing who would join him now. You don't know, he wants to tell his father. I decided years ago I wouldn't be you, I wouldn't be the fool who got caught, I would play their game better than any of them and I would win. You don't know how hard I *tried.*

He can't see his father's face, but he can still feel the scorn. *Who,* the ghost seems to say, *could understand that better than I?*

They give him a private cell at Newgate to await his hearing before the sessions. The warder, before closing the door, tells him nastily that he won't have long to wait, that it's been a slow series of weeks for the magistrate and he's eager to fill his time by sending a brace of murderers to the gallows. Then the warder slams the door and locks it after, and Jacob is left alone in the silence.

After the chaos in the street and the rattling of the prison van, silence is terrifying. It feels as though he's been dropped off the edge of the world.

It's several moments before he raises his head to look around. The room is cramped, about six feet square, with a set of triangular shelves wedged into one corner and two hooks on opposite walls from which to hang the rolled-up hammock on the bottom shelf. Beyond that and a framed placard bearing a Bible verse he doesn't take the time to read, the room is bare. He leans his back against the wall and fixes his gaze on the iron hook.

He would give a great deal for the comfort of ghosts just now, but he's never been so alone. His father abandoned him as soon as the doors to the prison van opened—the opposite of any ghost he's ever read about, happy to haunt anywhere but the place of its own death. If other ghosts would like a word with him, they evidently decided solitude will be a worse punishment for him now.

Jacob clenches his fists until his nails bite his palms. Any moment, he'll open his eyes and be at the house in Bell Court, waking from the worst dream of his life, and Nan will be sitting at the table with her hat in her hand, trading insults with Dodger, and they will all of them be as free as the birds that peck grain between the cobblestones of the Haymarket.

Please, he thinks. Let me wake up.

The iron hook glints back like an eye, but otherwise there is no answer.

Days pass. Endless days in which he eats little and speaks to no one, not even when he's routed out of his cell once a day to take twenty minutes of exercise in the prison yard with the others. It's his only time out of those four walls, and he uses it to glance about without getting caught, trying to piece together what has become of the world while he's been locked up. Somewhere in the rings of prisoners tracing dull circles around the dull yard, he thinks, he'll spot the familiar form of Bill Sikes, and then he'll know. He is destined to be disappointed. A hundred faces avert their eyes from his in the prison yard, but not one of them is Bill.

To avoid the thought of his own trial, he worries the question endlessly: What happened to Bill? There are many possibilities, each as unlikely and undesirable as the last. Maybe he's warming his own cell in Newgate, planning his escape, finding a shadow that will hide him until he can throttle Jacob with his bare hands. Maybe he's staring in silence at the wall of his cell, wearing that haunted look. Maybe he gave the police the slip and is sleeping in a cow pen somewhere in Surrey. Maybe he was killed in the scuffle. Maybe he's already been sentenced. Maybe the bells tolling each midnight hour sound for him.

Once, in the prison yard, he thinks he spots Bill out of the corner of his eye and nearly trips over his own feet from the shock. When he steadies himself, he can see it's only another tall, broad man with a dirty cravat and a short dark beard, who scowls and continues to trace the perimeter of his own circle until they are out of each other's sights.

"Move along," says a warder, shoving Jacob back into motion.

He ducks his head and walks, bent against the wind.

34

The warders were wrong when they said he'd soon be called to the Old Bailey. Or not—Jacob takes pride in his minimal knowledge of how fast the machinery of justice usually moves. Regardless, it's two weeks before a pair of men return to tell him his case will be brought before the judge in fifteen minutes. They don't offer Jacob the chance to wash, and he is still wearing the clothes in which he arrived. Even to his own nose, he's not a sympathetic defendant.

"Couldn't I . . ." Jacob begins, but gives up halfway through as the warder laughs.

His wrists are handcuffed again—it hurts less now than when they brought him in, though the iron still jolts against bone—and the two men escort him down the long halls of Newgate. The prison connects directly to the sessions-house, though he didn't think the way between the two would be so tortuous. It feels as though they walk for hours, turning each corner only to see an identical set of doors, the same windowless stretch of wall. At last, the warders reach the door they're looking for. One catches a tight grip on Jacob's collar while the other slips through the door, too fast for Jacob to see what lies beyond. Jacob's heart pounds so loudly he thinks it must echo off the walls.

The warder returns moments later and nods. "They're ready for you," he says.

It doesn't matter in the slightest whether he is ready for them.

The door opens directly into the dock, a space some seven

feet wide and set apart from the rest of the courtroom by a low wooden wall that reminds him, stupidly, of the prow of a ship. There's a single bench toward the front, and he sinks onto it, his knees weak, though part of him wishes he were the type of man to take his own doom standing. The room is full: the judge in the high-backed chair at the far end of the court, barristers beside, and galleries on both sides filled with faces he can't bring himself to look at, for fear he might know them. He glances at the judge, who takes one look at his filthy appearance and frowns. Jacob winces and drops his gaze. Respectability is everything when negotiating, and he's never been worse positioned for sympathy than he is now.

The business of calling the sessions to order is a blur. The bailiff's voice is loud and ringing and posh, and though Jacob is too rattled to follow the words, the disdain comes through clearly. When his name is spoken as the accused, a woman hisses from the gallery. He keeps his eyes on his shoes. If he focuses there, he might not be in the dock of the Old Bailey. He might in fact be on the deck of some ship, with the waves cresting beneath him as he leaves England and its hangmen behind. It's not running away when a man is on a ship. It's adventure then.

"Jacob Fagin," the judge says. "You have heard the charge brought against you, that of murder in the first degree. How do you plead?"

He didn't hear it. He isn't listening. He is a hundred miles away, off the coast, gazing across slate-gray water in search of land.

"You must plead," the judge says, annoyed now. "God's sake," he says, in a barely lowered voice, to the bailiff. "Is the man an imbecile as well as a vagrant?"

Pride is useless for a man in Jacob's position, but he has always been easy to goad.

"Not guilty, my lord," he says, quietly but firmly.

The gallery erupts in hisses and jeers, and he glances up. A vertiginous mistake, like looking down from the top of St. Paul's. There are dozens of faces here, as if the greater part of Clerkenwell came to watch him meet his end. The hate there freezes him, and he cannot look away. There are so many of them. So many more than the day he was arrested, though some are the same—those who like to see a grisly story through to the end. Most, he assumes, know nothing about him. A trial is public entertainment the same way a hanging is, and "the murderous old Jew of Saffron Hill" sounds like a stock character from a gothic novel, so it's little wonder a crowd has formed. He is going to panic, he is going to be ill, he is going to start screaming here in the dock and the judge will have to rethink his sentence, the noose or the asylum each as likely as the other. It's through this rush of thoughts that he sees one face, among the dozens, that doesn't look angry. A Black man dressed simply but cleanly in blue cambric and a flat cap. Large dark eyes Jacob has looked into more times than he can count, though not lately. Sitting in the back row of the gallery, his shoulders against the wood paneling, as quiet and thoughtful as when he was a child. Jacob stares into the man's face as though it's all that tethers him to life.

Ned Brooks looks back, and almost imperceptibly, he nods.

Never say die, says that nod.

"Not guilty," Jacob says again, firmly, and the proceedings begin.

The barrister for the prosecution comes forward first, a great gaunt man who looks as if he rose from the grave to practice law. He clears his throat before making a grandiloquent opening statement to the jury. Jacob cannot follow a word of it. Fear renders his brain useless, and the barrister speaks in circles and Latin flourishes until his head spins. Isolated phrases leap out at intervals—*plague of crime and violence perpetuated by common villains, leniency being tantamount to encouragement, a mode of living from which our genteel sensibilities recoil.* It all sounds like an essay plucked from the *Spectator,* some champion of the Poor Laws advocating for workhouses that double as charnel houses. The gallery is nodding; they are not the ones the prosecution needs to convince, but nevertheless they are nodding, these common people who are no better than Jacob.

Then the barrister turns to him. "The accused may rise."

He grips the rail of the dock and wills his knees to stop shaking. Jacob is not here, it is some other person on trial, and he knows no more than anyone else in the sessions-house what that man is going to say.

"The morning of September the twenty-third," the barrister says, "you were where, precisely?" The whorls and flourishes have melted away from his words. He speaks as if unconvinced Jacob understands English.

"At home," Jacob whispers.

"The accused is reminded that the court must hear him," the bailiff says loudly.

"At home," he repeats, face burning. "On Bell Court, in Saffron Hill."

"The precise address, if you please," says the barrister.

"There isn't one." There's never been any need. No postman would dare venture so far into the darkness, and any messenger would need only to ask for "the Jew's house at the bottom of the hill" to find his mark.

"Interesting," the barrister says, though it's not clear to whom. "A distinction I do not associate with the finer strains of society."

If Jacob had a proper barrister to defend him, that person would intervene, demand the relevance of this remark, convince the judge to sustain his objection. What Jacob has instead is an elderly man in tiny spectacles who is dozing at his seat and will collect his fee from the court whether his client walks or swings. He has to speak for himself, if anyone is to speak for him.

"I wasn't aware my lodgings were on trial, sir," Jacob says.

The gallery doesn't approve of his being clever. Neither does the barrister. "You will answer questions put to you respectfully," he says, "or you will find yourself additionally charged with contempt of court. So. You were at home. With whom?"

"With Nan."

"With Miss Nancy Reed of Bethnal Green, deceased," the barrister clarifies loftily.

The room is so hot the air seems to ripple. The barrister hasn't asked him another question, and so he doesn't say that Miss Nancy Reed of Bethnal Green would have laughed herself to tears to hear herself so addressed, as if the barrister is announcing her arrival at Clarence House to a ballroom of nobility. The word *deceased* threatens to undo him.

"Tell me in your own words what happened in your house that morning."

Jacob cannot look at the barrister, and so he turns to the gallery, desperate for a single face he can speak to. Ned remains sitting still as marble at the very back. His dark brown eyes are the only ones in the room Jacob is not afraid to meet. He will tell Ned the story, Ned who has come because he wants to know.

"Nan and I had waited all night for Bill," he says. "He was due back days before, and we hadn't heard a word from him. We thought something terrible had happened, so she and I were waiting."

"You are referring, naturally, to William Sikes, also of Bethnal Green," the barrister interrupts. A murmur races through the gallery. Jacob is a curiosity at best, but Bill is well-known to this crowd, his name worth remembering as he always promised it would be. "What is the nature of your relationship with Sikes?"

If Jacob knew the answer to that question, how gladly he would tell the barrister. How different his life would be if a single word could convey the whole of it.

"He's a very old friend," Jacob says.

The barrister hums, unconvinced, but does not press.

"When he came back, finally, he was agitated," Jacob continues. "He and I argued."

"About what?"

"About me," Jacob answers. Half an answer, but a true one. "I'd let him down."

"He was angry with you," the barrister says. The man is beginning to pace now, as though he can hunt down the answers he wants and pounce before they escape.

"Yes."

"How angry?"

"He hated me."

"Your very old friend."

"As a friend hates, yes."

The barrister tightens his lips but does not speak further. It falls to Jacob to go on.

"He was angry. Drew the gun. It wasn't planned. The moment, that was all, the moment."

"Fagin," the barrister interrupts again. "I urge you to be very careful about your next answer. Do you mean to claim that it was Sikes who shot Miss Reed, and that in doing so he was aiming for you?"

It is impossible to agree to a statement presented so bluntly. Jacob's head sags forward, and he draws an unsteady breath. The answer to this question will be a murder, and there's no chance of a lighter sentence this time. When he opens his mouth, it will be to place a pistol at Bill's temple and invite the judge to pull the trigger.

But someone must be guilty, so that he can live.

"I do," he says. "I would never have hurt Nan. I've done many things in my life I know are wicked, but never that, sir. I swear."

I wish I died instead of her, he could say, but doesn't, because he is in a court of law, where lying is forbidden.

"You may be seated, for the present," the barrister says coldly. "Bailiff, kindly introduce the first witness."

This witness, a young woman in a black muslin dress, is a person he recognizes, though he doesn't know her well. A flower seller by the name of Anna, whom he passed in the street a thousand times. Once, she sold him a posy to tuck into the brim of Nan's hat, before they made their way to the theater to rob the audience clean. The girl shakes as she takes her place at the stand, and when she attempts to take the oath, her voice is so quiet the barrister must tell her three times to speak up. The reprimand is delivered kindly, however—Anna is so frightened that for a moment it distracts Jacob from his own fear, wondering how she can stand without collapsing.

"I knew Miss Nancy well," she says, when she recovers herself. "Knew that man of hers too, Sikes. So when I heard shouting in the streets, I went straightaway. I don't know why. Not as if I could help, she'd never let me help before, when he got the way he was. She was a proud one, never liked accepting help from nobody. But I couldn't not go, my lord. You see."

"I do," the barrister says. "A credit to your sex, Miss Gilmore. Can you tell me where you went?"

"The Jew's house on Bell Court," she says, though she doesn't look at him in the dock. "If she weren't in Bethnal Green with her man, that's where she always was, the old house at the bottom of the hill. The Jew had some sort of hold on her, I never was able to work out what it was, whether she owed him money or something worse. But when I heard people in the street saying Miss Nancy's name, I knew she'd be there."

The barrister doesn't interrupt her. Her voice shrank to nothing by the end, and she takes what feels like five minutes to collect herself. Though he refuses to look, Jacob can feel each person in the gallery leaning forward, waiting for Anna's next words. The court doesn't distribute rulings based on public opinion, or so it claims, but in that domain, he has already lost.

"They'd taken the men away when I got there," Anna says. "But I went into that filthy little house, the police had knocked the door down, and there she was, lying on the floor. Her eyes still open. She had the most beautiful eyes, I thought that every time she looked at me."

This is either a polite exaggeration due to the dead or an outright lie. Nan wasn't beautiful. It was part of what made her so dreadfully good at what she did. A person built to disappear. If Anna saw the real beauty of Nan Reed the way Jacob did, she's describing something altogether different.

"The bullet hit her clean in the heart. She can't have lasted long, but the blood was everywhere. I've never seen—"

She gets no further before dissolving into sobs. The barrister waits several moments before intervening, giving the jury adequate time to absorb the spectacle of the crying girl. Jacob wonders how many witnesses they considered and dismissed before finding one tailor-made for the purpose. Bet, who loved Nan like a sister, could tell the same story in a clear voice with her head held high. He scans the gallery again, but no, Bet is nowhere to be seen. He shudders to imagine her reaction when she heard, the violence she must have promised in the name of vengeance. Bet has never been one to bear a loss quietly.

"And this is the Jew whose house your friend died in?" the barrister says.

Anna cannot answer. She merely nods, still without looking at him.

"Thank you, Miss Gilmore," the barrister says, "for your courage in coming today. You may rest assured your friend will find justice, if it is within my power to deliver it."

Anna continues nodding, though the time for questions has passed. She is still weeping as the bailiff ushers her away. The gallery is a steady murmur of hushed voices, *who would believe* and *the poor girl* and *hardly deserves to live.* He can't make out more than one or two words before his ears ring again with panic, and there's nothing but a voice in his ear whispering *guilty, guilty,* never anything but *guilty.*

"Next witness," the judge says.

Jacob forces himself to look up. His stomach drops when he sees little Charley Bates approach the bench, drowning in his man's-length coat. Charley looks even younger than he is before the powerful presence of the judge. The boy is so frightened Jacob can see his knees shaking all the way from the dock. But he stands tall, or as tall as someone who has only just broken four feet can stand. A distant twinge of pride fills Jacob. He taught his boys well, if they can face the world when they have something to gain from it. Taught them when to stand and when to run. Bravo, Charley.

"State your name," the barrister says.

"Charley Bates," Charley says. "And I'm here to say that Mr. Fagin ain't killed nobody."

The gallery doesn't appreciate the opening statement, and the murmur rises toward a roar. The judge is forced to shout to bring the room back to order. All the while, Charley stands firm. He doesn't look at the dock, leaving Jacob to stare at the back of his head. It's better this way. He suspects neither of them has the courage to look the other in the eyes.

"Your relationship to the accused?" the barrister asks.

Jacob winces. Charley has a good heart, but he is not Dodger, is not Ned. He isn't quick enough to come up with words to describe their relationship that won't sound depraved and wicked, if such words even exist, which at the moment Jacob isn't sure they do.

"I live with him," Charley says staunchly. "He teaches me things."

"And what," the barrister says, "has Fagin taught you?"

What indeed.

Jacob sits there in the dock of the Old Bailey, handcuffs chafing his wrists, as Charley Bates describes for the court everything he learned in his two years in Saffron Hill. Charley speaks quickly, as if they told him it will be his body dangling from a rope by nightfall if he doesn't give all the details in the space of a minute. The full story spills out: the lessons, the rotating cast of boys, the stolen goods passing through, the fences and the silver pot and the nights spent picking monograms out of handkerchiefs by the light of a candle stub. Even the barrister seems startled by the level of detail Charley is handing over. It's a smart strategy, Jacob will grant Charley that. Make himself so useful to the court that the odds of his being prosecuted for his own lawbreaking dwindle to nothing. He can respect it, even as he wants to leap to his feet and shout, *No,* shout, *What are you doing, you'll kill me, you ungrateful boy, you've already sent me to die and now you're kicking the bloody stool out from under my feet.* Your own neck before anyone else's. Proof, as if he still needs it, that he's a very good teacher.

"But that day," Charley says, "I heard everything. Came with my mate to listen at the door when we heard shouting, though we kept clear to be safe. It was Bill Sikes with the gun, Bill shouting bloody murder at both Mr. Fagin and Miss Nancy. Bill was in a state, shaken up something awful, and they both was trying to talk him down, and then it was Bill that shot the gun."

Jacob is no longer breathing.

"You're certain?" the barrister says.

"God save me," Charley says. "Dodge and I opened the door, because we was afraid, and we saw it. Was Bill Sikes that killed Miss Nancy. Who he was aiming for I can't say, but this much I know, that Mr. Fagin never touched that gun."

The barrister pauses for a long moment. At last, he nods, the light catching his spectacles and flashing like lightning through the room.

"Boy," he says, "kindly recall that perjuring yourself in a court of law is not only a crime, it is a sin before God. Now. Is this your sworn testimony?"

"Didn't I say it is?" Charley says indignantly.

"None of that," the bailiff says, and he takes Charley by the arm.

"Thank you," the barrister says tightly. "That will be all."

The bailiff ushers Charley away. Through the loud humming in his brain, Jacob finds an inch of himself still capable of amusement as he watches Charley brush off the bailiff's hand like a stately gentleman nudging away an overeager puppy. A sight to behold, how much dignity can be packed into such a little body.

Jacob ducks his head and says nothing as the session proceeds. Other witnesses are called, some he recognizes and others he doesn't, all speaking with relish about the times they saw Jacob creep through the shadows with weighted-down pockets, opining that they never heard a good word about him from anyone. One woman he's never seen in his life takes the stand to declare that she forbade her four children from wandering the streets of Clerkenwell after dark, lest "the monstrous old Jew" snatch them up and enlist them in his army of underage thieves. He wonders how the prosecution came across her, or if she turned up at the

Old Bailey uninvited and asked for the opportunity to vent her hatred. It seems as likely as anything else. The sleepy old barrister tasked with Jacob's defense asks a few pointless questions in a reedy voice, then waves a hand to indicate he has nothing further. Jacob still does not know the man's name.

"Fagin," the judge says at last, once the witness box is cleared for the final time and order is restored to the room. "Is there anything you would add to the testimony we have heard provided here?"

He stands again, as straight as he can manage. "Charley told it as it happened," he says. "That's how it was."

"And the rest of what the boy told us? That's also how it was?"

He could lie. But there are so many people who know the truth of him, so many lives that intersected with his own, that denying it will only invite them to come forward, and he'll be caught out as a perjurer on top of the rest. Besides, it will be Bill's turn before the bench soon, if it hasn't happened already. Bill will tell the story just the same, only more bitterly than Charley, and with more intent to damn. Charley Bates gave him the best framing he's likely to receive before the judge. He must take it, and brace for the worst.

"It is."

The room erupts as if he proclaimed himself to be the devil. The judge must hammer vigorously at the bench to bring them back to order, and even then, the hum of indignation ripples from corner to corner.

"Is there anything you would like to say to the jury in the face of this charge?" the judge says. "Any circumstances it would befit them to know?"

It's a laughable question. The law has made it clear throughout history that circumstances are of no importance. But it is his final chance to say something, and so he draws on his last remaining reserve of courage and says it, as clear as he can manage.

"I took them in," he says. "Charley and the others. I only took in the children no one else wanted. And our trade was to live, by any means necessary. I'm an old man, sir, and a poor one, but I still have the right to live."

He pushed too far, and the judge must fight for order again. If they were in the street and not under the high ceiling of the Old Bailey, the crowd would start to throw stones. He should have kept quiet, should have abased himself and flung himself on the mercy of the judge. A life full of mistakes, and this is to be the one that costs him: the one time he decided to tell the truth.

Jacob is jogging his heel against the floor, so rapidly the floorboards of the dock are creaking, when the judge invites the two barristers to deliver their closing statements to the jury. He hardly hears either man. Every eye in the room feels bright upon him, until he's certain that he's burning, a gas jet alight with the force of their attention. *An unrepentant criminal,* the prosecutor is saying, *a dangerous thief, and certainly an accomplice to violence, if not the perpetrator of the deed itself, which, personally, I find more than probable, but the facts of the matter are for the esteemed members of the jury to determine.* The barrister for the defense takes a tremendous pinch of snuff and sneezes loudly; the prosecutor continues on as if nothing interrupted him.

Then—too soon—the judge invites the jury to confer.

The gallery shifts and talks among itself impatiently, their chatter drowning out the voices of the jury as they huddle on their benches to discuss. In complicated cases, he's heard, jurors retire from the courtroom to deliberate, but for open-and-shut crimes, they reach a verdict where they sit. The public, at least, agrees with the jurors that the case is simple. They all issued their own guilty verdicts the moment they saw his face, cannot believe the jury needs to confer at all before reaching the same obvious conclusion. Jacob peers at the jury, attempting to make out the faces of those who have not turned fully away from him. The man he can see best from his position is sandy-haired and about forty, a prominent mole on the side of his nose. A single hair extends from the mole, which Jacob can see clearly when it catches the light. The world telescopes down to this man's face, this mole, this hair. Jacob feels nothing. Jacob is in agony, every inch of him writhing with it.

The foreman of the jury stands. A deathlike stillness falls over the Old Bailey.

"My lord," says the foreman. "We request permission to retire and to pronounce a verdict in this case after the end of this session, following the trial of William Sikes. We do not feel we can issue an informed verdict without hearing Sikes's testimony."

The building rings with protest. At first, the judge cannot bring them back to order. It is the work of several minutes before an irritable hush descends over the gallery, though dissatisfied murmuring continues. Jacob isn't certain he's breathing. They don't know which man to believe capable of murder. Their fates are tied together, his and Bill's, as they have always been. If one sinks, will he not drag down the other?

"Granted," the judge says. "The trial for Sikes is to be held tomorrow morning. The jury will confer and determine its ruling on both charges upon the conclusion of the proceedings, at which time Fagin will also be called back for sentencing. Are there any final words from the accused before this session is adjourned?"

The terrible radiance of a roomful of eyes. His heart sounds like a hammer against wood, a scaffold constructed under dark of night. There is nothing else to say that won't make his condemnation certain.

"Adjourned," the judge says, and the session is closed.

35

They take him by the shoulders and march him back the way he came, through the stone door and into the maze that connects the Old Bailey to Newgate. He hears the fall of his own footsteps more loudly than before. His body feels as though the skeleton were stripped out of it. He stumbles over nothing, and the warder must haul him to his feet again, cursing, practically dragging him forward.

"You're one of the lucky ones," the warder says. "One more day breathing than you deserve. I'll tell them to start building the gallows early, save them the time."

Jacob says nothing. He isn't sure when his voice will return, if it ever will.

Somehow, though he hardly remembers the journey, he returns to the room he now thinks of as his own. They shove him into the cell, only removing the handcuffs after locking him in by reaching through the bars, but there's no need to take such precautions against his running away. He'd have locked himself up with relief to escape the terrible weight of eyes on him.

The outer door slams over the bars. At last, he is alone.

After the crowded sessions-house, the darkness and silence feel embodied, familiar companions once again. All the energy he poured into staying upright drains from him in a great rush, and he is all at once more tired than he's ever been in his life. He leans forward to hold his head in his hands and is surprised when his palms encounter dampness on his cheeks. He's crying. Was he crying as the warders brought him back? In front of the judge? He hopes not, but he can't be sure. Even now, his tears are silent, as if afraid to disturb the stillness of the cell.

The jury will deliberate. They will listen to Bill and hear the whole story. He will live tonight, at least. After that, they will come together again and decide who will die. But until then, he will wait.

The hours pass strangely, now like sand through fingers and then with muleheaded slowness, and though he's certain he's too frightened to close his eyes, he dozes nonetheless. The body cannot operate under such strain for so long. He doesn't care enough to sling the hammock, curling up instead on the cold floor with his cheek leaned against the wall. It's as much as he deserves, to sleep against cold stone, and to find ghosts waiting for him there.

In his dream, Jacob is in the back room of the Three Cripples. The windows are in their proper places, the curtains pulled back, but instead of the dirty courtyard he knows so well, he looks out onto a dark, thick forest, one he's never seen but that seems perfectly natural where it is. Trees press up against the public-house, rattling their branches against the glass in a wind he cannot feel. Beams of light shoot down irregularly through some distant wooded canopy, filtered into a patchwork of night and day. Inside, a magpie sits on the mantel where, in a gentleman's house, one might find a coat of arms. The bird watches him as he hunches his shoulders. It is colder than he expects, in the dream.

In front of the ashen hearth, the magpie watching over her shoulder, is Nan.

She looks just the same as ever, the curls in her hair steadily going limp, crushed hat in one hand. If not for the blood that stains the bodice of her dress, it might be any other day. From the look on her face, he's not sure she's come to terms with the fact that she is dead. She looked at him with similar disappointment many times before in life.

"Fagin," she says.

"I'm sorry," he says automatically.

"You aren't," she tells him, and of course she's right. He's sorry it happened, but not for anything he did. Or rather, he's sorry for everything he did, but he'd do nothing differently if given a second chance, and remorse like that isn't worth the words used to describe it.

"Sit down," he says after a moment, though he doesn't move toward the table, remains standing and huddled against the cold.

Her laugh is punctuated by branches tapping against the glass. "I'm not here, Fagin, I can't. What did they do with my body?"

No voice should ever be able to ask that question. She moves away from the mantel, toward him, and though he draws back, he's still relieved by her nearness. So long as she's haunting him, it's not final, not yet.

"I don't know," he says, and then, because he's ashamed of that answer, "Dodger stayed with you."

"Is this your way of telling me to go haunt Jack?" The tilt of her head is familiar, almost playful. The blood still seems to flow from her chest. The stain over her heart is now twice the size it was when he arrived.

"No," he says. She takes a step nearer, until she's so close he could dip his fingertips in her blood. "No, don't leave me, Nan."

"You deserve to be left," she says, and now her voice is layered through with Bill's like the threat of thunder. "It was meant to be you."

"I know," he says.

What kind of monster does it make him that beneath his grief, he's glad Bill missed?

The trees rattle against the windows of the Three Cripples, the forest itself edging nearer. Nan takes one step toward Jacob, her face set.

The magpie surges up from the mantel in a hurricane of feathers and plunges its beak into his chest, piercing through to gouge out his heart.

The pain is so real it shocks him awake.

He sits bolt upright in his cell with a shout, a single beam of moonlight filtering through the narrow window. He's breathing hard, drenched in sweat. His heart burns. The silence is as complete as it's ever been, but he still hears her voice, as clear as though she sits beside him.

"I won't come again, Fagin. But I'll haunt you the rest of your life. I can promise you that."

He doesn't sleep again that night. Nan's face reappears every time he closes his eyes, until at last the light through the narrow window begins to shift, and it is dawn, and then it is day. Breakfast appears through the slat in the door, a mug of cocoa and a dish of gruel he leaves untouched where they place it. When the outer door beyond the bars opens at last, he assumes the warder came to take away the untouched food, or to bring him back to the Old Bailey, to tell him his time is up. He keeps his gaze on his knees. If the judge wants him back, they will have to tell Jacob it's time: he won't sign his own death warrant. But no one says anything. He feels their presence, but they wait, and much as he hates to give them the satisfaction, curiosity gets the better of him in the end.

Through the bars, he can see into the corridor, which remains dim but nonetheless shows a light he judges to be late afternoon. One warder stands near the door, a youngish man he does not recognize. Beside him are two people, well-dressed and visibly out of place in the squalor of the prison. One is an utter stranger: an elderly gentleman with fine white whiskers and an elegant black frock coat, who looks down his nose at Jacob with the familiar distaste of the wealthy. He could be any rich fellow Jacob robbed over the decades, no more memorable than any of the shillings that filled his pockets.

The second person, Jacob very much does recognize.

For a moment, he's not sure he's truly awake. The ghost before his eyes seems every bit as real as the ones in his mind.

"This is him, Oliver, my boy?" says the white-haired man.

And little Oliver Twist—dressed as a Mayfair gentleman, clean as a new penny, his wide blue eyes the picture of childhood innocence, Oliver Twist with his nine lives—he looks up at the old man and nods solemnly. "Yes, Mr. Brownlow, sir," Oliver says. "That's Mr. Fagin."

This thieving little sneak who Bill swore up and down was pierced with bullet holes and bleeding out in a ditch, the little boy who is the cause of so much death, now standing proud and swell as anything, with that sanctimonious stare. Jacob could embrace him in relief. Could throttle the boy with his bare hands just as easily.

"Oliver, my dear," he says, and then must clear his throat, for he's spoken perhaps twenty words in as many hours. He hoists himself up from the floor but does not approach the boy. Nonetheless, the gentleman tightens his grip on Oliver's arm, as though Jacob could wrench the bars apart and come for their throats. "You look well. We were worried."

"I'll eat my hat if you were," Mr. Brownlow says. "Master Oliver was insistent we come, to confirm his kidnapper has found justice at last."

Jacob can only stare. Kidnapper indeed. But of course what else would they call it, a boy like this and a man like him? From kidnapping it is a quick step to murder, to grinding boys' bones and blood into matzos. Mr. Brownlow is congratulating himself for helping Oliver escape becoming another Little Saint Hugh, captured and tortured and crucified by a cabal of wicked Hebrews as punishment for the fervor of his blue-eyed faith in Christ. Jacob doesn't blame Oliver for upholding the tale—had they switched places, he would have done the same. Life is for the living, after all. And he's too far gone for any of it to matter anymore.

"Tell me this, at least, my boy," he says, and now he does approach them, bracing himself on the wall. Mr. Brownlow tightens his grip on Oliver's shoulder. His legs do not work properly anymore. Neither does his tongue, to ask the question, but he forces it out before he loses his nerve. "Bill's sentence. Has it come down?"

He knows the answer from the satisfied gleam behind Mr. Brownlow's spectacles, but it still cuts to the heart when the man says it. "Guilty. Sentenced to hang on Friday. It's in all the papers."

"Here," Oliver says quietly. "I thought you would like to see."

Oliver extends one hand through the bars, a piece of newsprint in his fingers. Jacob lunges for it like a starving tiger in a zoo, before the warder or Mr. Brownlow can usher Oliver safely beyond his reach. His fist crushes the newsprint, and he snatches it into the cell, as determined to hold on to it as any beast with a scrap of meat. He is breathing hard now, though he scarcely exerted himself. Oliver watches him soberly. He will not, he knows, ever lay eyes on this boy again.

"You had the makings of someone great, you know," he says to the boy. "I've an eye for such things. If you'd let me teach you, you could've been better than any of them."

Oliver raises his chin until he looks Jacob in the eyes. It feels, for a moment, like looking directly into the sun.

"I mean to be a virtuous gentleman, Mr. Fagin," he says. "I mean to fear God, and do good, and live an honest life."

Jacob has known his share of liars and thieves and sinners, but none of them ever held a candle to Oliver Twist. He smiles faintly. "Do you know, my boy," he says, "you just might, at that."

"Come now," Mr. Brownlow says, taking Oliver by the hand. He is already ushering the boy away, and the warder is turning to close the outer door, which the old man's last words slip past just before it shuts. "You've seen what you came to. That fiend can't harm you anymore."

The moment the door closes, Jacob rushes to the narrow beam of light from the window, which barely lets him make out the words. Smoothing the crumpled newspaper against the wall, he scans the stories, until the one he is searching for leaps from the page.

BETHNAL GREEN HOUSEBREAKER TO HANG FOR MURDER

AT THIS MORNING'S SESSIONS at the Old Bailey, famed burglar and notorious criminal William Sikes was condemned to hang by the neck until dead for a grisly murder committed two weeks since in a thieves' den in Little Saffron Hill. The victim, one Nancy Reed, was a thief and woman of low character, aged thirty, and according to testimony the paramour of the thirty-seven-year-old housebreaker for several years, though no formal or legal relationship was ever established between the pair. Sikes bore his sentence stoically and said nothing to the judge as he was escorted from the room, though his silence stood in stark contrast to his behavior throughout the trial, during which Sikes swore wildly and seemed to start at small noises. Sikes will be hanged at the Newgate gallows on Friday at midday. His conspirator, fifty-one-year-old Jacob Fagin, the Jew and petty thief in whose house the murder took place and who is also charged for his role in the crime, will be sentenced this afternoon. We will faithfully report the verdict of this related trial in our evening edition.

He crumples the paper and throws it aside, though there isn't far for it to go. It bounces once against the wall and comes to rest at his feet, where it looks up at him accusingly. He stands there useless, staring back at it.

Bill deserves his sentence.

With Nancy gone, Bill is all Jacob has left in the world.

This time Friday, both Bill and Nancy will be dead.

All three of these facts can be true at once.

He is alone and he is not, because his father stands beside him now. Silent. Observing only. There, at last, is the emotion Jacob hasn't allowed himself to feel since the walls of Newgate closed in around him. There, at last, is the anger.

"Say something," he yells. "You could speak well enough, couldn't you, when you thought I was dead? Well, I'm for the gallows now, just like you. Speak, if there's something you want me to hear!"

Jacob has spoken so little these past two weeks that the shout grates at his throat, like each word rakes sandpaper through him on its way out. His father looks at him with the sort of pity reserved for creatures that cannot save themselves, rats and insects and half-drowned things. The man opens his mouth as if to speak, but at that moment the bell tolls from the church nearby, counting the hour. Two strokes, slow and ponderous. His father does not close his mouth until the echoes die away.

Somewhere, Jacob knows, Bill is sitting in the same prison, listening to the same bells.

36

They return for him before the hour is out, as the newspapers promised. This time, he is ready for them. Before they finish opening the door, he's on his feet, only the crumpled newspaper proof he ever spent a moment here. Whatever happens in the Old Bailey, he won't be coming back to this cell. Either he will be turned loose, which he can't allow himself to hope for, or he will be taken to the cells reserved for those condemned to die. Maybe he'll be able to hear Bill cursing from the cell beside his while they wait. He isn't sure how thick the walls are. By their nature, he's never met anyone who's seen them and lived to tell of it.

Jacob mutely extends his wrists and allows the warders to cuff them and lead him out. No one speaks. There doesn't seem to be much point.

The courtroom is as full as it was during the previous session, the crowd in the galleries falling to a hush on their own initiative as he enters. He feels the weight of their macabre interest, like pedestrians hoping to see a crushed leg through the wheel spokes of an overturned carriage. Jacob stands at the front of the dock, ignoring the bench. He allows himself one brief scan of the galleries, but he recognizes no one. Ned, it seems, has decided not to return, and Charley's role in the trial has been as witness only, not as spectator. Better that way. He can't be certain what he will do when the judge passes sentence. Better they remember him as they knew him, and not as whatever he's going to be today.

For the judge is here, now, bringing the session to order, and soon there will be no more time to wonder. The judge turns to the jury, the same motley assemblage of men who watched Jacob's trial only the day before.

"Has the jury reached its verdict?" the judge asks.

The foreman stands and clears his throat. "We have, my lord."

Every head in the gallery turns to the foreman. A few lean off the edge of their seats so as not to miss a word. Jacob isn't sure he'll be able to hear the man over the roaring of his own heart.

"Deliver it, then," says the judge.

The foreman clears his throat again, then speaks, and each word reaches the farthest corners of the Old Bailey, clear as any actor on the stage.

"On the charge of murder in the first degree, we the jury find the defendant Jacob Fagin not guilty."

All the iron vanishes from Jacob's legs. If not for the wooden rail of the dock, which he grips with both chained hands, he'd sink to his knees.

Not guilty. It doesn't matter that it's true. It's the last thing he expected to hear.

The crowd is of the same mind, for the courtroom becomes a riot. The people here made the trip to the Old Bailey for the second day in a row to see a man condemned to death, and the foreman snatched the gift of a double hanging from their hands. The judge hammers away at the bench with his gavel, demanding quiet, but it doesn't matter. Let them shout. Let the whole world scream itself hoarse, for all Jacob cares.

Not guilty, they said.

The foreman raises one hand, and the crowd quiets again. There is, it seems, more.

"On the additional counts of theft and receiving of stolen goods, with which the defendant has subsequently been charged based on the evidence presented at trial, we the jury find Jacob Fagin guilty."

How the crowd responds, he cannot say. Can barely hear

the judge, as though the next words arrive from an impossible distance.

"The sentence for these charges is fourteen years' transportation to the penal colonies of New South Wales, to be carried out as soon as is reasonable. Fagin will be transferred to Millbank Prison in the interim, to await the next ship departing for the colonies. The court is hereby adjourned."

Fourteen years' transportation.

In fourteen years, he will be sixty-five.

In more than fifty years of life, he has never gone farther from London than Epsom. He has never set foot on a ship larger than a Thames ferry. He has never seen the ocean. For every day of his life, London has filled his veins like blood and his lungs like breath. For the first moment after he hears the sentence, fourteen years abroad feels like a fate worse than hanging.

There's no time to gauge how the crowd responds. The warders take him by the collar and march him out of the courtroom, through the little door into the halls of Newgate. Somewhere he finds it in him to be grateful for the protection. He saw it in their eyes, these people who came to be sure he hangs—if he had to pass under their noses to reach the street, they would kill him themselves. But he is back in the labyrinth of Newgate, and they cannot touch him here.

And then he is out of the courtroom, flung back into his cell, for what he now knows to be one of a dwindling number of nights he will spend in the only country he has ever known.

But he is here. In this cell. Again. It should be impossible, but he is here.

It rises slowly in him, a feeling he can't name, while he sits awake in his darkened cell waiting for he doesn't know what. A sort of electricity in his chest, charging every breath so that his ribs spark and contract. It makes him want to scream, sing, weep, laugh, makes him want to feel everything a man can feel all at once and surfeit himself on the excess. It is, he realizes with a jolt, relief.

He is going to live.

It's not a life he understands, not one he can imagine, but it is life, which means it isn't death, and all at once he is possessed by a relief so great and terrible that he bursts into tears like a child. If it makes him a coward, then he is a coward. All his life he feared nothing more than the noose, and though he will still die someday, perhaps soon, it will not be tomorrow. The bells now tolling through the city are a preemptive knell for tomorrow's executed criminals, these bells are for Bill Sikes, but they are not for him.

Jacob hugs his knees to his chest, shivering with joy and fear and grief and cold and a thousand emotions he does not have the wit left to name, and he sobs until his head aches and his face is tearstained and swollen. The warders without, if they hear him—and they hear him—let him be.

The bells toll on through the dark, measuring out the final hours of Bill's life. Jacob sits awake all night to count them.

37

Jacob prays the next day as the sun comes up. The last time he prayed was nearly forty years ago, but as the beams of light inch into his cell heralding the arrival of Friday morning, he prays with single-minded, near-demented focus. Tears stain his cheeks as he murmurs the words under his breath, knowing that if any of the warders hear him they will consider him fully mad, and not caring in the slightest what they think.

He has never said this particular prayer aloud—his first occasion to use it, the death of his mother, was also the occasion of his severance from God—but the words come nonetheless, close at hand when they are needed. They have always been there, in his bones and his blood, in the cheaply bound books he brought away from his mother's house. Maybe Leah is the one speaking the words, not him. He doesn't know why else God might listen to anything he has to say.

His father does not join him in the cell, but even so, Jacob doesn't lack company. There in the sunlight beside him sits a child of thirteen, his bruised face smeared with dirt. The boy hugs his knees and listens to the rhythm of the prayer, though he doesn't understand a word of it. He watches Jacob unblinkingly as the minutes tick away, unflinching and stubborn as a bull terrier. Occasionally, Jacob thinks he sees the boy's eyes grow damp, but it's only a trick of the light. They are only glittering, forged hard like diamonds. Even at thirteen, this boy would not cry for such a trifle.

The girl sits opposite them both, her back to the bars. Both she and the magpie on her shoulder watch Jacob with iron eyes as he prays. God alone knows what she is thinking.

Today's hanging is to take place at noon precisely. He continues to pray long after the hour, in case it takes longer than usual for the prisoner to die. In case a few extra words will tip the scales, for any of them.

"Amen," he says to the boy and the girl and the empty room.

The bell tolls one, as if in agreement.

38

Next day—apparently the law does no other work on a hanging day—a pair of warders arrive in lieu of breakfast and strong-arm him into the corridor and through the front gate, into the waiting prison van. He allows them to manhandle him without protest. He still feels as though he's inhabiting a body that's not his own, each movement as stiff as borrowed clothes.

The journey through the city is silent. Before long, the warders pile him unceremoniously through the gates of what must, he supposes, be Millbank Prison. There's hardly a moment to glance up at the building's broad stone edifice before they usher him through the door, down a narrow corridor, and into a receiving room of some sort. Here, it seems, he is expected.

The room is freezing. Not only has the young clerk at the desk left his greatcoat on, but he also wears a pair of knitted fingerless gloves, so that he can still make use of a pen. The man barely glances up at Jacob and the warders escorting him before twitching a new sheet of paper onto the blotter, making a few desultory notes at the top. Jacob—his own wrists still chained—directs the whole of his attention to the man's gloves, the fine soft palms they enclose. Most likely a sweetheart knitted them, thinking of her fellow's blue and chapped hands chilled all day in the house of detention. He has never before felt such disdain for a pair of gloves.

"Name?" the clerk says, bored.

"Jacob Fagin," says one warder. The elder of the two assigned him in Newgate, though still fifteen years Jacob's junior.

The clerk purses his lips and notes it down. "Age?"

"Fifty-one."

"Prior convictions?"

"None." Jacob smiles to himself. It's still something to be proud of.

"Of what parish?"

The warder doesn't answer; clearly this one he doesn't know. Jacob clears his throat. He hasn't spoken a word since yesterday, when he prayed to an empty room until his body ached.

"None," he says—not meaning to be clever, but also not interested in being helpful—though as the clerk looks up from the paper with a rapidly expiring store of patience, he amends: "Jewish, of Saffron Hill, Clerkenwell."

The clerk's brow lowers. "All prisoners at Millbank are expected to attend daily prayers of the Established Church as well as Sunday chapel, unless they receive express dispensation from the governor. I shall make a note to forward the case for review."

"Thank you," Jacob says. "Although it will be a shame to miss what I'm told is the best chaplain of all the London prisons. I like a bit of poetry as much as the next man."

Now he's being difficult on purpose, with a giddy recklessness that crept up when he wasn't paying attention. The other warder cuffs him on the back of the head, but he hardly feels the blow. What does it matter? What else can they do to him? He is only stopping here on the way off the edge of the world. Bill Sikes is dead, and Nancy. No one here can hurt him more than he's already been hurt. It is an unhinged, ungovernable feeling that fills him to the tips of his fingers, glowing like an illuminated street.

"Crime and sentence," the clerk says coldly.

"Theft and receiving stolen goods," the first warder says. "Fourteen years' transportation."

"Very good," the clerk says, which strikes Jacob as a somewhat perverse response. "He will be housed at Millbank until his papers are complete and the next ship is ready to depart. Until then, he will be set to labor at a task suited to his age and sentence, at the pleasure of the governor. Does he know his letters?"

It's ridiculous, that of all the degradations he faced in the past week, this is the one that makes him lose his temper. "Read and write in two languages," he snaps, before the warder can answer, "and better than you in both."

The clerk's lips thin to such an extent he seems to have swallowed them. "Read that, then," he says, and points over Jacob's shoulder.

He follows the clerk's finger to a gilt frame that hangs above the unlit hearth. The letters within are small, and his eyesight from a distance is not what it once was, but he'll be damned if he gives the clerk with his fine knitted gloves another reason to feel superior, and so he squints and reads aloud.

"'There are six things that the Lord hates, seven that are an abomination to him: haughty eyes, a lying tongue, and hands that shed innocent blood, a heart that devises wicked plans, feet that make haste to run to evil, a false witness who breathes out lies, and one who sows discord among brothers.' Which ought to be a relief to me," he says, turning back to the clerk, "as nowhere in that list do I see receiving stolen goods, certainly *my* feet aren't the ones that ran anywhere—"

"If you don't hold your tongue," the second warder says, gripping Jacob by the back of the neck, "I'll see you lose it."

"He will not be enrolled in the prison school, then," the clerk says waspishly, "though he may make use of the lending library. There are a number of religious tracts there for his edification. Move him on to the next room."

It's a small, useless pleasure, to rile the clerk and get away with it. But he takes that minor satisfaction with him as the warders hustle him forward and hand him over to a Millbank guard in a small stone-floored chamber. The new warder, a heavyset man who towers over Jacob like a great tree, takes charge at once: removes his manacles, orders him to strip naked, and pushes him into a cold bath; shoves a bundle of gray prison clothes into his arms; forces him onto a stool to shear off his hair and beard until only a reddish stubble remains. Even the rough handling of the warder can't take his last ounce of pride, which Jacob clutches like a treasure. At least one man in Millbank has been forced to acknowledge him as a person.

It's not a victory, but it's more than he deserves, and he holds it close in the corridors, in the workroom, in his own narrow cell, like a candle flame in the dark.

He is a person, and he is alive.

Millbank is built for oblivion. Every day is the same, the long hours spent in one high-ceilinged room with fifty other men picking oakum fibers out of great coils of rope until the calluses at the tips of his fingers are hard and white and his joints ache in ways he didn't know were possible. Meals on tin trays pushed through the slat in the door, exercise in the yard, lights off as soon as the clock strikes eight, complete darkness until seven the next morning. The monotony is meant to torment, and for others no doubt it does, but to Jacob it has a soporific effect. He is only marking time here. It's barely a life, and so he wastes no thoughts on how he is meant to live it.

He eats every bite of what they give him and still feels his clothes growing looser, yet he is hardly aware of being hungry. He receives no letters, no special privileges, is prohibited under the separate system from speaking to the other prisoners and barely exchanges a word with any of the warders. So it is a consummate surprise when one of the guards comes to his door and informs him he has a visitor.

"I don't want to see anyone," he says. No doubt it's a lady from one of the charitable societies who's read about him in the papers and is eager to convert him before he's sent away.

The guard rolls his eyes and unlocks the door. "You don't write to anyone, you don't read, you don't go to chapel, if you weren't eating your rations I'd think you were a ghost. Can't you be an ordinary person for one moment and be glad when someone comes to visit?"

Jacob cannot think of a person he'd like to see who isn't already dead. His heart jolts toward panic as the guard secures the cuffs around his wrists. The old instinct to fight back rises up again, and he digs in his heels, refusing to be led.

"Who is it?"

"Damned if I know," the guard says. "Some Black fellow. Brought a dog. Told him a hundred times it wasn't allowed, but he wasn't having none of it. And I didn't like my odds fighting either him or the dog. Nice friends you have, can tell you that much."

Jacob follows the guard out.

The visitation room is divided into cells on the prisoners' side of the wall, each fronted by a small, barred window that looks out onto the open hallway where the visitors wait to speak to the inmates. In the cell beside his, before the guard shunts him into the small alcove and he can see nothing to either side, he spots a man who looks no more than twenty, speaking in a low voice to a woman who seems to be his mother. The prisoner presses his palm to the grate, and his mother raises her own in kind, but the bars are such that though they can no doubt feel the warmth of each other's hands, they cannot quite touch. He wonders for a moment what they're saying, whether the young man will have a place to return to after his sentence, if his sentence is the kind that has an *after*. And then the door to his visitation cell is locked behind him, and he can only look straight ahead at the familiar face who has come, for reasons unknown, to see him.

"Ned, my dear," he says. "You look well."

It's true, surprisingly. Ned Brooks settled into manhood with unexpected ease. There's a healthy beard on his chin, and he fills out the broader line of his shoulders as though he has in recent years had enough to eat. His clothes are simple, but they are clean and well-made. He wonders if Ned has a young woman at home who takes charge of the mending. It would be no surprise if so:

Ned has always been handsome, and more than that he's kind. And a good hand with a needle himself, Jacob suddenly recalls, from the nights they used to spend picking monograms out of silk handkerchiefs before bundling them for sale. Ned might still be doing his own mending after all.

"You look like death warmed over," Ned says frankly.

Jacob's laugh sounds like it ought to come out of a grave. "The fact I look like anything at all is worth celebrating," he says. "Did you really bring the bloody dog?"

Ned grins—it seems almost vulgar, that such a bright smile should exist in such a place—and bends down. If Jacob cranes his neck just right, he can see Bullseye's broad white body sitting at Ned's side, leaning up into Ned's hand for a scratch between the ears. The dog is wearing a collar and a leash, he notes. Jacob has never seen that before, but Bullseye seems taken with it. He even sits up a little more proudly, like a new-minted gentleman wearing a silk cravat for the first time.

"Turned up at my door the night after you were arrested," Ned says. "Wouldn't stop scratching until I let him in. I thought he was the police at first, but Jane wouldn't let me send him away. Said he'd never done anyone any harm."

That sentiment might be true for most stray dogs, but it's certainly not the case for Bullseye. Even so, the picture of it pleases Jacob. Ned sitting with his feet up in front of a fire, and Bullseye napping at his side, and someone named Jane reading the paper, someone with enough spirit in her to tell Ned what to do.

"Do the police still turn up at your door?" he asks, by which he means *Are you still in the trade I taught you,* and *Will you be in here yourself before too long?*

"Not anymore," Ned says. "A Chancery clerk in Billingsgate took me on as apprentice. Pay's not much, but it's easy work, and I don't mind it."

"A Chancery clerk," Jacob repeats, and whistles. "First time one of mine ever saw the court from that side of the dock, I can promise you that."

He means it as a joke, but it's hard for anything to come off lightly in Millbank, and the brightness in Ned's eyes fades. They're sharing the same thought, he's quite sure. He doesn't like to ask it, but he knows Ned will never tell him on his own.

"Did you go?" he asks.

He isn't sure what he hopes to hear. He already read about Bill Sikes's final hours in the paper, which Millbank's schoolmaster kindly brought for him; it seems impossible that hearing it in the voice of someone he knows will make the image any more palatable. Still, Ned was there in the gallery the day of his own trial. Multiple times that familiar face was all that kept him from breaking down in tears. Did Bill have such a face in the crowd for him too?

Ned shakes his head. "Was only you I cared what happened to," he says. "That man killed one of the best people I've ever known, and I'm glad he's dead. You weren't ever like him, Mr. Fagin. Not like that."

The visiting room is designed in such a way that if he leans, he can see the mother of the young prisoner beside him, though he can no longer see her son. The woman is crying now. She fights a valiant battle to do so without sound, but every so often, he hears the catch of her breath. Jacob wants to ask Ned to reach out to the woman, to take her hand and squeeze it. *It'll be all right, love,* he wants to say. *Your boy will be out in under a year, see if he isn't. It could be worse. You could have a son like me.*

"You didn't really know him, Ned," Jacob says. "He was just like me."

The blaze is up in Ned's face now. Bullseye growls from just out of sight. Ned tightens his grip on the dog's collar, and the growl quiets.

"You're making excuses for him," Ned says. "After what he did. You're still here, saying it's all right. Saying it's nothing, that he killed her. That he would have killed you."

"I'm not," Jacob says. "He was a wicked man who did the worst things that can be done, and if you believe in hell, he's there burning right now. He was shameful, small, selfish, cruel, vicious, and there's no forgiveness for that. But he was a man," he says, quietly, "and my friend, and I loved him. That's all I mean to say."

For several long minutes, the only sound is the stifled sobs of the woman standing beside Ned. Jacob cannot look at him, but there is nowhere else to look, and so his eyes go soft and lose focus, until the difference between the metal grate and Ned's face is nothing more than a guess.

"There's a ship at Gravesend now making ready for Sydney Cove," Ned says at last. "Captain means to set off within the fortnight."

This is new information to Jacob, despite the fact that he and his fellow prisoners will be the ones to fill the hull of that ship. "How do you know?"

"Asked," Ned says with a shrug. "Been asking, since your sentence came down."

"I'll imagine you seeing me off," he says. "Waving some bloody white handkerchief."

Ned scoffs, but there's a softness to the sound. "I won't be there."

"I know," Jacob says. "I said I'll imagine it, that's all."

The woman beside them dries her eyes on the back of her hand and gathers her coat. Ned glances over his shoulder—whatever catches his attention is out of Jacob's line of sight, but it must tell him that visiting hours are soon over, and that if he knows what's good for him he too will leave Millbank directly. He shifts his weight, trapped between staying and going.

"Go," Jacob says, and tries for a smile. "Back to your posh job and your pretty girl. Thank you for coming. But don't you ever come through this door again, Ned, do you understand me?"

Ned winks, and it's as if Jacob is looking through two decades collapsed on themselves, to a young boy with bloodied feet and no coat, hungry to make a name for himself in the world. They've both done so, in their own way. At some point, their paths split, his and Ned's, and he can't for the life of him point to the moment where he went wrong.

"Don't you worry, Mr. Fagin," Ned says. "You taught me well."

Ned drifts after the crying mother, sauntering easily across the stone floor. One hand is casually in the pocket of his coat. The other keeps a loose hold on the dog's leash. Just before they pass through the door, Bullseye barks, only once, as if determined to have the last word. To Jacob's ears, it sounds like Bill Sikes laughing.

39

1839

SYDNEY COVE, NEW SOUTH WALES

Through the dimly lit hold of the *Prince Regent* comes the sound of someone shouting abovedecks.

Jacob forces himself to sit up properly, though it makes every muscle ache. He has grown used to the rhythms of the ship's crew after more than four months aboard, and now he knows their voices and curses and footsteps as well as he knows the sound of his own heart. He can recognize the rush of activity before a storm, the quick scattering of crewmen before they drop anchor to resupply and stretch their legs ashore, the laughter and snatches of song when the crew allow themselves a night to forget their duties and revel in drunken freedom. Whatever is happening now, it's something new.

The shouts are growing louder, followed by the tramp of feet venturing below. All around him, his fellow convicts murmur to one another, and more than one breaks into quiet prayer, but Jacob remains still and silent. If the Royal Navy has come for him, he will face them like a man. At least it will be a change. The voyage was a nightmare, every day of it, spent chained by the ankles to a dozen other men in a hold too low for them even to stand. The chains, above all, he finds ridiculous: as if there were anywhere they could run to in the middle of the Atlantic, or halfway round the Cape of Good Hope. The smell, too, is unbearable. One bucket for every dozen men, dumped over the side of the ship only when the crew can be bothered to remember. The sea beneath them was so different from the Thames that it felt dishonest to call them both water, and he was violently ill for the first four days, which earned him no friends until the ship hit a proper storm and then they were all sick, all at once, and there was no longer any point in holding a grudge over it.

"You think this is it?" says Marsden. He is a counterfeiter from Leeds, likewise sentenced to fourteen years, who decided that he and Jacob are the kind of friends who talk casually at such moments, despite Jacob's lack of encouragement. Still, Jacob answers, because they've been joined at the ankle for four months and there's nothing else left to do in this darkened space under the sea but answer questions put to him. He has so adjusted to the shadows that when he feels the sun again he wonders if he'll simply crumble like dry paper to flame.

"Must be," he says.

"Reckon this is goodbye, then," Marsden says. "They'll have me at hard labor, but Christ knows what use they'll find for your ancient bones, old man. I'd say bait for the sharks, but there ain't enough meat on you to feed a baby one."

Marsden's attempt at reassurance leaves something to be desired. Before Jacob can tell him so, the booted feet of the *Prince Regent*'s crew descend into the hold. Whatever future awaits them, the time has come to face it.

Jacob's first thought when he sets foot on deck is that there's been a mistake, that they have not sailed to the southern edge of the world but into the very arms of the sun. He cannot see anything, and the pain of keeping his eyes open is unbearable, so he relies on the steady tug of the chains around his ankles to guide him forward, across the deck and into a longboat, which feels precarious after acclimating to a vessel twenty times its size. The boat tips as twelve chained men settle themselves awkwardly, sailors shouting curses but making no effort to help the men keep their balance. Slowly, bit by bit, he allows himself to crack his eyes open, and the pain is still sharp but he forces himself to bear it, because the terror of sitting in the heaving dark is worse.

The land rises up above the impossibly blue water, a tiny city at the end of the world. Reddish roofs over low whitewashed houses, scattered at irregular intervals up a low rise, surrounded by half-sown fields and twisted black trees. At the highest point he can see sits the tallest building, a church with a rough-and-ready steeple that hoists its cross up into a sky that has never heard of such a thing before, proclaiming the grace of a God that Jacob can't imagine holds any interest for the native people who behold it.

And beyond the little settlement, nothing. Vast, empty land, stretching on beyond the horizon. There are people there, he's heard tell, ones that ships like his will continue to push back as they empty more convicted English and Irish and Scots into this vast island. But from here, after months spent breathing the stale air of other men, it feels that the dozen people in this boat are the only living beings under the sky. The Union Jack, fluttering from the flagpole at the end of the dock, has never seemed more out of place. Against the universe of land behind it, it looks like a child's toy.

Jacob leans forward until he is more out of the longboat than in it. He has never seen so far in his life. There are no walls here, no courts, no buildings layered three deep off twisting streets with windows that open onto the bricks of their neighbors. Just trees and hills and grasses that dance in a breeze unbroken by any obstacle, and the calls of birds overhead, songs he has never heard before. He tilts his head back to watch them wheel above, searching for fish under the waves around the longboat. All his life, he was at most three feet away from another person, breathing their air, listening to the pounding of their heart. The expanse of sky above him and the sea below is emptiness of a sort he has never considered.

It is terrifying, and yet he is not afraid.

"Watch it," says one of the crewmen, who grabs Jacob by the collar and yanks him back into the longboat. "Didn't keep you alive for four months only for you to drown yourself."

He says nothing. For once, he doesn't feel the need to have the last word.

His legs are shaky when they guide him onto the dock. More than one of his fellow convicts falls to their knees at their first touch of dry land, unsettled and enraptured by the stillness. But Jacob stands as tall as he is able, and he breathes as deep as his lungs will let him.

They will find a use for him. He will work, building roads or making bricks or working the fields of a colonist whom the crown considers his better, and he will be beaten when he fails to meet expectations and ignored entirely when he satisfies them. He will work this way for fourteen years, or as many of them as he's able to survive on meager rations in an unfamiliar climate rife with diseases he is not prepared for, and when he dies, they will chip out a little patch of hot clay and leave him there, under the songs of foreign birds, fourteen thousand miles from the little room on Copley Street where he was born. It's the end the world has always foreseen for him, a criminal's end, a grave no one will visit.

But he is alive today.

Jacob looks behind him, back toward the *Prince Regent.* He already knows what he will see before he turns. Knows the familiar eyes that will look out at him from beneath the broad-brimmed hat, knows the iron manacles that will gleam more brightly under the sun of New South Wales than they ever did against the London fog. Part of him even looks forward to a glimpse of his father—one familiar sight in a world that has become so wholly uncharted.

But there is no one there. He is, possibly for the first time, entirely alone.

His gaze passes unbroken across the pier to the ship, and beyond it the sea. He didn't know water could be so blue. When the sun sets behind it, the stars will rise in numbers uncountable, in shapes and patterns he never imagined. He wonders what stories they will tell, those stars his father never laid eyes on. Whether they will unfold in a language he understands, or one he will have to learn.

There is, he supposes, only one way to find out.

"Move on," says the crewman, shoving Jacob forward along the dock.

And Jacob does, still thinking of the stars.

AUTHOR'S NOTE

Charles Dickens published *Oliver Twist* serially in *Bentley's Miscellany* between 1837 and 1839. It was a hit right away, though some pearl-clutching readers decried it as sensationalized, melodramatic, and inappropriate. In his preface to the 1867 edition of the novel, Dickens addressed his critics and denied all accusations of exaggeration. Of Bill Sikes, he wrote: "I fear there are in the world some insensible and callous natures, that do become utterly and incurably bad." And of Nancy: "It is useless to discuss whether the conduct and character of the girl seems natural or unnatural, probable or improbable, right or wrong. IT IS TRUE."

About Fagin, now one of the most famous antisemitic caricatures in English literature, Dickens's preface is silent. The word *Jew,* which appears 318 times in the version of the novel I consulted, is never used in the preface. But that's not to say the novel's almost-comical levels of antisemitism went unnoticed in the book's own time. In 1863, Dickens received a letter from Eliza Davis, a Jewish woman soliciting charitable contributions for a "Convalescent Home for the Jewish Poor." Davis took Dickens to task for Fagin, arguing that a sizable donation was only appropriate after the anti-Jewish hate Dickens encouraged: "Charles Dickens, the large hearted, whose works plead so eloquently and so nobly for the oppressed of his country . . . has encouraged a vile prejudice against the despised Hebrew."

Dickens was defensive at first, but gradually, it seems, Davis's critique got to him. The character of Riah in *Our Mutual Friend* is commonly read as Dickens's apology for Fagin: a harmless, dull, self-sacrificing pushover of a Jew who silently accepts the insults and indignities heaped on him by Fledgeby, a conniving, unscrupulous, lying, vile moneylending Christian. The scholar James D. Mardock described Riah as an "anti-Shylock," and to me this rings painfully true. If you prick Riah, he does not bleed; if you wrong him, nothing is less likely than revenge.

Every modern adaptation of *Oliver Twist* has to deal with the Fagin problem somehow. One option is to make a Riah of him: the quirky grandfather, a devout Jew backed into a corner who tries to defend his boys against the world. The other option is what Dickens did in later editions of *Oliver Twist,* which removed more than two hundred instances of the word *Jew*. Fagin still gets to prowl the narrow London streets this way, a colorful and captivating villain with his ten-dollar words and silk handkerchiefs. But in order to be interesting, he can't be Jewish in any way that matters.

Both of these options—sanitizing Fagin or disowning him—feel like a loss to me.

While *Fagin the Thief* keeps close to the plot of *Oliver Twist* in most aspects, I've diverged in some. Most obviously, I removed the bulk of the Brownlow-Maylie-Monks thread of the plot, though Dickens had Fagin play a role in that too. Nancy's death is intentionally framed differently in my version than in Dickens's. Dickens also never gives Fagin a first name, so I had to pick one. Jacob, the trickster patriarch who pickpockets his brother's birthright and has an inconceivable number of sons trailing him around Canaan, seemed the right namesake.

Fagin the Thief is largely aligned with historical fact in its setting, with a few exceptions for the sake of storytelling. There were Jewish enclaves in London as far back as the mid-seventeenth century, with Stepney forming a hub for the community later in the 1800s. I have no particular evidence of a Jewish community in the exact place and time I've situated Jacob's or Leah's childhoods, but it's certainly possible and representative. I tried to situate Jacob's adult home more or less where Dickens placed it, though

Bell Court is a fictional street. (If you're looking at Charles Booth's incredible 1889 map of London, I placed it just north of Charterhouse Street, in the black square labeled "vicious, semi-criminal.") The debate over Baron de Rothschild's oath of office that Bill and Jacob discuss was a real news item that culminated in the passage of the Jewish Disabilities Act, but the scandal started in 1847, not 1825 as I've written it. It was too perfect an event not to include, so I hope readers will forgive the anachronism. Any further errors are entirely my own.

The ending of this book deviates from *Oliver Twist,* but in a way that stays true to historical fact. By 1837, when the story's serialization began, the only crimes in England punishable by death were high treason, murder, arson, piracy, rape, and (curiously) causing a shipwreck. While Dickens sentences Fagin to death, the actual punishment for his crimes would have been transportation.

Two last thoughts.

First: There are Jews who hurt others. There are Jews who are kind. There are Jews who believe nine contradictory things before breakfast, who love the wrong people in the wrong ways, who perpetrate horrors, who stand up for justice, who make the best of the hand they're dealt. All of these can be true of the same Jewish person. No demographic is a reliable shorthand for what a person believes. The only way to find out is if you ask and listen.

Second: I don't know whether, as Dickens says, there are "some insensible and callous natures, that do become utterly and incurably bad." But if writing fiction is an exercise in imaginative empathy, I think we at least have to ask *why.*

ACKNOWLEDGMENTS

Thanking everyone who helped bring this book to life would require another hundred pages, but I'm particularly grateful to:

Carolyn Williams, editor extraordinaire, for your unfailing support, your brilliant instincts, and for helping me fix my silliest mistakes with patience and good humor.

Bridget Smith, my agent, for always being in my corner and for responding to my email that read, "I want to write this book but I'm scared," with "Don't be scared, do it."

The entire team at Doubleday, whose time and talent elevated this story beyond what I could ever have hoped for: Amy Ryan for heroic copyediting support, Andrea Monagle for production editing, Emily Mahon for cover design, LeeAnn Pemberton and Maggie Carr for proofreading, Pei Loi Koay for interior design, Peggy Samedi for production, Julie Erl for publicity, and Milena Brown for marketing.

Aubyn Keefe, my first reader, problem whisperer, and this book's biggest cheerleader. They're all worse now. Thanks.

The friends and loved ones I'm lucky enough to have on this ride with me, especially Katie Brill, Kim Ellsworth, Audrey Fierberg, Ann Foster, Olesya Salnikova Gilmore, Genevieve Gornichec, Lana Wood Johnson, Elsinore Kuo, Molly Lyons, Mary McMyne, Jessica Ross, Val Utter, and Nina Kryza Walsh. Also to the ever-expanding list of group chats, private servers, and online communities that keep me sane, motivated, and hydrated: the Northwestern Coven, Team B, Nerd Ventures, Dirtbag Nation, the Tits-Out Brigade.

The writers, musicians, and artists I've never met who would be bewildered if I tried to explain to them how much influence they had on this book, including Raúl Esparza, Tom Hardy, Jonathan Pryce, Annaleigh Ashford, Johnny Cash, Jack White, the Arctic Monkeys, Jethro Tull, Olga Tokarczuk, Jac Jemc, Sacha Lamb, Percival Everett, and Barbara Kingsolver.

The booksellers and librarians who keep up the magical work of connecting communities to books and books to communities.

Every person who bought, borrowed, found, lent, reviewed, or recommended this book, or any of my books, or any book. I genuinely can never thank you enough.

My family—immediate, extended, and expanding—for everything.

My parents, Ann Marie and Mike. Always, but especially this one.

Charles Dickens. You made a mistake with Bullseye. Don't worry. I fixed it.

ABOUT THE AUTHOR

Allison Epstein earned a BA in creative writing from the University of Michigan and her MFA in fiction from Northwestern University. A Michigan native, she now lives in Chicago, where she enjoys good theater, bad puns, and fancy jackets. She is the author of the historical novels *A Tip for the Hangman* and *Let the Dead Bury the Dead.*